D0965704

LAST OF THE DUANES

LAST OF THE DUANES

A Western Story

by

Zane Grey ™

Five Star Western
Thorndike, Maine

Five Star Western
Published in conjunction with
Golden West Literary Agency.

AUGUST 1996

First Edition, second printing.

Five Star Standard Print Western Series.

The text of this editon is unabridged.

Set in 11 pt. Century Schoolbook by Juanita Macdonald.

Printed in the United States on permanent paper.

Library of Congress Cataloging in Publication Data

Grey, Zane, 1872–1939.
    Last of the Duanes : a Western story / Zane Grey.
        p.   cm.
    "A Five star western."
    ISBN 0-7862-0627-6 (hc)
    1. Title.
    [PS3513.R6545L26   1996]
    813'.52—dc20   95-47156

LAST OF THE DUANES

Foreword

The legend of Zane Grey is so pervasive that, once it seems the *last* novel or story he wrote is to be published, another one seems to spring up. In June, 1994, his supposedly final novel, GEORGE WASHINGTON, FRONTIERSMAN, was published by the University of Kentucky Press. Though this was the first release of this book in any form, as we now see, it was by no means his last unpublished manuscript.

LAST OF THE DUANES, one of my father's most powerful and memorable novels, is now being published in book form for the first time, unexpurgated, transferred directly from the original holographic manuscript. The reason this great novel was never before published, other than in bits and pieces early on in magazines, is not entirely clear. Dad wrote LAST OF THE DUANES during the summer of 1913, not long after he had completed his visit with Captain Hughes of the Texas Rangers in San Antonio, and sent it off immediately to his friend, Bob Davis, the editor of *Munsey's Magazine*. The letter Dad received from him, reproduced below, quite literally stunned him.

October 17, 1913

Zane Grey, Esq.
Cottage Point,
Lackawaxen, Pennsylvania

My dear Zane:

"The Last of the Duanes": This story has been considered from every standpoint and it is the unanimous opinion of all of us that death comes too thick and fast. Buck is an interesting character and I am quite certain you have drawn a true picture of the type who would drift like water into the camps of the outlaws and run red-handed through his saturnalian career.

There are parts of the story that would interest and entertain any reader, but it is impossible to work up much sympathy or admiration for the hero. Neither does Jennie get a very strong hold upon the heart of the reader.

If you will stop a moment, Zane, and figure on the circumstance of killing nineteen men, it will become plain to you that the public as a whole cannot become very much attached to that type of individual.

The fact that Buck yearns all his outlawed years to regain his respectability is a mitigating circumstance in favor of the accused, but it does not absolve him by any means.

I am sorry to have kept the story so long, Zane, but there was no other way for me to give it full consideration.

I am returning it under separate cover.

Always sincerely,

Bob Davis

When one views the amount of blood spilled during just one day of today's television shows, this letter is almost amusing, to say the least. But to Dad a rejection of this sort was shocking and not a little painful. Even with his dramatic successes, such as RIDERS OF THE PURPLE SAGE and THE HERITAGE OF THE DESERT, he was still not yet at all sure of his greatness as an author.

A few days later, on November 13th, he also received a letter from Ripley Hitchcock, editor at Harper & Bros. Although he had not read the story, he patted Zane on the head in his usual "fatherly" fashion and agreed with Davis's thesis that there might be too much "pistol play" in the book and that Dad would be better advised to write something more like LORNA DOONE. Possibly for that reason the serial, "The Lone Star Rangers," was born early in 1914. Though it found fairly quick acceptance by *Cavalier/All-Story Weekly Magazine*, it is in my opinion far inferior to LAST OF THE DUANES both in plot and character.

"The Lone Star Rangers" is also the only story Dad wrote in the first person and is probably more autobiographical than fictional. Most of the heroic action is done by someone else other than the main character, Ranger Vaughan Steele. Though I could find no direct correspondence regarding this, my guess is that Harper & Bros. was not too enamored of "The Lone Star Rangers" either and may have suggested that Dad combine the two stories to make up the book published in 1915 as THE LONE STAR RANGER. It was, at best, a hastily constructed "marriage" between the first half of "Last of the Duanes" and the last half of "The Lone Star Rangers" with the names being changed to make Buck Duane an ex-outlaw turned ranger who finally wipes out the evil gangs in Pecos County. But along the way Buck

Duane's real sweetheart, Jennie Lee, simply disappears in favor of Alice Longstreth whose father, incidentally, turns out to be one of the major villains of the opus.

Notwithstanding, the mighty house of Harper & Bros. seemed satisfied with this "shotgun" wedding, and it has been virtually a bestseller among Westerns during the past seventy years. It may even have inspired a radio show in the early days of this medium, "The Lone Ranger," a character that eventually became a folk hero on radio and later on television and in the movies.

Since I first read the original manuscript of LAST OF THE DUANES, I have also reread the second half of THE LONE STAR RANGER. I realize now that THE LONE STAR RANGER was adulterated, probably by demand of the book publisher rather than by my father's wishes, perhaps because they didn't really *want* to look at the character of Buck Duane as presented in LAST OF THE DUANES. Yet, in THE LONE STAR RANGER there are many loose ends left dangling — such as what happened to Jennie Lee or why Alice Longstreth could so quickly and completely fall in love with the gunman who had destroyed her father and killed several of his followers! There are also other subplots not really relevant to the story, and these are totally absent in LAST OF THE DUANES.

In psychological terms the genesis of this book, in my view, might easily be called "The Anatomy of a Gunfighter." I think somehow there was far too much raw realism in this novel for the editors at Harper & Bros. — in fact it might even have proven a little frightening to these effete drawing-room Easterners, living as they did in their fancy Park Avenue-style apartments in New York City. At the time, of course, they all wanted to exploit the extremely lucrative phenomenon of Zane Grey, but I don't think they really wanted to believe much of what he wrote. Today's writers occasionally draw on psychological terms to describe the inner thoughts of their protagonists, but the debate still rages on as to whether the Darwinian principle of "kill or be killed" is an instinctual or a learned attribute of human nature. LAST OF THE DUANES in this form is a most intimate and dramatic study of the trauma of a gunman with a conscience who, though he turns his guns to the service of justice, still seems unable to curb the impulse to kill under some of the circumstances he faces. In this book, augmented perhaps by Lassiter in RIDERS OF THE PURPLE SAGE and "Killer" Kells in THE BORDER LEGION, Zane Grey defined the character of the Western gunman. Buck Duane, however, surely stands out from this group as one of my father's most uniquely compelling characters.

For all of the problems LAST OF THE DUANES encountered with editors, it did not fare badly on film. It was produced four times between 1919 and 1941, just as also occurred with film adaptations during the same period of THE LONE STAR RANGER. If you keep in mind that all eight of these full-length movies featured Buck Duane, this certainly constitutes some kind of record for films and remakes based on a single Zane Grey character. THE BORDER LEGION was filmed five times, so it holds Zane Grey's record for screen adaptations based on a single book.

In spite of these four motion pictures, however, LAST OF THE DUANES, until now has never before appeared in its entirety in book form. I regard it as Zane Grey's definitive study, not only of the bloodshed and gun play true of the early West, but also a depiction with great insight of the inner turmoil of a man indirectly made an

11

anti-hero by his actions, one who struggles not only with his own violent nature but with his past in his final hope to achieve redemption as a Texas Ranger.

Loren Grey,

Woodland Hills, California

Chapter One

So it was in him, then — an inherited fighting instinct, a driving intensity to kill. He was the last of the Duanes, that old fighting stock of Texas. But not the memory of his dead father, nor the pleading of his soft-voiced mother, nor the warning of this uncle who stood before him now, had brought to Buck Duane so much realization of the dark passionate strain in his blood. It was the recurrence, a hundredfold increased in power, of a strange emotion that for the last three years had arisen in him.

"Yes, Cal Bain's in town, full of bad whiskey an' huntin' for you," repeated the elder man gravely.

"It's the second time," muttered Duane, as if to himself.

"Son, you can't avoid a meetin'. Leave town till Cal sobers up. He ain't got it in for you when he's not drinkin'."

"But what's he want me for?" demanded Duane. "To insult me again? I won't stand that twice."

"He's got a fever that's rampant in Texas these days, my boy. He wants gun play. If he meets you, he'll try to kill you."

Here it stirred in Duane again, that bursting gush of blood, like a wind of flame shaking all his inner being and subsiding to leave him strangely chilled.

"Kill me! What for?" he asked.

"Lord knows there ain't any reason. But what's that to do with most of the shootin' these days? Didn't five cowboys over to Everall's kill one another dead all because they got to jerkin' at a quirt among themselves? An' Cal has no reason to love you. His girl was sweet on you."

"I quit when I found out she was his girl."

"I reckon *she* ain't quit. But never mind her or reasons. Cal's here, just drunk enough to be ugly. He's achin' to kill somebody. He's one of them four-flush gunfighters. He'd like to be thought bad. There's a lot of wild cowboys who're ambitious for a reputation. They talk about how quick they are on the draw. They ape Bland an' King Fisher an' Hardin an' all the big outlaws. They make threats about joinin' the gangs along the Rio Grande. They laugh at the sheriffs an' brag about how they'd fix the rangers. Cal's sure not much for you to bother with, if you only keep out of his way."

"You mean for me to run?" asked Duane in scorn.

"I reckon I wouldn't put it that way. Just avoid him. Buck, I'm not afraid Cal would get you if you met down there in town. You've got your father's eye an' his slick hand with a gun. What I'm most afraid of is that you'll kill Bain."

Duane was silent, letting his uncle's earnest words sink in, trying to realize their significance.

"If Texas ever recovers from that fool war an' kills off these outlaws, why, a young man will have a lookout," went on the uncle. "You're twenty-three now, an' a powerful sight of a fine fellow, barrin' your temper. You've got a chance in life. But if you go gunfightin', if you kill a man, you're ruined. Then you'll kill another. It'll be the same old story. An' the rangers would make you an outlaw. The rangers mean law an' order for Texas. This even-break business doesn't work with them. If you resist arrest, they'll kill you. If you submit to arrest, then you go to jail, an' mebbe you hang."

"I'd never hang," muttered Duane darkly.

"I reckon you wouldn't," replied the old man. "You'd be like your father. He was ever ready to draw . . . too ready. In times like these, with the Texas Rangers enforcin' the law, your dad would have been driven to the river. An' son, I'm afraid you're a chip off the old block. Can't you hold in . . . keep your temper . . . run away from trouble? Because it'll only result in you gettin' the worst of it in the end. Your father was killed in a street fight. An' it was told of him that he shot twice after a bullet had passed through his heart. Think of the terrible nature of a man to be able to do that. If you have any such blood in you, never give it a chance."

"What you say is all very well, Uncle," returned Duane, "but the only way out for me is to run, and I won't do it. Cal Bain and his outfit have already made me look like a coward. He says I'm afraid to come out and face him. A man simply can't stand that in this country. Besides, Cal would shoot me in the back someday if I didn't face him."

"Well, then, what're you goin' to do?" inquired the elder man.

"I haven't decided . . . yet."

"No, but you're comin' to it mighty fast. That damned spell is workin' in you. You're different today. I remember how you used to be moody an' lose your temper an' talk wild. Never was much afraid of you then. But now you're gettin' cool an' quiet, an' you think deep, an' I don't like the light in your eyes. It reminds me of your father."

"I wonder what Dad would say to me today if he were alive and here," said Duane.

"What do you think? What could you expect of a man who never wore a glove on his right hand for twenty years?"

"Well, he'd hardly have said much. Dad never talked.

15

But he would have done a lot. And I guess I'll go downtown and let Cal Bain find me."

Then followed a long silence, during which Duane sat with downcast eyes, and the uncle appeared lost in sad thought of the future. Presently he turned to Duane with an expression that denoted resignation and yet a spirit which showed wherein they were of the same blood.

"You've got a fast horse . . . the fastest I know of in this country. After you meet Bain, hurry back home. I'll have a duffel bag packed for you and the horse ready."

With that he turned on his heel and went into the house, leaving Duane to resolve in his mind his singular speech. Buck wondered presently if he shared his uncle's opinion of the result of a meeting between himself and Bain. His thoughts were vague. But on the instant of final decision, when he had settled with himself that he would meet Bain, such a storm of passion assailed him that he felt as if he was being shaken with rage. Yet it was all internal, inside his breast, for his hand was like a rock and, for all he could see, not a muscle about him quivered. He had no fear of Bain or of any other man; but a vague fear of himself — of this strange force in him — made him ponder and shake his head. It was as if he had not all to say in this matter. There appeared to have been in him a reluctance to let himself go, and some voice, some spirit from a distance, something he was not accountable for had compelled him. That hour of Duane's life was like years of actual living, and in it he became a thoughtful man.

He went into the house and buckled on his belt and gun. The gun was a Colt .45, six-shot and heavy, with an ivory handle. He had packed it, on and off, for five years. Before that it had been used by his father. There were a number of notches filed in the bulge of the ivory handle. This gun

16

was the one his father had fired twice after being shot through the heart, and his hand had stiffened so tightly upon it in the death grip that his fingers had to be pried open. It had never been drawn upon any man since it had come into Duane's possession. But the cold, bright polish of the weapon showed how it had been used. Duane could draw it with inconceivable rapidity, and at twenty feet he could split a card pointing edgewise toward him.

Duane wished to avoid meeting his mother. Fortunately, as he thought, she was away from home. He went out and down the path toward the gate. The air was full of the fragrance of blossoms and the melody of birds. Outside in the road a neighbor woman stood talking to a country man in a wagon. They spoke to him; he heard but did not reply. Then he began to stride down the road toward the town.

Wellston was a small town but important in that unsettled part of the great state because it was the trading center for several hundred miles of territory. On the main street there were perhaps fifty buildings, some brick, some frame, mostly adobe, and one third of the lot, and by far the most prosperous, were saloons. From the road Duane turned into this street. It was a wide thoroughfare lined by hitching rails and saddled horses and vehicles of various kinds. Duane's eye ranged down the street, taking in all at a glance, particularly persons moving leisurely up and down. Not a cowboy was in sight. Duane slackened his stride, and by the time he reached Sol White's place, which was the first saloon, he was walking slowly. Several people spoke to him and turned to look back after they had passed. He paused at the door of White's saloon, took a sharp survey of the interior, then stepped inside.

The saloon was large and cool, full of men and noise and smoke. The noise ceased upon his entrance, and the silence ensuing presently broke to the clink of Mexican silver dollars at a monte table. Sol White, who was behind the bar, straightened up when he saw Duane; then, without speaking, he bent over to rinse a glass. All eyes except those of the Mexican gamblers were turned upon Duane; and these glances were keen, speculative, questioning. These men knew Bain was looking for trouble; they probably had heard his boasts. But what did Duane intend to do? Several of the cowboys and ranchers present exchanged glances. Duane had been weighed by unerring Texas instinct, by men who all packed guns. The boy was the son of his father. Whereupon they greeted him and returned to their drinks and cards. Sol White stood with his big red hands out upon the bar. He was a tall, raw-boned Texan with a long mustache waxed to sharp points.

"Howdy, Buck," was his greeting to Duane. He spoke carelessly and averted his dark gaze for an instant.

"Howdy, Sol," replied Duane slowly. "Say, Sol, I hear there's a gent in town looking for me bad."

"Reckon there is, Buck," replied White. "He came in heah aboot an hour ago. Shore he was some riled an' a-roarin' for gore. Told me confidential a certain party had given you a white silk scarf, an' he was hell-bent on wearin' it home spotted red."

"Anybody with him?" queried Duane.

"Burt an' Sam Outcalt an' a little cowpuncher I never seen before. They all was coaxin' him to leave town. But he's looked on the flowin' glass, Buck, an' he's heah for keeps."

"Why doesn't Sheriff Oaks lock him up if he's that bad?"

"Oaks went away with the rangers. There's been another raid at Flesher's ranch. The King Fisher gang, likely. An' so the town's shore wide open."

Duane stalked outdoors and faced down the street. He walked the whole length of the long block, meeting many people — farmers, ranchers, clerks, merchants, Mexicans, cowboys, and women. It was a singular fact that when he turned to retrace his steps the street was almost empty. He had not returned a hundred yards on his way but that now the street was wholly deserted. A few heads protruded from doors and around corners. That main street of Wellston saw some such situation every few days. If it was an instinct for Texans to fight, it was also instinctive for them to sense with remarkable quickness the signs of a coming gun play. Rumor could not fly so swiftly. In less than ten minutes everybody who had been on the street or in the shops knew that Buck Duane had come forth to meet his enemy.

Duane walked on. When he came to within fifty paces of a saloon, he swerved out into the middle of the street, stood there for a moment, then went ahead and back to the sidewalk. He passed on in this way the length of the block. Sol White was standing in the door of his saloon.

"Buck, I'm a-tippin' you off," he said, quickly and low-voiced. "Cal Bain's over at Everall's. If he's a-huntin' you bad, as he brags, he'll show there."

Duane crossed the street and started down. Notwithstanding White's statement Duane was wary and slow at every door. Nothing happened, and he traversed almost the whole length of the block without seeing a person. Everall's place was on the corner.

Duane knew himself to be cold, steady. He was conscious of a strange fury that made him want to leap ahead. He seemed to long for this encounter more than anything he had ever wanted. But, vivid as were his sensations, he felt as if in a dream. Before he reached Everall's, he heard loud voices, one of which was raised high. Then the short door swung outward as if impelled by a vigorous hand. A bowlegged cowboy wearing woolly chaps burst out upon the sidewalk. At sight of Duane he seemed to bound into the air, and he uttered a savage roar.

Duane stopped in his tracks at the outer edge of the sidewalk, perhaps a dozen rods from Everall's door. If Bain was drunk, he did not show it in his movements. He swaggered forward, rapidly closing up the gap. Red, sweaty, disheveled, and hatless, his face distorted and expressive of the most malignant intent, he was a wild and sinister figure. He had already killed a man, and this showed in his demeanor. His hands were extended before him, the right hand a little lower than the left. At every step he bellowed his rancor in speech, mostly curses. Gradually he slowed his walk, then halted. A good twenty-five paces separated the men.

"Won't nothin' make you draw, you son of a bitch!" he shouted fiercely.

"I'm waitin' on you, Cal," replied Duane.

Bain's right hand stiffened — moved. Duane threw his gun as a boy throws a ball underhand — a draw his father had taught him. He pulled twice, his shots almost as one. Bain's big Colt boomed while it was pointed downward and he was falling. His bullet scattered dust and gravel at Duane's feet. He fell loosely, without contortion.

In a flash all was reality for Duane. He went forward and held his gun ready for the slightest movement on the part of Bain. But Bain lay upon his back, and all that moved were his breast and his eyes. How strangely the red had left his face — and also the distortion! The devil that had showed in Bain was gone. He was sober and conscious. He tried to speak but failed. His eyes expressed

20

something pitifully human. They changed — rolled — set blankly.

Duane drew a deep breath and sheathed his gun. He felt calm and cool, glad the fray was over. One violent expression burst from him. "The fool!" When he looked up, there were men around him.

"Plum center," said one.

Another, a cowboy who evidently had just left the gaming table, leaned down and pulled open Bain's shirt. He had the ace of spades in his hand. He laid it on Bain's breast, and the black figure on the card covered the two bullet holes just over Bain's heart.

Duane wheeled and hurried away. He heard another man say: "Reckon Cal got what he deserved. Buck Duane's first gun play. Like father, like son!"

Chapter Two

A thought kept repeating itself to Duane, and it was that he might have spared himself concern through his imagining how awful it would be to kill a man. He had no such feeling now. He had rid the community of a drunken, bragging, quarrelsome cowboy.

When he came to the gate of his home and saw his uncle there with a mettlesome horse, saddled, with canteen, rope, and bags all in place, a subtle shock pervaded his spirit. It had slipped his mind — the consequence of his act. But sight of the horse and the look of his uncle recalled the fact that he must now become a fugitive. An unreasonable anger took hold of him.

"The damned fool!" he exclaimed hotly. "Meeting Bain wasn't much, Uncle Jim. He dusted my boots, that's all. And for that I've got to go on the dodge."

"Son, you killed him then . . . ?" asked the uncle huskily.

"Yes. I stood over him . . . watched him die. I did as I would have been done by."

"I knew it. Long ago I saw it comin'. But now we can't stop to cry over spilt blood. You've got to leave town an' this part of the country."

"Mother!" exclaimed Duane.

"She's still away from home. You can't wait. I'll break it to her . . . it's what she always feared."

Suddenly Duane sat down and covered his face with his hands. "My God! Uncle, what have I done?" His broad shoulders shook.

"Listen, son, an' remember what I say," replied the elder man earnestly. "Don't ever forget. You're not to blame. I'm glad to see you take it this way, because maybe you'll never grow hard an' callous. You're not to blame. This is Texas. You're your father's son. These are wild times. The law as the rangers are laying it down now can't change life all in a minute. Even your mother, who's a good woman, has had her share in making you what you are this moment. For she was one of the pioneers . . . the fightin' pioneers of this state. Those years of wild times, before you was born, developed in her instinct to fight, to save her life, her children, an' that instinct has cropped out in you. It will be many years before it dies out of the boys born in Texas."

"I'm a murderer," said Duane, shuddering.

"No, son, you're not. An' you never will be. But you've got to be an outlaw till time makes it safe for you to come home."

"An outlaw?"

"I said it. If we had money an' influence, we'd risk a trial. But we've neither. An' I reckon the scaffold or jail is no place for Buckley Duane. Strike for the wild country, an' wherever you go an' whatever you do . . . be a man. Live honestly, if that's possible. If it isn't, be as honest as you can. If you have to herd with outlaws, try not to become bad. There are outlaws who're not all bad . . . many who have been driven to the river by such a deal as this you had. When you get among these men, avoid brawls. Don't drink, don't gamble. I needn't tell you what to do if it comes to gun play, as likely it will. You can't come home. When this thing is lived down, if that time ever comes, I'll get word into the unsettled country. It'll reach you some day. That's all. Remember, be a man. Good bye."

Duane, with blurred sight and contracting throat, gripped his uncle's hand and bade him a wordless farewell. Then he leaped astride the black and rode out of town.

As swiftly as was consistent with a care for his steed, Duane put a distance of fifteen or eighteen miles behind him. With that he slowed up, and the matter of riding did not require all his faculties. He passed several ranches and was seen by men. This did not suit him, and he took an old trail across country. It was a flat region with a poor growth of mesquite and prickly pear cactus. Occasionally he caught a glimpse of low hills in the distance. He had hunted often in that section and knew where to find grass and water. When he reached this higher ground, he did not, however, halt at the first favorable camping spot but went on and on. Once he came out upon the brow of a hill and saw a considerable stretch of country beneath him. It had the gray sameness characterizing all that he had traversed. He seemed to want to see wide spaces — to get a glimpse of the great wilderness lying somewhere beyond the southwest. It was sunset when he decided to camp at a likely spot he came across. He led the horse to water and then began searching through the shallow valley for a suitable place to camp. He passed by old camp sites that he well remembered. These, however, did not strike his fancy this time, and the significance of the change in him did not occur at the moment. At last he found a secluded spot, under cover of thick mesquites and oaks, at a goodly distance from the old trail. He took saddle and pack off the horse. He looked among his effects for a hobble and, finding that his uncle had failed to put one in, he suddenly remembered that he seldom used a hobble and never on this horse. He cut a few feet off the end of his lasso and used that. The horse, unused to such hampering of his free movements, had to be driven out upon the grass.

Duane made a small fire, prepared, and ate his supper. This done, ending the work of that day, he sat down and filled his pipe. Twilight had waned into dusk. A few wan stars had just begun to show and brighten. Above the low continuous hum of insects sounded like the evening carol of robins. Presently the birds ceased their singing, and then the quiet was more noticeable. When night set in, and the place seemed all the more isolated and lonely for that, Duane had a sense of relief.

It dawned upon him all at once that he was nervous, watchful, sleepless. The fact caused him surprise, and he began to think back, to take note of his late actions and their motives. The change one day had wrought amazed him. He who had always been free, easy, happy, especially when out alone in the open, had become in a few short hours bound, serious, preoccupied. The silence that had once been sweet now meant nothing to him except a medium whereby he might the better hear the sounds of pursuit. The loneliness, the night, the wild that had always been beautiful to him now only conveyed a sense of safety for the present. He watched; he listened; he thought. He felt tired yet had no inclination to rest. He intended to be off by dawn, heading toward the southwest. Had he a destination? It was vague as his knowledge of the great waste of mesquite and rock bordering the Rio Grande. Somewhere out there was a refuge. For he was a fugitive from justice, an outlaw.

This being an outlaw, then, meant eternal vigilance. No home, no rest, no sleep, no content, no life worth the living! He must be a lone wolf, or he must herd among men obnoxious to him. If he worked for an honest living, he still must hide his identity and take risks of detection. If he did not work on some distant outlying ranch, how was he to live? The idea of stealing was repugnant to him. The future seemed gray and somber enough. And he was twenty-three years old.

Why had this hard life been imposed upon him? The bitter question seemed to start a strange iciness that stole along his veins. What was wrong with him? He stirred the few sticks of mesquite into a last flickering blaze. He was cold, and for some reason he wanted some light. The black circle of darkness weighed down upon him, closed in around him. Suddenly he sat bolt upright and then froze in that position. He had heard a step. It was behind him — no! — on the side. Someone was there. He forced his hand down to his gun, and the touch of cold steel was another icy shock. Then he waited. But all was silent — silent as only a wilderness arroyo can be, with its low murmuring of wind in the mesquite. Had he heard a step? He began to breathe again.

But what was the matter with the light of his camp fire? It had taken on a strange green luster and seemed to be waving off into the outer shadows. Duane heard no step, saw no movement; nevertheless, there was another present at that camp-fire vigil. Duane saw him. He lay there in the middle of the green brightness, prostrate, motionless, dying. Cal Bain! His features were wonderfully distinct, clearer than any cameo, more sharply outlined than those of any picture. It was a hard face softening at the threshold of eternity. The red tan of sun, the coarse signs of drunkenness, the ferocity and hate so characteristic of Bain were no longer there. This face represented a different Bain, showed all that was human in him fading, fading as swiftly

26

as it blanched white. The lips wanted to speak but had not the power. The eyes held an agony of thought. They revealed what might have been possible for this man if he had lived — that he saw his mistake too late. Then they rolled, set blankly, and closed in death.

That haunting visitation left Duane sitting there in a cold sweat, a remorse gnawing at his vitals, realizing the curse that was on him. He divined that never would he be able to keep off that phantom. He remembered how his father had been eternally pursued by the furies of accusing guilt, how he had never been able to forget in work or in sleep those men he had killed.

The hour was late when Duane's mind let him sleep, and then dreams troubled him. In the morning he bestirred himself so early that in the gray gloom he had difficulty in finding his horse. Day had just broken when he struck the old trail again.

He rode hard all morning and halted in a shady spot to rest and graze his horse. In the afternoon he took to the trail at an easy trot. The country grew wilder. Bald, rugged mountains broke the level of the monotonous horizon. About three in the afternoon he came to a little river which marked the boundary line of his hunting territory.

The decision he made to travel upstream for a while was owing to two facts: the river was high with quicksand bars on each side, and he felt reluctant to cross into that region where his presence alone meant that he was a marked man. The bottomlands through which the river wound to the southwest were more inviting than the barrens he had traversed. The rest of that day he rode leisurely upstream. At sunset he penetrated the brakes of willow and cottonwood to spend the night. It seemed to him that in this lonely cover he would feel easy and content, but he did not. Every feeling, every imagining he had experienced the previous night, returned somewhat more vividly and accentuated by newer ones of the same intensity and color.

In this kind of travel and camping he spent three more days, during which he crossed a number of trails and one road where cattle — stolen cattle, probably — had recently passed. Thus time exhausted his supply of food, except salt, pepper, coffee, and sugar, of which he had a quantity. There were deer in the brakes but, as he could not get close enough to kill them with a revolver, he had to satisfy himself with a rabbit. He knew he might as well content himself with the hard fare that assuredly would be his lot.

Somewhere up this river there was a village called Huntsville. It was distant about a hundred miles from Wellston and had a reputation throughout southwestern Texas. He had never been there. The fact was this reputation was such that honest travelers gave the town a wide berth. Duane had what for him was considerable money in his possession, and he concluded to visit Huntsville, if he could find it, and buy a stock of provisions.

The following day, toward evening, he happened upon a road which he believed might lead to the village. There were a good many fresh horse tracks in the sand, and these made him thoughtful. Nevertheless, he followed the road, proceeding cautiously. He had not gone very far when the sound of rapid hoofbeats caught his ears. They came from his rear. In the darkening twilight he could not see any great distance back along the road. Voices, however, warned him that these riders, whoever they were, had approached closer than he liked. To go farther down the road was not to be thought of, so he turned a little way in among the mesquites and halted, hoping to escape being

28

seen or heard. As he was now a fugitive, it seemed every man was his enemy and pursuer.

The horsemen were fast approaching. Presently they were abreast of Duane's position, so near that he could hear the creak of saddles, the clink of spurs.

"Shore he crossed the river below," said one man.

"I reckon you're right, Bill. He's slipped us," replied another.

Rangers, or a posse of ranchers, in pursuit of a fugitive! The knowledge gave Duane a strange thrill. Certainly they could not have been hunting him, but the feeling their proximity gave him was identical to what it would have been had he been this particular hunted man. He held his breath; he clenched his teeth; he pressed a quieting hand upon his horse. Suddenly he became aware that these horsemen had halted. They were whispering. He could just make out a dark group closely massed. What had made them halt so suspiciously?

"You're wrong, Bill," said a man, in a low but distinct voice. "The idea of hearin' a hoss heave. You're wuss'n a ranger. An' you're hell-bent on killin' that rustler. Now I say, let's go home an' eat."

"Wal, I'll just take a look at the sand," replied the man called Bill.

Duane heard the clink of spurs on steel stirrup and the thud of boots on the ground. There followed a short silence which was broken by a sharply breathed exclamation.

Duane waited for no more. They had found his trail. He spurred his horse straight into the brush. At the second crashing bound there came yells from the road and then shots. Duane heard the hiss of a bullet close by his ear and, as it struck a branch, it made a peculiar singing sound. These shots and the proximity of that lead missile

aroused in Duane a quick, hot resentment which mounted
into a passion almost ungovernable. He must escape, yet
it seemed that he did not care whether he did or not.
Something grim kept urging him to halt and return the
fire of these men. After running a couple of hundred yards,
he raised himself from over the pommel, where he had
bent to avoid the stinging branches, and tried to guide his
horse. In the dark shadows under mesquites and cottonwoods he was hard put to find open passage; however, he
succeeded so well and made so little noise that, gradually,
he drew away from his pursuers. The sound of their horses'
crashing through the thickets died away. Duane reined in
and listened. He had distanced them. Probably they would
go into camp till daylight then follow his tracks. He started
on again, walking his horse, and peered sharply at the
ground, so that he might take advantage of the first trail
he crossed. It seemed a long while until he came upon
one. He followed it until a late hour when, striking the
willow branches again and hence the neighborhood of the
river, he picketed his horse and lay down to rest. He did
not sleep. His mind bitterly revolved the fate that had
come upon him. He made efforts to think of other things
but in vain. Every moment he expected the chill, the sense
of loneliness that yet was ominous of a strange visitation,
the peculiarity imagined lights and shades of the night —
these things that presaged the coming of Cal Bain. Doggedly
Duane fought against the insidious phantom. He kept telling himself that it was just imagination, that it would
wear off in time. If in his heart he did not believe what
he hoped, still he would not give up. He would not accept
the ghost of his victim as a reality.

Gray dawn found him in the saddle again, headed for
the river. Half an hour of riding brought him to the dense

chaparral and willow thickets. These he threaded to come at length to the ford. It was a gravel bottom and therefore an easy crossing. Once upon the opposite shore he reined in his horse and looked darkly back. This action marked his acknowledgment of his situation: he had voluntarily sought the refuge of the outlaws. He was beyond the pale. A bitter and passionate curse passed his lips as he spurred his horse into the brakes on that alien shore.

He rode perhaps twenty miles, not sparing his horse nor caring whether or not he left a plain trail. When the heat of the day began to be oppressive and hunger and thirst made themselves manifest, Duane began to look about him for a place to halt for the noon hour. The trail led into a road which was hard packed and smooth from the tracks of cattle. He doubted not that he had come across one of the roads used by border raiders. He headed into it and had scarcely traveled a mile when, turning a curve, he came point-blank upon a single horseman riding toward him. Both riders wheeled their mounts sharply and were ready to run and shoot back. Not more than a hundred paces separated them. They stood then for a moment, watching each other.

"Mawnin', stranger," called the man, dropping his hand from his hip.

"Howdy," replied Duane shortly.

They rode toward each other, closing half the gap, then they halted again.

"I see you ain't no ranger," called the rider, "an' shore I ain't none." He laughed loudly, as if he had made a joke.

"How'd you know I wasn't a ranger?" asked Duane curiously. Somehow he had instantly divined that this horseman was no officer or even a rancher trailing stolen stock.

"Wal," said the fellow, starting his horse forward at a

walk, "a ranger'd never git ready to run the other way from one man."

He laughed again. He was small and wiry, slouchy of attire, and armed to the teeth, and he bestrode a fine bay horse. He had quick, dancing, brown eyes, at once frank and bold, and a coarse, bronzed face. Evidently he was a good-natured ruffian.

Duane acknowledged the truth of the assertion and turned over in his mind how shrewdly the fellow had guessed him to be a hunted man.

"My name's Luke Stevens, an' I hail from the river. Who're you?" said the stranger.

Duane was silent.

"I reckon you're Buck Duane," went on Stevens. "I heard you was a damn' badman with a gun."

This time Duane laughed, not at the doubtful compliment but at the idea that the first outlaw he met should know him. Here was proof of how swiftly facts about gun play traveled on the Texas border.

"Wal, Buck," said Stevens in a friendly manner, "I ain't presumin' on your time or company. I see you're headin' fer the river. But will you stop long enough to stake a feller to a bite of grub?"

"I'm out of grub and pretty hungry myself," admitted Duane.

"Been pushin' your hoss, I see. Wal, I reckon you'd better stock up before you hit thet stretch of country."

He made a wide sweep of his right arm, indicating the southwest, and there was that in his action which seemed significant of a vast and barren region.

"Stock up?" queried Duane thoughtfully.

"Shore. A feller has jest got to eat. I can rustle along without whiskey but not without grub. Thet's what makes it so embarrassin', travelin' these parts, dodgin' your shadow. Now, I'm on my way to Mercer. It's a little two-bit town up the river a ways. I'm goin' to pack out some grub."

Stevens's tone was inviting. Evidently he would welcome Duane's companionship, but he did not openly say so. Duane kept silent, however, and then Stevens went on.

"Strange, in this here country two's a crowd. It's safer. I never was much on this lone-wolf dodgin', though I've done it of necessity. It takes a damn' good man to travel alone any length of time. Why, I've been thet sick I was jest achin' fer some ranger to come along and plug me. Give me a pardner any day. Now, mebbe you're not thet kind of a feller, an' I'm shore not presumin' to ask. But I just declares myself sufficient."

"You mean you'd like me to go with you?" asked Duane.

Stevens grinned. "Wal, I should smile. I'd be particular proud to be braced with a man of your reputation."

"See here, my good fellow, that's all nonsense," declared Duane in some haste.

"Shore I think modesty becomin' to a youngster," replied Stevens. "I hate a brag. An' I've no use fer these four-flush cowboys thet're always lookin' fer trouble an' talkin' gun play. Buck, I don't know much about you. But every man who's lived along the Texas border remembers a lot about your dad. It was expected of you, I reckon, an' much of your rep was established before you throwed your gun. I jest heard thet you was lightnin' on the draw, an' when you cut loose with a gun, why the figger on the ace of spades would cover your cluster of bullet holes. Thet's the word thet's gone down the border. It's the kind of reputation most sure to fly far an' swift ahead of a man in this country. An' the safest, too, I'll gamble on thet. It's the land of the draw. I see now you're only a boy, though

33

you're shore a strappin' husky one. Now, Buck, I'm not a spring chicken, an' I've been long on the dodge. Mebbe a little of my society won't hurt you none. You'll need to learn the country."

There was something sincere and likable about this outlaw.

"I dare say you're right," replied Duane quietly. "And I'll go to Mercer with you."

Next moment he was riding down the road with Stevens. Duane had never been much of a talker, and now he found speech difficult. But his companion did not seem to mind that. He was a jocose, voluble fellow, probably glad now to hear the sound of his own voice. Duane listened, and sometimes he thought with a pang of the distinction of name and heritage of blood his father had left to him.

Chapter Three

Late that day, a couple of hours before sunset, Duane and Stevens, having rested their horses in the shade of some mesquites near the town of Mercer, saddled up and prepared to move.

"Buck, as we're lookin fer grub an' not trouble, I reckon you'd better hang up out here," Stevens was saying as he mounted. "You see, towns an' sheriffs an' rangers are always lookin' fer new fellers gone bad. They sort of forget most of the old boys, except those as are plumb bad. Now, nobody in Mercer will take notice of me. Reckon there's been a thousand men run into the river country to become outlaws since yours truly. You jest wait here an' be ready to ride hard. Mebbe my besettin' sin will go operatin' in spite of my good intentions. In which case there'll be. . . ."

His pause was significant. He grinned, and his brown eyes danced with a kind of wild humor.

"Stevens, have you got any money?" asked Duane.

"Money!" exclaimed Luke blankly. "Say, I haven't owned a two-bit piece since . . . wal fer some time."

"I'll furnish money for grub," returned Duane. "And for whiskey, too, providing you hurry back here . . . without making trouble."

"Shore you're a down right good pard," declared Stevens in admiration, as he took the money. "I'll give my word, Buck, an' I'm here to say I never broke it yet. Lay low an' look fer me back quick."

With that he spurred his horse and rode out of the mesquites toward town. At that distance, about a quarter of a mile, Mercer appeared to be a cluster of low adobe houses set in a grove of cottonwoods. Pastures of alfalfa were dotted by horses and cattle. Duane saw a sheepherder driving in a meager flock.

Presently Stevens rode out of sight into the town. Duane waited, hoping the outlaw would make good his word. Probably not a quarter of an hour had elapsed when Duane heard the clear reports of a Winchester rifle, the clatter of rapid hoofbeats, and yells unmistakably the kind to mean danger for a man like Stevens. Duane mounted and rode to the edge of the mesquites.

He saw a cloud of dust down the road and a bay horse running fast. Stevens apparently had not been wounded by any of the shots, for he had a steady seat in his saddle and his riding, even at that moment, struck Duane as admirable. He carried a large pack over the pommel, and he kept looking back. The shots had ceased, but the yells increased. Duane saw several men running and waving their arms. Then he spurred his horse and got into a swift stride, so Stevens would not pass him. Presently the outlaw caught up with him. Stevens was grinning, but there was now no fun in the dancing eyes. It was a devil that danced in them. His face seemed a shade paler.

"Was jest comin' out of the store," yelled Stevens. "Run plumb into a rancher . . . who knowed me. He opened up with a rifle. Think they'll chase us."

They covered several miles before there were any signs of pursuit and, when horsemen did move into sight out of the cottonwoods, Duane and his companion steadily drew farther away.

"No hosses in thet bunch to worry us," called out Stevens.

Duane had the same conviction, and he did not look back again. He rode somewhat to the fore and was constantly aware of the rapid thudding of hoofs behind, as Stevens kept close to him. At sunset they reached the willow brakes and the river. Duane's horse was winded and lashed with sweat and lather. It was not until the crossing had been accomplished that Duane halted to rest his animal. Stevens was riding up the low, sandy bank. He reeled in the saddle. With an exclamation of surprise, Duane leaped off and ran to the outlaw's side.

"You're shot!" cried Duane.

"Wal, who'n hell said I wasn't? Would you mind givin' me a lift . . . with this here pack?"

Duane lifted the heavy pack down and then helped Stevens to dismount. The outlaw had a bloody foam on his lips, and he was spitting blood.

"Oh, why didn't you say so!" cried Duane. "I never thought. . . . You seemed all right."

"Wal, Luke Stevens may be as gabby as an old woman, but sometimes he doesn't say anythin'. It wouldn't have done no good."

Duane bade him sit down, removed his shirt, and washed the blood from his breast and back. Stevens had been shot in the breast, fairly low down, and the bullet had gone clear through him. His ride, holding himself and that heavy pack in the saddle, had been a feat little short of marvelous. Duane did not see how it had been possible, and he felt no hope for the outlaw. But he plugged the wounds and bound them tightly.

"Feller's name was Brown," Stevens said. "Me an' him fell out over a hoss I stole from him over in Huntsville. We had a shootin' scrape then. Wal, as I was straddlin' my hoss back there in Mercer, I seen this Brown, an' seen

37

him before he seen me. Could have killed him, too. But I wasn't breakin' my word to you. I kind of hoped he wouldn't spot me. But he did . . . an' fust shot he got me here. What do you think of this hole?"

"It's pretty bad," replied Duane, and he could not look the cheerful outlaw in the eyes.

"I reckon it is. Wal, I've had some bad wounds I lived over. Guess mebbe I can stand this one. Now, Buck, get me some place in the brakes, leave me some grub an' water at my hand, an' then you clear out."

"Leave you here alone?" asked Duane sharply.

"Shore. You see, I can't keep up with you. Brown an' his friends will foller us across the river a ways. You've got to think of number one in this game."

"What would you do in my case?" asked Duane curiously.

"Wal, I reckon I'd clear out an' save my hide," replied Stevens.

Duane felt inclined to doubt the outlaw's assertion. For his own part he decided his conduct without further speech. First he watered the horses, filled canteens and water-bag, and then tied the pack upon his own horse. That done, he lifted Stevens upon his horse and, holding him in the saddle, turned into the brakes, being careful to pick out hard or grassy ground that left little signs of tracks. Just about dark he ran across a trail that Stevens said was a good one to take into the wild country.

"Reckon we'd better keep right on in the dark . . . till I drop," concluded Stevens with a laugh.

All that night Duane, gloomy and thoughtful, attentive to the wounded outlaw, walked the trail and never halted till daybreak. He was tired then and very hungry. Stevens seemed in bad shape, although he was still spirited and cheerful. Duane made camp. The outlaw refused food but asked for both whiskey and water. Then he stretched out.

"Buck, will you take off my boots?" he asked with a faint smile on his pallid face.

Duane removed them, wondering if the outlaw had the thought that he did not want to die with his boots on. Stevens seemed to read his mind.

"Buck, my old daddy used to say thet I was born to be hanged. But I wasn't . . . an' dyin' with your boots on is the next wust way to croak."

"You've a chance to . . . to . . . get over this," said Duane.

"Shore. But I want to be correct about the boots . . . an' say, pard, if I do go over, jest you remember thet I was appreciatin' of your kindness."

Then he closed his eyes and seemed to sleep.

Duane could not find water for the horses, but there was an abundance of dew-wet grass upon which he hobbled them. After that was done, he prepared himself a much needed meal. The sun was getting warm when he lay down to sleep but, when he awoke, it was sinking in the west. Stevens was still alive, for he breathed heavily. The horses were in sight. All was quiet except the hum of insects in the brush. Duane listened a while then rose and went for the horses.

When he returned with them, he found Stevens awake, bright eyed, cheerful as usual, and apparently stronger.

"Wal, Buck, I'm still with you an' good fer another night's ride," he said. "Guess about all I need now is a big pull on thet bottle. Help me, will you? There! . . . thet was bully. I ain't swallowin' my blood this evenin'. Mebbe I've bled all there was in me."

While Duane got a hurried meal for himself, packed up the little outfit, and saddled the horses, Stevens kept on talking. He seemed to be in a hurry to tell Duane all about this country. Another night ride would put them beyond fear of pursuit, within striking distance of the Rio Grande and the hiding places of the outlaws.

When it came time for mounting the horses, Stevens said: "Reckon you can pull on my boots once more." In spite of the laugh accompanying the words Duane detected a subtle change in the outlaw's spirit.

On this night travel was facilitated by the fact that the trail was broad enough for two horses abreast, enabling Duane to ride while upholding Stevens in the saddle. The difficulty most persistent was in keeping the horses in a walk. They were used to a trot, and that kind of gait would not do for Stevens. The red died out of the west; a pale afterglow prevailed for a while; darkness set in; then the broad expanse of blue darkened, and the stars brightened. After a while Stevens ceased talking and drooped in his saddle. Duane kept the horses going, however, and the slow hours wore away. Duane thought the quiet night would never break to dawn, and there seemed no end to the melancholy, brooding plain. But a length of grayness blotted out the stars and mantled the level of mesquite and cactus.

Dawn caught the fugitives at a green camping site on the bank of a rocky little stream. Stevens fell, a dead weight into Duane's arms, and one look at the haggard face showed Duane that the outlaw had taken his last ride. He knew it, too. Yet that cheerfulness prevailed.

"Buck, my feet are awful tired packin' them heavy boots," he said and seemed immensely relieved when Duane had removed them.

This matter of the outlaw's boots was strange, Duane thought. He made Stevens as comfortable as possible then attended to his own needs. The outlaw took up the thread of his conversation where he had left off the night before.

"This trail splits up a ways from here, an' every branch of it leads to a hole where you find men . . . a few, mebbe, like yourself . . . some like me . . . and gangs of no-good hoss thieves, rustlers, an' such. It's easy livin', Buck. I reckon, though, that you'll not find it easy. You'll never mix in. You'll be a lone wolf. I seen that right off. Wal, if a man can stand the loneliness an' if he's quick on the draw, mebbe lone wolf is the best bet. Shore I don't know. But these fellers in here will be suspicious of a man who goes it alone. If they get a chance, they'll kill you."

Stevens asked for water several times. He had forgotten, or he did not want the whiskey. His voice grew perceptibly weaker.

"Be quiet," said Duane. "Talking uses up your strength."

"Aw, I'll talk till . . . I'm done," he replied doggedly. "See here, pard, you can gamble on what I'm tellin' you . . . an' it'll be useful. From this camp we'll . . . you'll meet men right along. An' none of them will be honest men. All the same, some are better'n others. I've lived along the river for twelve years. There's three big gangs of outlaws. King Fisher . . . you know him, I reckon, fer he's half the time livin' among respectable folks. King is a pretty good feller. It'll do to tie up with him an' his gang. Now, there's Cheseldine, who hangs out in the Rim Rock way up the river. He's an outlaw chief. I never seen him, though I stayed once right in his camp. Late years he's got rich an' keeps back pretty well hid. But Bland . . . I knowed Bland fer years. An' I haven't any use for him. Bland has the biggest gang. You ain't likely to miss strikin' his place sometime or other. He's got a regular town, I might say. Shore there's some gamblin' an' gunfightin' goin' on at Bland's camp all the time. Bland has killed some twenty men, an' thet's not countin' greasers."

Here Stevens took another drink and then rested for a while.

"You ain't likely to get on with Bland," he resumed. "You're too strappin' big an' good lookin' to please the chief. Fer he's got women in his camp. Then he'd be jealous of your possibilities with a gun. Shore I reckon he'd be careful, though. Bland's no fool, an' he loves his hide. I reckon any of the other gangs would be better fer you when you ain't goin' it alone."

Apparently that exhausted the fund of information and advice Stevens had been eager to impart. He lapsed into silence and lay with closed eyes. Meanwhile the sun rose warmly; the breeze waved the mesquites; the birds came down to splash in the shallow stream. Duane dozed in a comfortable seat. By and by something aroused him. Stevens was once more talking but with a changed tone.

"Feller's name . . . was Brown," he rambled. "We fell out . . . over a hoss I stole from him . . . in Huntsville. He stole it fust. Brown's one of them sneaks . . . afraid of the open . . . he steals an' pretends to be honest. Say, Buck, mebbe you'll meet Brown some day. You an' me are pards now."

"I'll remember, if I ever meet him," said Duane.

That seemed to satisfy the outlaw. Presently he tried to lift his head but had not the strength. A strange shade was creeping across the bronzed, rough face.

"My feet are pretty heavy. Shore you got my boots off?"

Duane held them up but was not certain that Stevens could see them. The outlaw closed his eyes again and muttered incoherently. Then he fell asleep. Duane believed that sleep was final. The day passed with Duane watching and waiting. Toward sundown Stevens awoke, and his eyes

42

seemed clearer. Duane went to get some fresh water, thinking his comrade would surely want some. When he returned, Stevens made no sign that he wanted anything. There was something bright about him.

"Pard, you . . . stuck . . . to me!" the outlaw whispered.

Duane caught a hint of gladness in the voice. He traced a faint surprise in the haggard face. Stevens seemed like a child. To Duane the moment was sad, elemental, big, with a burden of mystery he could not understand.

He buried him in a shallow arroyo and heaped up a pile of stones to mark the grave. That done, he saddled his comrade's horse, hung the weapons over the pommel and, mounting his own steed, he rode down the trail in the gathering twilight.

Chapter Four

Two days later, about the middle of the forenoon, Duane dragged the two horses up the last ascent of an exceedingly rough trail and found himself on top of the Rim Rock with a beautiful green valley at his feet, the yellow, sluggish Rio Grande shining in the sun, and the great, wild, mountainous barrens of Mexico stretching to the south. Duane had not fallen in with any travelers. He had taken the likeliest looking trail he had come across. Where it had led him, he had not the slightest idea except that here was the river, and probably the enclosed valley was the retreat of some famous outlaw.

No wonder outlaws were safe in that wild refuge! Duane had spent the last two days climbing the roughest and most difficult trail he had ever seen. From the looks of the descent he imagined the worst part of his travel was yet to come. Not improbably it was two thousand feet down to the river. The wedge-shaped valley, green with alfalfa and cottonwood and nestled down amid the bare walls of yellow rock, was a delight and a relief to his tired eyes. Eager to get down to a level and to find a place to rest, Duane began the descent.

The trail proved to be the kind that could not be descended slowly. He kept dodging rocks which his horses loosed behind him, and in a short time he reached the valley, entering at the apex of the wedge. A stream of clear water tumbled out of the rocks here, and most of it ran into irrigation ditches. His horses drank thirstily. And he drank with that fullness and gratefulness common to the desert traveler finding sweet water. Then he mounted and rode down the valley, wondering what would be his reception.

The valley was much larger than it had appeared from the high elevation. Well watered, green with grass and trees, and farmed evidently by good hands, it gave Duane a considerable surprise. Horses and cattle were everywhere. Every clump of cottonwoods surrounded a small adobe house. Duane saw Mexicans working in the fields and horsemen going to and fro. Presently he passed a house bigger than the others with a porch attached. A woman, young and pretty he thought, watched him from a door. No one else appeared to notice him.

Presently the trail widened into a road, and that into a kind of square lined by a number of adobe and log buildings of rudest structure. Within sight were horses, dogs, a couple of steers, Mexican women with children, and white men, all of whom appeared to be doing nothing. His advent created no interest until he rode up to the white men who were lolling in shade on the verandah. This place evidently was a store and saloon, and from the inside came a lazy hum of voices.

As Duane reined to a halt, one of the loungers in the shade rose with a loud exclamation: "Bust me if thet ain't Luke's hoss!"

The others accorded their interest, if not assent, by rising to advance toward Duane.

"How about it, Euchre? Ain't thet Luke's bay?" queried the first man.

"Plain as your nose," replied the fellow called Euchre.

"There ain't no doubt about thet, then," laughed another, "fer Bosomer's nose is shore plain on the landscape."

These men lined up before Duane and, as he coolly regarded them, he thought they could have been recognized anywhere as desperadoes. The man called Bosomer, who had stepped forward, had a forbidding face which showed yellow eyes, an enormous nose, and skin the color of dust, with a thatch of sandy hair.

"Stranger, who are you an' where in the hell did you git thet bay hoss?" he demanded. His yellow eyes took in Stevens's horse, then the weapons hung on the saddle, and finally turned their glinting, hard light upward to Duane.

Duane did not like the tone in which he had been addressed, and he remained silent. At least half his mind seemed busy with curious interest in regard to something that leaped inside him and made his breast feel tight. He recognized it as that strange emotion which had shot through him often of late and which had decided him to go out to the meeting with Bain. Only now it was different, more powerful.

"Stranger, who are you?" asked another man, somewhat more vividly.

"My name's Duane," replied Duane curtly.

"An' how'd you come by the hoss?"

Duane answered briefly, and his words were followed by a short silence, during which the men looked at him. Bosomer began to twist the ends of his beard.

"Reckon he's dead, all right, or nobody'd hev his hoss an' guns," Euchre said presently.

"Mister Duane," began Bosomer, in low, stinging tones, "I happen to be Luke Stevens's side-pardner."

Duane looked him over, from dusty, worn-out boots to his slouchy sombrero. That look seemed to inflame Bosomer.

"An' I want the hoss an' them guns," he shouted.

"You or anybody else can have them, for all I care. I just

fetched them in. But the pack is mine," replied Duane. "And say, I befriended your pard. If you can't use a civil tongue, you'd better cinch it."

"Civil? Haw, haw!" rejoined the outlaw. "I don't know you. How do we know you didn't plug Stevens, stole his hoss, an' jest happened to stumble down here?"

"You'll have to take my word, that's all," replied Duane sharply.

"Damn it! I ain't takin' your word! Savvy thet? An' *I* was Luke's pard!"

With that Bosomer wheeled and, pushing his companions aside, he stamped into the saloon where his voice broke out in a roar.

Duane dismounted and threw his bridle.

"Stranger, Bosomer is shore hot headed," said Euchre. He did not appear unfriendly nor were the others hostile.

At this juncture several more outlaws crowded out of the door, and the one in the lead was a tall man of stalwart physique. His manner proclaimed him a leader. He had a long face, a flaming red beard, and clear, cold, blue eyes that fixed in close scrutiny upon Duane. He was not a Texan — in truth, Duane did not recognize one of these outlaws as native to his state.

"I'm Bland," said the tall man authoritatively. "Who're you, and what're you doing here?"

Duane looked at Bland as he had at the others. This outlaw chief appeared to be reasonable, if he was not courteous. Duane told his story again, this time a little more in detail.

"I believe you," replied Bland at once. "Think I know when a fellow is lying."

"I reckon you're on the right trail," put in Euchre. "Thet about Luke wantin' his boots took off . . . thet satisfies

47

me. Luke had a mortal dread of dyin' with his boots on."

At this sally the chief and his men laughed.

"You said Duane . . . Buck Duane?" queried Bland. "Are you a son of that Duane who was a gunfighter some years back?"

"Yes," replied Duane.

"Never met him, and glad I didn't," said Bland with a grim humor. "So you got in trouble and had to go on the dodge? What kind of trouble?"

"Had a fight."

"Fight? Do you mean gun play?" questioned Bland. He seemed eager, curious, speculative.

"Yes. It ended in gun play, I'm sorry to say," answered Duane.

"Guess I needn't ask the son of Duane if he killed his man," went on Bland ironically. "Well, I'm sorry you bucked against trouble in my camp. But as it is, I guess you'd be wise to make yourself scarce."

"Do you mean I'm politely told to move on?" asked Duane quietly.

"Not exactly that," said Bland, as if irritated. "If this isn't a free place, there isn't one on earth. Every man is equal here. Do you want to join my band?"

"No, I don't."

"Well, even if you did, I imagine that wouldn't stop Bosomer. He's an ugly fellow. He's one of the few gunmen I've met who wants to kill somebody all the time. Most men like that are four-flushers. But Bosomer is all one color, and that's red. Merely for your own sake I advise you to hit the trail."

"Thanks. But if that's all, I'll stay," returned Duane. Even as he spoke, he felt that he did not know himself.

Bosomer appeared at the door, pushing men who tried

48

to detain him and, as he jumped clear of a last reaching hand, he uttered a snarl like an angry dog. Manifestly the short while he had spent inside the saloon had been devoted to drinking and talking himself into a frenzy. Bland and the other outlaws quickly moved aside, letting Duane stand alone. When Bosomer saw Duane standing motionless and watchful, a strange change passed quickly in him. He halted in his tracks and, as he did that, the men who had followed him out piled over one another in their hurry to get to one side.

Duane saw all the swift action, felt intuitively the meaning of it and in Bosomer's sudden change of front. The outlaw was keen, and he had expected a shrinking, or at least a frightened, antagonist. Duane knew he was neither. He felt like iron, and yet thrill after thrill ran through him. It was almost as if this situation had been one long familiar to him. Somehow he understood the yellow-eyed Bosomer. The outlaw had come out to kill him. And now, though somewhat checked by the stand of the stranger, he still meant to kill. Like so many desperadoes of his ilk, he was victim of a passion to kill for the sake of killing. Duane divined that no sudden animosity was driving Bosomer. It was just his chance. In that moment murder would have been joy to him. Very likely he had forgotten his pretext for a quarrel. Very probably his faculties were absorbed in conjecture as to Duane's possibilities. He did not speak a word. He remained motionless for a long moment, his eyes pale and steady, his right hand like a claw.

That instant gave Duane a power to read in his enemy's eyes the thought that preceded action. Duane did not want to kill another man. Still he would have to fight, and he decided to cripple Bosomer. When Bosomer's hand moved, Duane's gun was spouting fire. Two shots only — both from Duane's gun — and the outlaw fell with his right arm shattered. Bosomer cursed harshly and floundered in the dust, trying to reach the gun with his left hand. His comrades, however, seeing that Duane would not kill unless forced, closed in upon Bosomer and prevented any further madness on his part.

Chapter Five

Of the outlaws present Euchre appeared to be the one most inclined to lend friendliness to curiosity, and he led Duane and the horses away to a small adobe shack. He tied the horses in an open shed and removed their saddles. Then, gathering up Stevens's weapons, he invited his visitor to enter the house.

It had two rooms — windows without coverings — bare floors. One room contained blankets, weapons, saddles, and bridles, the other a stone fireplace, rude table and bench, two bunks, a box cupboard, and various blackened utensils.

"Make yourself to home as long as you want to stay," said Euchre. "I ain't rich in this world's goods, but I own what's here, an' you're welcome."

"Thanks. I'll stay a while and rest. I'm pretty well played out," replied Duane.

Euchre gave him a keen glance. "Go ahead an' rest. I'll take your horses to grass."

Euchre left Duane alone in the house. Duane relaxed then, and mechanically he wiped the sweat from his face. He was laboring under some kind of a spell or shock which did not pass off quickly. When it had worn away, he took off his coat and belt and made himself comfortable on the blankets. He had a thought that, if he rested or slept, what difference would it make on the morrow? No rest, no sleep could change the gray outlook of the future. He felt glad when Euchre came bustling in, and for the first time he took notice of the outlaw.

Euchre was old in years. What little hair he had was gray, his face clean shaven and full of wrinkles; his eyes were half shut from long gazing through the sun and dust. He stooped. But his thin frame denoted strength and endurance still unimpaired.

"Hev a drink or a smoke?" he asked.

Duane shook his head. He had not been unfamiliar with whiskey, and he had used tobacco moderately since he was sixteen. But now, strangely, he felt a disgust at the idea of stimulants. He did not understand clearly what he felt. There was that vague idea of something wild in his blood, something that made him fear himself.

Euchre wagged his old head sympathetically. "Reckon you feel a little sick. When it comes to shootin', I run. What's your age?"

"I'm twenty-three," replied Duane.

Euchre showed surprise. "You're only a boy! I thought you thirty anyways. Buck, I heard what you told Bland an', puttin' thet with my own figurin', I reckon you're no criminal yet. Throwin' a gun in self-defense . . . thet ain't no crime!"

Duane, finding relief in talking, told more about himself.

"Huh," replied the old man. "I've been on this river fer years, an' I've seen hundreds of boys come in on the dodge. Most of them, though, was no good. An' thet kind don't last long. This river country has been an' is the refuge fer criminals from all over the States. I've bunked with bank cashiers, forgers, plain thieves, an' out-an'-out murderers, all of which had no bizness on the Texas border. Fellers like Bland are exceptions. He's no Texan . . . you seen thet. The gang he rules here come from all over, an' they're tough cusses, you can bet on thet. They live fat an' easy.

52

If it wasn't fer the fightin' among themselves, they'd shore grow populous. The Rim Rock is no place for a peaceable, decent feller. I heard you tell Bland you wouldn't join his gang. Thet'll not make him take a likin' to you. Have you any money?"

"Not much," replied Duane.

"Could you live by gamblin'? Are you any good at cards?"

"No."

"You wouldn't steal hosses or rustle cattle?"

"No."

"When your money's gone, how'n hell will you live? There ain't any work a decent feller could do. You can't herd with greasers. Why, Bland's men would shoot at you in the fields. What'll you do, son?"

"God knows," replied Duane hopelessly. "I'll make my money last as long as possible . . . then starve."

"Wal, I'm pretty pore, but you'll never starve while I got anythin'."

Here it struck Duane again — that same something human and kind and eager which he had seen in Stevens. Duane's estimate of outlaws had lacked this quality. He had not accorded them any virtues. To him, as to the outside world, they had been merely vicious men without one redeeming feature.

"I'm much obliged to you, Euchre," replied Duane. "But, of course, I won't live with anyone unless I can pay my share."

"Have it any way you like, my son," said Euchre good humoredly. "You make a fire, an' I'll set about gettin' grub. I'm a sourdough, Buck. Thet man doesn't live who can beat my bread."

"How do you ever pack supplies in here?" asked Duane, thinking of the almost inaccessible nature of the valley.

"Some comes across from Mexico, an' the rest down the river. Thet river trip is a bird. It's more'n five hundred miles to any supply point. Bland has *mozos,* greaser boatmen. Sometimes, too, he gets supplies in from downriver. You see, Bland sells thousands of cattle in Cuba. An' all this stock has to go down by boat to meet the ships."

"Where on earth are the cattle driven down to the river?" asked Duane.

"Thet's not my secret," replied Euchre shortly. "Fact is, I don't know. I've rustled cattle for Bland, but he never sent me through the Rim Rock with them."

Duane experienced a sort of pleasure in the realization that interest had been stirred in him. He was curious about Bland and his gang and glad to have something to think about. For every once in a while he had a sensation that was almost like a pang. He wanted to forget. In the next hour he did forget and enjoyed helping in the preparation and eating of the meal. Euchre, after washing and hanging up the several utensils, put on his hat and turned to go out.

"Come along or stay here, as you want," he said to Duane.

"I'll stay," rejoined Duane slowly.

The old outlaw left the room and trudged away, whistling cheerfully.

Duane looked around him for a book or paper, anything to read; but all the printed matter he could find consisted of a few words on cartridge boxes and an advertisement on the back of a tobacco pouch. There seemed to be nothing for him to do. He had rested; he did not want to lie down any more. He began to walk to and fro, from one end of the room to the other. And as he walked, he fell into the lately acquired habit of brooding over his misfortune.

Suddenly he straightened up with a jerk. Unconsciously

he had drawn his gun. Standing there with the bright cold weapon in his hand, he looked at it in consternation. How had he come to draw it? With difficulty he traced his thoughts backward but could not find any that was accountable for his act. He discovered, however, that he had a remarkable tendency to drop his hand to his gun. That might have come from the habit long practice in drawing had given him. Likewise, it might have come from a subtle sense, scarcely thought of at all, of the late, close, and inevitable relation between that weapon and himself. He was amazed to find that, bitter as he had grown at fate, the desire to live burned strongly in him. If he had been as unfortunately situated, but with the difference that no man wanted to put him in jail or take his life, he felt that this burning passion to be free, to save himself, might not have been so powerful. Life certainly held no bright prospects for him. Already he had begun to despair of ever getting back to his home. But to give up like a white-hearted coward, to let himself be handcuffed and jailed, to run from a drunken, bragging cowboy or be shot in cold blood by some border brute who merely wanted to add another notch to his gun — these things were impossible for Duane, because there was in him the temper to fight. In that hour he yielded only to fate and the spirit inborn in him. Hereafter this gun must be a living part of him. Right then and there he returned to a practice he had long discontinued — the draw. It was now a stern, bitter, deadly business with him. He did not need to fire the gun, for accuracy was a gift and had become assured. Swiftness on the draw, however, could be improved, and he set himself to acquire the limit of speed possible to any man. He stood still in his tracks; he paced the room; he sat down, lay down, put himself in awkward positions; and from every position he practiced throwing his gun — practiced it till he was hot and tired and his arm ached and his hand burned. That practice he determined to keep up every day. It was one thing, at least, that would help pass the weary hours.

Later, he went outdoors to the cooler shade of the cottonwoods. From this point he could see a good deal of the valley. Under different circumstances Duane felt that he would have enjoyed such a beautiful spot. Euchre's shack sat against the first rise of the slope of the wall, and Duane, by climbing a few rods, got a view of the whole valley. Assuredly it was an outlaw settlement. He saw a good many Mexicans who, of course, were hand and glove with Bland. Also he saw enormous flat-boats, crude of structure, moored along the banks of the river. The Rio Grande rolled away between high bluffs. A cable, sagging deeply in the middle, was stretched over the wide yellow stream, and an old scow, evidently used as a ferry, lay anchored on the far shore.

The valley was an ideal retreat for an outlaw band operating on a big scale. Pursuit scarcely need be feared over the broken trails of the Rim Rock. And the open end of the valley could be defended against almost any number of men coming down the river. Access to Mexico was easy and quick. What puzzled Duane was how Bland got cattle down to the river, and he wondered if the rustler really did get rid of his stolen stock by use of boats.

Duane must have idled away considerable time up on the hill for, when he returned to the shack, Euchre was busily engaged around the camp fire.

"Wal, glad to see you ain't so pale about the gills as you was," he said by way of greeting. "Pitch in an' we'll soon have grub ready. There's shore one consolin' fact 'round this here camp."

"What's that?" asked Duane.

"Plenty of good juicy beef to eat. An' it doesn't cost a short bit."

"But it costs hard rides and trouble, bad conscience, and life, too, doesn't it?"

"I ain't shore about the bad conscience. Mine never bothered me none. An' as for life, why, thet's cheap in Texas."

"Who *is* Bland?" asked Duane, quickly changing the subject. "What do you know about him?"

"We don't know who he is, or where he hails from," replied Euchre. "Thet's always been somethin' to interest the gang. He must have been a young man when he struck Texas. Now he's middle age. I remember how years ago he was soft spoken an' not rough in talk or act like he is now. Bland ain't likely his right name. He knows a lot. He can doctor you, an' he's shore a knowin' feller with tools. He's the kind thet rules men. Outlaws are always ridin' in here to join his gang an', if it hadn't been fer the gamblin' an' gun play, he'd have a thousand men around him."

"How many in his gang now?"

"I reckon there's short of a hundred now. The number varies. Then Bland has several small camps up an' down the river. Also he has men back on the cattle ranges."

"How does he control such a big force?" asked Duane. "Especially when his band's composed of badmen. Luke Stevens said he had no use for Bland. And I heard once somewhere that Bland was a devil."

"Thet's it. He is a devil. He's as hard as flint, violent in temper, never made any friends except his right-hand men, Dave Rugg an' Chess Alloway. Bland'll shoot at a wink. He's killed a lot of fellers an' some fer nothin'. The reason thet outlaws gather 'round him an' stick is because he's a safe refuge, an' then he's well heeled. Bland is rich. They

57

say he has a hundred thousand *pesos* hid somewhere an' lots of gold. But he's free with money. He gambles when he's not off with a shipment of cattle. He throws money around. An' the fact is there's always plenty of money where he is. Thet's what holds the gang. Dirty, bloody money!"

"It's a wonder he hasn't been killed. All these years on the border!" exclaimed Duane.

"Wal," replied Euchre dryly, "he's been quicker on the draw than the other fellers who hankered to kill him, thet's all."

Euchre's reply rather chilled Duane's interest for the moment. Such remarks always made his mind revolve around facts pertaining to himself.

"Speakin' of this here swift wrist game," went on Euchre, "there's been considerable talk in camp about your throwin' of a gun. You know, Buck, thet among us fellers . . . us hunted men . . . there ain't anythin' calculated to 'rouse respect like a slick hand with a gun. I heard Bland say this afternoon . . . an' he said it serious-like an' speculative . . . thet he'd never seen your equal. He was watchin' you close, he said, an' just couldn't follow your hand when you drawed. All the fellers who seen you meet Bosomer had somethin' to say. Bo was about as handy with a gun as any man in this camp, barrin' Chess Alloway an' mebbe Bland himself. Chess is the captain with a Colt . . . or he was. An' he shore didn't like the references made about your speed. Bland was honest in acknowledgin' it, but he didn't like it, neither. Some of the fellers allowed your draw might have been just accident. But most of them figgered different. An' they all shut up when Bland told who an' what your dad was. 'Pears to me I once seen your dad in a gun scrape over at Stanton, years ago. Wal, I put my oar in today among the fellers, an' I says: 'What ails you locoed gents? Did young Duane budge an inch when Bo came roarin' out, blood in his eye? Wasn't he cool an' quiet, steady of lips, an' weren't his eyes readin' Bo's mind? An' thet lightnin' draw . . . can't you all see thet's a family gift?'"

Euchre's narrow eyes twinkled, and he gave the dough he was rolling a slap with a flour-whitened hand. Manifestly he had proclaimed himself a champion and partner of Duane's, with all the pride an old man could feel in a young one whom he admired.

"Wal," he resumed presently, "thet's your introduction to the border, Buck. An' your card was a high trump. You'll be let severely alone by real gunfighters an' men like Bland, Alloway, Rugg, an' the bosses of the other gangs. After all, these real men *are* men, you know an', unless you cross them, they're no more likely to interfere with you than you are with them. But there's a sight of fellers like Bosomer in the river country. They'll all want your game. An' every town you ride into will scare up some cowpuncher full of booze or a long-haired four-flush gunman or a sheriff . . . an' these men will be playin' to the crowd an' yellin' for your blood. Thet's the Texas of it. You'll have to hide ferever in the brakes, or you'll have to kill such men. Buck, I reckon this ain't cheerful news to a decent chap like you. I'm only tellin' you because I've taken a likin' to you, an' I seen right off thet you ain't border wise. Let's eat now, an' afterward we'll go out so the gang can see you're not hidin'.'"

When Duane went out with Euchre, the sun was setting behind a blue range of mountains across the river in Mexico. They valley appeared to open to the southwest. It was a tranquil, beautiful scene. Somewhere in a house near at hand a woman was singing. In the road Duane saw a little Mexican boy driving home some cows, one of which wore a bell. The sweet, happy voice of a woman and a whistling barefoot boy — these seemed utterly out of place here.

Euchre presently led to the square and the row of rough houses Duane remembered. He almost stepped on a wide imprint in the dust where Bosomer had confronted him. A sudden fury beset him that he should be affected strangely by the sight of it.

"Let's have a look in here," said Euchre.

Duane had to bend his head to enter the door. He found himself in a very large room enclosed by adobe walls and roofed with brush. It was full of rude benches, tables, seats. At one corner a number of kegs and barrels lay side by side in a rack. A Mexican boy was lighting lamps hung on posts that sustained the log rafters of the roof.

"The only feller who's goin' to put a close eye on you is Benson," said Euchre. "He runs the place an' sells drinks. The gang calls him Jackrabbit Benson, because he's always got his eye peeled an' his ear cocked. Don't notice him if he looks you over, Buck. Benson is scared to death of every new-comer who rustles into Bland's camp. An' the reason, I take it, is because he's done somebody dirt. He's hidin'. Not from a sheriff or ranger! Men who hide from them don't act like Jackrabbit Benson. He's hidin' from some guy who's huntin' him to kill him. Wal, I'm always expectin' to see some feller ride in here an' throw a gun on Benson. Can't say I'd be grieved."

Duane casually glanced in the direction indicated, and he saw a spare, gaunt man with a face strikingly white beside the red and bronze and dark skins of the men around him. It was a cadaverous face. The black mustache hung down; a heavy lock of black hair dropped down over the brow; deep-set, hollow, staring eyes looked out piercingly. The man had a restless, alert, nervous manner. He put his hands on the board that served as a bar and stared at Duane. But when he met Duane's glance, he turned hurriedly to go on serving liquor.

"What have you got against him?" inquired Duane as he sat down beside Euchre. He asked more for something to say than from real interest. What did he care about a mean, haunted, craven-faced criminal?

"Wal, mebbe I'm cross-grained," replied Euchre apologetically. "Shore an outlaw an' rustler such as me can't be touchy. But I never stole nothin' but cattle from some rancher who never missed 'em anyway. Thet sneak Benson . . . he was the means of puttin' a little girl in Bland's way."

"Girl?" queried Duane, now with real attention.

"Shore. Bland's great on women. I'll tell you about this girl when we get out of here. Some of the gang are goin' to be sociable, an' I can't talk about the chief."

During the ensuing half hour a number of outlaws passed by Duane and Euchre, halted for a greeting or sat down for a moment. They were all gruff, loud voiced, merry, and good natured. Duane replied civilly and agreeably when he was personally addressed, but he refused all invitations to drink and gamble. Evidently he had been accepted, in a way, as one of their clan. No one made any hint of an allusion to his affair with Bosomer. Duane saw readily that Euchre was well liked. One outlaw borrowed from him; another asked for tobacco.

By the time it was dark the big room was full of outlaws and Mexicans, most of whom were engaged at monte. These gamblers, especially the Mexicans, were intense and quiet.

The noise in the place came from the drinkers, the loungers. Duane had seen gambling resorts — some of the famous ones in San Antonio and El Paso, a few in border towns where license went unchecked. But this place of Jackrabbit Benson's impressed him as one where guns and knives were accessories to the game. To his perhaps rather distinguishing eye the most prominent thing about the gamesters appeared to be their weapons. On several of the tables were piles of silver — Mexican *pesos* — as large and high as the crown of his hat. There were also piles of gold and silver in United States coin. Duane needed no experienced eyes to see that betting was heavy and that heavy sums exchanged hands. The Mexicans showed a sterner obsession, an intense passion. Some of the Americans staked freely, nonchalantly, as befitted men to whom money was nothing. These latter were manifestly winning, for there were brother outlaws who wagered coin with grudging, sullen, greedy eyes. Boisterous talk and laughter among the drinking men drowned, except at intervals, the low, brief talk of the gamblers. The clink of coin sounded incessantly, sometimes just low, steady musical rings and again, when a pile was tumbled quickly, there was a silvery crash. Here an outlaw pounded on a table with the butt of his gun; there another noisily palmed a roll of dollars while he studied his opponent's face. The noises, however, in Benson's den did not contribute to any extent to the sinister aspect of the place. That seemed to come from the grim and reckless faces, from the bent, intent heads, from the dark lights and shades. There were bright lights, but these served only to make the shadows. And in the shadows lurked unrestrained lust of gain, a spirit ruthless and reckless, something at once suggesting lawlessness, theft, murder, and hell.

"Bland's not here tonight," Euchre was saying. "He left today on one of his trips, takin' Alloway an' some others. But his other man, Rugg, he's here. See him standin' with them three fellers, all close to Benson. Rugg's the little bow-legged man with the half of his face shot off. He's one eyed. But he can shore see out of the one he's got. An', darn me, there's Hardin. You know him? He's got an outlaw gang as big as Bland's. Hardin is standin' next to Benson. See how quiet an' unassumin' he looks. Yes, thet's Hardin. He comes here once in a while to see Bland. They're friends, which's shore strange. Do you see thet greaser there . . . the one with gold an' lace on his sombrero? Thet's Manuel, a Mexican bandit. He's a great gambler. Comes here often to drop his coin. Next to him is Bill Marr . . . the feller with the bandanna 'round his head. Bill rode in the other day with some fresh bullet holes. He's been shot more'n any feller I ever heard of. He's full of lead. Funny, because Bill's no trouble hunter, an' like me he'd rather run than shoot. But he's the best rustler Bland's got . . . a grand rider an' a wonder with cattle. An' see the tow-headed youngster. Thet's Kid Fuller, the kid of Bland's gang. Fuller has hit the pace hard, an' he won't last the year out on the border. He killed his sweetheart's father, got run out of Staceytown, took to stealin' hosses. An' next he's here with Bland. Another boy gone wrong an' now shore a hard nut."

Euchre went on calling Duane's attention to other men, just as he happened to glance over them. Any one of them would have been a marked man in a respectable crowd. Here each took his place with more or less distinction, according to the record of his past wild prowess and his present possibilities. Duane, realizing that he was tolerated here, received in carelessly friendly spirit by this terrible

63

class of outcasts, experienced a feeling of revulsion that amounted almost to horror. Was his being here not an ugly dream? What had he in common with such ruffians? Then in a flash of memory came the painful proof . . . he was a criminal in sight of Texas law. He, too, was an outcast.

For the moment Duane was wrapped up in painful reflections, but Euchre's heavy hand, clapping with a warning hold on his arm, brought him back to outside things. The hum of voices, the clink of coin, the loud laughter had ceased. There was a silence that manifestly had followed some unusual word or action sufficient to still the room. It was broken by a harsh curse and the scrape of a bench on the floor. Some man had risen.

"You stacked the cards, you son of a bitch!"

"Say that twice," another voice replied, so different in its cool, ominous tone from the other.

"I'll say it twice," returned the first gamester in hot haste. "I'll say it three times. I'll whistle it. Are you deaf? You light-fingered gent! You stacked the cards!"

Silence ensued, deeper than before, pregnant with meaning. For all that Duane saw, not an outlaw moved for a full moment. Then suddenly the room was full of disorder as men rose and ran and dived everywhere.

"Run or duck!" yelled Euchre, close to Duane's ear. With that he dashed for the door. Duane leaped after him. They ran into a jostling mob. Heavy gunshots and hoarse yells hurried the crowd Duane was with pell-mell out into the darkness. There they all halted, and several peeped in at the door.

"Who was the Kid callin'?" asked one outlaw.

"Bud Marsh," replied another.

"I reckon them fust shots was Bud's. *Adíos,* Kid. It was

comin' to him," went on yet another.

"How many shots?"

"Three or four, I counted."

"Three heavy an' one light. The light one was the Kid's Thirty-Eight. Listen! There's the Kid hollerin' now. He ain't cashed anyway."

At this juncture most of the outlaws began to file back into the room. Duane thought he had seen and heard enough in Benson's den for one night, and he started slowly down the walk. Presently Euchre caught up with him.

"Nobody's hurt much, which's shore some strange," he said. "The Kid . . . young Fuller thet I was tellin' you about . . . he was drinkin' an' losin'. Lost his nut, too, callin' Bud Marsh thet way. Bud's as straight at cards as any of 'em. Somebody grabbed Bud, who shot into the roof. An' Fuller's arm was knocked up. He only hit a greaser."

Chapter Six

Next morning Duane found that a moody and despondent spell had fastened on him. Wishing to be alone, he went out and walked a trail leading around the river bluff. He thought and thought. After a while he made out that the trouble with him probably was that he could not resign himself to his fate. He abhorred the possibility chance seemed to hold in store for him. He could not believe there was no hope. But what to do appeared beyond his power to tell.

Duane had intelligence and keenness enough to see his peril — the danger threatening his character as a man just as much as that which threatened his life. He cared vastly more, he discovered, for what he considered honor and integrity than he did for life. He saw that it was bad for him to be alone. But, it appeared, lonely months and perhaps years inevitably must be his. Another thing puzzled him. In the bright light of day he could not recall the state of mind that was his at twilight or dusk or in the dark night. By day these visitations became to him what they really were — phantoms of his conscience. He could dismiss the thought of them then. He could scarcely remember or believe that this strange feat of fancy or imagination had troubled him, pained him, made him sleepless and sick.

That morning Duane spent an unhappy hour wrestling decision out of the unstable condition of his mind. But at length he determined to create interest in all that he came across and so forget himself as much as possible. He had an opportunity now to see just what the outlaw's life really was. He meant to force himself to be curious, sympathetic, clear sighted. He would stay here in the valley until its possibilities had been exhausted or until circumstances sent him out upon his uncertain way.

When he returned to the shack, Euchre was cooking dinner.

"Say, Buck, I've news for you," he said, and his tone conveyed either pride in his possession of such news or pride in Duane. "Feller named Bradley rode in this mornin'. He's heard some about you. Told about the ace of spades they put over the bullet holes in thet cowpuncher, Bain, you plugged. Then there was a rancher shot at a water hole twenty miles south of Wellston. Reckon you didn't do it?"

"No, I certainly did not," replied Duane.

"Wal, you get the blame. It ain't nothin' for a feller to be saddled with gun plays he never made. An' Buck, if you ever get famous, as seems likely, you'll be blamed for many a crime. The border'll make an outlaw an' murderer out of you. Wal, thet's enough of thet. I've more news. You're goin' to be popular."

"Popular? What do you mean?"

"I met Bland's wife this mornin'. She seen you the other day when you rode in. She shore wants to meet you an' so do some of the other women in camp. They always want to meet the new fellers who've just come in. It's lonesome for women here, an' they like to hear news from the towns."

"Well, Euchre, I don't want to be impolite, but I'd rather not meet any women," rejoined Duane.

"I was afraid you wouldn't. Don't blame you much. Women are hell. I was hopin', though, you might talk a little to

67

thet poor lonesome kid."

"What kid?" inquired Duane in surprise.

"Didn't I tell you about Jennie . . . the girl Bland's holdin' here . . . the one Jackrabbit Benson had a hand in stealin'?"

"You mentioned a girl. That's all. Tell me now," replied Duane abruptly.

"Wal, I got it this way. Mebbe it's straight, an' mebbe it ain't. Some years ago Benson made a trip over the river to buy mescal an' other drinks. He'll sneak over there once in a while. An' as I get it, he run across a gang of greasers with some *gringo* prisoners. I don't know, but I reckon there was some barterin' perhaps murderin'. Anyway, Benson fetched the girl back. She was more dead than alive, but it turned out she was only starved an' scared half to death. She hadn't been harmed. I reckon she was then about fourteen years old. Benson's idea, he said, was to use her in his den sellin' drinks an' the like. But I never went much on Jackrabbit's word. Bland seen the kid right off and took her . . . bought her from Benson. You can gamble Bland didn't do thet from notions of chivalry. I ain't gainsayin', however, but thet Jennie was better off with Kate Bland. She's been hard on Jennie, but she's kept Bland an' the other men from treatin' the kid shameful. Late Jennie has growed into an all-fired pretty girl, an' Kate is powerful jealous of her. I can see hell brewin' over there in Bland's cabin. Thet's why I wish you'd come over with me. Bland's hardly ever home. His wife's invited you. Shore, if she gets sweet on you, as she has on. . . . Wal, thet'd complicate matters. But you'd get to see Jennie, an' mebbe you could help her. Mind, I ain't hintin' nothin.' I'm just wantin' to put her in your way. You're a man an' can think fer yourself. I had a baby girl once an', if she'd lived, she be as big as Jennie now, an' by Gawd I wouldn't want her here in Bland's camp."

"I'll go, Euchre. Take me over," replied Duane. He felt Euchre's eyes upon him. The old outlaw, however, had no more to say.

In the afternoon Euchre set off with Duane, and soon they reached Bland's cabin. Duane remembered it as the one where he had seen the pretty woman watching him ride by. He could not recall what she looked like. The cabin was the same as the other adobe structures in the valley, but it was larger and pleasantly located rather high up in a grove of cottonwoods. In the windows and upon the porch were evidences of a woman's hand. Through the open door Duane caught a glimpse of bright Mexican blankets and rugs.

Euchre knocked upon the side of the door.

"Is that you, Euchre?" asked a girl's voice, low, hesitatingly. The tone of it, rather deep and with a note of fear, struck Duane. He wondered what she would be like.

"Yes, it's me, Jennie. Where's Missus Bland?" asked Euchre.

"She went over to Deger's. There's somebody sick," replied the girl.

Euchre turned and whispered something about luck. The snap of the outlaw's eyes was added significance to Duane.

"Jennie, come out or let us come in. Here's the young man I was tellin' you about," Euchre said.

"Oh, I can't! I look so . . . so . . . !"

"Never mind how you look," interrupted the outlaw in a whisper. "It ain't no time to care fer thet. Here's young Duane, Jennie. He's no rustler, no thief. He's different. Come out, Jennie, an' mebbe he'll. . . ."

Euchre did not complete his sentence. He had spoken low, with his glance shifting from side to side, but what he said was sufficient to bring the girl quickly. She appeared in the doorway with downcast eyes and a stain of red on her white cheeks. She had a pretty, sad face and bright hair.

"Don't be bashful, Jennie," said Euchre. "You and Duane have a chance to talk a little. Now, I'll go fetch Missus Bland, but I won't be hurryin'."

With that Euchre went away through the cottonwoods.

"I'm glad to meet you, Miss . . . Miss Jennie," said Duane. "Euchre didn't mention your last name. He asked me to come over to. . . ."

Duane's attempt at pleasantry halted short when Jennie lifted her lashes to look at him. Some kind of a shock went through Duane. Her gray eyes were beautiful, but it had not been beauty that cut short his speech. He seemed to see a tragic struggle between hope and doubt that shone in her piercing gaze. She kept looking, and Duane could not break the silence. It was no ordinary moment.

"What did you come here for?" she asked at last.

"To see you," replied Duane, glad to speak.

"Why?"

"Well, Euchre thought . . . he wanted me to talk to you, cheer you up a bit," replied Duane, somewhat lamely. The earnest eyes embarrassed him.

"Euchre's good. He's the only person in this awful place who's been good to me. But he's afraid of Bland. He said you were different. Who are you?"

Duane told her.

"You're not a robber or rustler or murderer or some badman come here to hide?"

"No, I'm not," replied Duane, trying to smile.

"Then why are you here?"

"I'm on the dodge. You know what that means. I got in

70

a shooting scrape at home and had to run off. When it blows over, I hope to go back."

"But you can't be honest here!"

"Yes, I can."

"Oh, I know what these outlaws are. Yes, you're different." She kept the strained gaze upon him, but hope was kindling, and the hard lines of her youthful face were softening. Something sweet and warm stirred deeply in Duane as he realized the unfortunate girl was experiencing a birth of trust in him.

"Oh God! Maybe you're the man to save me . . . to take me away before it's too late!"

Duane's spirit leaped. "Maybe I am," he said instantly.

She seemed to check a blind impulse to run into his arms. Her cheeks flamed, her lips quivered, her bosom swelled under her ragged dress. Then the glow began to fade; doubt once more assailed her.

"It can't be. You're only . . . after me, too, like Bland . . . like all of them."

Duane's long arms went out, and his hands clasped her shoulders. He shook her. "Look me straight in the eye. There are decent men. Haven't you a father . . . a brother?"

"They're dead . . . killed by raiders. We lived in Dimmit County. I was carried away," Jennie replied hurriedly. She put up an appealing hand to him. "Forgive me. I believe . . . I *know* you're good. It was only . . . I live so much in fear . . . I'm half crazy . . . I've almost forgotten what good men are like. Mister Duane, you'll help me?"

"Yes, Jennie, I will. Tell me how. What must I do? Have you any plan?"

"Oh, no. But take me away."

"I'll try," said Duane simply. "That won't be easy, though. I must have time to think. You must help me. There are

71

many things to consider. Horses, food, trails, and then the best time to make the attempt. Are you watched . . . kept prisoner?"

"No. I could have run off lots of times, but I was afraid. I'd only have fallen into worse hands. Euchre has told me that. Missus Bland beats me, half starves me, but she has kept me from her husband and these other dogs. She's been as good as that, and I'm grateful. She hasn't done it for love of me, though. She always hated me. And lately she's growing jealous. There was a man came here by the name of Spence . . . so he called himself. He tried to be kind to me, but she wouldn't let him. She was in love with him. She's a bad woman. Bland finally shot Spence, and that ended that. She's been jealous ever since. I hear her fighting with Bland about me. She swears she'll kill me before he gets me. And Bland laughs in her face. Then I've heard Chess Alloway try to persuade Bland to give me to him. But Bland doesn't laugh then. Just lately before Bland went away things almost came to a head. I couldn't sleep. I wished Missus Bland would kill me. I'll certainly kill myself if they ruin me. Duane, you must be quick, if you'd save me."

"I realize that," replied Duane thoughtfully. "I think my difficulty will be to fool Missus Bland. If she suspected me, she'd have the whole gang of outlaws on me at once."

"She would that. You've got to be careful . . . and quick."

"What kind of a woman is she?" inquired Duane.

"She's . . . she's brazen. I've heard her with her lovers. They get drunk sometimes when Bland's away. She's got a terrible temper. She's vain. She likes flattery. Oh, you could fool her easy enough if you'd lower yourself to . . . to. . . ."

"To make love to her?" interrupted Duane.

72

Jennie bravely turned shamed eyes to meet his.

"My girl, I'd do worse than that to get you away from here," he said bluntly.

"But . . . Duane," she faltered, and again she put out the appealing hand. "Bland will kill you."

Duane made no reply to this. He was trying to still a rising, strange tumult in his breast. The old emotion — the rush of an instinct to kill. He turned cold all over.

"Chess Alloway will kill you if Bland doesn't," went on Jennie, her tragic eyes on Duane's.

"Maybe he will," said Duane. It was difficult for him to force a smile, but he achieved one.

"Oh, better take me off at once," she said. "Save me without risking so much . . . without making love to Missus Bland!"

"Surely, if I can. There! I see Euchre coming with a woman."

"That's her. Oh, she mustn't see me with you."

"Wait a moment," whispered Duane, as Jennie slipped indoors. "We've settled it. Don't forget. I'll find some way to get word to you, perhaps through Euchre. Meanwhile keep up your courage. Remember I'll save you somehow. We'll try strategy first. Whatever you see or hear me do, don't think less of me."

Jennie checked him with a gesture and a wonderful gray flash of eyes. "I'll bless you with every drop of blood in my heart," she whispered passionately.

It was only as she turned away into the room that Duane saw she was lame and that she wore Mexican sandals over bare feet. He sat down upon a bench on the porch and directed his attention to the approaching couple. The trees of the grove were thick enough for him to make reasonably sure that Mrs. Bland had not seen him talking to Jennie.

When the outlaw's wife drew near, Duane saw that she was a tall, strong, full-bodied woman, rather good looking with a full-blown, bold attractiveness. Duane was more concerned with her expression than with her good looks and, as she appeared unsuspicious, he felt relieved. The situation then took on a singular zest.

Euchre came up on the porch and awkwardly introduced Duane to Mrs. Bland. She was young, probably not over twenty-five, and not quite so prepossessing at close range. Her eyes were large, rather prominent, and brown in color. Her mouth, too, was large, with the lips full, and she had white teeth.

Duane took her proffered hand and remarked frankly that he was glad to meet her. Mrs. Bland appeared pleased. Her laugh, which followed, was loud and rather musical.

"Mister Duane . . . Buck Duane, Euchre said, didn't he?" she asked.

"Buckley," corrected Duane. "The nickname's not of my choosing."

"I'm certainly glad to meet you, Buckley Duane," she said, as she took the seat Duane offered her. "Sorry to have been out. Kid Fuller's lying over at Deger's. You know he was shot last night? He's got fever today. When Bland's away, I have to nurse all these shot-up boys, and it sure takes my time. Have you been waiting here alone? Didn't see that slattern girl of mine?"

She gave him a sharp glance. The woman had an extraordinary play of features, Duane thought, and unless she was smiling was not pretty at all.

"I've been alone," replied Duane. "Haven't seen anybody but a sick-looking girl with a bucket. And she ran when she saw me."

"That was Jen," said Mrs. Bland. "She's the kid we keep

here, and she sure hardly pays for her keep. Did Euchre tell you about her?"

"Now that I think of it, he did say something or other."

"What did he tell you about me?" bluntly asked Mrs. Bland.

"Wal, Kate," replied Euchre, speaking for himself, "you needn't worry none, for I told Buck nothin' but compliments."

Evidently the outlaw's wife liked Euchre, for her keen glance rested with amusement upon him.

"As for Jen, I'll tell you her story some day," went on the woman. "It's a common enough story along this river. Euchre here is a tender-hearted old fool, and Jen has taken him in."

"Wal, seein' as you've got me figgered correct," said Euchre dryly, "I'll go in an' talk to Jennie, if I may?"

"Certainly. Go ahead. Jen calls you her best friend," said Mrs. Bland amiably. "You're always fetching some Mexican stuff, and that's why, I guess."

When Euchre had shuffled into the house, Mrs. Bland turned to Duane with curiosity and interest in her gaze.

"Bland told me about you."

"What did he say?" queried Duane in pretended alarm.

"Oh, you needn't think he's done you dirt. Bland's not that kind of a man. He said: 'Kate, there's a young fellow in camp . . . rode in here on the dodge. He's no criminal, and he refused to join my band. Wish he would. Slickest hand with a gun I've seen for many a day! I'd like to see him and Chess meet out there in the road.' Then Bland went on to tell how you and Bosomer came together."

"What did you say?" inquired Duane as she paused.

"Me? Why, I asked him what you looked like," she replied gaily.

"Well?" went on Duane.

" 'Magnificent chap,' Bland said. 'Bigger than any man in the valley. Just a great, blue-eyed, sunburned boy!' "

"Humph!" exclaimed Duane, "I'm sorry he led you to expect somebody worth seeing."

"But I'm not disappointed," she returned archly. "Duane, are you going to stay long here in camp?"

"Yes, till I run out of money and have to move. Why?"

Mrs. Bland's face underwent one of the singular changes. The smiles and flushes and glances, all that had been coquettish about her, had lent her a certain attractiveness, almost beauty and youth. But with some powerful emotion she changed and instantly became a woman of discontent, Duane imagined, of deep, violent nature.

"I'll tell you, Duane," she said earnestly, "I'm sure glad if you mean to bide here a while. I'm a miserable woman, Duane. I'm an outlaw's wife, and I hate him and the life I have to lead. I come of a good family in Brownsville. I never knew Bland was an outlaw till long after he married me. We were separated at times. I imagined he was away on business, but the truth came out. Bland shot my own cousin who told me. My family cast me off, and I had to flee with Bland. I was only eighteen then. I've lived here since. I never see a decent woman or man. I never hear anything about my old home or folks or friends. I'm buried here . . . buried alive with a lot of thieves and murderers. Can you blame me for being glad to see a young fellow . . . a gentleman . . . like the boys I used to go with? I tell you it makes me feel full . . . I want to cry. I'm sick for somebody to talk to. I have no children, thank God! If I had, I'd not stay here. I'm sick of this hole. I'm lonely. . . ."

There appeared to be no doubt about the truth of all this. Genuine emotion checked, then halted, the hurried speech. She broke down and cried. It seemed strange to Duane that an outlaw's wife — and a woman who fitted her consort and the wild nature of their surroundings — should have weakness enough to weep. Duane believed and pitied her.

"I'm sorry for you," he said.

"Don't be *sorry* for me," she said. "That only makes me see the . . . the difference between you and me. And don't pay any attention to what these outlaws say about me. They're ignorant. They couldn't understand me. You'll hear that Bland killed men who ran after me, but that's a lie. Bland, like all the other outlaws along this river, is always looking for somebody to kill. He *swears* not, but I don't believe him. He explains that gun play gravitates to men who are the real thing . . . that it is provoked by the four-flushers, the badmen. I don't know. All I know is that somebody is being killed every other day. He hated Spence before Spence ever saw me."

"Would Bland object if I called on you occasionally?" inquired Duane.

"No, he wouldn't. He likes me to have friends. Ask him yourself when he comes back. The trouble has been that two or three of his men fell in love with me and, when half drunk, got to fighting. You're not going to do that."

"I'm not going to get half drunk, that's certain," said Duane.

He was surprised to see her eyes dilate then glow with fire. Before she could reply, Euchre returned to the porch, and that put an end to the conversation.

Duane was content to let the matter rest there and had little more to say. Euchre and Mrs. Bland talked and joked, while Duane listened. He tried to form some estimate of her character. Manifestly she had suffered a wrong, if not

77

worse, at Bland's hands. She was bitter, morbid, overemotional. If she was a liar, which seemed likely enough, she was a frank one and believed herself. She had no cunning. The thing which struck Duane so forcibly was that she thirsted for respect. In that, better than in her weakness of vanity, he thought he had discovered a trait through which he would manage her. Once, while he was revolving these thoughts, he happened to glance into the house, and deep in the shadow of a corner he caught a pale gleam of Jennie's face with great, staring eyes on him. She had been watching him, listening to what he said. He saw from her expression that she had realized what had been so hard for her to believe. Watching his chance, he flashed a look at her; and then it seemed to him the change in her face was wonderful.

Later, after he had left Mrs. Bland with a meaningful — *"Adíos, hasta mañana"* — and was walking along beside the old outlaw, he found himself thinking of the girl instead of the woman, and of how he had seen her face blaze with hope and gratitude.

Chapter Seven

That night Duane was not troubled by ghosts haunting his waking and sleeping hours. He awoke feeling bright and eager and grateful to Euchre for having put something worth while into his mind. During breakfast, however, he was unusually thoughtful, working over the idea of how much or how little he would confide in the outlaw. He was aware of Euchre's scrutiny.

"Wal," began the old man at last, "how'd you make out with the kid?"

"Kid?" inquired Duane tentatively.

"Jennie, I mean. What'd you an' she talk about?"

"We had a little chat. You know you wanted me to cheer her up."

Euchre sat with coffee cup poised and narrowed eyes studying Duane. "Reckon you cheered her, all right. What I'm a-feared of is mebbe you done the job too well."

"How so?"

"Wal, when I went in to Jen last night, I thought she was half crazy. She was burstin' with excitement, an' the look in her eyes hurt me. She wouldn't tell me a darn word you said, but she hung onto my hands, an' showed every way without speakin' how she wanted to thank me fer bringin' you over. Buck, it was plain to me thet you'd either gone the limit or else you'd been kinder prodigal of cheer an' hope. I'd hate to think you'd led Jennie to hope more'n ever would come true." Euchre paused and, as there seemed no reply forthcoming, he went on: "Buck, I've seen some outlaws whose word was good. Mine is. You can trust me. I trusted you, didn't I, takin' you over there an' puttin' you wise to my tryin' to help thet poor kid?"

Thus enjoined by Euchre, Duane began to tell the conversation with Jennie and Mrs. Bland word for word. Long before he had reached an end, Euchre set down the coffee cup and began to stare, and at the conclusion of the story his face lost some of its red color and beads of sweat stood out thickly on his brow.

"Wal, if thet doesn't floor me!" he ejaculated, blinking at Duane. "Young man, I figgered you was some swift an' sure to make your mark on this river, but I reckon I missed your real caliber. So thet's what it means to be a man! I guess I'd forgot. Wal, I'm old an', even if my heart was in the right place, I never was built fer big stunts. Do you know what it'll take to do all you promised Jen?"

"I haven't any idea," replied Duane gravely.

"You'll have to pull the wool over Kate Bland's eyes an', even if she falls in love with you, which's shore likely, thet won't be easy. An' she'd kill you in a minnit, Buck, if she ever got wise. You ain't mistaken her none, are you?"

"Not me, Euchre. She's a woman. I'd fear her more than any man."

"Wal, you'll have to kill Bland an' Chess Alloway an' Rugg, an' mebbe some others, before you can ride off into the hills with thet girl."

"Why? Can't we plan to be nice to Missus Bland and then at an opportune time sneak off without any gun play?"

"Don't see how on earth," returned Euchre earnestly. "When Bland's away, he leaves all kinds of spies an' scouts watchin' the valley trails. They've all got rifles. You couldn't git by them. But when the boss is home, there's a difference.

Only, of course, him an' Chess keep their eyes peeled. They both stay to home pretty much, except when they're playin' monte or poker over at Benson's. So I say the best bet is to pick out a good time in the afternoon, drift over care-less-like with a couple of hosses, choke Missus Bland or knock her on the head, take Jennie with you, an' make a rush to git out of the valley. If you had luck, you might pull thet stunt without throwin' a gun. But I reckon the best figgerin' would include dodgin' some lead an' leavin' at least Bland or Alloway dead behind you. I'm figgerin', of course, thet when they come home an' find out you're visitin' Kate frequent, they'll jest naturally look fer results. Chess don't like you, fer no reason except you're swift on the draw . . . mebbe swifter'n him. Thet's the hell of this gun play business. No one can ever tell who's the swifter of two gunmen till they meet. Thet fact holds a fascination mebbe you'll learn some day. Bland would treat you civil unless there was reason not to, an' then I don't believe he'd invite himself to a meetin' with you. He'd set Chess or Rugg to put you out of the way. Still Bland's no coward an', if you came across him at a bad moment, you'd have to be quicker'n you was with Bosomer."

"All right. I'll meet what comes," said Duane quickly. "The great point is to have horses ready, pick the right moment, then rush the trick through."

"Thet's the *only* chance fer success. An' you can't do it alone."

"I'll have to. I wouldn't ask you to help me. Leave you behind!"

"Wal, I'll take my chances," replied Euchre gruffly. "I'm goin' to help Jennie, you can gamble your last *peso* on thet. There's only four men in this camp who would shoot me . . . Bland, an' his right-hand pards, an' thet rabbit-faced

Benson. If you happened to put out Bland and Chess, I'd
stand a good show with the other two. Anyway, I'm old
an' tired . . . what's the difference if I do git plugged? I
can risk as much as you, Buck, even if I am afraid of gun
play. You said correct, 'Hosses ready, the right minnit,
then rush the trick.' Thet much's settled. Now let's figger
all the little details."

They talked and planned, though in truth it was Euchre
who planned, Duane who listened and agreed. While await-
ing the return of Bland and his lieutenants, it would be
well for Duane to grow friendly with the other outlaws, to
sit in a few games of monte, or show a willingness to spend
a little money. The two schemers were to call upon Mrs.
Bland every day — Euchre to carry messages of cheer and
warning to Jennie, Duane to blind the elder woman at
any cost. These preliminaries decided upon, they proceeded
to put them into action.

No hard task was it to win the friendship of most of
those good-natured outlaws. They were used to men of a
better order than theirs coming to the hidden camps and
sooner or later sinking to their lower level. Besides, with
them everything was easy come, easy go. That was why
life itself went on so carelessly and usually ended so
cheaply. There were men among them, however, that made
Duane feel that terrible, inexplicable wrath rise in his
breast. He could not bear to be near them. He could not
trust himself. He felt that any instant a word, a deed,
something might call too deeply to that instinct he could
no longer control. Jackrabbit Benson was one of these men.
Because of him and other outlaws of his ilk, Duane could
scarcely ever forget the reality of things. This was a hidden
valley, a robbers' den, a rendezvous for murderers, a wild

place stained red by deeds of wild men. And because of that there was always a charged atmosphere. The merriest, idlest, most careless moment might in the flash of an eye end in ruthless and tragic action. In an assemblage of desperate characters it could not be otherwise. The terrible thing that Duane sensed was this. The valley was beautiful, sunny, fragrant, a place in which to dream. The mountaintops were always blue or gold rimmed; the yellow river slid by slowly and majestically; the birds sang in the cottonwoods; the horses grazed and pranced; children played, and women longed for love, freedom, happiness; the outlaws rode in and out, free with money and speech; they lived comfortably in their adobe homes, smoked, gambled, talked, laughed, whiled away the idle hours — and all the time life there was wrong, and the simplest moment might be precipitated by that evil into the most awful of contrasts. Duane felt rather than saw a dark, brooding shadow over the valley.

Then, without any solicitation or encouragement from Duane, the Bland woman fell passionately in love with him. His conscience was never troubled about the beginning of that affair. She launched herself. It took no great perspicuity on his part to see that. The thing which evidently held her in check was the newness, the strangeness, and for the moment the all-satisfying fact of his respect for her. Duane exerted himself to please, to amuse, to interest, to fascinate her, and always with deference. That was his strong point, and it had made his part easy so far. He believed he could carry the whole scheme through without involving himself any deeper.

He was playing at a game of love — playing with life and death. Sometimes he trembled, not that he feared Bland or Alloway or any other man, but at the depths of a life into which he had come to see. He was carried out of his old mood. Not once since this daring motive had stirred him had he been haunted by the phantom of Bain beside his bed. Rather had he been haunted by Jennie's sad face, her wistful smile, her eyes. He never was able to speak a word to her. What little communication he had with her was through Euchre who carried short messages. But he caught glimpses of her every time he went to the Bland house. She contrived somehow to pass door or window, to give him a look when chance afforded. Duane discovered with surprise that these moments were more thrilling to him than any with Mrs. Bland. Often Duane knew Jennie was sitting just inside the window, and then he felt inspired in his talk, and it was all made for her. So at least she came to know him while as yet she was almost a stranger. Jennie had been instructed by Euchre to listen, to understand that this was Duane's only chance to help keep her mind from constant worry, to gather the import of every word which had a double meaning.

Euchre said that the girl had begun to wither under the strain, to burn up with intense hope which had flamed within her. But all the difference Duane could see was a paler face and darker, more wonderful eyes. The eyes seemed to be entreating him to hurry, that time was flying, that soon it might be too late. Then there was another meaning in them, a light, a strange fire wholly inexplicable to Duane. It was only a flash, gone in an instant, but he remembered it because he had never seen it in any other woman's eyes. All through those waiting days he knew that Jennie's face and especially the warm, fleeting glances she gave him were responsible for a subtle and gradual change in him. This change, he fancied, was only that through remembrance of her he got rid of his pale, sickening ghosts.

One day a careless Mexican threw a lighted cigarette up into the brush matting that served as a ceiling for Benson's den, and there was a fire which left little more than the adobe walls standing. The result was that, while repairs were being made, there was no gambling and drinking. Time hung very heavily on the hands of some two score outlaws. Days passed by without a brawl, and Bland's valley saw more successive hours of peace than ever before. Duane, however, found the hours anything but empty. He spent more time at Mrs. Bland's. He walked miles on all the trails leading out of the valley. He had a care for the condition of his two horses.

Upon his return from the latest of these tramps Euchre suggested that they go down to the river to the boat landing. "Ferry couldn't run ashore this mornin'," said Euchre. "River gettin' low an' sand bars makin' it hard fer hosses. There's a greaser freight wagon stuck in the mud. I reckon we might hear news from the freighters. Bland's supposed to be in Mexico."

Nearly all the outlaws in camp were assembled on the river bank, lolling in the shade of the cottonwoods. The heat was oppressive. Not an outlaw offered to help the freighters, who were trying to dig a heavily freighted wagon out of the quicksand. Few outlaws would work for themselves, let alone for the despised Mexicans.

Duane and Euchre joined the lazy group and sat down with them. Euchre lighted a black pipe and, drawing his hat over his eyes, lay back in comfort after the manner of the majority of the outlaws. But Duane was alert, observing, thoughtful. He never missed anything. It was his belief that any moment an idle word might be of benefit to him.

Moreover, these rough men were always interesting.

"Bland's been chased acrost the river," said one.

"Naw, he's deliverin' cattle to thet Cuban ship," replied another.

"Big deal on, hey?"

"Some big. Rugg says the boss had an order fer fifteen thousand."

"Say, that order'll take a year to fill."

"Naw. Hardin is in cahoots with Bland. Between 'em they'll fill orders bigger'n thet."

"Wondered what Hardin was rustlin' in here fer."

Duane could not possibly attend to all the conversations among the outlaws. He endeavored to get the drift of talk nearest to him.

"Kid Fuller's goin' to cash," said a sandy-whiskered little outlaw.

"So Jim was tellin' me. Blood poison, ain't it? Thet hole wasn't bad, but he took the fever," rejoined a comrade.

"Deger says the Kid might pull through if he had nursin'."

"Wal, Kate Bland ain't nursin' any shot-up boys these days. She hasn't got time."

A laugh followed this sally then came a penetrating silence. Some of the outlaws glanced good naturedly at Duane. They bore him no ill will. Manifestly they were aware of Mrs. Bland's infatuation.

"Pete, 'pears to me you've said thet before."

"Shore. Wal, it's happened before."

This remark drew louder laughter and more significant glances at Duane. He did not choose to ignore them any longer.

"Boys, poke all the fun you like at me but don't mention any lady's name again. My hand is nervous and itchy these days."

He smiled as he spoke, and his speech was drawled, but the good humor in no ways weakened it. His latter remark was significant to a class of men who from inclination and necessity practiced at gun drawing until they wore callous and sore places on their thumbs and inculcated in the very deeps of their nervous organization a habit that made even the simplest and most innocent motion of the hand end at or near the hip. There was something remarkable about a gunfighter's hand. It never seemed to be gloved, never to be injured, never out of sight, or in an awkward position.

There were grizzled outlaws in that group, some of whom had many notches on their gun handles, and they with their comrades accorded Duane silence that carried conviction of the regard in which he was held. Duane could not recall any other instance where he had let fall a similar speech to these men, and certainly he had never before hinted of his possibilities. He saw instantly that he could not have done better.

"Orful hot, ain't it?" remarked Bill Black presently. Bill could not keep quiet for long. He was a typical Texas desperado, had never been anything else. He was stoop shouldered and bowlegged from much riding, a wiry little man, all muscle, with a square head, a hard face partly black from scrubby beard and red from sun, and a bright, roving, cruel eye. His shirt was open at the neck, showing a grizzled breast.

"Is there any guy in this heah outfit sport enough to go swimmin'?" he asked.

This raised a laugh in which Black joined, but no one seemed eager to join him in a bath.

"Laziest outfit I ever rustled with," went on Bill discontentedly. "Nuthin' to do! Say, if nobody wants to swim, maybe some of you'll gamble?"

He produced a dirty pack of cards and waved them at the motionless crowd.

"Bill, you're too good at cards," replied a lanky outlaw.

"Now, Jasper, you say thet powerful sweet, an' you look sweet, or I might take it to heart," replied Black, with a sudden change of tone.

Here it was again — that upflashing passion. What Jasper saw fit to reply would mollify the outlaw, or it would not. There was an even balance.

"No offense, Bill," said Jasper placidly, without moving.

Bill grunted and forgot Jasper, but he seemed restless and dissatisfied. Duane knew him to be an inveterate gambler. As Benson's place was out of running order, Black was like a fish on dry land.

"Wal, if you all are afraid of the cards, what will you bet on?" he asked in disgust.

"Bill, I'll play you a game of mumbly peg fer two bits," replied one.

Black eagerly accepted. Betting to him was a serious matter. The game obsessed him, not the stakes. He entered into the mumbly-peg contest with a thoughtful mien and a corded brow. He won. Other comrades tried their luck with him and lost. Finally, when Bill had exhausted their supply of two-bit pieces or their desire for that particular game, he offered to bet on anything.

"See thet turtle dove there?" he said, pointing. "I'll bet he'll scare at one stone or he won't. Five pesos he'll fly, or he won't fly, when someone chucks a stone. Who'll take me up?"

That appeared to be more than the gambling spirit of several outlaws could withstand.

"Take thet. Easy money," said one.

"Who's goin' to chuck the stone?" asked another.

"Anybody," replied Bill.

"Wal, I'll bet you can scare him with one stone," said the first outlaw.

"We're in on thet, Jim to fire the darnick," chimed in the others.

The money was put up, the stone thrown. The turtle dove took flight to the great joy of all the outlaws except Bill.

"I'll bet you all he'll come back to thet tree inside of five minnets," he offered imperturbably.

Hereupon the outlaws did not show any laziness in their alacrity to cover Bill's money as it lay on the grass. Somebody had a watch, and they all sat down, dividing attention between the timepiece and the tree. The minutes dragged by to the accompaniment of various jocular remarks anent a fool and his money. When four and three-quarter minutes had passed, a turtle dove alighted in the cottownwood. Then ensued an impressive silence while Bill calmly pocketed the fifty dollars.

"But it ain't the same dove!" exclaimed one outlaw excitedly. "This'n is smaller, dustier, not so purple."

Bill eyed the speaker loftily. "Wal, you'll have to ketch the other one to prove thet. *Sabe,* pard? Now I'll bet any gent heah the fifty I won thet I can scare thet dove with one stone."

No one offered to take his wager.

"Wal, then, I'll bet any of you even money thet you can't scare him with one stone."

Not proof against this chance, the outlaws made up a purse, in no wise disconcerted by Bill's contemptuous allusions to their banding together. The stone was thrown. The dove did not fly. Thereafter, in regard to that bird, Bill was unable to coax or scorn his comrades into any kind of wager.

He tried them with a multiplicity of offers and in vain. Then he appeared at a loss for some unusual and seductive wager. Presently a little ragged Mexican boy came along the river trail, a particularly starved and poor-looking little fellow. Bill called to him and gave him a handful of silver coins. Speechless, dazed, he went his way, hugging the money.

"I'll bet he drops some before he gits to the road," declared Bill. "I'll bet he runs. Hurry, you four-flush gamblers."

Bill failed to interest any of his companions and forthwith became sullen and silent. Strangely his good humor departed in spite of the fact that he had won considerably. Duane, watching the disgruntled outlaw, marveled at him and wondered what was in his mind. These men were more variable than children, as unstable as water, as dangerous as dynamite.

"Bill, I'll bet you ten you can't spill whatever's in the bucket thet peon's packin'," said the outlaw called Jim.

Black's head came up with the action of a hawk about to swoop. Duane glanced from Black to the road, where he saw a crippled peon carrying a tin bucket toward the river. This peon was a half-witted Indian who lived in a shack and did odd jobs for the Mexicans. Duane had met him often.

"Jim, I'll take you up," replied Black.

Something, perhaps a harshness in his voice, caused Duane to whirl. He caught a leaping gleam in the outlaw's eye.

"Aw, Bill, thet's too fur a shot," said Jasper, as Black rested an elbow on his knee and sighted over the long, heavy Colt. The distance to the peon was about fifty paces, too far for even the most expert shot to hit a moving object so small as a bucket.

Duane, marvelously keen in the alignment of sights, was positive that Black held too high. Another look at the hard face, now tense and dark with blood, confirmed Duane's suspicion that the outlaw was not aiming at the bucket at all. Duane leaped and struck the leveled gun out of his hand. Another outlaw picked it up.

Black fell back astounded. Deprived of his weapon, he did not seem the same man, or else he was cowed by Duane's significant and formidable affront. Sullenly he turned away without even asking for his gun.

Chapter Eight

What a contrast, Duane thought, the evening of that day presented to the state of his soul! The sunset lingered in golden glory over the distant Mexican mountains; twilight came slowly; a faint breeze blew from the river, cool and sweet; the late cooing of a dove and the tinkle of a cowbell were the only sounds; a serene and tranquil peace lay over the valley. Inside Duane's body there was strife. This third facing of a desperate man had thrown him off his balance. It had not been fatal, but it threatened so much. The better side of his nature seemed to urge him to die rather than to go on fighting or opposing ignorant, unfortunate, savage men. But the perversity of him was so great that it dwarfed reason, conscience. He could not resist it. He felt something dying in him. He suffered. Hope seemed far away. Despair had seized upon him and was driving him into a reckless mood when he thought of Jennie.

He had forgotten her. He had forgotten that he had promised to save her. He had forgotten that he meant to snuff out as many lives as might stand between her and freedom. The very remembrance sheered off his morbid introspection. She made a difference. How strange for him to realize that! He felt grateful to her. He had been forced into outlawry; she had been stolen from her people and carried into captivity. They had met in the river fastness, he to instill hope into her despairing life, she to be the means, perhaps, of keeping him from sinking to the level of her captors. He became conscious of a strong and beating desire to see her, talk with her.

These thoughts had run through his mind while on his way to Mrs. Bland's house. He had let Euchre go on ahead because he wanted more time to compose himself. Darkness had about set in when he reached his destination. There was no light in the house. Mrs. Bland was waiting for him on the porch.

She embraced him, and the sudden, violent, unfamiliar contact sent such a shock through him that he all but forgot the deep game he was playing. She, however, in her agitation did not notice his shrinking. From her embrace and the tender, incoherent words that flowed with it, he gathered that Euchre had acquainted her of his action with Black.

"He might have killed you!" she whispered, more clearly now.

If Duane had ever heard love in a voice, he heard it then. It softened him. After all, she was a woman, weak, fated through her nature, unfortunate in her experience of life, doomed to unhappiness and tragedy. He met her advance so far that he returned the embrace and kissed her. Emotion such as she showed would have made any woman sweet, and she had a certain charm. It was easy, even pleasant, to kiss her; but Duane resolved that, whatever her abandonment might become, he would not go farther than the lie she made him act.

"Buck, you love me?" she whispered.

"Yes . . . yes," he burst out, eager to get it over and, even as he spoke, he caught the pale gleam of Jennie's face through the window. He felt a shame he was glad she could not see. Did she remember that she had promised not to misunderstand any action of his? What did she

93

think of him, seeing him out there in the dusk with this bold woman in his arms? Somehow that dim sight of Jennie's pale face, the big dark eyes, thrilled him, inspired him to his hard task of the present.

"Listen, dear," he said to the woman — but he meant his words for the girl. "I'm going to take you away from this outlaw den if I have to kill Bland, Alloway, Rugg . . . anybody who stands in my path. You were dragged here. You *are* good. I know it. There's happiness for you somewhere . . . a home among good people who will care for you. Just wait till. . . ."

His voice trailed off and failed from excess of emotion. Kate Bland closed her eyes and leaned her head on his breast. Duane felt her heart beat against his, and conscience smote him a keen blow. If she loved him so much! But memory and understanding of her character hardened him again, and he gave her such commiseration as was due her sex but no more.

"Boy, that's good of you," she whispered, "but it's too late. I'm done for. I can't leave Bland. All I ask is that you love me a little and stop your gun throwing."

The moon had risen over the eastern bulge of dark mountain, and now the valley was flooded with mellow light, and shadows of cottonwoods wavered against the silver. Suddenly the clip-clop, clip-clop of hoofs caused Duane to raise his head and listen. Horses were coming down the road from the head of the valley. The hour was unusual for riders to come in. Presently the narrow, moonlit lane was crossed at its far end by black moving objects. Duane discerned two horses.

"It's Bland!" whispered the woman, grasping Duane with shaking hands. "You must run! No, he'd see you. That'd be worse. It's Bland! I know his horse's trot."

94

"But you said he wouldn't mind my calling here," protested Duane. "Euchre's with me. It'll be all right."

"Maybe so," she replied with visible effort at self-control. Manifestly she had a great fear of Bland. "If I could only think!"

Then she dragged Duane to the door, pushed him in. "Euchre, come out with me! Duane, you stay with the girl! I'll tell Bland you're in love with her. Jen, if you give us away, I'll wring your neck."

The swift action and fierce whisper told Duane that Mrs. Bland was herself again. Duane stepped close to Jennie, who stood near the window. Neither spoke, but her hands were outstretched to meet his own. They were small, trembling hands, cold as ice. He held them close, trying to convey what he felt — that he would protect her. She leaned against him, and they looked out of the window. Duane felt calm and sure of himself. His most pronounced feeling besides that for the frightened girl was a curiosity as to how Mrs. Bland would rise to the occasion. He saw the riders dismount down the lane and wearily come forward. A boy led away the horses. Euchre, the old fox, was talking loud and with remarkable ease, considering what he claimed was his natural cowardice.

". . . that was way back in the 'Sixties, about the time of the war," he was saying. "Rustlin' cattle wasn't nuthin' then to what it is now. An' times is rougher these days. This gun throwin' has come to be a disease. Men have an itch for the draw same as they used to have fer poker. The only real gambler outside of greasers we ever had here was Bill, an' I presume Bill is burnin' now."

The approaching outlaws, hearing voices, halted a rod or so from the porch. Then Mrs. Bland uttered an exclamation, ostensibly meant to express surprise, and hurried out to meet them. She greeted her husband warmly and gave welcome to the other man. Duane could not see well enough in the shadow to recognize Bland's companion, but he believed it was Alloway.

"Dog-tired we are and starved," said Bland heavily. "Who's here with you?"

"That's Euchre on the porch. Duane is inside at the window with Jen," replied Mrs. Bland.

"Duane!" he exclaimed. Then he whispered low — something Duane could not catch.

"Why, I asked him to come," said the chief's wife. She spoke easily and naturally and made no change in tone. "Jen has been ailing. She gets thinner and whiter every day. Duane came here one day with Euchre, saw Jen, and went loony over her pretty face, same as all you men. So I let him come."

Bland cursed low and deeply under his breath. The other man made a violent action of some kind and apparently was quieted by a restraining hand.

"Kate, you let Duane make love to Jennie?" queried Bland incredulously.

"Yes, I did," replied the wife stubbornly. "Why not? Jen's in love with him. If he takes her away and marries her, she can be a decent woman."

Bland kept silent a moment, then his laugh pealed out loud and harsh. "Chess, did you get that? Well, by God! what do you think of my wife?"

"She's lyin', or she's crazy," replied Alloway, and his voice carried an unpleasant ring.

Mrs. Bland promptly and indignantly told her husband's lieutenant to keep his mouth shut.

"Ho, ho, ho!" rolled out Bland's laugh.

Then he led the way to the porch, his spurs clinking, the

weapons he was carrying rattling, and he flopped down on a bench.

"How are you, Boss?" asked Euchre.

"Hello, old man. I'm well, but all in."

Alloway slowly walked onto the porch and leaned against the rail. He answered Euchre's greeting with a nod. Then he stood there, a dark, silent figure.

Mrs. Bland's full voice in eager questioning had a tendency to ease the situation. Bland replied briefly to her, reporting a remarkably successful trip.

Duane thought it time to show himself. He had a feeling that Bland and Alloway would let him go for the moment. They were plainly nonplused, and Alloway seemed sullen, brooding.

"Jennie," whispered Duane, "that was clever of Missus Bland. We'll keep up the deception. Any day now, be ready."

She pressed closely to him and a barely audible "Hurry!" came breathing into his ear.

"Good night, Jennie," he said aloud. "Hope you feel better tomorrow."

Then he stepped out into the moonlight and spoke. Bland returned the greeting and, though he was not amiable, he did not show resentment.

"Met Jasper as I rode in," said Bland presently. "He told me you made Bill Black mad, and there's liable to be a fight. What did you go off the handle about?"

Duane explained the incident. "I'm sorry I happened to be there," he went on. "It wasn't my business."

"Scurvy trick that'd've been," muttered Bland. "You did right. All the same, Duane, I want you to stop quarreling with my men. If you were one of us, . . . that'd be different. I can't keep my men from fighting, but I'm not called on to let an outsider hang around my camp and plug my rustlers."

"I guess I'll have to be hitting the trail for somewhere," said Duane.

"Why not join my band? You've got a bad start already, Duane, and, if I know this border, you'll never be a respectable citizen again. You're a born killer. I know every badman on this frontier. More than one of them has told me that something exploded in their brain and, when sense came back, there lay another dead man. It's not so with me. I've done a little shooting, too, but I never wanted to kill another man just to rid myself of the last one. My dead men don't sit on my chest at night. That's the gunfighter's trouble. He's crazy. He has to kill a new man . . . he's driven to it to forget the last one."

"But I'm no gunfighter," protested Duane. "Circumstances made me. . . ."

"No doubt," interrupted Bland, with a laugh. "Circumstances made me a rustler. You don't know yourself. You're young. You've got a temper. Your father was one of the most dangerous men Texas ever had. I don't see any other career for you. Instead of going it alone . . . a lone wolf, as the Texans say . . . why not make friends with other outlaws? You'll live longer."

Euchre squirmed in his seat. "Boss, I've been givin' the boy exactly thet same line of talk. Thet's why I took him to bunk with me. If he makes pards among us, there won't be any more trouble. An' he'd be a grand feller fer the gang. I've seen Wild Bill Hickok throw a gun, an' Billy the Kid, an' Hardin, an' Chess here . . . all the fastest men on the border. An' with apologies to present company, I'm here to say Duane has them all skinned. His draw is different. You can't see how he does it."

Euchre's admiring praise served to create an effective little silence. Alloway shifted uneasily on his feet, his spurs jangling faintly, and did not lift his head. Bland seemed thoughtful.

"That's about the only qualification I have to make me eligible for your band," said Duane easily.

"It's good enough," replied Bland shortly. "Will you consider the idea?"

"I'll think it over. Good night."

He left the group, followed by Euchre. When they reached the end of the lane and before they had exchanged a word, Bland called Euchre back. Duane proceeded slowly along the moonlit road to the cabin and sat down under the cottonwoods to wait for Euchre. The night was intense and quiet, a low hum of insects giving the effect of a congestion of life. The beauty of the soaring moon, the ebony cañons of shadow under the mountain, the melancholy serenity of the perfect night, made Duane shudder in the realization of how far aloof he now was from enjoyment of these things. Never again so long as he lived could he be natural. His mind was clouded. His eye and ear henceforth must register impressions of nature, but the joy of them had fled.

Still, as he sat there with foreboding of more and darker work ahead of him, there was yet a strange sweetness left to him, and it lay in thought of Jennie. The pressure of her cold little hands lingered in his. He did not think of her as a woman, and he did not analyze his feelings. He just had vague, dreamy thoughts and imagination that were interspersed in the constant and stern revolving of plans to save her.

A shuffling step aroused him. Euchre's dark figure came crossing the moonlit grass under the cottonwoods. The moment the outlaw reached him Duane saw that he was laboring under great excitement. It scarcely affected Duane. He seemed to be acquiring patience, calmness, strength.

99

"Bland kept you pretty long," he said.

"Wait till I git my breath," replied Euchre. He sat silently a little while, fanning himself with his sombrero, though the night was cool, and then he went into the cabin to return presently with a lighted pipe.

"Fine night," he said, and his tone further acquainted Duane with Euchre's quaint humor. "Fine night for love affairs, by gum!"

"I'd noticed that," rejoined Duane dryly.

"Wal, I'm a son of a gun if I didn't stand an' watch Bland choke his wife till her tongue stuck out an' she got black in the face."

"No!" ejaculated Duane.

"Hope to die if I didn't. Buck, listen to this here yarn. When I got back to the porch, I seen Bland was wakin' up. He'd been too fagged out to figger much. Alloway an' Kate had gone in the house, where they lit up the lamps. I heard Kate's high voice, but Alloway never chirped. He's not the talkin' kind, an' he's damn dangerous when he's thet way. Bland asked me some questions right from the shoulder. I was ready for them, an' I swore the moon was green cheese. He was satisfied. Bland always trusted me, an' liked me, too, I reckon. I hated to lie black thet way. But he's a hard man with bad intentions toward Jennie, an' I'd double-cross him any day.

"Then we went into the house. Jennie had gone to her little room, an' Bland called her to come out. She said she was undressin'. An' he ordered her to put her clothes back on. Then, Buck, his next move was some surprisin'. He deliberately throwed a gun on Kate. Yes sir, he pointed his big blue Colt right at her, an' he says: 'I've a mind to blow out your brains.'

" 'Go ahead,' says Kate, cool as could be.

" 'You lied to me,' he roars.

"Kate laughed in his face. Bland slammed the gun down an' made a grab fer her. She fought him but wasn't a match fer him, an' he got her by the throat. He choked her till I thought she was strangled. Alloway made him stop. She flopped down on the bed an' gasped fer a while. When she come to, them hard-shelled cusses went after her, trying to make her give herself away. I think Bland was jealous. He suspected she'd got thick with you an' was foolin' him. I reckon thet's a sore feelin' fer a man to have . . . to guess pretty nice but not to be sure. Bland gave it up after a while. An' then he cussed an' raved at her. One sayin' of his worth pinnin' in your sombrero: 'It ain't nuthin' to kill a man. I don't need much fer thet. But I want to *know,* you hussy!'

"Then he went in an' dragged poor Jen out. She'd had time to dress. He was so mad he hurt her sore leg. You know Jen got thet injury fightin' off one of them devils in the dark. An' when I seen Bland twist her . . . hurt her . . . I had a queer hot feelin' deep down in me, an' fer the only time in my life I wished I was a gunfighter.

"Wal, Jen amazed me. She was whiter'n a sheet, an' her eyes were big an' starry, but she had nerve. Fust time I ever seen her show any.

" 'Jennie,' he said, 'my wife said Duane came here to see you. I believe she's lyin'. I think she's been carryin' on with him, an' I want to *know.* If she's been an' you tell me the truth, I'll let you go. I'll send you out to Huntsville, where you can communicate with your friends. I've give you money.'

"Thet must hev been a hell of a minnit fer Kate Bland. If ever I seen death in a man's eye, I seen it in Bland's. He loves her. Thet's the strange part of it.

" 'Has Duane been comin' here to see my wife?' Bland asked, fierce-like.

" 'No,' said Jennie.

" 'He's been after you?'

" 'Yes.'

" 'He has fallen in love with you? Kate said thet.'

" 'I'm not . . . I don't know . . . he hasn't told me.'

" 'But you're in love with him?'

" 'Yes,' she said. An', Buck, if you only could have *seen* her! She throwed up her head, an' her eyes were full of fire. Bland seemed dazed at sight of her. An' Alloway, why, thet little skunk of an outlaw cried right out. He was hit plumb center. He's in love with Jen. An' the look of her then was enough to make any feller quit. He jest slunk out of the room. I told you, mebbe, thet he'd been tryin' to git Bland to marry Jen to him. So even a tough like Alloway can love a woman!

"Bland stamped up an' down the room. He sure was dyin' hard.

" 'Jennie,' he said, once more turnin' to her. 'You swear in fear of your life thet you're tellin' truth. Kate's not in love with Duane? She's let him come to see *you?* There's been nuthin' between them?'

" 'No, I swear,' answered Jennie.

"Bland sat down like a man licked. 'Go to bed, you white faced . . . !' Bland choked on some word or other . . . a bad one, I reckon . . . an' he positively shook in his chair.

"Jennie went then, an' Kate began to have hysterics, an' your Uncle Euchre ducked his nut out of the door an' come home."

Duane did not have a word to say at the end of Euchre's long harangue. He experienced relief. As a matter of fact, he had expected a good deal worse. He thrilled at the thought of Jennie perjuring herself to save that abandoned woman. What mysteries these feminine creatures were!

"Wal, there's where our little deal stands now," resumed Euchre meditatively. "You know, Buck, as well as me thet, if you'd been some feller who hadn't shown he was a wonder with a gun, you'd now be full of lead. If you'd happen to kill Bland an' Alloway, I reckon you'd be as safe on this here border as you would in Santone. Such is gun fame in this land of the draw."

Chapter Nine

Both men were awake early, silent with the premonition of trouble ahead, thoughtful of the fact that the time for the long-planned action was at hand. It was remarkable that a man as loquacious as Euchre could hold his tongue so long; and this was significant of the deadly nature of the intended deed. During breakfast he said a few words customary in the service of food. At the conclusion of the meal he seemed to come to an end of deliberation.

"Buck, the sooner the better now," he declared, a glint in his eye. "The more time we use up now the less surprised Bland'll be."

"I'm ready when you are," replied Duane quietly, and he rose from the table.

"Wal, saddle up then," went on Euchre gruffly. "Tie on them two packs I made, one fer each saddle. You can't tell . . . mebbe either hoss will be carryin' double. It's good they're both big, strong hosses. Guess thet wasn't a wise move of your Uncle Euchre's . . . bringin' in your hosses an' havin' them ready?"

"Euchre, I hope you're not going to get in bad here, but I'm afraid you are. Let me do the rest now," said Duane.

The old outlaw eyed him sarcastically. "Thet'd be turrible now, wouldn't it? If you want to know why, I'm in bad already. I didn't tell you thet Alloway called me out last night. He's gettin' wise pretty quick."

"Euchre, you're going with me?" queried Duane, suddenly divining the truth.

"Wal, I reckon. Either to hell or safe over the mountain! I wish I was a gunfighter. I hate to leave here without takin' a peg at Jackrabbit Benson. Now, Buck, you do some hard figgerin' while I go nosin' 'round. It's pretty early, which is all the better."

Euchre put on his sombrero and, as he went out, Duane saw that he wore a gun and cartridge belt. It was the first time Duane had ever seen the outlaw armed.

Duane packed his few belongings into his saddlebags and then carried the saddles out to the corral. An abundance of alfalfa in the corral showed that the horses had fared well. They had gotten almost fat during his stay in the valley. He watered them, put on the saddles loosely cinched, and then the bridles. His next move was to fill the two canvas water bottles. That done, he returned to the cabin to wait.

At the moment he felt no excitement or agitation of any kind. There was no more thinking and planning to do. The hour had arrived, and he was ready. He understood perfectly the desperate chances he must take. His thoughts became confined to Euchre and the surprising loyalty and goodness in the hardened old outlaw. Time passed slowly. Duane kept glancing at his watch. He hoped to start the thing and get away before the outlaws were out of their beds. Finally he heard the shuffle of Euchre's boots on the hard path. The sound was quicker than usual.

When Euchre came around the corner of the cabin, Duane was not so astounded as he was concerned to see the outlaw white and shaking. Sweat dripped from him. He had a wild look.

"Luck ours . . . so . . . fur, Buck!" he panted.

"You don't look it," replied Duane.

"I'm turrible sick. Jest killed a man. Fust one I ever killed!"

"Who?" asked Duane startled.

"Jackrabbit Benson. An' sick as I am, I'm gloryin' in it. I went nosin' 'round up the road. Saw Alloway goin' into Deger's. He's thick with the Degers. Reckon he's askin' questions. Anyway, I was sure glad to see him away from Bland's. An' he didn't see me. When I dropped into Benson's, there wasn't nobody there but Jackrabbit an' some greasers he was startin' to work. Benson never had no use fer me. An' he up an' said he wouldn't give a two-bit piece for my life. I asked him why.

" 'You're double-crossin' the boss an' Chess,' he said.

" 'Jack, what'd you give fer your own life?' I asked him.

"He straightened up, surprised an' mean-lookin'. An' I let him have it, plumb center! He wilted, an' the greasers run. I reckon I'll never sleep again. But I had to do it."

Duane asked if the shot had attracted any attention outside.

"I didn't see anybody but the greasers, an' I sure looked sharp. Comin' back, I cut across through the cottonwoods, past Bland's cabin. I meant to keep out of sight, but somehow I had an idea I might find out if Bland was awake yet. Sure enough, I run plumb into Beppo, the boy who tends Bland's hosses. Beppo likes me. An' when I inquired of his boss, he said Bland had been up all night fightin' with the *señora*. An', Buck, here's how I figger. Bland couldn't let up last night. He was sore, an' he went after Kate again, tryin' to wear her down. Jest as likely he might have went after Jennie, with wuss intentions. Anyway, he an' Kate must have had it hot an' heavy. We're pretty lucky."

"It seems so. Well, I'm goin'," said Duane tersely.

106

"Lucky! I should smile! Bland's been up all night after a most draggin' ride home. He'll be fagged out this mornin', sleepy, sore, an' he won't be expectin' hell before breakfast. Now, you walk over to his house. Meet him how you like. Thet's your game. But I'm suggestin', if he comes out an' you want to parley, you can jest say you'd thought over his proposition an' was ready to join his band, or you ain't. You'll have to kill him, an' it'd save time to go fer your gun on sight. Might be wise, too, fer it's likely he'll do thet same."

"How about the horses?"

"I'll fetch them an' come along about two minutes behind you. 'Pears to me you ought to have the job done an' Jennie outside by the time I git there. Once on them hosses, we can ride out of camp before Alloway or anybody else gits into action. Jennie ain't much heavier'n a rabbit. Thet big black could carry you both."

"All right. But once more let me persuade you to stay . . . not to mix any more in this," said Duane earnestly.

"Nope, I'm goin'. You heard what Benson told me. Alloway wouldn't give me the benefit of any doubts. Buck, a last word . . . look out fer thet Bland woman!"

Duane merely nodded and then, saying that the horses were ready, he strode away through the grove. Accounting for the short cut across grove and field, it was about five minutes' walk up to Bland's house. To Duane it seemed long in time and distance, and he had difficulty in restraining his pace. As he walked, there came a gradual and subtle change in his feelings. Again he was going out to meet a man in conflict. He could have avoided this meeting. But despite the fact of his courting the encounter, he had not as yet felt that hot, inexplicable rush of blood. The motive of this deadly action was not personal, and

107

somehow that made a difference.

No outlaws were in sight. He saw several Mexican herders with cattle. Blue columns of smoke curled up over some of the cabins. The fragrant smell of it reminded Duane of his home and cutting wood for the stove. He noted a cloud of creamy mist rising above the river, dissolving in the sunlight. Then he entered Bland's lane.

While yet some distance from the cabin, he heard loud, angry voices of man and woman — Bland and Kate still quarreling! He took a quick survey of the surroundings. There was now not even a Mexican in sight. Then he hurried a little. Half way down the lane he turned his head to peer through the cottonwoods. This time he saw Euchre coming with the horses. There was no indication that the old outlaw might lose his nerve at the end. Duane had feared this.

Duane now changed his walk to a leisurely saunter. He reached the porch and then distinguished what was said inside the cabin.

"If you do, Bland, by heaven I'll fix you and her!" That was panted out in Kate Bland's full voice.

"Let me loose! I'm going in there, I tell you!" replied Bland hoarsely.

"What for?"

"I want to make a little love to her. Ha! ha! It'll be fun to have the laugh on her new lover."

"You lie!" cried Kate Bland.

"I'm not saying what I'll do to her *afterward!*" His voice grew hoarser with passion. "Let me go now!"

"No! no! I won't let you go. You'll choke the . . . the truth out of her . . . you'll kill her."

"The *truth!*" hissed Bland.

"Yes. I lied. Jen lied. But she lied to save me. You needn't

. . . murder her . . . for that."

Bland cursed horribly. Then followed a wrestling sound of bodies in violent straining contact — the scrape of feet — the jangle of spurs — a crash of sliding table or chair, and then the cry of a woman in pain.

Duane stepped into the open door, inside the room. Kate Bland lay half across a table where she had been flung, and she was trying to get to her feet. Bland's back was turned. He had opened the door into Jennie's room and had one foot across the threshold. Duane caught the girl's low, shuddering cry. Then he called out loud and clear.

With cat-like swiftness Bland wheeled, then froze on the threshold. His sight, quick as his action, caught Duane's menacing, unmistakable position.

Bland's big frame filled the door. He was in a bad place to reach for his gun, but he would not have time for a step. Duane read in his eyes the desperate calculation of chances. For a fleeting instant Bland shifted his glance to his wife. Then his whole body seemed to vibrate with the swing of his arm.

Duane shot him. He fell forward, his gun exploding as it hit into the floor, and dropped loose from stretching fingers. Duane stood over him, stooped to turn him on his back. Bland looked up with clouded gaze, then gasped his last.

"Duane, you've killed him!" cried Kate Bland huskily. "I knew you'd have to!"

She staggered against the wall, her eyes dilating, her strong hands clenching, her face slowly whitening. She appeared shocked, half stunned, but showed no grief.

"Jennie!" called Duane sharply.

"Oh . . . Duane!" came a halting reply.

"Yes. Come out. Hurry!"

She came out with uneven steps, seeing only him, and she stumbled over Bland's body. Duane caught her arm, swung her behind him. He feared the woman when she realized how she had been duped. His action was protective, and his movement toward the door was equally as significant.

"Duane!" cried Mrs. Bland.

It was no time for talk. Duane edged on, keeping Jennie behind him. At that moment there was a pounding of iron-shod hoofs out in the lane. Kate Bland bounded to the door. When she turned back, her amazement was changing to realization.

"Where are you taking Jen?" she cried, her voice like a man's.

"Get out of my way," replied Duane. His look, perhaps without speech, was enough for her. In an instant she was transformed into a fury.

"You hound! All the time you were fooling me! You made love to me! You let me believe . . . you swore you loved me! Now I see what was queer about you. All for that girl! But you can't have her. You'll never leave here alive. Give me that girl! Let me . . . get at her! She'll never win any more men in this camp."

She was a powerful woman, and it took all Duane's strength to ward off her onslaughts. She clawed at Jennie over his upheld arm. Every second her fury increased.

"Help! Help! Help!" she shrieked, in a voice that must have penetrated to the remotest cabin in the valley.

"Let go! Let go!" cried Duane, low and sharply. He still held his gun in his right hand, and it began to be hard for him to ward the woman off. His coolness had gone with her shriek for help. "Let go!" he repeated, and he shoved her fiercely.

110

Suddenly she snatched a rifle off the wall and backed away, her strong hands fumbling at the lever. As she jerked it down, throwing a shell into the chamber and cocking the weapon, Duane leaped upon her. He struck up the rifle as it went off, the powder burning his face.

"Jennie, run out! Get on a horse!" he said.

Jennie flashed out of the door.

With an iron grasp Duane held the rifle barrel. He had grasped it with his left hand, and he gave such a pull that he swung the crazed woman off the floor, but he could not loose her grip. She was as strong as he.

"Kate! Let go!"

He tried to intimidate her. She did not see his gun thrust in her face, or reason had given way to such an extent to passion that she did not care. She cursed. Her husband had used the same curses, and from her lips they seemed strange, unsexed, more deadly. Like a tigress she fought him. Her face no longer resembled a woman's. The evil of that outlaw life, the wildness and rage, the intention to kill, was even in such a moment terribly impressed upon Duane.

He heard a cry from outside — a man's cry, hoarse and alarming. It made him think of loss of time. This demon of a woman might yet block his plan.

"Let go!" he whispered and felt his lips stiffen. In the grimness of that instant he relaxed his hold on the rifle barrel.

With a sudden, redoubled, irresistible strength she wrenched the rifle down and discharged it. Duane felt a blow — a shock — a burning agony tearing through his breast. Then in a frenzy he jerked so powerfully upon the rifle that he threw the woman against the wall. She fell and seemed stunned.

111

Duane leaped back, whirled, flew out of the door to the porch. The sharp cracking of a gun halted him. He saw Jennie holding to the bridle of his bay horse. Euchre was astride the other, and he had a Colt leveled, and he was firing down the lane. Then came a single shot, heavier, and Euchre's ceased. He fell from the horse.

A swift glance showed to Duane a man coming down the lane. Chess Alloway! His gun was smoking. He broke into a run. Then in an instant he saw Duane and tried to check his pace as he swung up his arm. But that slight pause was fatal. Duane shot, and Alloway was falling when his gun went off. His bullet whistled close to Duane and thudded into the cabin.

Duane bounded down to the horses. Jennie was trying to hold the plunging bay. Euchre lay flat on his back, dead, a bullet hole in his shirt, his face set hard, and his hands twisted around gun and bridle.

"Jennie, you've nerve, all right!" cried Duane, as he dragged down the horse she was holding. "Up with you now! There! Never mind . . . long stirrups! Hang on somehow!"

He caught his bridle out of Euchre's clutching grip and leaped astride. The frightened horses jumped into a run and thundered down the lane into the road. Duane saw men running from cabins. He heard shouts, but there were no shots fired. Jennie seemed able to stay on her horse, but without stirrups she was thrown about so much that Duane rode closer and reached out to grasp her arm.

Thus they rode through the valley to the trail that led up over the steep and broken Rim Rock. As they began to climb, Duane looked back. No pursuers were in sight.

"Jennie, we're going to get away!" he cried, exultation for her in his voice.

She was gazing horror stricken at his breast, as in turning to look back he faced her.

"Oh, Duane, your shirt's all bloody!" she faltered, pointing with trembling fingers.

With her words Duane became aware of two things — the hand he instinctively placed to his breast still held his gun, and he had sustained a terrible wound. Duane had been shot through the breast far enough down to give him grave apprehension of his life. The clean-cut hole made by the bullet bled freely both at its entrance and, where it had come out, but with no signs of hemorrhage. He did not bleed at the mouth; however, he began to cough up a reddish-tinged foam. As they rode on, Jennie, with pale face and mute lips, kept looking at him.

"I'm badly hurt, Jennie," he said then, "but I guess I'll stick it out."

"The woman . . . did she shoot you?"

"Yes, she was a devil. Euchre told me to look out for her. I wasn't quick enough."

"You didn't have to . . . to . . . ?" shivered the girl.

"No, no!" he replied.

They did not stop climbing while Duane tore a scarf and made compresses, which he bound tightly over his wounds. The fresh horses made fast time up the rough trail. From open places Duane looked down. When they surmounted the steep ascent and stood on top of the Rim Rock, with no signs of pursuit down in the valley and with the wild, broken vastness before them, Duane turned to the girl and assured her that they now had every chance of escape.

"But . . . your . . . wound!" she faltered with dark, troubled eyes. "I see the blood . . . dripping from your back."

"Jennie, I'll take a lot of killing," he said.

Then he became silent and attended to the uneven trail.

He was aware presently that he had not come into Bland's camp by this route. But that did not matter; any trail leading out beyond the Rim Rock was safe enough. What he wanted was to get far away into some wild retreat where he could hide till he recovered from his wound. He seemed to feel a fire inside his breast, and his throat burned so that it was necessary for him to take a swallow of water every little while. He began to suffer considerable pain, which increased as the hours went by and then gave way to a numbness. Gradually, he lost his steadiness and his keen sight; and he realized that if he were to meet foes, or if pursuing outlaws should come up with him, he could make only a poor stand. So he turned off on a trail that appeared seldom traveled.

Soon after this move he became conscious of a further thickening of his senses. He felt able to hold onto his saddle for a while longer, but he was failing. Then he thought he ought to advise Jennie, so in case she was left alone she would have some idea of what to do.

"Jennie, I'll give out soon," he said. "No . . . I don't mean . . . what you think. But I'll drop soon. My strength's going. If I die . . . you ride back to the main trail. Hide and rest by day. Ride at night. That trail goes to water. I believe you could get across the Nueces, where some rancher will take you in."

Duane could not get the meaning of her incoherent reply. He rode on, and soon he could not see the trail or hear his horse. He did not know whether they traveled a mile or many times that far. But he was conscious when the horse stopped and had a vague sense of falling and feeling Jennie's arms before all became dark to him.

When consciousness returned, he found himself lying in

114

a little hut of mesquite branches. It was well built and evidently some years old. There were two doors or openings, one in front and the other at the back. Duane imagined it had been built by a fugitive — one who meant to keep an eye both ways and not to be surprised. Duane felt weak and had no desire to move. Where was he, anyway? A strange, intangible sense of time, distance, of something far behind weighed upon him. Sight of the two packs Euchre had made brought his thoughts to Jennie. What had become of her? There was evidence of her work in a smoldering fire and a little blackened coffee pot. Probably she was outside, looking after the horses or getting water. He thought he heard a step and listened, but he felt tired, and presently his eyes closed, and he fell into a doze.

Awakening from this, he saw Jennie sitting beside him. In some way she seemed to have changed. When he spoke, she gave a start and turned eagerly to him.

"Duane!" she cried.

"Hello. How're you, Jennie, and how am I?" he said, finding it a little difficult to talk.

"Oh, I'm all right," she replied. "And you've come to . . . your wound's healed, but you've been sick. Fever, I guess. I did all I could."

Duane saw now that the difference in her was a whiteness and tightness of skin, a hollowness of eye, a look of strain.

"Fever? How long have we been here?" he asked.

She took some pebbles from the crown of his sombrero and counted them.

"Nine. Nine days," she answered.

"Nine days!" he exclaimed incredulously. Another look at her assured him that she meant what she said. "I've been sick all the time? You nursed me?"

"Yes."

"Bland's men didn't come along here?"

"No."

"Where are the horses?"

"I keep them grazing down in a gorge back of here. There's good grass and water."

"Have you slept any?"

"A little. Lately I couldn't keep awake."

"Good Lord! I should think not. You've had a time of it, sitting here day and night nursing me, watching for the outlaws. Come, tell me all about it."

"There's nothing much to tell."

"I want to know anyway, just what you did . . . how you felt."

"I can't remember very well," she replied simply. "We must have ridden forty miles that day we got away. You bled all the time. Toward evening you lay on your horse's neck. When we came to this place, you fell out of the saddle. I dragged you in here and stopped your bleeding. I thought you'd die that night, but in the morning I had a little hope. I had forgotten the horses, but luckily they didn't stray far. I caught them and kept them down in the gorge. When your wounds closed and you began to breathe stronger, I thought you'd get well quick. It was fever that put you back. You raved a lot, and that worried me, because I couldn't stop you. Anybody trailing us could have heard you a good ways. I don't know whether I was scared most then or when you were quiet, and it was so dark and lonely and still all around. Every day I put a stone in your hat."

"Jennie, you saved my life," said Duane.

"I don't know. Maybe. I did all I knew how to do," she replied. "You saved mine . . . more than my life."

Their eyes met in a long gaze and then their hands in a close clasp.

116

"Jennie, we're going to get away," he said with gladness. "I'll be well in a few days. You don't know how strong I am. We'll hide by day and travel by night. I can get you across the river."

"And then?" she persisted.

"Why," he began slowly, "that's as far as my thoughts ever got. It was pretty hard, I tell you, to assure myself of so much. It means your safety. You'll tell your story. You'll be sent to some village or town and be taken care of until a relative or friend is notified."

"And you?" she inquired in a strange voice.

Duane kept silent.

"What will you do?" she went on.

"Jennie, I'll go back to the brakes. I daren't show my face among respectable people. I'm an outlaw."

"You're no criminal!" she declared with deep passion.

"Jennie, on this border the little difference between an outlaw and a criminal doesn't count for much."

"You won't go back among those terrible men? You, with your gentleness and sweetness . . . all that's good about you? Oh, Duane, don't . . . don't go!"

"I can't go back to the outlaws, at least not Bland's band. No, I'll go alone. I'll be a lone wolf, as they say on the border. What else can I do, Jennie?"

"Oh, I don't know. Couldn't you hide? Couldn't you slip out of Texas . . . go far away?"

"I could never get out of Texas without being arrested. I could hide, but a man must live. Never mind about me, Jennie."

In three days Duane was able with great difficulty to mount his horse. During daylight, by short relays, he and Jennie rode back to the main trail, where they hid again

117

till he had rested. Then in the dark they rode out of the cañons and gullies of the Rim Rock, and early in the morning halted at the first water to camp.

From that point they traveled after nightfall and went into hiding during the day. Once across the Nueces River, Duane was assured of safety for her and great danger for himself. They had crossed into a country he did not know. Somewhere east of the river there were scattered ranches, but he was as liable to find the rancher in touch with the outlaws as he was likely to find him honest. Duane hoped his good fortune would not desert him in this last service to Jennie. Next to the worry of that was realization of his condition. He had gotten up too soon. He had ridden too far and hard, and now he felt that any moment he might fall from his saddle. At last, far ahead over a barren mesquite-dotted stretch of dusty ground, he espied a patch of green and a little flat, red ranch house. He headed his horse for it and turned a face he tried to make cheerful for Jennie's sake. She seemed both happy and sorry.

When near at hand he saw that the rancher was a thrifty farmer, and thrift spoke for honesty. There were fields of alfalfa, fruit trees, corrals, windmill pumps, irrigation ditches, all surrounding a neat little adobe house. Some children were playing in the yard. The way they ran at sight of Duane hinted of both the loneliness and the fear of their isolated lives. Duane saw a woman come to the door, then a man. The latter looked keenly, then stepped outside. He was a sandy-haired, freckled Texan.

"Howdy, stranger," he called as Duane halted. "Get down, you an' your woman. Say, now, air you sick or shot or what? Let me. . . ."

Duane, reeling in his saddle, bent searching eyes upon the rancher. He thought he saw good will, kindness, hon-

118

esty. He risked all on that one sharp glance, then he almost plunged from the saddle.

The rancher caught him, helped him to a bench. "Martha, come out here!" he called. "This man's sick. No, he's shot, or I don't know blood stains."

Jennie had slipped off her horse and to Duane's side. Duane appeared about to faint.

"Air you his wife?" asked the rancher.

"No. I'm only a girl he saved from outlaws. Oh, he's so pale! Duane, Duane!"

"Buck Duane!" exclaimed the rancher excitedly. "The man who killed Bland an' Alloway? Say, I owe him a good turn, an' I'll pay it, young woman."

The rancher's wife came out and, with a manner at once kind and practical, essayed to make Duane drink from a flask. He was not so far gone that he could not recognize its contents, which he refused, and weakly asked for water. When that was given him, he found his voice.

"Yes, I'm Duane. I've only overdone myself . . . just all in. The wounds I got at Bland's are healing. Will you take this girl in . . . hide her a while till the excitement's over among the outlaws?"

"I shore will," replied the Texan.

"Thanks. I'll remember you . . . I'll square it."

"What're you goin' to do?"

"I'll rest a bit . . . then go back to the brakes."

"Young man, you ain't in any shape to travel. See here . . . any rustlers on your trail?"

"I think we gave Bland's gang the slip."

"Good. I'll tell you what. I'll take you in along with the girl, an' hide both of you till you get well. It'll be safe. My nearest neighbor is five miles off. We don't have much company."

"You risk a great deal. Both outlaws and rangers are hunting me," said Duane.

"Never seen a ranger yet in these parts. An' have always got along with outlaws, mebbe exceptin' Bland. I tell you I owe you a good turn."

"My horses might betray you," added Duane.

"I'll hide them in a place where there's water an' grass. Nobody goes to it. Come now, let me help you indoors."

Duane's last fading sensations of that hard day were the strange feel of a bed, a relief at the removal of his heavy boots, and of Jennie's soft, cool hands on his hot face.

He lay ill for three weeks before he began to mend, and it was another week then before he could walk out a little in the dusk of the evenings. After that his strength returned rapidly. And it was only at the end of this long siege that he recovered his spirits. During most of his illness he had been silent, moody.

"Jennie, I'll be riding off soon," he said one evening. "I can't impose on this good man, Andrews, much longer. I'll never forget his kindness. His wife, too . . . she's been so good to us. Yes, Jennie, you and I will have to say good bye very soon."

"Don't hurry away," she replied.

Lately Jennie had appeared strange to him. She had changed from the girl he used to see at Mrs. Bland's house. He took her reluctance to say good bye as another indication of her regret that he must go back to the brakes. Yet, somehow, it made him observe her more closely. She wore a plain white dress, made from material Mrs. Andrews had given her. Sleep and good food had improved her. If she had been pretty out there in the outlaw den, now she was more than that, but she had the same paleness, the same strained look, the same dark eyes full of haunting shadows. After Duane's realization of the change in her, he watched her more, with a growing certainty that he would be sorry not to see her again.

"It's likely we won't ever be together again," he said. "That's strange to think of. We've been through some hard days, and I seem to have known you a long time."

Jennie appeared shy, almost sad, so Duane changed the subject to something less personal.

Andrews returned one evening from a several days' trip to Huntsville. "Duane, everybody's talkin' about how you cleaned up the Bland outfit," he said, feeling important and full of news. "It's some exaggerated, accordin' to what you told me, but you've shore made friends on this side of the Nueces. I reckon there ain't a town where you wouldn't find people to welcome you. Huntsville, you know, is some divided in its ideas. Half the people are crooked. Likely enough, all them who was so loud in praise of you are the crookedest. For instance, I met King Fisher, the boss outlaw of these parts. Well, King thinks he's a decent citizen. He was tellin' me what a grand job yours was for the border an' honest cattlemen. Now that Bland and Alloway are done for, King Fisher will find rustlin' easier. There's talk of Hardin movin' his camp over to Bland's, but I don't know how true it is. I reckon there ain't much to it. In the past, when a big outlaw chief went under, his band almost always broke up an' scattered. There's no one left who could run the outfit."

"Did you hear of any outlaws hunting me?" asked Duane.

"Nobody from Bland's outfit is huntin' you, thet's shore." replied Andrews. "Fisher said there never was a hoss straddled to go on your trail. Nobody had any use for Bland. Anyhow, his men would be afraid to trail you. An' you

121

could go right into Huntsville, where you'd be some popular. Reckon you'd be safe, too, except when some of them fool saloon loafers or bad cowpunchers would try to shoot you for the glory in it. Them kind of men will bob up everywhere you go, Duane."

"I'll be able to ride and take care of myself in a day or two," Duane said. "Then I'll go . . . I'd like to talk to you about Jennie."

"She's welcome to a home here with us."

"Thank you, Andrews. You're a kind man, but I want Jennie to get farther away from the Rio Grande. She'd never be safe here. Besides, she may be able to find relatives. She has some, though she doesn't know where they are."

"All right, Duane. Whatever you think best. I reckon now you'd better take her to some town. Go north an' strike for Shelbyville or Crockett. Them's both good towns. I'll tell Jennie the names of men who'll help her. You needn't ride into town at all."

"Which place is nearer, and how far is it?"

"Shelbyville. I reckon about two days' ride. Poor stock country, so you ain't liable to meet rustlers. All the same, better hit the trail at night an' go careful."

At sunset two days later Duane and Jennie mounted their horses and said good bye to the rancher and his wife. Andrews would not listen to Duane's thanks.

"I tell you I'm beholden to you yet," he declared.

"Well, what can I do for you?" asked Duane. "I may come along here again some day."

"Get down an' come in, then, or you're no friend of mine. I reckon there ain't nothin' I can think of . . . I just happen to remember!" Here he led Duane out of earshot of the women and went on in a whisper. "Buck, I used to be well-to-do. Got skinned by a man named Brown . . . Rodney Brown. He lives in Huntsville, an' he's my enemy. I never was much on fighting, or I'd've fixed him. Brown ruined me . . . stole all I had. He's a hoss an' cattle thief, an' he has pull enough at home to protect him. I reckon I needn't say any more."

"Is this Brown a man who shot an outlaw named Stevens?" queried Duane curiously.

"Shore, he's the same. I heard the story. Brown swears he plugged Stevens through the middle, but the outlaw rode off, an' nobody ever knew for shore."

"Luke Stevens died of that shot. I buried him," said Duane.

Andrews made no further comment, and the two men returned to the women.

"The main road for about three miles then, where it forks, take the left-hand road and keep on straight. That what you said, Andrews?"

"Shore. An' good luck you both!"

Duane and Jennie trotted away into the gathering twilight. At the moment an insistent thought bothered Duane. Both Luke Stevens and the rancher Andrews had hinted to Duane to kill a man named Brown. Duane wished with all his heart that they had not mentioned it, let alone taken for granted the execution of the deed. What a bloody place Texas was! Men who robbed and men who were robbed both wanted murder. It was in the spirit of the country. Duane certainly meant to avoid ever meeting this Rodney Brown. And that very determination showed Duane how dangerous he really was — to men and to himself. Sometimes he had a feeling of how little stood between his sane and better self and a self utterly wild and terrible. He reasoned that only intelligence could save him — only a thoughtful understanding of his danger and a hold upon some ideal.

Then he fell into low conversation with Jennie, holding out hopeful views of her future, and presently darkness set in. The sky was overcast with heavy clouds; there was no air moving; the heat and oppression threatened storm. By and by Duane could not see a rod in front of him, though his horse had no difficulty in keeping to the road. Duane was bothered by the blackness of the night. Traveling fast was impossible, and any moment he might miss the road that led off to the left. So he was compelled to give all his attention to peering into the thick shadows ahead. As good luck would have it, he came to higher ground where there was less mesquite and therefore not such impenetrable darkness. And at this point he came to where the road split.

Once headed in the right direction, he felt easier in mind. To his annoyance, however, a fine, misty rain set in. Jennie was not well dressed for wet weather and, for that matter, neither was he. His coat, which in that dry, warm climate he seldom needed, was tied behind his saddle, and he put it on Jennie.

They traveled on. The rain fell steadily, if anything growing heavier. Duane grew uncomfortably wet and chilly. Jennie, however, fared somewhat better by reason of the heavy coat. The night passed quickly, despite the discomfort, and soon a gray, dismal, rainy dawn greeted the travelers.

Jennie insisted that he find some shelter where a fire could be built to dry his clothes. He was not in a fit condition to risk catching cold. In fact, Duane's teeth were chattering. To find a shelter in that barren waste seemed a futile task. Quite unexpectedly, however, they happened

124

upon a deserted adobe cabin situated a little off the road. Not only did it prove to have a dry interior, but also there was firewood. Water was available in pools everywhere, but there was no grass for the horses. A good fire and hot food and drink changed the aspect of their condition as far as comfort went. Jennie lay down to sleep. For Duane, however, there must be vigilance. This cabin was no hiding place. The rain fell harder all the time, and the wind changed to the north. "It's a norther, all right," muttered Duane. "Two or three days." And he felt that his extraordinary luck had not held out. Still one point favored him, and it was that travelers were not likely to come along during the storm.

Jennie slept while Duane watched. The saving of this girl meant more to him than any task he had ever assumed. First it had been partly from a human feeling to succor an unfortunate woman and partly a motive to establish clearly to himself that he was no outlaw. Lately, however, had come a different sense, a strange one, with something personal and warm and protective in it.

As he looked down upon her, a slight, slender girl with bedraggled dress and disheveled hair, her face pale and quiet, a little stern in sleep, and her long, dark lashes lying on her cheek, he seemed to see her fragility, her prettiness, her femininity as never before. But for him she might at that very moment have been a broken, ruined girl lying back in that cabin of the Blands'. The fact gave him a feeling of his importance in this shifting of her destiny. She was unharmed, still young. She would forget and be happy. She would live to be a good wife and mother. Somehow the thought swelled his heart. His act, death dealing as it had been, was a noble one and helped him to hold on to his drifting hopes. Hardly once since Jennie had entered into his thoughts had those ghosts returned to torment him. Tomorrow she would be gone among good, kind people with a possibility of finding her relatives. He thanked God for that. Nevertheless, he felt a pang.

She slept more than half the day. Duane kept guard, always alert, whether he was sitting, standing, or walking. The rain pattered steadily on the roof and sometimes came in gusty flurries through the door. The horses were outside in a shed that afforded poor shelter, and they stamped restlessly. Duane kept them saddled and bridled.

About the middle of the afternoon Jennie awoke. They cooked a meal and afterward sat beside the little fire. She had never been, in his observation of her, anything but a tragic figure, an unhappy girl, the farthest removed from serenity and poise. That characteristic capacity for agitation struck him as stronger in her this day. He attributed it, however, to the long strain, the suspense nearing an end. Yet sometimes, when her eyes were on him, she did not seem to be thinking of her freedom, of her future.

"This time tomorrow you'll be in Shelbyville," he said.

"Where will you be?" she asked quickly.

"Me? Oh, I'll be making tracks for some lonesome place," he replied.

The girl shuddered. "I've been brought up in Texas. I remember what a hard lot the men of my family had. But poor as they were, they had a roof over their heads, a hearth with a fire, a warm bed . . . somebody to love them. And you, Duane . . . oh, my God! What must your life be? You must ride and hide and watch eternally. No decent food, no pillow, no friendly word, no clean clothes, no woman's hand! Horses, guns, trails, rocks, holes . . . these must be the important things in your life. You must go on riding, hiding, killing until you meet. . . ."

She ended with a sob and dropped her head on her knees. Duane was amazed, deeply touched.

"My girl, thank you for that thought of me," he said, with a tremor in his voice. "You don't know how much that means to me."

She raised her face, and it was tear stained, eloquent, beautiful. "I've heard tell . . . the best of men go to the bad out there. You won't. Promise me you won't. I never . . . knew any man . . . like you. I . . . I . . . we may never see each other again . . . after today. I'll never forget you. I'll pray for you, and I'll never give up trying to . . . to do something. Don't despair. It's never too late. It was my hope that kept me alive . . . out there at Bland's . . . before you came. I was only a poor weak girl, but if *I* could hope . . . so can you. Stay away from men. Be a lone wolf. Fight for your life. Stick out your exile . . . and maybe . . . some day. . . ."

Then she lost her voice. Duane clasped her hand and with feeling as deep as hers promised to remember her words. In her despair for him she had spoken wisdom — pointed out the only course.

Duane's vigilance, momentarily broken by emotion, had no sooner reasserted itself than he discovered the bay horse, the one Jennie rode, had broken his halter and gone off. The soft wet earth had deadened the sound of his hoofs. His tracks were plain in the mud. There were clumps of mesquite in sight, among which the horse might have strayed. It turned out, however, that he had not done so.

Duane did not want to leave Jennie alone in the cabin so near the road. So he put her up on his horse and bade her follow. The rain had ceased for the time being, though evidently the storm was not yet over. The tracks led up a wash to a wide flat where mesquite, prickly pear, and thorn bush grew so thickly that Jennie could not ride into it. Duane was thoroughly concerned. He must have her horse. Time was flying. It would soon be night. He could not expect to scramble quickly through that brake on foot. Therefore, he decided to risk leaving her at the edge of the thicket and go in alone.

As he went in a sound startled him. Was it the breaking of a branch he had stepped on or thrust aside? He heard the impatient pound of his horse's hoofs. Then all was quiet. Still he listened, not wholly satisfied. He was never satisfied in regard to safety. He knew too well that there never could be safety for him in this country.

The bay horse had threaded the aisles of the thicket. Duane wondered what had drawn him there. Certainly it had not been grass, for there was none. Presently he heard the horse trampling along, and then he ran. The mud was deep, and the sharp thorns made going difficult. He came up with the horse and at the same moment crossed a multitude of fresh horse tracks.

He bent lower to examine them and was alarmed to find that they had been made very recently, even since it had ceased raining. They were tracks of well-shod horses. Duane straightened up with a cautious glance all around. His instant decision was to hurry back to Jennie, but he had come a goodly way through the thicket, and it was impossible to rush back. Once or twice he imagined he heard crashing in the brush but did not halt to make sure. Certain he was now that some kind of danger threatened.

Suddenly there came an unmistakable thump of horses' hoofs off somewhere to the fore. Then a scream rent the air. It ended abruptly. Duane leaped forward, tore his way through the thorny brake. He heard Jennie cry again — an appealing call, quickly hushed. It seemed more to his right, and he plunged that way. He burst into a glade where a smoldering fire and ground covered with footprints and tracks showed that campers had lately been. Rushing across this, he broke his passage out to the open, but he was too late. His horse had disappeared. Jennie was gone. There were no riders in sight. There was no sound. There was a heavy trail of horses going north. Jennie had been carried off — probably by outlaws. Duane realized that pursuit was out of the question — that Jennie was lost.

Chapter Ten

A hundred miles from the haunts most familiar with Duane's deeds, far up where the Nueces ran a trickling clear stream between yellow cliffs, stood a small deserted shack of covered mesquite poles. It had been made long ago but was well preserved. A door faced the overgrown trail, and another faced down into a gorge of dense thickets. On the border fugitives from law and men who hid in fear of someone they had wronged never lived in houses with only one door.

It was a wild spot, lonely, not fit for human habitation except for the outcast. He, perhaps, might have found it hard to leave for most of the other wild nooks in that barren country. Down in the gorge there was never failing sweet water, grass all the year around, cool, shady retreats, deer, rabbits, turkeys, fruit, and miles and miles of narrow-twisting, deep cañons full of broken rocks and impenetrable thickets. The scream of the panther was heard there, the squall of the wildcat, the cough of the jaguar. Innumerable bees buzzed in the spring blossoms and, it seemed, scattered honey to the winds. All day there was continuous song of birds, that of the mockingbird, sweet and yet mockingly loud above the rest.

On clear days — and rare indeed were cloudy days — with the subsiding of the wind at sunset, a hush seemed to fall around the little hut. Far distant dim-blue mountains stood gold-rimmed, gradually to fade with the shading of light.

At this quiet hour a man climbed up out of the gorge and sat in the westward door of the hut. This lonely watcher of the west and listener to the silence was Duane. And this hut was the one where, three years before, Jennie had nursed him back to life.

The killing of a man named Sellers, and the combination of circumstances that had made the tragedy a memorable regret, had marked, if not a change, at least a cessation in Duane's activities. He had trailed Sellers to kill him for the supposed abduction of Jennie. He had trailed him long after he had learned Sellers traveled alone. Duane wanted absolute assurance of Jennie's death. Vague rumors, a few words here and there, inauthenticated stories, were all Duane had gathered in years to substantiate his belief — that Jennie died shortly after the beginning of her second captivity, but Duane did not know for sure. Sellers might have told him. Duane expected, if not to force it from him at the end, to read it in his eyes, but the bullet went too unerringly. It locked his lips and fixed his eyes.

After that meeting Duane lay long at the ranch house of a friend and, when he recovered from the wound Sellers had given him, he started with two horses and a pack for the lonely gorge on the Nueces. There he had been hidden for months, a prey to remorse, a dreamer, a victim of phantoms.

It took work for him to find subsistence in that rocky fastness. And work, action, helped to pass the hours, but he could not work all the time, even if he had found it to do. Then in his idle moments and at night his task was to live with the hell in his mind.

The sunset and the twilight hour made all the rest bearable. The little hut on the rim of the gorge seemed to hold Jennie's presence. It was not as if he felt her spirit. If it had been, he would have been sure of her death. He hoped Jennie had not survived her second misfortune; and that intense hope had burned into belief, if not surety. Upon his return to that locality, on the occasion of his first visit to the hut, he had found things just as they had left them, and a poor, faded piece of ribbon Jennie had used to tie around her bright hair. No wandering outlaw or traveler had happened upon the lonely spot, which further endeared it to Duane.

A strange feature of this memory of Jennie was the freshness of it — the failure of years, toil, strife, death-dealing to dim it — to deaden the thought of what might have been. He had a marvelous gift of visualization. He could shut his eyes and see Jennie before him just as clearly as if she had stood there in the flesh. For hours he did that, dreaming, dreaming of life he had never tasted and now never would taste. He saw Jennie's slender, grace-ful figure, the old brown ragged dress in which he had seen her first at Bland's, her little feet in Mexican sandals, her fine hands coarsened by work, her round arms and swelling throat, and her pale, sad, beautiful face with its staring dark eyes. He remembered every look she had given him, every word she had spoken to him, every time she had touched him. He thought of her beauty and sweet-ness, of the few things which had come to mean to him that she must have loved him; and he trained himself to think of these in preference to her life at Bland's, the escape with him, and then her recapture, because such memories led to bitter, fruitless pain. He had to fight suffering because it was eating out his heart.

Sitting there, eyes wide open, he dreamed of the old homestead and his white-haired mother. He saw the old home life, sweetened and filled by dear new faces and added joys, go on before his eyes with him a part of it.

Then in the inevitable reaction, the reflux of bitter reality, he would send out a voiceless cry no less poignant because it was silent: *Poor fool! No, I shall never see mother again . . . never go home . . . never have a home. I am Duane, the lone wolf! Oh, God! I wish it were over! These dreams torture me! What have I to do with a mother, a home, a wife? No bright-haired boy, no dark-eyed girl will ever love me. I am an outlaw, an outcast, dead to the good and decent world. I am alone . . . alone. Better be a callous brute or better dead! I shall go mad thinking! Man, what is left to you? A hiding place like a wolf's . . . lonely silent days, lonely nights with phantoms! Or the trail and the road with their blood tracks, and then the hard ride, the sleepless, hungry ride to some hole in the rocks or brakes. What hellish thing drives me? Why can't I end it all? What is left? Only that damned unquenchable spirit of the gunfighter to live . . . to hang onto a miserable life . . . to have no fear of death, yet to cling like a leach . . . to die as gunfighters seldom die, with boots off! Bain, you were first, and you're long avenged. I'd change with you. And Sellers, you were last, and you're avenged. And you others . . . you're avenged. Lie quiet in your graves and give me peace!*

But they did not lie quietly in their graves and give him peace. A group of specters trooped out of the shadows at dusk and, gathering around him, escorted him to his bed.

When Duane had been riding the trails passion-bent to escape pursuers, or passion-bent in his search, the constant action and toil and exhaustion made him sleep. But when in hiding, as time passed, gradually he required less rest and sleep, and his mind became more active. Little by little his phantoms gained hold on him, and at length, but for the saving power of his dreams, they would have claimed him utterly.

How many times he had said to himself: *I am an intelligent man. I'm not crazy. I'm in full possession of my faculties. All this is fancy . . . imagination, conscience. I've no work, no duty, no ideal, no hope . . . and my mind is obsessed, thronged with images. And these images naturally are of the men with whom I have dealt. I can't forget them. They come back to me, hour after hour. When my tortured mind grows weak, then maybe I'm not just right till the mood wears out and lets me sleep.*

So he reasoned as he lay down in his comfortable camp. The night was star bright above the cañon walls, darkly shadowing down between them. The insects hummed and chirped and thrummed a continuous thick song, low and monotonous. Slow-running water splashed softly over stones in the stream bed. From far down the cañon came the mournful hoot of an owl. The moment he lay down, thereby giving up action for the day, all these things weighed upon him like a great, heavy mantle of loneliness. In truth, they did not constitute loneliness.

He could no more have dispelled thought than he could have reached out to touch a cold, bright star. He wondered how many outcasts like him lay under this star-studded, velvety sky across the fifteen hundred miles of wild country between El Paso and the mouth of the river. A vast wild territory — a refuge for outlaws. Somewhere he had heard or read that the Texas Rangers kept a book with names and records of outlaws — three thousand known outlaws! Yet these could scarcely be half of that unfortunate horde which had been recruited from all over the States. Duane had traveled from camp to camp, den to den, hiding place to hiding place, and he knew these men. Most of them were hopeless criminals; some were avengers; a few were wronged wanderers; and among them occasionally was a man, human in his way, honest as he could be, not yet lost to good.

But all of them were akin in one sense — their outlawry; and that starry night they lay with their dark faces up, some in packs like wolves, others alone like the gray wolf who knew no mate. It did not make much difference in Duane's thought of them that the majority were steeped in crime and brutality, more often than not stupid from rum, incapable of a fine feeling, just lost, wild dogs.

Duane doubted that there was a man among them who did not realize his moral wreck and ruin. He had met poor, half-witted wretches who knew it. He believed he could enter into their minds and feel the truth of all their lives — the hardened outlaw, coarse, ignorant, bestial, who murdered as Bill Black had murdered, who stole for the sake of stealing, who craved money to gamble and drink, defiantly ready for death like that terrible outlaw, Helm, who cried out on the scaffold: "Let her rip!"

The wild youngsters seeking notoriety and reckless adventure, the cowboys with a notch on their guns, with boastful pride in the knowledge that they were marked by rangers, the crooked men from the North, defaulters, forgers, murderers, all pale-faced, flat-chested men not fit for that wilderness and not surviving, the dishonest cattlemen, hand in glove with outlaws, driven from their homes; the old grizzled, bowlegged genuine rustlers — all these Duane had come in contact with, had watched and known. As he felt at one with them, he seemed to see that as their lives were bad, sooner or later to end dismally or tragically, so they must pay some kind of earthly penalty — if not of conscience, then of fear, or if not of fear, then of that most

terrible of all things to restless, active men — pain, the
pang of flesh and bone.

Duane knew, for he had seen them pay. Best of all,
moreover, he knew the internal life of the gunfighter, of
that select but by no means small class of which he was
representative. The world that judged him and his kind
judged him as a machine, a killing machine, with only
mind enough to hunt, to meet, to slay another man. It had
taken three endless years for Duane to understand his
own father. Duane knew beyond all doubt that the gunfighters like Bland, like Alloway, like Sellers, men who
were evil and had no remorse, no spiritual accusing neme-
sis, had something far more torturing to the mind, more
haunting, more murderous of rest and sleep and peace,
and that something was abnormal fear of death. Duane
knew this, for he had shot these men; he had seen the
quick, dark shadow in eyes, the presentiment that the will
could not control, and then the horrible certainty. These
men must have been in agony at every meeting with a
possible or certain foe — more agony than the hot rend
of a bullet. They were haunted, too, haunted by this fear,
by every victim calling from the grave that nothing was
so inevitable as death, which lurked behind every corner,
hid in every shadow, lay deep in the dark barrel of every
gun. These men could not have a friend; they could not
love or trust a woman. They knew their one chance of
holding onto life lay in their own distrust, watchfulness,
dexterity, and that hope, by the very nature of their
lives, could not be lasting. They had doomed themselves.
What, then, could possibly have dwelt in the depths of
their minds as they went to their beds on a starry night
like this, with mystery in silence and shadow, with time
passing surely, and the dark future and its secret ap-

proaching every hour — what, then, but hell?

The hell in Duane's mind was not fear of man or fear of death. He would have been glad to lay down the burden of life, providing death came naturally. Many times he had prayed for it. But that overdeveloped, superhuman spirit of defense in him precluded suicide or the inviting of an enemy's bullet. Sometimes he had a vague, scarcely analyzed idea that this spirit was what had made the Southwest habitable for the white man.

Every one of his victims, singly and collectively, returned to him forever, it seemed, in cold, passionless, accusing domination of these haunted hours. They did not accuse him of dishonor or cowardice or brutality or murder; they only accused him of death. It was as if they knew more than when they were alive, had learned that life was a divine mysterious gift not to be taken. They thronged about him with their voiceless clamoring, drifted around him with their fading eyes.

Chapter Eleven

After nearly six months in the Nueces gorge the loneliness and inaction of this life drove Duane out upon the trails seeking anything rather than to hide longer alone, a prey to the scourge of his thoughts. The moment he rode into sight of men a remarkable transformation occurred in him. A strange warmth stirred in him — a longing to see the faces of people, to hear their voices — a pleasurable emotion, sad and strange, but it was only a precursor of his old bitter, sleepless, and eternal vigilance. When he hid alone in the brakes, he was safe from all except his deeper, better self; when he escaped from this into the haunts of men, his force and will went to the preservation of his life.

Mercer was the first village into which he rode. He had many friends there. Mercer claimed to owe Duane a debt. On the outskirts of the village there was a grave overgrown by brush so that the rude-lettered post which marked it was scarcely visible to Duane as he rode past. He had never read the inscription, but he thought now of Hardin, no other than the erstwhile ally of Bland. For many years Hardin had harassed the stockmen and ranchers in and around Mercer. On an evil day for him he or his outlaws had beaten and robbed a man who once succored Duane when sore in need. Duane met Hardin in the little plaza of the village, called him every name known to border men, taunted him to draw, and killed him in the act.

Duane went to the house of one Jones, a Texan who had

138

known his father, and there he was warmly received. The feel of an honest hand, the voice of a friend, the prattle of children who were not afraid of him or his gun, good wholesome food, and change of clothes — these things for the time being made a changed man of Duane. To be sure, he did not often speak. The price on his head and the weight of his burden made him silent, but eagerly he drank in all the news that was told him. In the years of his absence from home he had never heard a word about his mother or uncle. Those who were his real friends on the border would have been the last to make inquiries, to write or receive letters that might give a clue to Duane's whereabouts.

Duane remained all day with this hospitable Jones and, as twilight fell, was loath to go and yielded to a pressing invitation to remain overnight. It was seldom indeed that Duane slept under a roof. Early in the evening, while Duane sat on the porch with two awed and hero-worshipping sons of the house, Jones returned from a quick visit down at the post office. Summarily he sent off the boys. He labored under intense excitement.

"Duane, there's rangers in town," he whispered. "It's all over town, too, that you're here. You rode in long after sunup. Lots of people saw you. I don't believe there's a man or boy that'd squeal on you, but the women might. They gossip, and these rangers are handsome fellows . . . devils with the women."

"What company of rangers?" asked Duane quickly.

"Company A, under Captain MacNelly, that new ranger. He made a big name in the war. And since he's been in the ranger service, he's done wonders. He's cleaned up some bad places south, and he's working north."

"MacNelly. I've heard of him. Describe him to me."

"Slight built chap but wiry and tough. Clean face, black mustache and hair. Sharp black eyes. He's got a look of authority. MacNelly's a fine man, Duane. Belongs to a good Southern family. I'd hate to have him look you up." Duane did not speak.

"MacNelly's got nerve, and his rangers are all experienced men. If they find out you're here, they'll come after you. MacNelly's no gunfighter, but he wouldn't hesitate to do his duty, even if he faced sure death. Which he would in this case. Duane, you mustn't meet Captain MacNelly. Your record is clean, if it is terrible. You never met a ranger or any officer except a rotten sheriff now and then, like Rod Brown."

Still Duane kept silent. He was not thinking of danger but of the fact of how fleeting must be his stay among friends.

"I've already fixed up a pack of grub," went on Jones. "I'll slip out to saddle your horse. You watch here."

He had scarcely uttered the last word when soft, swift footsteps sounded on the hard path. A man turned in at the gate. The light was dim yet clear enough to disclose an unusually tall figure. When it appeared nearer, he was seen to be walking with both arms raised, hands high. He slowed his stride.

"Does Burt Jones live here?" he asked in a low, hurried voice.

"I reckon. I'm Burt. What can I do for you?" replied Jones.

The stranger peered around, stealthily came closer, still with his hands up.

"It is known that Buck Duane is here. Captain MacNelly's camping on the river just out of town. He sends word to Duane to come out there after dark."

The stranger wheeled and departed as swiftly and

strangely as he had come.

"Bust me! Duane, whatever do you make of that?" exclaimed Jones.

"A new one on me," replied Duane thoughtfully.

"First fool thing I ever heard of MacNelly doing. Can't make head nor tails of it. I'd have said offhand that MacNelly wouldn't double-cross anybody. He struck me as a square man, sand all through. But, hell! He must mean treachery. I can't see anything else in that deal."

"Maybe the captain wants to give me a fair chance to surrender without bloodshed," observed Duane. "Pretty decent of him, if he meant that."

"He *invites* you out to his camp *after dark*. Something strange about this, Duane. But MacNelly's a new man out here. He does some queer things. Perhaps he's getting a swelled head. Well, whatever his intentions, his presence around Mercer is enough for us. Duane, you hit the road and put some miles between you and the amiable captain before daylight. Tomorrow I'll go out there and ask him what in the devil he meant."

"That messenger he sent . . . he was a ranger?" said Duane.

"Sure he was, a nervy one! It must have taken sand to come bracing you that way. Duane, the fellow didn't pack a gun, I'll swear to that. Pretty odd, this trick. But you can't trust it. Hit the road, Duane."

A little later a black horse with muffled hoofs, bearing a tall, dark rider who peered keenly into every shadow, trotted down a pasture lane back of Jones's house, turned into the road, and then, breaking into swifter gait, rapidly left Mercer behind.

Fifteen or twenty miles out Duane drew rein in a forest of mesquite, dismounted, and searched about for a glade

141

with a little grass. Here he staked his horse on a long lariat and, using his saddle for a pillow, his saddle-blanket for covering, he went to sleep. Next morning he was off again, working south. During the next few days he paid brief visits to several villages that lay in his path. In each some one particular friend had a piece of news to impart that made Duane profoundly thoughtful. A ranger had made a quiet, unobtrusive call upon these friends and left this message, "Tell Buck Duane to ride into Captain Mac-Nelly's camp some time after night."

Duane concluded, and his friends all agreed with him, that the new ranger's main purpose in the Nueces country was to capture or kill Buck Duane, and that this message was simply an original and striking ruse, the daring of which might appeal to certain outlaws. It did not appeal to Duane. Although his curiosity was aroused, it did not, however, tempt him to any foolhardy act. He turned southwest and rode a hundred miles until he again reached the sparsely settled country. Here he heard no more of rangers. It was a barren region he had never but once ridden through, and that ride had cost him dearly. He had been compelled to shoot his way out. Outlaws were not in accord with the few ranchers and their cowboys who ranged here. He learned that both outlaws and Mexican raiders had long been at bitter enmity with these ranchers. Being unfamiliar with roads and trails, Duane had pushed on into the heart of this district, when all the time he really believed he was traveling around it. A rifle shot from a ranch house, a deliberate attempt to kill him because he was an unknown rider in those parts, discovered to Duane his mistake; and a hard ride to get away persuaded him to return to his old methods of hiding by day and traveling by night.

He got into rough country, rode for three days without covering much ground, but believed that he was getting on safer territory. Twice he came to a wide bottomland green with willow and cottonwood and thick as chaparral, somewhere through the middle of which ran a river he decided must be the lower Nueces.

One evening, as he stole out from a covert where he had camped, he saw the lights of a village. He tried to pass it on the left but was unable to because the brakes of this bottomland extended in almost to the outskirts of the village, and he had to retrace his steps and go around to the right. Wire fences and horses in pasture made this a task, so it was well after midnight before he accomplished it. He made ten miles or more then by daylight and after that proceeded cautiously along a road which appeared to be well worn from travel. He passed several thickets where he would have halted to hide during the day but for the fact that he had to find water. He was a long while in coming to it, and then there was no thicket or clump of mesquite near the water hole that would afford him covert. So he kept on.

The country before him was ridgy and began to show cottonwoods here and there in the hollows and yucca and mesquite on the higher ground. As he mounted a ridge, he noted that the road made a sharp turn, and he could not see what was beyond it. He slowed up and was making the turn, which was downhill between high banks of yellow clay, when his mettlesome horse heard something to frighten him or shied at something and bolted.

The few bounds he took before Duane's iron arm checked him were enough to reach the curve. One flashing glance showed Duane the open once more, a little valley below with a wide, shallow, rocky stream, a clump of cottonwoods beyond, a somber group of men facing him, and two dark, limp, strangely grotesque figures hanging from branches. The sight was common enough in southwest Texas, but Duane had never before found himself so unpleasantly close.

A hoarse voice pealed out: "By hell! There's another one!"

"Stranger, ride down an' account fer yourself!" yelled another.

"Hands up!"

"Thet's right, Jack. Don't take no chances. Plug him!"

These remarks were so swiftly uttered as almost to be continuous. Duane was wheeling his horse when a rifle cracked. The bullet struck his left forearm, and he thought broke it, for he dropped the rein. The frightened horse leaped. Another bullet whistled past Duane. Then the bend in the road probably saved him from certain death. Like the wind his fleet steed went down the long hill.

Duane was in no hurry to look back. He knew what to expect. His chief concern of the moment was for his injured arm. He found that the bones were still intact, but the wound, having been made by a soft bullet, was an exceedingly bad one. Blood pored from it. Giving the horse his head, Duane wound his scarf tightly around the holes and with teeth and hand tied it tightly. That done, he looked back over his shoulder.

Riders were making the dust fly on the hillside road. There were more coming around the cut where the road curved. The leader was perhaps a quarter of a mile back, and the others strung out behind him. Duane needed only one glance to tell him that they were fast and hard-riding cowboys in a land where all riders were good. They would not have owned any but strong, swift horses. Moreover, it was a district where ranchers had suffered beyond all

144

endurance the greed and brutality of outlaws. Duane had simply been so unfortunate as to run right into a lynching party at a time of all times when any stranger would be in danger and any outlaw put to his limit to escape with his life.

Duane did not look back again till he had crossed the ridgy piece of ground and had gotten to the level road. He had gained upon his pursuers. When he ascertained this, he tried to save his horse, to check a little that killing gait. This horse was a magnificent animal, big, strong, fast, but his endurance had never been put to a grueling test. That worried Duane. His life had made it impossible to keep one horse very long at a time, and this one was an unknown quantity.

Duane had but one plan — the only plan possible in this case — and that was to make the river bottoms, where he might elude his pursuers in the willow brakes. Fifteen miles or so would bring him to the river, and this was not a hopeless distance for any good horse if not too closely pressed. Duane concluded presently that the cowboys behind were losing a little in the chase because they were not extending their horses. It was decidedly unusual for such riders to save their mounts. Duane pondered over this, looking backward several times to see if their horses were stretched out. They were not, and the fact was disturbing. Only one reason presented itself to Duane's conjecturing, and it was that with him headed straight on that road his pursuers were satisfied not to force the running. He began to hope and look for a trail or a road turning off to right or left. There was none. A rough, mesquite-dotted, and yucca-spiked country extended away on either side. Duane believed that he would be compelled to take to this hard going. One thing was certain — he had to go around the village. The river, however, was on the outskirts of the village, and once in the willows he would be safe.

Dust clouds far ahead caused his alarm to grow. He watched with his eyes strained; he hoped to see a wagon, a few stray cattle. But no, he soon descried several horsemen. Shots and yells behind him attested to the fact that his pursuers likewise had seen these newcomers on the scene. More than a mile separated these two parties, yet that distance did not keep them from soon understanding each other. Duane waited only to see this new factor show signs of sudden quick action, and then, with a muttered curse, he spurred his horse off the road into the brush.

He chose the right side, because the river lay nearer that way. There were patches of open sandy ground between clumps of cactus and mesquite, and he found that despite a zigzag course he made better time. It was impossible for him to locate his pursuers. They would come together, he decided, and take to his tracks. What, then, was his surprise and dismay to run out of a thicket right into a low ridge of rough, broken rock, impossible to get a horse over! He wheeled to the left along its base. The sandy ground gave place to a harder soil, where his horse did not labor so. Here the growths of mesquite and cactus became scantier, affording better travel but poor cover. He kept sharp eyes ahead and, as he had expected, soon saw moving dust clouds and the dark figures of horses. They were half a mile away and swinging obliquely across the flat, which fact proved that they entertained a fair idea of the country and the fugitive's difficulty.

Without an instant's hesitation Duane put his horse to his best efforts, straight ahead. He had to pass those men. When this was seemingly made impossible by a deep wash from which he had to turn, Duane began to feel cold and sick. Was this the end? Always there had to be an end to an outlaw's career. He wanted then to ride straight at these pursuers, but reason outweighed instinct. Although he was fleeing for his life, nevertheless the strongest instinct at the time was his desire to fight.

He knew when these three horsemen saw him, and a moment afterward he lost sight of them as he got into the mesquite again. He meant now to try to reach the road and pushed his mount severely, though still saving him for a final burst. Rocks, thickets, bunches of cactus, washes — all operated against his following a straight line. He almost lost his bearing and finally would have ridden toward his enemies had not good fortune favored him in the matter of an open, burned-over stretch of ground.

Here he saw both groups of pursuers, one on each side and almost within gunshot. Their sharp yells, as much as his cruel spurs, drove his horse into that pace which now meant life or death for him. And never had Duane bestrode a gamer, swifter, stauncher beast. He seemed about to accomplish the impossible. In the dragging sand he was far superior to any horse in pursuit, and on this sandy open stretch he gained enough to spare a little in the brush beyond. Heated now and thoroughly terrorized, he kept the pace through thickets that almost tore Duane from his saddle. Something weighty and grim eased off Duane. He was going to get out in front! The horse had speed, fire, stamina.

Duane dashed out into another open place dotted by few trees and here, right in his path within pistol-range, stood horsemen waiting. They yelled. They spurred toward him but did not fire at him. He turned his horse — faced to the right. Only one thing kept him from standing his ground to fight it out. He remembered those dangling limp figures hanging from the cottonwoods. These ranchers would rather hang an outlaw than do anything. They might draw all his fire and then capture him. His horror of hanging was so great as to be all out of proportion compared to his gunfighter's instinct of self preservation.

A race began then, a dusty, crashing drive through gray mesquite. Duane could scarcely see, he was so blinded by stinging branches across his eyes. The hollow wind roared in his ears. He lost his sense of the nearness of his pursuers, but they must have been close. Did they shoot at him? He imagined he had heard shots, but that might have been the crackling of dead snags. His left arm hung limply, almost useless; he handled the rein with his right; and most of the time he hung low over the pommel. The gray walls flashing by him, the whip of twigs, the rush of wind, the heavy, rapid pound of hoofs, the violent motion of his horse — these vied in sensation with the smart of sweat in his eyes, the rack of his wound, the cold, sick cramp in his stomach. With these also was dull, raging fury. He had to run when he wanted to fight. It took all his mind to force back that bitter hate of himself, of his pursuers, of this race for his useless life.

Suddenly he burst out of a line of mesquite into the road — a long stretch of lonely road. How fiercely, with hot, strange joy, he wheeled his horse upon it! Then he was sweeping along, sure now that he was out in front. His horse still had strength and speed but showed signs of breaking. Presently Duane looked back. Pursuers — he could not count how many — were loping along in his rear. He paid no more attention to them, and with teeth set he faced ahead, grimmer now in his determination to foil them.

148

He passed a few scattered ranch houses where horses whistled from corrals, and men curiously watched him fly past. He saw one rancher running, and he felt intuitively that this fellow was going to join in the chase. Duane's steed pounded on, not noticeably slower but with a lack of former smoothness, with a strained, convulsive, jerking stride that showed he was almost done.

Sight of the village ahead surprised Duane. He had reached it sooner than he expected. Then he made a discovery — he had entered the zone of wire fences. As he dared not turn back now, he kept on, intending to ride through the village. Looking backward, he saw that his pursuers were half a mile distant, too far to alarm any villagers in time to intercept him in his flight. As he rode by the first houses, his horse broke and began to labor. Duane did not believe he would last long enough to go through the village.

Saddled horses in front of a store gave Duane an idea, not by any means new, and one he had carried out successfully before. As he pulled in his heaving mount and leaped off, a couple of ranchers came out of the place, and one of them stepped to a clean-limbed, fiery bay. He was about to get into his saddle when he saw Duane, and then he halted, a foot in the stirrup.

Duane strode forward, grasped the bridle of this man's horse. "Mine's done . . . but not killed," he panted. "Trade with me."

"Wal, stranger, I'm shore always ready to trade," drawled the man. "But ain't you a little swift?"

Duane glanced back up the road. His pursuers were entering the village. "I'm Duane . . . Buck Duane," he cried, menacingly. "Will you trade? Hurry!"

The rancher, turning white, dropped his foot from the

149

stirrup and fell back. "I reckon I'll trade," he said.

Bounding up, Duane dug spurs into the bay's flanks. The horse snorted in fright, plunged into a run. He was fresh, swift, half wild. Duane flashed by the remaining houses on the street out into the open. But the road ended at that village or else led out from some other quarter, for he had ridden straight into the fields and from them into rough desert. When he reached the cover of mesquite once more, he looked back to find six horsemen within rifle shot of him and more coming behind them.

His new horse had not had time to get warm before Duane reached a high sandy bluff below which lay the willow brakes. As far as he could see extended an immense flat strip of red-tinged willow. How welcome it was to his eye! He felt like a hunted wolf that, weary and lame, had reached his hole in the rocks. Zigzagging down the soft slope, he put the bay into the dense wall of leaf and branch, but the horse balked.

There was little time to lose. Dismounting, he dragged the stubborn beast into the thicket. This was harder and slower work than Duane cared to risk. If he had not been rushed, he might have had better success. So he had to abandon the horse — a circumstance to which only such sore straits could have driven him. Then he went slipping swiftly through the narrow aisles.

He had not gotten under cover any too soon. For he heard his pursuers piling over the bluff, loud voiced, confident, brutal. They crashed into the willows.

"Hi, Sid! Heah's your hoss!" called one, evidently to the man Duane had forced into a trade.

"Say, if you locoed gents'll hold up a little, I'll tell you somethin'," replied a voice from the bluff.

"Come on, Sid! We got him corralled," said the first speaker.

"Wal, mebbe, an' if you hev, it's liable to be damn' hot. *Thet feller was Buck Duane!*"

Absolute silence followed that statement. Presently it was broken by a rattling of loose gravel and then low voices.

"He can't git acrost the river, I tell you," came to Duane's ears. "He's corralled in the brake. I know thet hole."

Then Duane, gliding silently and swiftly through the willows, heard no more from his pursuers. He headed straight for the river. Threading a passage through a willow brake was an old task for him. Many days and nights had gone to the acquiring of a skill that might have been envied by an Indian.

The Rio Grande and its tributaries for the most of their length in Texas ran between wide, low, flat lands covered by a dense growth of willow. Cottonwood, mesquite, prickly pear, and other growths mingled with the willow, and altogether they made a matted, tangled copse, a thicket that an inexperienced man would have considered impenetrable. From above, these wild brakes looked green and red; from the inside they were gray and yellow — a striped wall. Trails and glades were scarce. There were a few deer runways and sometimes little paths made by peccaries — the *jabali,* or wild pigs of Mexico. The ground was clay and unusually dry, sometimes baked so hard that it left no imprint of a track. Where a growth of cottonwood had held back the encroachment of the willows, there usually was thick grass and underbrush. The willows were short, slender poles with stems so close together that they almost touched and with the leafy foliage forming a thick covering.

The depths of this break Duane had penetrated was a silent, dreamy, strange place. In the middle of the day the light was weird and dim. When a breeze fluttered the

151

foliage, then slender shafts and spears of sunshine pierced the green mantle and danced like gold on the ground.

Duane had always felt the strangeness of this kind of place, and likewise he had felt a protecting, harboring something which always seemed to him to be the sympathy of the brake for a hunted creature. Any unwounded creature, strong and resourceful, was safe when he had glided under the low, rustling green roof of this wild covert. It was not hard to conceal tracks; the springy soil gave forth no sound; and men could hunt each other for weeks, pass within a few yards of each other, and never know it. The problem of sustaining life was difficult, but then hunted men and animals survived on very little.

Duane wanted to cross the river if that was possible and, keeping in the brake, work his way upstream till he had reached country more hospitable. Remembering what the man had said in regard to the river, Duane had his doubts about crossing. But he would take any chance to put the river between him and his hunters. He pushed on. His left arm had to be favored, as he could scarcely move it. Using his right to spread the willows, he slipped sideways between them and made fast time. There were narrow aisles and washes and holes low down and paths brushed by animals, of all of which he took advantage, running, walking, crawling, stooping any way to get along. To keep in a straight line was not easy — he did it by marking some bright sunlit stem or tree ahead and, when he reached it, looked straight on to mark another. His progress necessarily grew slower, for as he advanced the brake became wilder, denser, darker. Mosquitoes began to whine about his head. He kept on without pause. Deepening shadows under the willows told him that the afternoon was far advanced. He began to fear he had wandered in a wrong direction. Finally a strip of light ahead relieved his anxiety, and after a toilsome penetration of still denser brush he broke through to the bank of the river.

He faced a wide, shallow, muddy stream with brakes on the opposite bank extending like a green and yellow wall. Duane perceived at a glance the futility of his trying to cross at this point. Everywhere the sluggish water laved quicksand bars. In fact, the bed of the river was all quicksand, and very likely there was not a foot of water anywhere. He could not swim; he could not crawl; he could not push a log across. Any solid thing touching that smooth yellow sand would be grasped and sucked down. To prove this he seized a long pole and, reaching down from the high bank, thrust it into the stream. Right near the shore there apparently was no bottom to the treacherous quicksand. He abandoned any hope of crossing the river. Probably for miles up and down it would be just the same as here. Before leaving the bank, he tied his hat upon the pole and lifted enough water to quench his thirst. Then he worked his way back to where thinner growth made advancement easier and kept on upstream till the shadows were so deep he could not see. Feeling around for a place big enough to stretch out on, he lay down. For the time being he was as safe there as he would have been beyond in the Rim Rock. He was tired, though not exhausted, and in spite of the throbbing pain in his arm he dropped at once into sleep.

Chapter Twelve

Some time during the night Duane awoke. A stillness seemingly so thick and heavy as to have substance blanketed the black willow brake. He could not see a star or a branch or tree trunk or even his hand before his eyes. He lay there waiting, listening, sure that he had been awakened by an unusual sound. Ordinary noises of the night in the wilderness never disturbed his rest. His faculties, like those of old fugitives and hunted creatures, had become trained to a marvelous keenness. A long low breath of slow wind moaned through the willows, passed away; some stealthy, soft-footed beast trotted past him in the darkness; there was a rustling among dry leaves; a fox barked lonesomely in the distance. But none of these sounds had broken his slumber.

Suddenly, piercing the stillness, came a bay of a bloodhound. Quickly Duane sat up, chilled to his marrow. The action made him aware of his crippled arm. Then came other bays, lower, more distant. Silence enfolded him again, all the more oppressive and menacing in his suspense. Bloodhounds had been put on his trail, and the leader was not far away. All his life Duane had been familiar with bloodhounds. He knew that, if the pack surrounded him in this impenetrable darkness, he would be held at bay or dragged down as wolves dragged down a stag. Rising to his feet, prepared to flee as best he could, he waited to be sure of the direction he should take.

The leader of the hounds broke into cry again, a deep, full-toned, ringing bay, strange, ominous, terribly significant in its power. It caused a cold sweat to ooze out all over Duane's body. He turned from it, and with his uninjured arm outstretched to feel for the willows he groped his way along. As it was made impossible to pick out the narrow passages, he had to slip and squeeze and plunge between the yielding stems. He made such a crashing that he no longer heard the baying of the hounds. He had no hope to elude them. He meant to climb the first cottonwood that he stumbled upon in his blind flight, but it appeared he never was going to be lucky enough to run against one. Often he fell, sometimes flat, at others upheld by the willows. What made the work so hard was the fact that he had only one arm to open a clump of close-growing stems and his feet would catch or tangle in the narrow crotches, holding him fast. He had to struggle desperately. It was as if the willows were clutching hands, his enemies, fiendishly impeding his progress. He tore his clothes on sharp branches, and his flesh suffered many a prick. But in a terrible earnestness he kept on until he brought up hard against a cottonwood tree.

There he leaned and rested. He found himself as nearly exhausted as he had ever been, wet with sweat, his hands torn and burning, his breast laboring, his legs stinging from innumerable bruises. While he leaned there to catch his breath, he listened for the pursuing hounds. For a long time there was no sound from them. This, however, did not deceive him into any hopefulness. There were bloodhounds that bayed often on a trail, and others that ran mostly silent. The former were more valuable to their owner, and the latter more dangerous to the fugitive. Presently Duane's ears were filled by a chorus of short ringing yelps. The pack had found where he had slept, and now the trail was hot. Satisfied that they would soon overtake him, Duane set about climbing the cottonwood, which in his condition was difficult of ascent.

It happened to be a fairly large tree, with a fork about fifteen feet up and branches thereafter in succession. Duane climbed until he got above the enshrouding belt of blackness. A pale gray mist hung above the brake, and through it shone a line of dim lights. Duane decided these were bonfires made along the bluff to render his escape more difficult on that side. Away, in the direction he thought was north, he imagined he saw more fires but, as the mist was thick, he could not be sure. While he sat there pondering the matter, listening for the hounds, the mist and the gloom on one side lightened; and this side he concluded was east and meant that dawn was near. Satisfying himself on this score, he descended to the first branch of the tree.

His situation now, though still critical, did not appear to be so hopeless as it had been. The hounds would soon close in on him, and he would kill them or drive them away. It was beyond the bounds of possibility that any men could have followed running hounds through that brake in the night. The thing that worried Duane was the fact of the bonfires. He had gathered from the words of one of his pursuers that the brake was a kind of trap, and he began to believe there was only one way out of it and that was along the bank where he had entered, and where obviously all night long his pursuers had kept fires burning. Further conjecture on this point, however, was interrupted by a crashing in the willows and the rapid patter of feet.

Underneath Duane lay a gray, foggy obscurity. He could not see the ground nor any object but the black trunk of the tree. Sight would not be needed to tell him when the

156

pack arrived. With a pattering rush through the willows, the hounds reached the tree and then, high above crash of brush and thud of heavy paws, rose a hideous clamor. Duane's pursuers far off to the south would hear that and know what it meant. At daybreak, perhaps before, they would take a shortcut across the brake, guided by the baying of hounds that had treed their quarry.

It was only a few moments, however, till Duane could distinguish the vague forms of the hounds in the gray shadow below. Still he waited. He had no shots to spare. And he knew how to treat bloodhounds. Gradually the obscurity lightened, and at length Duane had good enough sight of the hounds for his purpose. His first shot killed the huge brute leader of the pack. Then, with unerring shots, he crippled several others. That stopped the baying. Piercing howls arose. The pack took fright and fled, its course easily marked by the howls of the crippled members. Duane reloaded his gun and, making certain all the hounds had gone, he descended to the ground and set off at a rapid pace to the north.

The mist had dissolved under a rising sun when Duane made his first halt some miles north of the scene where he had waited for the hounds. A barrier to further progress, in shape of a precipitous rocky bluff, rose sheer from the willow brake. He skirted the base of the cliff, where walking was comparatively easy, around in the direction of the river. He reached the end finally to see there was absolutely no chance to escape from the brake at that corner. It took extreme labor, attended by some hazard and considerable pain to his arm, to get down where he could fill his sombrero with water. After quenching his thirst, he had a look at his wound. It was caked over with blood and dirt. When

157

washed off, the arm was seen to be inflamed and swollen around the bullet hole. He bathed it, experiencing a soothing relief in the cool water. Then he bandaged it as best he could and arranged a sling around his neck. This mitigated the pain of the injured member and held it in a quiet and restful position, where it had a chance to begin mending.

As Duane turned away from the river, he felt refreshed. His great strength and endurance had always made fatigue something almost unknown to him. However, tramping on foot day and night was as unusual to him as to any other riders of the Southwest, and it had begun to tell on him. Retracing his steps, he reached the point where he had abruptly come upon the bluff, and here he determined to follow along its base in the other direction until he found a way out or discovered the futility of such effort.

Duane covered ground rapidly. From time to time he paused to listen, but he was always listening, and his eyes were ever roving. This alertness had become second nature with him, so that except in extreme cases of caution he performed it while he pondered his gloomy and fateful situation. Such habits of alertness and thought made time fly swiftly.

By noon he had rounded the wide curve of the brake and was facing south. The bluff had petered out from a high, mountainous wall to a low abutment of rock, but it still held to its steep, rough nature and afforded no crack or slope where quick ascent could have been possible. He pushed on, growing warier as he approached the danger zone, finding that as he neared the river on this side it was imperative to go deeper into the willows. In the afternoon he reached a point where he could see men pacing to and fro on the bluff. This assured him that whatever place was guarded was one by which he might escape. He headed toward these men and approached within a hundred paces of the bluff where they were. There were several men and several boys, all armed and, after the manner of Texans, taking their task leisurely. Farther down Duane made out black dots on the horizon of the bluff-line, and these he concluded were more guards stationed at another outlet. Probably all the available men in the district were on duty. Texans took a grim pleasure in such work. Duane remembered that upon several occasions he had served such duty himself.

Duane peered through the branches and studied the lay of the land. For several hundred yards the bluff could be climbed. He took stock of those careless guards. They had rifles, and that made vain any attempt to pass them in daylight. He believed an attempt by night might be successful, and he was swiftly coming to a determination to hide there till dark and then try it, when the sudden yelping of a dog betrayed him to the guards on the bluff.

The dog had likely been placed there to give an alarm, and he was lustily true to his trust. Duane saw the men run together and begin to talk excitedly and peer into the brake, which was a signal for him to slip away under the willows. He made no noise, and he assured himself he must be invisible. Nevertheless, he heard shouts, then the cracking of rifles, and bullets began to zip and swish through the leafy covert. The day was hot and windless, and Duane concluded that whenever he touched a willow stem, even ever so slightly, it vibrated to the top and sent a quiver among the leaves. Through this the guards had located his position. Once a bullet hissed by him; another thudded into the ground before him. The shooting loosed a rage in Duane. He had to fly from these men, and he hated them and himself because of it. Always in the fury of such moments he wanted to give back shot for shot. But he slipped on through the willows, and at length the rifles ceased to crack.

He sheered to the left again, in line with the rocky barrier, and kept on, wondering what the next mile would bring. It brought worse, for he was seen by sharp-eyed scouts, and a hot fusillade drove him to run for his life, luckily to escape with no more than a bullet-creased shoulder.

Later that day, still undaunted, he sheered again toward the trap wall, and found that the nearer he approached to the place where he had come down into the brake the greater his danger. To attempt to run the blockade of that trail by day would be fatal. He waited for night and, after the brightness of the fires had somewhat lessened, he assayed to creep out of the brake. He succeeded in reaching the foot of the bluff, here only a bank, and had begun to crawl stealthily up under cover of a shadow when a hound again betrayed his position. Retreating to the willows was as perilous a task as had ever confronted Duane and, when he had accomplished it, right under what seemed a hundred blazing rifles, he felt that he had indeed been favored by Providence. This time men followed him a goodly ways into the brake, and the ripping of lead through the willows sounded on all sides of him.

When the noise of pursuit ceased, Duane sat down in the darkness, his mind clamped between two things — whether to try again to escape or wait for possible opportunity. He seemed incapable of decision. His intelligence told him that every hour lessened his chances for escape. He had little enough chance in any case, and that was what made another attempt so desperately hard. Still it was not love of life that bound him. There would come an

160

hour, sooner or later, when he would wrench decision out of his chaos of emotion and thought, but that time was not yet.

When he had remained quiet long enough to cool off and recover from his run, he found that he was tired. He stretched out to rest, but the swarms of vicious mosquitoes prevented sleep. The corner of the brake was low and near the river, a breeding ground for the blood-suckers. They sang and hummed and whined around him in an ever-increasing horde. He covered his head and hands with his coat and lay there patiently. That was a long and wretched night. Morning found him still strong physically but in a dreadful state of mind.

First he hurried for the river. He could withstand the pangs of hunger, but it was imperative to quench thirst. His wound made him feverish and therefore more than usually hot and thirsty. Again he was refreshed. That morning he was hard put to it to hold himself back from attempting to cross the river. If he could find a light log, it was within the bounds of possibility that he might ford the shallow water and bars of quicksand. But not yet! Wearily, doggedly, he faced about toward the bluff.

All that day and all that night, all the next day and all the next night, he stole like a hunted savage from river to bluff; and every hour forced upon him the bitter certainty that he was trapped. Duane lost track of days, of events. He had come to an evil pass. There arrived an hour when, closely pressed by pursuers at the extreme southern corner of the brake, he took to a dense thicket of willows, driven to what he believed was his last stand. If only these human bloodhounds would swiftly close in on him! Let him fight to the last bitter gasp and have it over! But these hunters, eager as they were to get him, had care of their own skins.

They took few risks. They had him cornered.

It was the middle of the day, hot, dusty, oppressive, threatening storm. Like a snake Duane crawled into a little space in the darkest part of the thicket and lay still. Men had cut him off from the bluff, from the river, seemingly from all sides. Even if his passage to the river had not been blocked, it might just as well have been.

"Come on fellers . . . down hyar," called one man from the bluff.

"Got him corralled at last," shouted another.

"Reckon you needn't be too shore. We thought thet more'n once," taunted another.

"I seen him, I tell you."

"Aw, thet was a deer."

"But Bill found fresh tracks an' blood on the willows."

"If he's winged, we needn't hurry."

"Hold on thar, you boys," came a shout in authoritative tones from farther up the bluff. "Go slow. You all air gittin' foolish at the end of a long chase."

"Thet's right, Colonel. Hold 'em back. There's nothin' shorer than somebody'll be stoppin' lead pretty quick. He'll be huntin' us soon!"

"Let's surround this corner an' starve him out."

"Fire the brake."

How clearly all this talk pierced Duane's ears! In it he seemed to hear his doom. This, then, was the end he had always expected, which had been close to him before yet never like now.

By God! thought Duane, *the thing for me to do now . . . is go out . . . meet them.*

That was prompted by the fighting, the killing instinct in him. In that moment it had almost superhuman power. If he must die, that was the way for him to die. What else could be expected of Buck Duane? He got to his knees and drew his gun. With his swollen and almost useless hand he held what spare ammunition he had left. He ought to creep out noiselessly to the edge of the willows, suddenly face his pursuers, then, while there was a beat left in his heart, kill, kill, kill. These men all had rifles. The fight would be short, but the marksmen did not live on earth who could make such a fight go wholly against him. Confronting them suddenly, he could kill a man for every shot in his gun.

Thus Duane reasoned. So he hoped to accept his fate — to meet his end. But when he tried to step forward, something checked him. He forced himself, yet he could not go on. The obstruction that opposed his will was as insurmountable as it had been physically impossible for him to climb the bluff.

Slowly he fell back, crouched low, and then lay flat. The grim and ghastly dignity that had been his a moment before fell away from him. He lay there stripped of his last shred of self respect. He wondered, was he afraid? — had he, the last of the Duanes, come to feel fear? No! Never in all his wild life had he so longed to go out and meet men face to face. It was not fear that held him back. He hated this hiding, this eternal vigilance, this hopeless life. The damnable paradox of the situation was that, if he went out to meet these men, there was absolutely no doubt of his doom. If he clung to his covert, there was a chance, a merest chance, for his life. These pursuers, dogged and unflagging as they had been, were mortally afraid of him. It was his fame that made them cowards. Duane's keenness told him that at the very darkest and most perilous moment there was still a chance for him. And the blood in him, the temper of his father, the years of his

163

outlawry, the pride of his unsought and hated career, the nameless, inexplicable something in him made him accept that slim chance.

Waiting then became a physical and mental agony. He lay under the burning sun, parched by thirst, laboring to breathe, sweating and bleeding. His neglected wound was like a red-hot prong in his flesh. Blotched and swollen from the never-ending attack of flies and mosquitoes, his face seemed twice its natural size, and it ached and stung.

On one side, then, was this physical torture, on the other the old hell, terribly augmented at this crisis in his mind. It seemed that thought and imagination had never been so swift. If death found him presently, how would it come? Would he get decent burial or be left for the peccaries and the coyotes? Would his people ever know where he had fallen? How wretched, how miserable his state? It was cowardly — it was monstrous — for him to cling longer to this doomed life. Then the hate in his heart, the hellish hate of these men on his trail — that was like a scourge. He felt no longer human. He had degenerated into an animal that could think. His heart pounded; his pulse beat; his breast heaved; and this internal strife seemed to thunder into his ears. He was now enacting the tragedy of all crippled, starved, hunted wolves at bay in their dens. Only his tragedy was infinitely more terrible because he had mind enough to see his plight, his resemblance to a lonely wolf, bloody fanged, dripping, snarling, fire eyed in a last instinctive defiance.

Mounted upon the horror of Duane's thought was a watching, listening intensity so supreme that it registered impressions which were creations of his imagination. He heard stealthy steps that were not there; he saw shadowy, moving figures that were only leaves. A hundred times, when he

164

was about to pull trigger, he discovered his error. Yet voices came from a distance, and steps and crackings in the willows, and other sounds real enough, but Duane could not distinguish the real from the false. There were times when the wind which had arisen sent a hot, pattering breath down the willow aisles, and Duane heard it as an approaching army.

This straining of Duane's faculties brought on a reaction which in itself was a respite. He saw the sun darkened by thick, slow-spreading clouds. A storm appeared to be coming. How slowly it moved! The air was like steam. If there broke one of those dark, violent storms occasional though rare to the country, Duane believed he might slip away in the fury of wind and rain. Hope, that seemed unquenchable in him, resurged again. He hailed it with a bitterness that was sickening.

Then at a rustling step he froze into the old strained attention. He heard a slow patter of soft feet. A tawny shape crossed a little opening in the thicket. It was that of a dog. The moment while that beast came into full view was an age. The dog was not a bloodhound and, if he had a trail or a scent, he seemed to be at fault on it. Duane waited for the inevitable discovery. Any kind of hunting dog could have found him in that thicket. Voices from outside could be heard urging on the dog. Rover, they called him. Duane sat up at the moment the dog entered the little shaded covert. Duane expected a yelping, a baying, or at least a bark that would tell of his hiding place. A strange relief swiftly swayed over him. The end was near now. He had no further choice. Let them come — a quick fierce exchange of shots — and then this torture past! He waited for the dog to give the alarm.

But the dog looked at him and trotted by into the thicket

165

without a yelp. Duane could not believe the evidence of his senses. He thought he had suddenly gone deaf. He saw the dog disappear, heard him running to and fro among the willows, getting farther and farther away, till all sound from him ceased.

"Thar's Rover," called a voice from the bluffside. "He's been through thet black patch."

"Nary a rabbit in there," replied another.

"Bah! Thet pup's no good," scornfully growled another man. "Put a hound at thet clump of willows."

"Fire's the game. Burn the brake before the rain comes."

The voices droned off as their owners evidently walked up the ridge. Upon Duane fell the crushing burden of the old waiting, watching, listening. After all, it was not to end just now. His chance still persisted — looked a little brighter — led him on, perhaps, to forlorn hope.

All at once twilight settled quickly down upon the willow brake, or else Duane noted it suddenly. He imagined it to be caused by the approaching storm. But there was little movement of air or cloud, and thunder still muttered and rumbled at a distance. The fact was the sun had set and, at this time of overcast sky, night was at hand.

Duane realized it with the awakening of all his old force. He would yet elude his pursuers. That was the moment when he seized the significance of all these fortunate circumstances which had aided him. Without haste and without sound he began to crawl in the direction of the river. It was not far, and he reached the bank before darkness set in. There were men up on the bluff carrying wood to build a bonfire. For a moment he half yielded to a temptation to try to slip along the river shore, close in under the willows. But when he raised himself to peer out, he saw that an attempt of this kind would be liable to failure.

166

At the same moment he saw a rough-hewn plank lying beneath him, lodged against some willows. The end of the plank extended in almost to a point beneath him. Quick as a flash he saw where a desperate chance invited him. Then he tied his gun in an oilskin bag and put it in his pocket. The bank was steep and crumbly. He must not break off any earth to splash into the water. There was a willow growing back some few feet from the edge of the bank. Cautiously he pulled it down, bent it over the water so that when he released it there would be no springing back. Then he trusted his weight to it, with his feet sliding carefully down the bank. He went into the water almost up to his knees, felt the quicksand grip his feet; then, leaning forward till he reached the plank, he pulled it toward him and lay upon it.

Without a sound one end went slowly under water and the farther end appeared lightly braced against the overhanging willows. Very carefully then Duane began to extricate his right foot from the sucking sand. It seemed as if his foot was encased in solid rock. But there was a movement upward, and he pulled with all the power he dared use. It came slowly and at length was free. The left one he released with less difficulty. The next few moments he put all his attention on the plank to ascertain if his weight would sink it into the sand. The far end slipped off the willows with a little splash and gradually settled to rest upon the bottom. But it sank no farther, and Duane's greatest concern was relieved. However, as it was manifestly impossible for him to keep his head up for long, he carefully crawled out upon the plank until he could rest an arm and shoulder upon the willows.

When he looked up, it was to find the night strangely luminous with fires. There was a bonfire on the extreme end of the bluff, another a hundred paces beyond. A great flare extended over the brake in that direction. Duane heard a roaring on the wind, and he knew his pursuers had fired the willows. He did not believe that would help them much. The brake was dry enough but too green to burn readily. As for the bonfires he discovered that the men, probably having run out of wood, were keeping up the light with oil and stuff from the village. A dozen men kept watch on the bluff scarcely fifty paces from where Duane lay concealed by the willows. They talked, cracked jokes, sang songs, and manifestly considered this outlaw hunting a great lark. As long as the bright light lasted, Duane dared not move. He had the patience and the endurance to wait for the breaking of the storm and, if that did not come, then the early hour before dawn when the gray fog and gloom were over the river.

Escape was now in his grasp. He felt it. And with that in his mind he waited, strong as steel in his conviction, capable of withstanding any strain endurable by the human frame. The wind blew in puffs, grew wilder, and roared through the willows, carrying bright sparks upward. Thunder rolled down over the river, and lightning began to flash. Then the rain fell in heavy sheets but not steadily. The flashes of lightning and the broad flares played so incessantly that Duane could not trust himself out on the open river. Certainly the storm rather increased the watchfulness of the men on the bluff. He knew how to wait, and he waited, grimly standing pain and cramp and chill. The storm wore away as desultorily as it had come, and the long night set in. There were times when Duane thought he was paralyzed, others when he grew sick, giddy, weak from the strained posture. The first paling of the stars quickened him with a kind of wild joy. He watched them grow paler, dimmer, disappear one by one. A shadow hovered down, rested upon the river, and gradually thickened. The bonfire on the bluff showed as through a foggy veil. The watchers were mere groping, dark figures.

Duane, aware of how cramped he had become from long inaction, began to move his legs and uninjured arm and body and at length overcame a paralyzing stiffness. Then, digging his hands in the sand and holding the plank with his knees, he edged it out into the river. Inch by inch he advanced until clear of the willows. Looking upward, he saw the shadowy figures of the men on the bluff. He realized they ought to see him, feared that they would, but he kept on, cautiously, noiselessly, with a heart-numbing slowness. From time to time his elbow made a little gurgle and splash in the water. Try as he might, he could not prevent this. It got to be like the hollow roar of a rapid, filling his ears with a mocking sound. There was a perceptible current out in the river, and it hindered straight advancement. Inch by inch he crept on, expecting to hear the bang of rifles, the spattering of bullets. He tried not to look backward but failed. The fire appeared a little dimmer, the moving shadows a little darker.

Once the plank stuck in the sand and felt as if it were settling. Bringing feet to aid his hand, he shoved it over the treacherous place. This way he made faster progress. The obscurity of the river seemed to be enveloping him. When he looked back again, the figures of the men were coalescing with the surrounding gloom. The fires were streaky, blurred patches of light, but the sky above was brighter. Dawn was not far off.

To the west all was dark. With infinite care and implacable spirit and waning strength, Duane shoved the plank along and, when at last he discerned the black border of the bank, it came just in time, he thought, to save him. He crawled out, rested till the gray dawn broke, and then headed north through the willows.

Chapter Thirteen

How long Duane was traveling out of that region he never knew, but he had finally reached familiar country and found a rancher who had befriended him before. Here his arm was attended; he had food and sleep; and in a couple of weeks he was himself again.

When the time came for Duane to ride away on his endless trail, his friend reluctantly imparted the information that some thirty miles south, near the village of Shirley, there was posted at a certain crossroads a reward for Buck Duane, dead or alive. Duane had heard of such notices, but he had never seen one. His friend's reluctance and refusal to state for what particular deed this reward was offered aroused Duane's curiosity. He had never been any closer to Shirley than this rancher's home. Doubtless some post office burglary, some shooting scrape had been attributed to him. He had been accused of worse deeds. Abruptly Duane decided to ride over there and find out who wanted him dead or alive, and why.

As he started south on the road, he reflected that this was the first time he had ever deliberately hunted trouble. Introspection awarded him this knowledge. During that last terrible flight on the lower Nueces and while he lay a-bed recuperating, he had changed. A fixed, immutable, hopeless bitterness abided within him. He had reached the end of his rope. All the power of his mind and soul were unavailable to turn him back from his fate. That fate was to become an outlaw in every sense of the term, to be what he was credited with being — that is to say, to embrace evil. He had never committed a crime. He wondered now was a life of crime closer to him? He reasoned finally that the desperation of crime had been forced upon him, if not its motive, and that, if driven, there was no limit to his possibilities. He understood now many of the hitherto inexplicable actions of certain noted outlaws — why they had returned to the scene of the crime that had outlawed them; why they took such strangely fatal chances; why life was no more to them than a breath of wind; why they rode straight into the jaws of death to confront wronged men or hunting rangers, vigilantes, to laugh in their very faces. It was such bitterness as this that drove these men.

Toward afternoon, from the top of a long hill, Duane saw the green fields and trees and shining roofs of a town he presumed must be Shirley. At the bottom of the hill he came upon an intersecting road. There was a placard nailed on the crossroads signpost. Duane drew rein near it and leaned close to read the faded print.

$1000 REWARD
FOR
BUCK DUANE
DEAD OR ALIVE

Peering closer to read the finer, more faded print, Duane learned that he was wanted for the murder of Mrs. Jeff Aiken at her ranch near Shirley. The month September was named, but the date was illegible. The reward was offered by the woman's husband, whose name appeared with that of a sheriff's at the bottom of the placard.

Duane read the thing twice. When he straightened, he was sick with horror at his fate, wild with passion at those misguided fools who could believe that he had harmed a woman. Then he remembered Kate Bland and, as always when she returned to him, he quaked inwardly. Years before word had gone abroad that he had killed her, and so it was easy for men wanting to fix a crime to name him. Perhaps it had been done often. Probably he bore on his shoulders a burden of numberless crimes.

A dark, passionate fury possessed him. It shook him like a storm shakes an oak. When it passed, leaving him cold, with clouded brow and piercing eye, his mind was set. Spurring his horse, he rode straight toward the village.

Shirley appeared to be a large, pretentious country town. A branch of some railroad terminated there. The main street was wide, bordered by trees and commodious houses, and many of the stores were of brick. A large plaza shaded by giant cottonwood trees occupied a central location.

Duane pulled his running horse and halted him, plunging and snorting, before a group of idle men who lounged on benches in the shade of a spreading cottonwood. How many times had Duane seen just that kind of lazy shirt-sleeved Texas group. Not often, however, had he seen such placid, lolling, good-natured men change their expression, their attitude so swiftly. His advent apparently was momentous. They evidently took him for an unusual visitor. So far as Duane could tell, not one of them recognized him, had a hint of his identity.

He slid off his horse and threw the bridle. "I'm Buck Duane," he said. "I saw that placard . . . out there on the sign post. It's a damned lie! Somebody find this man Jeff Aiken. I want to see him."

His announcement was taken in absolute silence. That

173

was the only effect he noted, for he avoided looking at these villagers. The reason was simple enough. Duane felt himself overcome with emotion. There were tears in his eyes. He sat down on a bench, put his elbows on his knees, and his hands to his face. For once he had absolutely no concern for his fate. This ignominy was the last straw.

Presently, however, he became aware of some kind of commotion among these villagers. He heard whisperings, low, hoarse voices, then the shuffle of rapid feet moving away. All at once a violent hand jerked his gun from its holster. When Duane rose, a gaunt man, livid of face, shaking like a leaf, confronted him with his own gun.

"Hands up, thar, you Buck Duane!" he roared, waving the gun.

That appeared to be the cue for pandemonium to break loose. Duane opened his lips to speak but, if he had yelled at the top of his lungs, he could not have made himself heard. In weary disgust he looked at the gaunt man and then at the others, who were working themselves into a frenzy. He made no move, however, to hold up his hands. The villagers surrounded him, emboldened by finding him now unarmed. Then several men lay hold of his arms and pinioned them behind his back. Resistance was useless even if Duane had the spirit. Someone fetched his halter from his saddle, and with this they bound him helpless.

People were running now from the street, the stores, the houses. Old men, cowboys, clerks, boys, ranchers came on the trot. The crowd grew. The increasing clamor began to attract women as well as men. A group of girls ran up, then hung back in fright and pity.

The presence of cowboys made a difference. They split up the crowd, got to Duane, and lay hold of him with rough, business-like hands. One of them lifted his fists

174

and roared at the frenzied mob to fall back, to stop the racket. He beat them back into a circle, but it was some little time before the hubbub quieted down so a voice could be heard.

". . . shut up, will you-all?" he was yelling. "Give us a chance to hear somethin'. Easy now . . . soho. There ain't nobody goin' to be hurt. Thet's right, everybody quiet now. Let's see what's come off."

This cowboy, evidently one of authority or at least one of strong personality, turned to the gaunt man, who still waved Duane's gun.

"Abe, put the gun down," he said. "It might go off. Here, give it to me. Now, what's wrong? Who's this roped gent, an' what's he done?"

The gaunt fellow, who appeared now about to collapse, lifted a shaking hand and pointed.

"Thet thar feller . . . he's Buck Duane!" he panted.

An angry murmur ran through the surrounding crowd.

"The rope! The rope! Throw it over a branch! String him up!" cried an excited villager.

"Buck Duane! Buck Duane!"

"Hang him!"

The cowboy silenced these cries. "Abe, how do you know this fellow is Buck Duane?" he asked sharply.

"Why . . . he said so," replied the man called Abe.

"What!" came the exclamation, incredulously.

"It's a tarnal fact," panted Abe, waving his hands importantly. He was an old man and appeared to be carried away with the significance of his deed. "He like to ride his hoss right over us all. Then he jumped off, says he was Buck Duane, an' he wanted to see Jeff Aiken bad."

This speech caused a second commotion as noisy though not so enduring as the first. When the cowboy, assisted

175

by a couple of his mates, had restored order again, someone had slipped the noose-end of Duane's rope over his head.

"Up with him!" screeched a wild-eyed youth.

The mob surged closer but was shoved back by the cowboys.

"Abe, if you ain't drunk or crazy, tell thet over," ordered Abe's interlocutor.

With some show of resentment and more of dignity, Abe reiterated his former statement.

"If he's Buck Duane, how'n hell did you get hold of his gun?" bluntly queried the cowboy.

"Why . . . he set down thar . . . an' he kind of hid his face in his hands. An' I grabbed his gun an' got the drop on him."

What the cowboy thought of this was expressed in a laugh. His mates likewise grinned broadly. Then the leader turned to Duane.

"Stranger, I reckon you'd better speak up for yourself," he said.

That stilled the crowd as no command had done.

"I'm Buck Duane, all right," said Duane quietly. "It was this way."

The big cowboy seemed to vibrate with a shock. All the ruddy warmth left his face; his jaw began to bulge; the corded veins in his neck stood out in knots. In an instant he had a hard, stern, strange look. He shot out a powerful hand that fastened in the front of Duane's shirt.

"Somethin' queer here. But if you're Duane, you're sure in bad. Any fool ought to know that. You mean it, then?"

"Yes."

"Rode in to shoot up the town, eh? Same old stunt of you gunfighters? Meant to kill the man who offered a reward? Wanted to see Jeff Aiken bad, huh?"

"No," replied Duane. "Your citizen here misrepresented things. He seems a little off his head."

"Reckon he is. Somebody is, that's sure. You claim to be Buck Duane, then, an' all his doings?"

"I'm Duane, yes, but I won't stand for the blame of things I never did. That's why I'm here. I saw that placard out there offering the reward. Until now I never was within half a day's ride of this town. I'm blamed for what I never did. I rode in here, told who I was, asked somebody to send for Jeff Aiken."

"An' then you set down an' let this old guy throw your own gun on you?" queried the cowboy in amazement.

"I guess that's it," replied Duane.

"Well, it's powerful strange, if you're *really* Buck Duane."

A man elbowed his way into the circle.

"It's Duane. I recognize him. I seen him in more'n one place," he said. "Sibert, you can rely on what I tell you. I don't know if he's locoed or what, but I do know he's the genuine Buck Duane. Anyone who'd ever seen him once would never forget him."

"What do you want to see Aiken for?" asked the cowboy, Sibert.

"I want to face him and tell him I never harmed his wife."

"Why?"

"Because I'm innocent, that's all."

"Suppose we send for Aiken, an' he hears you an' doesn't believe you, what then?"

"If he won't believe me . . . why, then my case's so bad . . . I'd be better off dead."

A momentary silence was broken by Sibert.

"If this isn't a queer deal! Boys, reckon we'd better send for Jeff."

"Somebody went for him. He'll be comin' soon," replied a man.

Duane stood a head taller than that circle of curious faces. He gazed out above and beyond them. It was in this way that he chanced to see a number of women on the outskirts of the crowd. Some were old, with hard faces, like the men. Some were young and comely, and most of these seemed agitated by excitement or distress. They cast fearful, pitying glances upon Duane as he stood there with that noose around his neck. *Women are more human than men,* Duane thought. He met eyes that dilated, seemed fascinated at his gaze, but were not averted. It was the old women who were voluble, loud in expression of their feelings.

Near the trunk of the cottonwood stood a slender woman in white. Duane's wandering glance rested upon her. Her eyes were riveted upon him. A soft-hearted woman, probably, who did not want to see him hanged!

"Thar comes Jeff Aiken now," called a man loudly.

The crowd shifted and trampled in eagerness.

Duane saw two men coming fast, one of whom, in the lead, was of stalwart build. He had a gun in his hand, and his manner was that of fierce energy.

The cowboy Sibert thrust open the jostling circle of men.

"Hold on, Jeff," he called, and he blocked the man with the gun. He spoke so low Duane could not hear what he said, and his form hid Aiken's face. At that juncture the crowd spread out, closed in, and Aiken and Sibert were caught in the circle. There was a pushing forward, a pressing of many bodies, hoarse cries and flinging hands — again the insane tumult was about to break out — the demand for an outlaw's blood, the call for a wild justice executed a thousand times before on Texas' bloody soil.

178

Sibert bellowed at the dark encroaching mass. The cowboys with him beat and cuffed in vain.

"Jeff, will you listen?" broke in Sibert, hurriedly, his hand on the other man's arm.

Aiken nodded coolly. Duane, who had seen many men in perfect control of themselves under circumstances like these, recognized the spirit that dominated Aiken. He was white, cold, passionless. There were lines of bitter grief deep around his lips. If Duane ever felt the meaning of death, he felt it then.

"Sure this's your game, Aiken," said Sibert, "but hear me a minute. Reckon there's no doubt about this man bein' Buck Duane. He seen the placard out at the crossroads. He rides into Shirley. He says he's Buck Duane, an' he's lookin' for Jeff Aiken. That's all clear enough. You know how these gunfighters go lookin' for trouble. But here's what stumps me. Duane sits down there on the bench and lets old Abe Strickland grab his gun an' get the drop on him. More'n that, he gives me some strange talk about how, if he couldn't make you believe he's innocent, he'd better be dead. You see for yourself. Duane ain't drunk or crazy or locoed. He doesn't strike me as a man who rode in here huntin' blood. So I reckon you'd better hold on till you hear what he has to say."

Then for the first time the drawn-faced, hungry-eyed giant turned his gaze upon Duane. He had intelligence which was not yet subservient to passion. Moreover, he seemed the kind of man Duane would care to have judge him in a critical moment like this.

"Listen," said Duane gravely, with his eyes steadily on Aiken's, "I'm Buck Duane. I never lied to any man in my life. I was forced into outlawry. I've never had a chance to leave the country. I've killed men to save my own life.

179

I never intentionally harmed any woman. I rode thirty miles today . . . deliberately to see what this reward was, who made it, what for. When I read the placard, I was sick to the bottom of my soul. So I rode in here to find you . . . to tell you this: I never saw Shirley before today. It was impossible for me to have . . . killed your wife. Last September I was two hundred miles north of here on the upper Nueces. I can prove that. Men who know me will tell you I couldn't murder a woman. I haven't any idea why such a deed should be laid at my hands. It's just that wild border gossip. I have no idea what reasons you have for holding me responsible. I only know you're wrong. You've been deceived. And see here, Aiken. You understand, I'm a miserable man. I'm about broken, I guess. I don't care any more for life, for anything. If you can't look me in the eyes, man to man believe what I say . . . why, by God! you can kill me!"

Aiken heaved a great breath. "Buck Duane, whether I'm impressed or not by what you say needn't matter. You've had accusers, justly or unjustly, as will soon appear. The thing is we can prove you innocent or guilty. My girl, Lucy, saw my wife's assailant." He motioned for the crowd of men to open up. "Somebody . . . you, Sibert . . . go for Lucy. That'll settle this thing."

Duane heard as a man in an ugly dream. The faces around him, the hum of voices, all seemed far off. His life hung by the merest thread. Yet he did not think of that so much as of the brand of a woman-murderer which might be soon sealed upon him by a frightened, imaginative child.

The crowd trooped apart and closed again. Duane caught a blurred image of a slight girl clinging to Sibert's hand. He could not see distinctly. Aiken lifted the child, whispered soothingly to her not to be afraid. Then he fetched her closer to Duane.

"Lucy, tell me. Did you ever see this man before?" asked Aiken huskily and low. "Is he the one . . . who came in the house that day . . . struck you down . . . and dragged Mama . . . ?" Aiken's voice failed.

A lightning flash seemed to clear Duane's blurred sight. He saw a pale, sad face and violet eyes fixed in gloom and horror upon his. No terrible moment in Duane's life ever equaled this one of silence — of suspense.

"It ain't him!" cried the child.

Then Sibert was flinging the noose off Duane's neck and unwinding the bonds around his arms. The spellbound crowd awoke to hoarse exclamations.

"See there, my locoed gents, how easy you'd hang the wrong man," burst out the cowboy, as he made the rope end hiss. "You-all are a lot of wise rangers. Haw! haw!" He freed Duane and thrust the bone-handled gun back in Duane's holster. "You, Abe, there. Reckon you pulled a stunt! But don't try the like again. And, men, I'll gamble there's a hell of a lot of bad work Buck Duane's named for . . . which all he never done. Clear away there. Where's his hoss? Duane, the road's open out of Shirley."

Sibert swept the gaping watchers aside and pressed Duane toward the horse, which another cowboy held. Mechanically Duane mounted, felt a lift as he went up. Then the cowboy's hard face softened in a smile.

"I reckon it ain't uncivil of me to say . . . hit that road quick!" he said frankly.

He led the horse out of the crowd. Aiken joined him, and between them they escorted Duane across the plaza. The crowd appeared irresistibly drawn to follow. Aiken paused with his big hand on Duane's knee. In it, unconsciously probably, he still held the gun.

"Duane, a word with you," he said. "I believe you're not so black as you've been painted. I wish there was time to say more. Tell me this, anyway. Do you know the ranger, Captain MacNelly?"

"I do not," replied Duane in surprise.

"I met him only a week ago over in Fairfield," went on Aiken hurriedly. "He declared you never killed my wife. I didn't believe him . . . argued with him. We almost had hard words over it. Now . . . I'm sorry. The last thing he said was: 'If you ever see Duane, don't kill him. Send him into my camp after dark!' He meant something strange. What . . . I can't say. But he was right, and I was wrong. If Lucy had batted an eye, I'd have killed you. Still, I wouldn't advise you to hunt up MacNelly's camp. He's clever. Maybe he believes there's no treachery in his new ideas of ranger tactics. I tell you for all it's worth. Good bye. May God help you further as he did this day!"

Duane said good bye and touched the horse with his spurs.

"So long, Buck!" called Sibert with that frank smile breaking warmly over his brown face, and he held his sombrero high.

Chapter Fourteen

When Duane reached the crossing of the roads, the name Fairfield on the signpost seemed to be the thing that tipped the oscillating balance of decision in favor of that direction. He answered here to unfathomable impulse. If he had been driven to hunt up Jeff Aiken, now he was called to find this unknown ranger captain. In Duane's state of mind clear reasoning, common sense, or keenness were out of the question. He went because he felt he was compelled.

Dusk had fallen when he rode into a town which inquiry proved to be Fairfield. Captain MacNelly's camp was stationed just out of the village limits on the other side. No one except the boy Duane questioned appeared to notice his arrival. Like Shirley, the town of Fairfield was large and prosperous compared to the innumerable hamlets dotting the vast extent of southwestern Texas. As Duane rode through, being careful to get off the main street, he heard the tolling of a church bell that was a melancholy reminder of his old home.

There did not appear to be any camp on the outskirts of the town, but as Duane sat his horse, peering around and undecided what farther move to make, he caught the glint of flickering lights through the darkness. Heading toward them, he rode perhaps a quarter of a mile to come upon a grove of mesquite. The brightness of several fires made the surrounding darkness all the blacker. Duane saw the moving forms of men and heard horses. He advanced naturally, expecting any moment to be halted.

"Who goes there?" came the sharp call out of the gloom.

Duane pulled his horse. The gloom was impenetrable.

"One man . . . alone," replied Duane.

"A stranger?"

"Yes."

"What do you want?"

"I'm trying to find the ranger camp."

"You've struck it. What's your errand?"

"I want to see Captain MacNelly."

"Get down and advance. Slow. Don't move your hands. It's dark, but I can see."

Duane dismounted and, leading his horse, slowly advanced a few paces. He saw a dully bright object — a gun — before he discovered the man who held it. A few more steps showed a dark figure blocking the trail. Here Duane halted.

"Come closer, stranger. Let's have a look at you," the guard ordered curtly.

Duane advanced again until he stood before the man. Here the rays of light from the fires flickered upon Duane's face.

"Reckon you're a stranger, all right. What's your name and your business with the captain?"

Duane hesitated, pondering what best to say. "Tell Captain MacNelly I'm the man he's been asking to ride into his camp . . . after dark," said Duane finally.

The ranger bent forward to peer hard at this night visitor. His manner had been alert, and now it became tense.

"Come here, one of you men, quick," he called without turning in the least toward the camp fire.

"Hello! What's up, Pickens?" came the swift reply. It was followed by a rapid thud of boots on soft ground. A dark

184

form crossed the gleams from the firelight. Then a ranger loomed up to reach the side of the guard. Duane heard whispering, the purport of which he could not catch. The second ranger swore under his breath. Then he turned away and started back.

"Here, ranger, before you go, understand this. My visit is peaceful . . . friendly if you'll let it be. Mind, I was asked to come here . . . after dark."

Duane's clear, penetrating voice carried far. The listening rangers at the camp fire heard what he said.

"Ho, Pickens! Tell that fellow to wait," replied an authoritative voice. Then a slim figure detached itself from the dark, moving group at the camp fire and hurried out.

"Better be foxy, Cap," shouted a ranger in warning.

"Shut up . . . all of you," was the reply.

This officer, obviously Captain MacNelly, soon joined the two rangers who were confronting Duane. He had no fear. He strode straight up to Duane.

"I'm MacNelly," he said. "If you're my man, don't mention your name . . . yet."

All this seemed so strange to Duane, in keeping with much that had happened lately. "I met Jeff Aiken today," he said. "He sent me. . . ."

"You've met Aiken!" exclaimed MacNelly, sharp, eager, low. "By all that's bully!" Then he appeared to catch himself, to grow restrained. "Men, fall back, leave us alone a moment."

The rangers slowly withdrew.

"Buck Duane! It's you?" he whispered eagerly.

"Yes."

"If I give my word you'll not be arrested . . . you'll be treated fairly . . . will you come into camp and consult with me?"

"Certainly."

"Duane, I'm sure glad to meet you," went on MacNelly, and he extended his hand.

Amazed and touched, scarcely realizing this actuality, Duane gave his hand and felt no unmistakable grip of warmth.

"It doesn't seem natural, Captain MacNelly, but I believe I'm glad to meet you," said Duane soberly.

"You will be. Now we'll go back to camp. Keep your identity mum for the present."

He led Duane in the direction of the camp fire.

"Pickens, go back on duty," he ordered, "and, Beeson, you look after this horse."

When Duane got beyond the line of mesquite, which had hidden a good view of the camp site, he saw a group of perhaps fifteen rangers sitting around the fires near a long low shed, where horses were feeding, and a small adobe house at one side.

"We've just had grub, but I'll see you get some. Then we'll talk," said MacNelly. "I've taken up temporary quarters here. Have a rustler job on hand. Now, when you've eaten, come right into the house."

Duane was hungry, but he hurried through the ample supper that was set before him, urged on by curiosity and astonishment. The only way he could account for his presence there in a ranger camp was that MacNelly hoped to get useful information out of him. Still that would hardly have made this captain so eager. There was a mystery here, and Duane could scarcely wait for it to be solved. While eating, he had bent keen eyes around him. After a first quiet scrutiny the rangers apparently paid no more attention to him. They were all veterans in service — Duane saw that — and rugged, powerful men of iron constitution. Despite the occasional joke and sally of the more youthful members, and a general conversation of camp fire nature, Duane was not deceived about the fact that his advent had been an unusual and striking one which had caused an undercurrent of conjecture and even consternation among them. These rangers were too well trained to appear openly curious about their captain's guest. If they had not deliberately attempted to be oblivious of his presence, Duane would have concluded they thought him an ordinary visitor, somehow of use to MacNelly. As it was, Duane felt a suspense that must have been due to a hint of his identity. He was not long in presenting himself at the door of the house.

"Come in and have a chair," said MacNelly, motioning for the one other occupant of the room to rise. "Leave us, Russell, and close the door. I'll be through these reports right off."

MacNelly sat at a table upon which was a lamp and various papers. Seen in the light, he was a fine-looking, soldierly man of about forty years, dark haired and dark eyed, with a bronzed face, shrewd, stern, strong, yet not wanting in kindliness. He scanned hastily over some papers, fussed with them, and finally put them in envelopes. Without looking up, he pushed a cigar case toward Duane and, upon Duane's refusal to smoke, he took a cigar, rose to light it at the lamp chimney, and then, settling back in his chair, he faced Duane, making a vain attempt to hide what must have been the fulfillment of a long-nourished curiosity.

"Duane, I've been hoping for this for two years," he began.

Duane smiled a little — a smile that felt strange on his face. He had never been much of a talker, and speech here seemed more than ordinarily difficult.

MacNelly must have felt that. He looked long and earnestly at Duane, and his quick, nervous manner changed to grave thoughtfulness. "I've lots to say, but where to begin," he mused. "Duane, you've had a hard life since you went on the dodge. I never met you before, don't know what you looked like as a boy. But I can see what . . . well, even ranger life isn't all roses." He rolled his cigar between his lips and puffed clouds of smoke. "Ever hear from home since you left Wellston?" he asked abruptly.

"No."

"Never a word?"

"Not one," replied Duane sadly.

"That's tough. I'm glad to be able to tell you that up to just lately your mother, sister, uncle . . . all your folks, I believe, were well. I've kept posted, but haven't heard lately."

Duane averted his face a moment, hesitated till the swelling left his throat, and then said, "It's worth what I went through today to hear that."

"I can imagine how you must feel about it. When I was in the war . . . but let's get down to the business of this meeting." He pulled his chair closer to Duane's. "You've had word more than once in the last two years that I wanted to see you?"

"Three times, I remember," replied Duane.

"Why didn't you hunt me up?"

"I supposed you imagined me one of those gunfighters who couldn't take a dare and expected me to ride up to your camp and be arrested."

"That was natural, I suppose," went on MacNelly. "You didn't know me, otherwise you would have come. I've been a long time getting to you, but the nature of my job, as far as you're concerned, made me cautious. Duane, you're aware of the hard name you bear all over the Southwest?"

188

"Once in a while I'm jarred into realizing it," replied Duane.

"It's the hardest, barring Murrell and Cheseldine, on the Texas border. But there's this difference. Murrell in his day was known to deserve his infamous name. Cheseldine in his day also. But I've found hundreds of men in southwest Texas who're your friends, who swear you never committed a crime. The farther south I get the clearer this becomes. What I want to know is the truth. Have you ever done anything criminal? Tell me the truth, Duane. It won't make any difference in my plan. And when I say crime, I mean what I would call crime or would any reasonable Texan."

"That way my hands are clean," replied Duane.

"You never held up a man, robbed a store for grub, stole a horse when you needed him bad . . . never anything like that?"

"Somehow I always kept out of that, even when pressed the hardest."

"Duane, I'm damn' glad!" MacNelly exclaimed, gripping Duane's hand. "Glad for your mother's sake! But, all the same, in spite of this, you are a Texas outlaw accountable to the state. You're perfectly aware that under existing circumstances, if you fell into the hands of the law, you'd probably hang, at least go to jail for a long term?"

"That's what kept me on the dodge all these years," replied Duane.

"Certainly." MacNelly removed his cigar. His eyes narrowed and glittered. The muscles along his brown cheeks set hard and tense. He leaned closer to Duane, laid sinewy, pressing fingers upon Duane's knee. "Listen to this," he whispered hoarsely. "If I place a pardon in your hand . . . make you a free, honest citizen once more, clear your name of infamy, make your mother, your sister proud of you . . .

will you swear yourself to a service, *any* service, I demand of you?"

Duane sat stock still, stunned.

Slowly, more persuasively, with show of earnest agitation, Captain MacNelly reiterated his startling query.

"My God!" burst from Duane. "What's this? MacNelly, you *can't* be in earnest!"

"Never more so in my life. I've a deep game. I'm playing it square. What do you say?"

He rose to his feet. Duane, as if impelled, rose with him. Ranger and outlaw then locked eyes that searched each other's souls. In MacNelly's Duane read truth, strong, fiery purpose, hope, even gladness, and a fugitive mounting assurance of victory.

"Any service? Every service! MacNelly, I give my word," said Duane.

A light played over MacNelly's face, warming out all the grim darkness. He held out his hand. Duane met it with his in a clasp that men unconsciously give in moments of stress.

When they unclasped, and Duane stepped back to drop into a chair, MacNelly fumbled for another cigar — he had bitten his other into shreds — and, lighting it as before, he turned to his visitor, now calm and cool. He had the look of a man who had just won something at considerable cost. His next move was to take a long leather case from his pocket and extract from it several folded papers.

"Here's your pardon from the governor," he said quietly. "You'll see, when you look it over, that it's conditional. When you sign this paper I have here, the condition will be met."

He smoothed out the paper, handed Duane a pen, ran his forefinger along a dotted line. Duane's hand was shaky.

Years had passed since he had held a pen. It was with difficulty that he achieved his signature. Buckley Duane — how strangely the name looked!

"Right here ends the career of Buck Duane, outlaw and gunfighter," said MacNelly and, seating himself, he took the pen from Duane's fingers and wrote several lines in several places upon the paper. Then with a smile he handed it to Duane.

"That makes you a member of Company A, Texas Rangers."

"So, that's it!" burst out Duane, a light breaking in upon his bewilderment. "You want me for ranger service?"

"Sure. That's it," replied the captain dryly. "Now to hear what service is to be. I've been a busy man since I took this job and, as you may have heard, I've done a few things. I don't mind telling you that political influence put me in here and that up Austin way there's a good deal of friction in the Department of State in regard to whether or not the ranger service is any good — whether it should be discontinued or not. I'm on the party side who's defending the ranger service. I contend that it's made Texas habitable. Well, it's been up to me to produce results. So far I have been successful. My great ambition is to break up the outlaw gangs along the river. I have never ventured in there yet because I've been waiting to get the lieutenant I needed. You, of course, are the man I had in mind. It's my idea to start up the Rio Grande and begin with Cheseldine. He's the strongest, the worst outlaw of the times. He's more than a rustler. It's Cheseldine and his gang who are operating on the banks. They're doing bank robbing. That's my private opinion, but it's not been backed up by any evidence. Cheseldine doesn't leave evidence. He's intelligent, cunning. No one seems to have seen him . . . to

191

know what he looks like. I assume, of course, that you are a stranger to the country he dominates. It's five hundred miles west of your ground. There's a little town over there called Fairdale. It's the nest of a rustler gang. They rustle and murder at will. Nobody knows who the leader is. I want you to find out. Well, whatever way you decide is best, you will proceed to act upon. You are your own boss. You know such men, and how they can be approached. You will take all the time needed, if it's months. It will be necessary for you to communicate with me, and that will be a difficult matter. For Cheseldine dominates several whole counties. You must find some way to let me know when I and my rangers are needed. The plan is to break up Cheseldine's gang. It's the toughest job on the border. Arresting him alone isn't to be heard of. He couldn't be brought out. Killing him isn't much better, for his select men, the ones he operates with, are as dangerous to the community as he is. We want to kill or jail this choice selection of robbers and break up the rest of the gang. To find them, to get among them somehow, to learn their movements, to lay your trap for us rangers to spring . . . that, Duane, is your service to me, and God knows it's a great one!"

"I have accepted it," replied Duane.

"Your work will be secret. You are now a ranger in my service, but no one except the few I choose to tell will know of it until we pull off the job. You will simply be Buck Duane till it suits our purpose to acquaint Texas with the fact that you're a ranger. You'll see there's no date on that paper. No one will ever know just when you entered the service. Perhaps we can make it appear that all or most of your outlawry has really been good service to the state. At that, I'll believe it'll turn out so."

MacNelly paused a moment in his rapid talk, chewed his cigar, drew his brows together in a dark frown, and went on. "No man on the border knows so well as you the deadly nature of this service. It's a thousand to one that you'll be killed. I'd say there was no chance at all for any other man besides you. Your reputation will go far among the outlaws. Maybe that and your nerve and your gun play will pull you through. I'm hoping so. But it's a long, long chance against your ever coming back."

"That's not the point," said Duane. "But in case I get killed out there . . . what . . . ?"

"Leave that to me," interrupted Captain MacNelly. "Your folks will know at once of your pardon and your ranger duty. If you lose your life out there, I'll see your name cleared . . . the service you render known. You can rest assured of that."

"I am satisfied," replied Duane. "That's so much more than I've dared to hope."

"Well, it's settled, then. I'll give you money for expenses. You'll start as soon as you like . . . the sooner the better. I hope to think of other suggestions, especially about communicating with me."

"Captain MacNelly, I'd like to know how this came about. I can't realize it yet. Some things are strange to me. Who interested you in my case? Won't you explain?"

"Sure I will," replied MacNelly, as he reached for another cigar. "It must have been three years ago when I first began to hear your name mentioned at Austin, in the adjutant general's office and elsewhere. Just casually, you understand, and I took no particular notice. Then I heard that women of your family were working to get influence for you. This was before you became famous as an outlaw. Of course, a little later, after the Bland affair, your name

193

grew to be a household mark in Texas. From then on your reputation grew. About this time, which was about the time I became exceedingly busy with my rangers, I got an anonymous letter. It was from a woman, and it entreated me not to go on your trail. It was a remarkable letter. I have it somewhere and shall find it for you. My idea was, of course, that it was from your mother or sister. The thing about it that struck me was the old Texas line drawn between the criminal and the outlaw. At that time I had no intention of going upon your trail. I was early in the ranger game and . . . well, it seemed wiser not to look up Buck Duane. But I got to thinking, and naturally in your favor.

"Different trails led me down toward the Nueces country, and here I learned a good deal about you. There were men who would not declare they were your friends, but all the same they championed you. It was in this southern trip that I first conceived the idea of making a proposition to you to become a ranger. However, at that stage of the game I never sent any word to you.

"Upon my return to Austin, where I go often to make reports to the adjutant general, I was visited by a young woman, who claimed to be a member of your household at Wellston. I took her for your sister, or near relative, in fact called her Miss Duane, which at the time she did not correct. She had been to see the governor. And, of course, he had turned her down. The governor is against outlaws, the same as he is against rangers. This girl wanted an audience with the adjutant general, and in his absence she ran across me.

"I want to say here that she electrified me. Before she left my office, I was ready to fight for her. I promised to speak to the adjutant general and to use what influence

I had in her behalf. She wanted a parole for you, if not a pardon. I was absent from Austin when she came the next time. She won the interest of Adjutant General Reed, and he even went to the governor with her. Sure they only got turned down. I learned from Reed's secretary that this girl was a Miss Lee instead of Miss Duane. Evidently, she was wealthy. It was a fact, however, that she lived at your mother's home in Wellston. If money could have helped your case there at the capital, it sure would have been forthcoming.

"All this interested me. I wrote to Miss Lee and told her that my duties would soon take me to the Nueces country again, and that I would find out all I could about you. She replied . . . a grateful, sweet, womanly letter. I wrote her from several towns on the border and heard from her. It was in this way that I kind of kept in touch with your family. And it was on this trip that I hatched out my plan to make a ranger of you.

"When I got back to Austin, I laid my plan before Adjutant General Reed. He hailed it with enthusiasm. I tell you your cousin, Miss Lee, . . . I presumed she was your cousin . . . certainly had won over Reed. We went to call upon the governor.

"I'm not likely to forget that intervention in a hurry. We called on him to give us a pardon for you and promised we would make you render the state a service as a ranger. We found ourselves precipitated into a fierce debate upon the old question of the ranger service. The governor got mad and flayed us alive. Most rangers were lazy, useless, gunfighting shysters! Reed lost his temper. He's hot for the service. But I kept cool and told the governor straight out that, if he'd pardon you, I'd break up Cheseldine's gang on the river. That sort of floored the governor. He got interested. I talked to him for an hour, explained how there were only two ways to exterminate Cheseldine and the like. Either with an army, or with the ranger service, employing such a scout as you. The army idea wasn't possible, but he was impressed by the other. He said: 'Set an outlaw to catch an outlaw, eh?' Then he pondered a while and at last rang for his secretary. 'My political enemies say I'm not liberal minded,' he went on. 'Now I'm going to make this a test case of the ranger service. I'll pardon this gun sharp, Duane, on condition you make him a ranger. That is, he'll not be pardoned until he *is* a ranger. Then we'll see how the scheme works out. . . .' So he made out the pardon and entrusted it to me with good wishes as sincere as he was doubtful of our success.

"The next thing was to locate you. That was not an easy job. A lone wolf, you know! It was absolutely necessary that I proceed cautiously. The success of my plan depended upon your becoming a secret ranger. This much I did not tell Miss Lee. But I encouraged her all I could, said I did not mean to arrest you. There was a whole year in which I lost track of you all together. We thought you had cashed in sure. Then I heard of you again. But your trail always faded in the sand. I sent rangers to different towns. At last in desperation I suggested to Miss Lee that your uncle, or somebody who could be trusted, go from town to town in the Neuces country and try to get track of you. Especially make known his identity to supposed friends of yours and leave them a message for you. Well, your uncle traveled all over the West, and I understand Miss Lee visited border towns herself. They found friends of yours, and yet you say you have heard of my wanting to see you but just three times. That's about all, I guess. . . . And it was Jeff Aiken who sent you to me?"

Duane made some slight motion of assent that signified he had at least heard the question. He seemed dazed. All this story was beyond his understanding. He found his mind groping in unfamiliar ground. For years it had been steeped in gloom, in the dark moods common to a fugitive exposed to the elements, alone, suspicious of everything, incapable of wholesome thought. The sudden contrast bewildered him. Out of it all struck one mounting fact — while he had thought himself a forgotten outcast there had been loyal and powerful influences at work.

"That woman . . . cousin, relative of mine? Who could she be? I remember so poorly. My sister was only a child." Suddenly, he started up violently. "*Miss Lee!* You said her name was Miss Lee!"

"Yes," replied MacNelly.

"That was the name Aiken called a woman who was distressed by the scene in Shirley . . . when the mob threatened to hang me. She held the mob back then interceded for me with Aiken . . . Miss Lee. He called her that."

"So she was over there. Well, tell me about it," said MacNelly, curious.

Swiftly Duane narrated the circumstances of his arrival, detention, and escape in Shirley.

"By all that's bully!" exclaimed the captain. "She would have done just that. A splendid young woman!"

"I imagined her just a hysterical girl . . . scared or sickened into the crazy way women act sometimes," said Duane. "Yet she looked so strange at me. Who was she? If I ever saw her before, I've forgotten. I remember so poorly. I almost forget now what she was like . . . medium height . . . slim . . . white faced, with dark eyes, very intent."

"Duane, you've sure described Miss Lee," replied Mac-Nelly. "Here, cudgel your memory. She must be a cousin, a near relative. Think."

"MacNelly, I can't remember what my mother was like! I think, though, I'd recognize Uncle Jim."

"Well, Duane, maybe you'll place Miss Lee after a while, when you can think clearly. You're upset now. But there's one thing sure. The best way to place her will be to think back and call up the girls who were fond of you as a boy . . . passionately fond of you."

"There never was one."

MacNelly laughed. "I'll gamble there was. There's *one,* and don't you forget it. You can't fool me on women." Then his face darkened. "The thing I regret is she'll have to know of this service you're bound to. That'll be tough on her and on your mother. It can't be helped. I wish there were no women on the border."

"MacNelly, I want to see this Miss Lee," said Duane.

"I was thinking of that. It's a good chance. Maybe there'll never be another one." He paused a moment, chewing his cigar. "All right, I see no reason against your meeting her," he went on. "But let me arrange the matter as suits me. Tomorrow I'll send a ranger over to Shirley. There's a train, and stage, too. Now let's turn in, Duane. We've talked a deal. And I was tired before we began. Make yourself a bed there. Good night."

Long after the lights were out and the low hum of voices had ceased around the camp fires, Duane lay wide awake, eyes staring into the blackness, marveling over the strange events of the day. He was humble, grateful to the depths of his soul. A huge and crushing burden had been lifted from his heart. He welcomed this hazardous service to the man who had saved him. Thoughts of his mother and sister and Uncle Jim, of his home, of old friends came rushing over him, the first time in years that he had happiness in these memories. The disgrace he had put upon them would now be removed and, in the light of that, his wasted life of the past and its probable tragic end in future service as atonement changed their aspects. Then, coming and going and ever returning, was the thought of Miss Lee, this forgotten relative, or friend, or school mate, this tender-hearted girl who had lived with his mother and growing, developing in the years of his exile, had thrown her heart into a fight for his freedom. Whoever she was, she had changed so that he could not recall her place in his boyhood surroundings. Whoever she was, the thought of meeting her again thrilled him to his depths. As he lay there, with the approach of sleep finally dimming the vividness of his thoughts, her white face, dark grave intent eyes, so full of mystery, floated in the blackness around him, haunting him as he had always been haunted by phantoms.

It was broad daylight when he awakened. MacNelly was calling him to breakfast. Outside sounded voices of men, crackling of fires, snorting and stamping of horses, the barking of dogs. Duane rolled out of his blankets and made good use of the soap and towel and razor and brush nearby on a bench — things of rare luxury to an outlaw on the run. The face he saw in the mirror was as strange as the past he had tried so hard to recall. Then he stepped to the door and went out.

The rangers were eating in a circle around a tarpaulin spread upon the ground.

"Fellows," said MacNelly, "shake hands with Buck Duane. He's on secret ranger service for me. Service that'll likely make you all hump soon! Mind you keep mum about it."

The rangers surprised Duane with a roaring greeting,

the warmth of which he soon divined was divided between pride of his acquisition to their ranks and eagerness to meet that violent service of which their captain hinted. They were jolly, wild fellows, with just enough gravity in their welcome to show Duane their respect and appreciation while not forgetting his lone wolf record. When he had seated himself in that circle, now one of them, a feeling, subtle and uplifting, pervaded his spirit.

MacNelly advised Duane to stay indoors during the day, especially in case there were any villagers loitering around. The captain and his company, with the exception of a couple of rangers, then rode off in the direction of the village.

For Duane that day seemed short. He did nothing but lounge around and think, yet the time flew by. Every moment of his new freedom he would have made longer. The rangers returned in several squads, the last of which included Captain MacNelly.

"Good news, Duane," he said, all smiles. "But let's eat first. Bet that never in your wolf days were you as hungry as I am. You do look hungry, though not for grub. Well, possess your soul in peace for a little."

After supper one of the rangers told Duane that Captain MacNelly wanted him in the house.

"Things going fine, Duane," was the captain's greeting. "We got those rustlers where we want them . . . and that's in jail. Also had a draft cashed. Money for you was bothering me. Now that's all right. My man came back from Shirley with news that'll please you. He had a talk with Jeff Aiken and Miss Lee. Of course it wouldn't do for you to go over to Shirley. And I didn't think it wise for Miss Lee to come over to meet you in Fairfield. Too close. Anyway, she grasped the situation at once. She's clever. She has friends or relatives, I forget which, up in Ensenada. She was going there before you turned up in Shirley. Let's see, she sent a paper with names, directions . . . Colonel Silas Waite, Ensenada . . . you can reach Ensenada by rail. It's more than a hundred miles, a big town north where you'll not stand much risk of being recognized. But in case any of these ambitious sheriffs try to hold you, instead of sticking a gun under their noses, just show your ranger certificate. You're to go to Colonel Waite's house and ask for Miss Lee. That's all of that except by George! I wouldn't mind being you for that call anyway! Here's the money. Make it go as far as you can. Better strike straight for El Paso, snook around there and hear things. Then go to Valentine. That's near the river and some fifty miles or so off the edge of the Rim Rock. Somewhere up there Cheseldine holds forth. But he doesn't hide all the time in the rocks. Only after some daring raid or hold-up. Cheseldine's got border towns on his staff, or scared of him, and these places we want to know about. Write me in care of the adjutant general at Austin. I don't have to warn you to be careful where you mail letters. Ride a hundred, two hundred miles, if necessary, or go clear to El Paso."

MacNelly stopped with an air of finality, and then Duane slowly rose.

"I'll start at once," he said, extending his hand to the captain. "I wish . . . I'd like to thank you!"

"Hell man, don't thank me!" replied MacNelly, crushing the proffered hand. "I've sent a lot of good men to their deaths, and maybe you're another. But as I said, you're one chance in a thousand. And by God! I'd hate to be Cheseldine or any other man you were trailing. No, and good bye! *Adíos,* Duane! May we meet again!"

Chapter Fifteen

Early the next morning Duane left Fairfield, proceeded to Hildreth, where he had to wait to change trains, and then traveled on, reaching Ensenada about ten o'clock at night. That being rather late for a call, he curbed his impatience and went to an inn. The following day he arose with a strange restless excitement, full of vague presentiments and conjectures.

After breakfast he went out into the street to find that there was a plaza, common to many Texas towns, opposite the hotel. He sauntered over, meeting pedestrians and horsemen on early morning errands. Here he sat down upon a bench and tried to realize the actuality of his presence.

The absence of his old and accustomed riding clothes, jeans, chaps, boots, spurs — the newness of a different plain garb — with its long coat that hid his belt and gun, to these matters he could not so soon accustom himself. It was impossible to shake off the old ever-present habit of vigilance. Equally impossible was it to feel natural. A deep joy at what he considered his deliverance from outlawry abided with him and was as strange as all the rest. Presently he would stand face to face with Miss Lee, this mysterious and unremembered person who was closely in touch with his family, and from her lips he would hear all about his mother, his sister, his home. That filled him so with unfamiliar emotion that he longed for the meeting with her yet also dreaded it. He had so long been a hunted, hated outcast.

But he was no more an outlaw. He was free, a man of honest calling, a ranger entrusted with a service as important to the state as its commission was perilous to him. For the first time in years he was in a community of honest men and not prepared to flee at a moment's notice. Ensenada lay many miles north of the territory associated with his name. Still, there was never any telling where or when he might meet recognition. Suppose a sheriff should see him, stride up to him, clap a hand on his shoulder, and say: "Buck Duane, outlaw, come with me!" Duane would not need that swiftness of wrist that had made him so dreaded on the border. He had in his pocket a stronger argument than a gun. An inexpressible wonder and gratitude flowed from his heart. Slowly, gradually, with some kind of pang, his bitter weight of ignominy seemed to be lifting from him, making him glad to look into the faces of passing men.

Presently he hailed a boy and proffered a coin to the bare-footed youngster.

"What's that, sonny?" he asked.

"Why, sir, it's two bits," the boy replied, a broad smile breaking over his face.

"Do you know where Colonel Waite lives?"

"Sure."

"Take me there."

Duane followed his guide across the plaza and down the main street. He passed various people, all of whom took no notice of him, but Duane felt warmth steal along his veins at the mere sight of them. How little they divined the meaning of their presence to him who had been an exile and an outlaw! A comely old lady, sweet faced and mild eyed, looked up at him, struck by his giant stature. He passed school boys and girls with bright faces. The street had awakened to business, and he met farmers, ranchers, stockmen, — all dusty, loud-voiced, cheery, with the deep red of Texas sun on their cheeks. Suddenly he espied a row of mettlesome horses haltered to a long hitching rail. The sleek and racy Thoroughbreds, the big saddles, the coiled lariats told of the town visit of cowboys. Another glance showed a wide high gaudy sign at the front of a saloon. Involuntarily Duane stiffened, seemed to be pierced from head to foot by the old cool alertness. How many hundreds of times had he been forced to walk in bitter expectation past drinking places such as this? How many times had he met, striding forth, a rum-crazed cowboy, wearing a gun? — Duane hurried along, conscious that no honest calling, no ranger service would ever make him exempt from the wild pursuits of men of that class. Somebody would always want to kill him because he was Buck Duane.

Presently the youthful guide turned off into a street where there were fine houses, well-kept lawns, and shade trees. A couple of blocks down the street, looking in common with most all Texas streets, abruptly on the plain and at this point sitting well back in a grove was a big white house. This, the boy designated, was the home of Colonel Waite.

The walk up to the big colonial porch seemed long to Duane. He heard the leaves fluttering and caught a sweet scent of flowers. Somebody at the back of the house was talking sharply to a horse, and there followed the familiar pound of iron hoofs on hard ground.

Duane stepped upon the porch and rang the bell. After what appeared to be a long time a Negro maid opened the door.

"A caller to see Miss Lee," said Duane.

The maid asked him in and led him to a parlor. It was a large room, light enough, yet full of unfamiliar shapes. He stood there uncertain, waiting. The maid returned to say that Miss Lee would be right in.

Whoever Miss Lee was, she must have connections with wealthy people. Duane felt long absent associations become vivid in his mind. The pictures, the curtains, the rich furniture, the long low windows opening like doors out into a garden of flowers recalled rooms at Wellston that he had forgotten. His utter strangeness in such environment manifested itself in the fact that he did not want to move. He thought of his boots, his spurs, the dust — which things, at the moment, he had not upon him at all.

How quiet the house! Duane felt oppressed, and he imagined it the atmosphere of that rich parlor. There was a painting of a soldier over the mantel, a gallant officer, wearing the gray. He wondered if it was a picture of Colonel Waite. He had never heard that name before.

This woman he expected to see — she would come in soon. What was he to say? He felt thick tongued. All he recalled was the appeal she had made to Jeff Aiken. If she had known him as a boy, which probably was the case, what difference would she see in him now? Then — so much she must have to tell him! He wished she would hurry. He had called too early. The house was so quiet. It was not the outdoor quiet so familiar to him but a closed-in, shut-up silence, somehow pregnant with meaning. He thought he heard something and listened all the more keenly.

Then came a faint rustle, a soft step. Somebody — probably Miss Lee — was in the parlor with him. Duane knew it, and the sense of her presence, or some strange fact pertaining to it, had the effect on him of the old phantoms that drifted in the darkness around his bed. An unaccountable certainty of a spirit held Duane momentarily stiff. There was a spirit in the room — the spirit of some one long dead — or . . . ?

Slowly he turned. A slender woman in white stood in the door, one hand clinging to the curtains, the other at her breast. She was whiter than her dress — as white as a flower. Her eyes were dark, strained, staring, beautiful. The look of them Duane had seen before! Yes, she was that Miss Lee of the Shirley episode. But she was somebody else — somebody more.

Duane's lips uttered her name, yet he had a vague sense of not hearing his own voice. The movement of his lips, his hand, seemed to animate her. She had been as still as a statue, and now she was as if shot through and through with life. That supporting hand upon the curtain appeared to uphold her quivering form. The other hand pressed deeply into her heaving bosom as if to stop a bursting heart. The dark and passionate fire of her eyes was now an agony or a glory, Duane could not tell which. He did know that she tried to speak — failed — failed again.

She was only another phantom. He imagined it — tortured his mind to place her.

"Oh, Duane . . . don't you . . . know?"

The low voice, deep, sweet as an old chord, faltered and broke and failed. Duane sustained a sudden shock and an instant of paralyzed confusion of thought, when the old cold sickness of fancy fought a resurging might of memory that awakened to the sweetness of a voice for years unheard, never forgotten.

"Oh, Duane, don't you . . . know me?"

She moved, she swept out her hands, and the wonder of

206

her eyes dimmed in a flood of tears. She stepped blindly. And Duane's sight, straining with all the abnormal keenness of stunned faculties leaping back to power, caught a slight but unmistakable limp in her step. In a flash all that had been strange about her vanished. He knew that faltering step. He was back in another world, one he had seared over in his heart and closed forever.

"My God! . . . who are you?" he cried.

Then she met him, arms outstretched.

"Jennie! . . . Jennie! . . . *Jen-nie!*" she sobbed.

Swift as light Duane caught her up and held her crushed to his breast. The past, like deadening scales, fell from him. He stood holding her tightly, with the feel of her warm, throbbing breast and the clasp of her clinging arms as flesh and blood realities, to fight a terrible fear that this was only another, and the worst, of those moments haunted by phantoms. Despite a stunned consciousness he never lost the true sense of the exquisite life of that moment. He felt her, and the might of it was stronger than all the demons of his unhappy years. Jennie was not dead. She was alive — alive — *alive!* And he held her as if she had been his soul — his strength on earth — his hope of heaven.

The strife of doubt all passed, the encroaching of old dark moods fell short and faded. He found his sight again. And there rushed over him a tide of emotion unutterably sweet and full, strong like an intoxicating wine, deep as his nature, something glorious and terrible as the blaze of the sun after being long in darkness. He had become an outcast, a wanderer, a gunman, a victim of circumstances — he had loved and lost and suffered worse than death in that loss — he had gone down the endless bloody trail, a killer of men, a fugitive whose mind slowly and

207

inevitably closed to all except that instinct to survive, and a black despair; and now, with this woman in his arms, her swelling breast against his, in this moment almost of resurrection he bent under a storm of passion and joy, possible only to him who has endured so much.

"Jennie! Jennie!" he whispered unsteadily. "No dream, no ghost, but *you!* I didn't know you."

"Yes, Jennie. And you never knew me!" She stirred and lifted her face from his breast. Her hands unclasped from his neck, fell to his shoulder, and caught there. A stain of red came into her white face. "Have I changed . . . so much . . . from that time over in the Rim Rock?"

"Changed! You're not the same girl! You've only that old look in your eyes. I saw you limp . . . that told me!"

"I'm still a little lame."

"It was that. God! how everything rushed back! I saw you as on that first day in the cabin. It's all clearer than the thousand times I've dreamed it. Euchre and Bland and that fierce woman, his wife, and Alloway! The little shack where you hid and nursed me. Jennie, I went back there . . . lived a whole year there with dreams and ghosts."

He shuddered and looked out of the window, far beyond, in cold and sick fancy, to the wilds of a desert gorge. Jennie lifted a hand and touched his cheek with tenderness.

"I lived there alone . . . alone like a crippled wolf. Oh, the hell of the lonely nights . . . the black nights with their faces. But, Jennie, I found one thing . . . my salvation there."

He bent over her, looking deeply into the dark eyes.

"What?" she whispered.

"I found I loved you . . . and one of my bitterest regrets was that you never knew it. Hear it *now!* I love you. I've always loved you. I learned to love you there at Bland's cabin when we planned to save you. But it never came to me till I'd lost you. Then the memory was all that kept my mind from going. . . . Your eyes used to haunt me, Jennie. I could see them, dark and sad and watchful, as you peered through the window at me with that woman, Kate Bland. It all comes back. Jennie, you must have much to tell me. And I have much to tell you. Can you tell me . . . do you care for me? When I think of what you must have done! Jennie, haven't you loved me . . . a little?"

She uttered a low laugh that was half sob and her arms slipped up to his neck again.

"A little! I nearly died of love for you," she whispered. "I've never lived an hour without loving you, longing for you, praying for you. Oh, Duane, Duane, I love you!"

Their lips met in their first kiss. The sweetness, the fire of her mouth, seemed so new, so strange, so irresistible to Duane. His sore and hungry heart throbbed with thick and heavy beats. He felt the outcast's need of love. And he gave up to the enthralling moment. She met him half way, returned kiss for kiss, clasp for clasp, her face scarlet, her eyes closed, till her passion and strength were spent. She fell back upon his shoulder.

Duane suddenly thought she was going to faint. He divined then that she had understood him, would have denied him nothing, not even her life, in that moment. But she was overcome, and he suffered a pang of regret at his unrestraint.

"Jennie . . . don't mind it. I'm rough. I was carried away," he said. "I never knew life could be so sweet."

"I don't mind . . . I'm glad," she replied, slipping out of his arms. "But my breath went . . . and . . . and . . . and . . . come, let's sit down here by the window."

She led him to a sofa, and they sat down. It seemed then

that each looked at the other with different eyes, hers dark and sad and troubled, his glowing and soft, full of wonder.

"Jennie, I know you now, yet you're a stranger," he said earnestly. "You were a pretty girl in a wild and neglected way. Now you're a beautiful woman with only your eyes and your voice to prove you the old Jennie. There have been many strange and amazing things in my life, but none like this meeting with you. I remember you well as I last saw you. Years ago . . . terrible years for me! You wore my coat over a white cotton dress stained by rain and mud. You had no hat. Your hair was like an Indian's. Your sat on my big bay horse and, as I made off into the mesquites to catch your horse, you said: 'Don't be long.' I lost you there. My God! Yet, here you are, stranger than any dream! Jennie, begin there . . . where I lost you at that old cabin . . . and tell me your story."

"Yes. I want to tell you," she began softly. As she took his hand in hers, tears blurred the glow of her eyes. "After all, my story isn't so strange. That day we were separated so long ago . . . there were cowboys hiding in the mesquites. Cowboys on the trail of a rustler that they thought was in the cabin. When you left me, they jumped out of the thicket and dragged me away with them. They were rough but kind. They took no stock in my story. They left me at a rancher's house and went on after rustlers. The country was overrun with cattle thieves at that time. The rancher's wife was good to me, helped me to the nearest town, and arranged for me to travel to Wellston. There I went to your mother and told her my story. She gave me a home with her, and I loved her as if she had been my own mother.

"I helped with the housework, learned to make my clothes, and besides went to school. I worked, and I studied, but

I never forgot. Your Uncle Jim advertised and searched for relatives of mine. He found no relatives, but he did find property of my father's and my uncle's, both of whom were killed by raiders in Mexico. All this property was being held at Dresen in Diminick County. It came to me and includes the farm where I was born, a big ranch of my uncle's, and city property, too. My uncle was a director in the Dresen bank. I was poor and forlorn when you found me out there in the Rim Rock. Now I'm rich. Think of that, Duane!

"I was eighteen when I came into the property. But I continued to live with your mother. You, Duane, were the common bond between us, and we needed each other. I suddenly found myself a young woman of consequence, and it was then I became active in my efforts to get you pardoned. Governor Stone hates the wild life of Texas. He's from the eastern boundary and has never understood the desert and river country. I made friends in Austin, but it took us a year to get the pardon from the governor. The adjutant general was strong for us, and Captain Mac-Nelly, of the rangers, brought the influence which won our case. I don't know the particulars, but I fancy Captain MacNelly said you might give him valuable information regarding the border. Anyway, we won. MacNelly had the pardon and set out to locate you. This was a long and anxious year for your mother and me. Captain MacNelly failed to find you. Then your Uncle Jim and I set out on the quest, under the hampering orders of the ranger. We must be secret. It was not to be generally known that you were pardoned. We did not understand the reasons for the secrecy, but we obeyed. And that's why you were so hard to find.

"I have been to most of the towns and villages of southwestern Texas this side of the Nueces. Wherever I heard that you had friends there, I stayed and made them my friends. It was no easy task. The men of the desert are no dumber than those loyal friends of yours on the border. I had to guess, and love was my guide. I left all with a message. But you must never have visited any of these people since I had. I would spend a month traveling about then go home to Wellston.

"It was on the beginning of one of these trips that I happened to go to Shirley two weeks ago. There you had enemies. I made friends with Jeff Aiken and his family. I tried to prove to him that you couldn't have harmed his wife. He was sensible but hard to move. He did not talk much. But he seemed to like me, and I made up my mind to go to Shirley again. I was about to leave . . . the other day . . . when you rode into the town. Duane, I recognized you on sight! No one could fail that . . . who had ever seen you. Yet how terribly changed you were! That mob! Oh, heaven, what horror that time was to me! I recognized you. But I couldn't tell them. I prayed they wouldn't prove your identity. Sibert, the cowboy, saved you that day. I had met him before . . . talked with him . . . interested him in my mission there. He fought the mob. Then Aiken came up, so cold and black. I believed that would be the end. My heart was bursting, but I flung myself before him, into that mob, tried to say something. Then I guess I fainted, for I had to be told the rest that happened. Sibert told me. He was glad. And Aiken said he believed you'd go to see MacNelly. So I waited in Shirley. When that ranger came to me with messages, I believe then that happiness began for me, the first I'd known for ten years. I thought it best to have you meet me here in Ensenada where I have friends. Colonel Waite was close to my uncle.

Then you are not known hereabouts. So I came . . . and waited."

She ended in a whisper, and Duane felt her hot tears fall upon the hand she clasped. He sat silently a little while, trying to comprehend.

"I'm so glad . . . so thankful . . . for you," he said huskily. "Now, tell me of home."

"You've never had a word from home in all these years?"

"Not till the other day when I saw MacNelly."

"Dear, I should have told you first of home, instead of myself. It's all good news, Duane. Your mother's growing old, but she's strong, vigorous, bright. She'll live many years yet. Uncle Jim is well. Kitty is growing up . . . she's pretty and clever . . . she has a beau. And they all love you, never forget you. . . .

"But to go back, when I first got to Wellston, your folks weren't living in the home you were brought up in. I did not know that then. Afterwards, I learned they'd seen some poor times and had lost the old home. There wasn't much money. Your Uncle Jim did what he could, but that wasn't much. When my windfall came, I soon changed all that. We went back to the old home, fixed it up, bought the fields and woods adjoining. It's now one of the prettiest places in Wellston. Kitty is in the high school. She's full of fun, very popular among the boys and girls and, as I said before, there's a beau. Uncle Jim has settled down, getting ready to be an old man he says. He sits on the porch and smokes a great deal. He's always cheerful, and he'll talk. But he never mentions you to anyone except me, and that's not often. I think long ago he gave up hope. Your father's end would be yours. Mother Duane is different. She has two sides to her, it seems. For the most part she's gentle, kind, sweet, always busy, always doing some-

213

thing for someone. But she has moods. And then it's easy to see she's your mother, Duane. For then she's thoughtful, dark, stern. She's quick as fire at those times. I've heard her say, when report of some deviltry was around, that if you were home it would soon be stopped. She was never ashamed of your gun record. And at any hint of your outlawry she was furious. 'Law!' she would cry. 'What's law, and what's the state? My grandfather and my father, and men of their kind, made wild Texas safe for homes. We fought the Indians and the Mexicans. We bled for years. And now because my son was a fighter, the state makes him a criminal. If there's a criminal, it's I . . . for I gave him birth and the blood to live on this border!' She has never given up hope of having you back home, free. She listened when we told her of your pardon, and she read it. But I think she felt scorn for the governor who granted it. She always watches, and often she says: 'He'll ride in some day!' "

All this was sweet to Duane, and his thankfulness was in keeping with his joy. Out of it, however, gradually grew a pang which, when he had tasted full of the one bitter drop, he divined was caused by the fact that he must tell Jennie he had been pardoned only to go on a service more perilous than his old lonely bloody trail. She must be told, but how could he do it? The thought brought a chilling sensation, as if a cold hand had been laid upon some warm place deeply within him. This thought loomed larger and darker, so that suddenly he was afraid.

"So your name is Lee . . . Jennie Lee?" he said, trying to make conversation. "You know, I never heard your last name out there on the river. And, after all, Sellers wasn't guilty."

"Sellers? I don't remember any man by that name,"

214

replied Jennie.

"That day, when the cowboys made off with you, I trailed the tracks of my horse which you rode. They led to a village. There I got on the trail of Sellers. I was made to believe he had you. I trailed him for years, long after I had any hope you were alive. At last I met him in a gambling room in Brownsville. We drew, and he died with his lips shut. I never knew what part he really played. I believed he had taken you, but I never proved it . . . and now I find him innocent!"

"Poor man! Oh, Duane it was terrible to kill him, not knowing," cried Jennie. "Who was he? I hope not any man. . . ."

"Sellers was bad enough. He was the worst kind of thief, a crooked cattleman. Then he was handy with guns and had used them freely. I'm carrying his bullet to this day, here in my shoulder. Sometimes it hurts me. But, God knows, I'm sorry now I killed him."

Jennie placed a quick and tender arm around the shoulder he indicated.

"Duane, forget him and all the others. *Forget!*" She whispered that in his ear and leaned her face against his cheek. He felt more than warmth, tenderness, sympathy in her voice and touch. Again some subtle suggestion conveyed to him the impression that she understood. Perhaps her love made her divine his remorse. But he prayed that she could not see into the gulf of his soul, that black pit of phantoms.

"Forget! Jennie, I've deliberately hunted men, faced them, made them draw upon me in my passion to forget. But I only killed them, and had more to remember!"

"I shall make you forget," she whispered, and slid upon his knee, and into his arms.

215

"I believe you could . . . if. . . ."

"If what?" she asked softly, as he hesitated.

Duane groaned. He who had endured mental and physical agony beyond the limit of man's strength grew suddenly weak, unable to repress his emotion. It was because he had to tell her. He bowed his head over her, as she clung closely to him, and then had not the courage to let her see his face.

"If what, Duane? You must forget your miseries. There *are* no ifs. I can make up to you much that you've lost. We can be happy. You will forget."

"Not . . . just yet," he said and could not control his voice.

He felt her start, then grow still and stiff in his arms, then slip from him. And he hid his face in his hands. There was a silence and, as it grew longer and that cold sick darkness blotted out the brightness of joy, he prayed she would never speak.

"Duane, there's something you've not told me?" she said bravely.

"Yes."

"What . . . what is it?"

He kept silent because he could not answer then.

"Something . . . to do . . . with MacNelly?" Her voice now was far away, low, and not natural.

He nodded with bowed head.

"Duane!"

That brought him up, thrilling, as might have a cry for help. If Jennie had been white at the moment of their meeting, she now looked like death. She had guessed the condition of the governor's pardon, the fatal service sworn to MacNelly.

216

Chapter Sixteen

Jennie slipped to her knees, and her trembling hands reached up to Duane. "Don't tell me MacNelly has made you a ranger?" she implored.

"That's it," replied Duane and brought himself to face her. He feared a breakdown or at least a storm of weeping, but apparently she grew calmer now that the truth was out.

"He didn't make you a ranger just for an excuse for the pardon?"

"No. It's secret special service."

"Ah! What is it, Duane?"

"I'm to make my way west, find where Cheseldine hides out with his picked men, get in with them and, when they're ready to ride out on another raid or bank robbery, I'm to plan a trap so MacNelly can kill them or capture them."

"Oh heaven! Duane, was it for that MacNelly got your pardon? He might as well have killed you. To send you on a mission like that . . . Duane, it's impossible! With your reputation . . . known hatred of border criminals . . . with the deaths of Bland, Alloway, Hardin, all those outlaws against you, why, it would be utterly hopeless. Impossible!"

"No, Jennie, not that. It could be done by good management and luck."

"I mean you'd never succeed . . . and then come back," said Jennie. "You might do the same out there as you did in Bland's camp, but the risk's greater. I remember all about Cheseldine. I've never heard his name since we got away from Bland, but now it all comes back. Bland was mortally jealous of Cheseldine, wanted to be like him, to have his power, to rule a gang as big. Cheseldine was then supposed to control all the outlaws up the river. No one knew the extent of his rule. No one knew who were or were not his friends. There were villages that lived off him."

"Jennie, did you ever hear the name of his hiding place?" queried Duane eagerly.

"Yes, I did. Oh, I can't remember. Bland knew it, but I never heard *him* say it. Somebody told me. Who? Let me think. I remember Alloway once said outlaws were faithful to Cheseldine. . . . *Euchre!* He told me. Poor old Euchre! If ever there was a good outlaw, he was one. He told me. He had been in every outlaw camp in Texas. Let me remember!"

With her hands on Duane's knees, her brow knitted, her dark eyes shadowy with memories of that tragic past she had tried to forget, Jennie remained still as a stone for a long moment.

"It all comes back," she said with a shudder and her eyes closed. "Euchre's talks to me. I remember every word. He used to try to keep my mind off my misery. He told me everything he ever knew . . . or saw or did. Cheseldine was an outlaw with brains, the planner but not the doer. Poggin was Cheseldine's lieutenant. Handy Poggin, rustler, murderer, bank robber, gunman, everything bad, the worst and most dangerous outlaw since the days of Murrell! Cheseldine plans . . . Poggin executes. There are Boldt, Fletcher . . . Jim Fletcher . . . Blossom Kane . . . Pan Handle Smith . . . Phil Knell, outlaws bad and cunning enough to work with Poggin.

"Cheseldine's hiding place is on Mount Ord in the Big Bend country. He has a beautiful ranch in a valley. It's well hidden. Euchre said he was there once. Cheseldine and his men work in Brewster, Presidio, and Jeff Davis Counties, sending cattle west along the Rio Grande. It's desert and mountain country with ranches on the plains and valleys. They rustle cattle west of this territory and operate in other ways to the south. Valentine, Marfa, these towns are more associated with Cheseldine's gang than any others, but all the towns are dominated by the outlaws. Euchre told me this many years ago. I suppose conditions are the same now, or even worse. MacNelly said as much. West of the Nueces is bad enough, but the Big Bend country! Duane, no rangers or sheriffs, even soldiers, have ever been in there."

"That's just why MacNelly picked me out to go, I suppose," replied Duane. "I can ride in there on my nerve and, if it comes to a showdown, my name may help me along. I'm not bothered about how I'll be received. It's accomplishing my job . . . and getting away alive . . . there's the rub."

"Duane, you can never do it. Now, honestly, don't you think MacNelly's ambition for the service has led him to give you a forlorn task?"

"Yes, but that was the condition under which the governor pardoned me. Jennie, I'm a free man now, a ranger with an honest calling. You ought to know what that means to me. I've had an infamous name for years. Presently that disgrace will be lifted."

"You exaggerate your disgrace. There are as many Texans proud of you now as there are others who believe you're bad or you're painted . . . Duane, the vital point with me

is not your pardon, your name, your sworn ranger service
. . . *but your life!*"

She rose and stood before him, still white, though calm
now, with steady hands. Underneath the shadows of love
and trouble in her dark eyes smoldered a fire. She looked
stronger, older then.

"Jennie, you mean this . . . that I have already received
more than my share of narrow scrapes? Logically I can't
look farther to a kind Providence? Sooner or later the
gunfighter, whether he be outlaw or ranger, must meet
his match . . . and the inevitable end?"

"I mean just that," she replied solemnly. "If you don't put
up your gun and get out of Texas, you're doomed. It can't
be otherwise."

"Get out of Texas!" echoed Duane. The idea was new to
him, though in his early days as a fugitive he had tried
to plan such a thing. Then he sighed. "*¿Quién sabe?* I dare
say you're right. But what's the use of talking any more
about it? You had to be told. My mother must be told. But
let's talk of other things . . . of our being together now
. . . of a possible future."

"I'm thinking of a possible future," she rejoined, with a
smile sweet and sad. "Duane, let me go back to MacNelly."

"What for?"

"To entreat him to release you."

"Why, he wouldn't. He's keen to do this thing. And I
don't blame him. MacNelly's a fine fellow. He's not wanting
in sympathy. But he's got a man's job, and you couldn't
move him."

"Yes, I could. At least, if I couldn't persuade him, I could
buy your release. The ranger service is poorly paid. They
need money. He could do much with money. I'll pay him
ten thousand dollars to release you."

"*Jennie!* Oh, you mustn't think of such a thing. He wouldn't consent. Remember, I'm practically bound to Governor Stone as well as to Captain MacNelly."

"What Governor Stone would never know wouldn't hurt him," muttered Jennie. The fire in her eyes had spread. Faint red spots appeared in her white cheeks. Her breast rose and fell with deep, hurried breaths. Duane saw in her the fighting spirit of Texas and sensed a bursting storm.

"Dear Jennie, look at it this way," he said in a persuasive tone. "Thank God I'm a free man now. Think how glad my mother will be. I've a hard job on hand, but you know I'm pretty well able to tackle it. I'll break up Cheseldine's band. And maybe I'll get away safe. There's a chance. Can't you imagine what I'll do with that chance . . . when all the time I'll know you love me . . . are waiting for me?"

For all the effect this speech produced he might as well have kept silent. Her eyes, black now and blazing, were on him.

"Duane, return the pardon to MacNelly and go back to the Nueces. Be an outlaw again! I'll go with you."

Duane stared at her in amazement. He hardly knew what to say. He felt how little he understood women. His heart began to pound and thrills ran over him. The sweetness of this woman . . . that she would go back to outlawing with him . . . appealed with strange power.

"That course wouldn't be dishonorable," she continued.

"No, but it's impossible. I'd die before I'd drag you into that life. You ought to remember an outlaw's days."

"I do. I'd rather have them again than lose you. Besides, we could hide in some cañon, some valley . . . and be happy."

"No . . . no . . . no." Duane felt the insidious creeping

221

strength of some hitherto unknown emotion. It came from her suggestion . . . to be alone with her . . . to have her . . . and he realized that he must not let the thing stay before his mind.

Jennie came closer to him then, so close that she almost touched him. Something about her presence, the look of her eyes or the heave of her breast, made that sweet vague emotion grow. "Duane, do you love me?" she asked.

"Jennie! You're going to make it impossible for me," he burst out in despair.

"Tell me," she insisted.

"Good God! Love you? I love you as no man ever loved a woman. Think of my lonely wretched life! What have I known of women, of the sweetness of one? And now it has burst upon me. Jennie, don't ask me that. I'm afraid of myself. I can't understand."

She came only the closer, until now she did touch him, her slender form reaching to his shoulder, and she leaned upon him with her face upturned. He felt her hands on his, and they were soft, clinging, strong, like steel under velvet. He felt the rise and fall — the warmth of her breast. A tremor ran over him. He tried to draw back and, if he succeeded a little, her form swayed with him, pressing closer. She did not speak. She held her face up, and he was compelled to look. It was wonderful now — white, yet glowing, with the red lips parted, the dark eyes alluring. But that was not all. There was passion, unquenchable spirit, woman's resolve deep and mighty as life.

"I love you, Duane," she said. "I could suffer anything for you. I'm not selfish in this. It's for you. I know what your life has been. I can't let you go back to it. Listen, you don't know me. You think you're with the old Jennie. But I'm different. I've suffered, and I've learned in these years. I

222

believe I'm right in asking you to give up this ranger service. Will you?"

"Jennie, I can't. How could you ask it?"

"How could you go if you love me?"

"If you were a man, you'd understand."

"But I'm a woman. *You* don't understand that!" she cried passionately.

"Can you expect a man who lived like a hunted wolf to understand the finer feelings of a woman? I am outside, Jennie, . . . the outcast . . . the outlaw. And even so I've kept myself different from the others. But, God knows, perhaps I'm coarse, hard, inhuman."

"Hush!" She put a hand over his lips. "I didn't mean to hurt you. I meant . . . oh, Duane, I'm here ready for your arms . . . a starved woman . . . and you don't know it."

Duane became suddenly weak and, when he did take her into his arms, he scarcely had strength to lift her to a seat beside him. She seemed more than a dead weight. Her calmness had fled. She was throbbing, palpitating, quivering, with hot wet cheeks, and arms that clung to him like vines. She lifted her mouth to him, whispering: "Kiss me!"

Duane bent down, and her arms went around his neck, and drew him close. With his lips on hers he seemed to float away. That kiss closed his eyes, and he could not lift his head. He sat motionless, holding her, blind and helpless, wrapped in a secret dark glory. She kissed him — one long endless kiss — or else a thousand times. Her lips, her wet cheeks, her hair, the softness, the fragrance of her, the tender moving clasp of her arms, the swell of her breast, — all these enclosed him, bound him. She whispered and murmured — broken and incoherent words — words that did not need to be understood — so full were they of sweetness and meaning and love.

Suddenly he found that he was listening to low, clear, vibrant speech that dispelled the thickness in his ears, impelled and drew him even more powerfully than had the tender wildness: "The only way! Oh, Duane, we can do it. Who could blame us! You will go straight on from Ensenada. You'll get a through train at Center Junction. You'll go through Santone, Austin, perhaps at night. No one would recognize you up there. Travel straight north to Saint Louis. There's a hotel I've heard of . . . the Buell House. Go there and wait. Wait for me! I'll be careful, quiet, no one will suspect anything, but I'll draw what money I have in the bank. I sold my uncle's ranch. I've been prepared. So if I can't sell the rest, we'll still have money . . . more than we need. I'll slip off and come to Saint Louis. Then, oh, Duane, we'll plan our future with this bloody Texas left out of account. We'll never come back. We'll never. We'll never be heard of again here where we've been known. We can go East. We can go abroad, or we can hunt for an out of the way place, somewhere in a pretty country, and make our home, and be at peace. Oh, Duane, don't refuse. We've suffered so much. This is our chance. Let's take it. I beg you. Duane, dear lonely wanderer, let me find you a home!"

"My God!" cried Duane, shaken to his soul. "You mustn't! If you love me, don't . . . don't! MacNelly, damn him! He *knew* his man. That's why he got my word."

Jennie enfolded him closer, stronger in her abandonment as he weakened. "Your word? Yes, but break it! What is your word to your life and my love? I beseech you, break it. No man could be blamed for that. No one will ever know what became of you. See! There's a straw, if you want to grasp it. But I . . . I say damn MacNelly! Damn the governor! Damn the state! I was an outlaw, too, Duane. That life influenced me, almost ruined me. It comes out now. I put your life before your honor. I believe your mother would do the same. You have paid for that pardon. You have rid the state of many a villain. I repeat no one will ever know what became of you. I'll leave an impression behind. I'll grow sick of Texas. I'll give up hope. I'll confide only in your mother and swear her to silence. MacNelly will think you were killed in your service. He'll never dream you . . . you. . . ."

"Yes, that's the hell of it. He'd never dream I'd double-cross him. Oh, Jennie, you're torturing me!"

She did not cease but seemed to gather more force in this crisis. He could not put her from him. She fell again to loving him, without shame, without joy, passionate, inflamed, unchangeable in her resolve to break his will. He yielded to her lips and arms, watching her, involuntarily returning her caresses, sure now of her intent, fascinated by the sweetness of her, bewildered, almost lost. This was what it was to be loved by a woman. His years of outlawing had blotted out any boyish love he might have known. This was what he had to give up — all this wonder of her sweet person, this strange fire he feared yet loved, this mate his deep and tortured soul recognized. Never until that moment had he divined the meaning of a woman to a man. That meaning was physical — in as much that he learned now what beauty was, what marvel in the touch of quickening flesh — and it was spiritual in that he saw there might have been for him, under happier circum-stances, a life of noble ideals to be lived for such a woman. If he kept his word, he must give up love along perhaps with his life. If he won love through dishonor, could he ever rise to the height otherwise possible for the sake of the woman who loved him? Some flash of insight told him, no. Perhaps that was the instant of decision.

Jennie wore herself out and lay on his breast, broken in strength but still indomitable of spirit. She seemed in this state more beautiful than ever, and her slenderness, the lightness of her body, its fragility, brought home a new thought to Duane. She was not strong. She needed a protector, some man to work for her, take care of her. He had to give that up, too. The more he thought the more he found to give up. It was she who had hurled into his mind all this possibility of love, companionship, happiness, home, children. Still, despite the pain of hopeless regret, he was glad she had made him feel that possibility.

Then a trip hammer warning beat into his brain the truth that he divined in Jennie's signs of recovery. If she ever found strength to abandon herself again to the storm of love and passion that she had spent upon him, he would be overwhelmed. The thought of it almost broke his will, as indeed it made him tremble.

He rose and let Jennie sit back against the cushions. Her fingers clung weakly to him. Her eyes hurt him. While he fumbled in his pocket for papers, to fetch forth the governor's pardon, Jennie watched him and, when he laid the paper in her hands, she let it drop.

"Give that to mother," he said huskily. "Tell her . . . maybe I'll come back . . . there's a chance."

"Don't go! Don't go!" she cried.

"I must. Dear, good bye . . . remember I love you! Jennie, let me go!"

He pulled her hands loose from his — stepped back. She fell upon her knees with outstretched arms.

"Duane! Duane!" she wailed.

Like a murderer he backed away.

"Jennie . . . dearest . . . I believe I'll come back!" he whispered.

These last words were falsehood. He reached the door — gave her a last piercing glance — to fix forever in memory that white face with its dark, staring, tragic eyes.

"Duane!"

He fled with that moan — like thunder, death, hell in his ears.

Chapter Seventeen

In Texas west of the Pecos River there extended a vast and wild region, barren in the north where the *Llano Estacado* spread its shifting spurs, fertile in the south along the Rio Grande. A railroad marked an undeviating course across five hundred miles of this country, and the only villages and towns lay on or near this line of steel. Unsettled as was this western part of Texas and despite the acknowledged dominance of the outlaw bands, the pioneers pushed steadily into it. First had come the lone rancher — then his neighbors in near and far valleys — then the hamlets — at last the railroad and the towns. And still the pioneers came, spreading deeper into the valleys, farther and wider over the plains. It was mesquite-dotted, cactus-covered desert, but there was also rich soil upon which water acted like magic. There was little grass to an acre, but there were millions of acres. The climate was wonderful. Cattle flourished, and ranchers prospered.

The Rio Grande flowed almost due south along the western boundary for a thousand miles and then, weary of its course, turned abruptly north, to make what was called the Big Bend. The railroad, running west, cut across this bend, and all that country bounded in the north by the railroad and in the south by the river was as wild as the Staked Plains. It contained not one settlement. Across the face of this Big Bend, as if to isolate it, stretched the Ord mountain range, of which Mount Ord, Cathedral Mountain, and Elephant Mountain raised bleak peaks above their fellows. In the valleys of the foothills and out across the plains were ranches, farther north villages and the towns of Alpine and Marfa.

Like other parts of the great Lone Star State this section of Texas was a world in itself — a world where the riches of the rancher were enriching the outlaw. The village closest to the gateway of this outlaw-infested region was a little place called Ord, named after the dark peak that loomed some miles to the south. It had been settled originally by Mexicans — there were still the ruins of adobe missions — but with the advent of the rustler and outlaw, many inhabitants were shot or driven away, so that at the height of Ord's prosperity and evil sway there were but few Mexicans living there, and these had their choice between holding hand and glove with the outlaws or furnishing target practice for that wild element. Towards the close of a day in September a stranger rode into Ord, and in a community where all men were remarkable, for one reason or another, he excited interest. His horse, perhaps, received the first and most engaging attention — horses in that region being apparently more important than men. This particular horse did not attract with beauty. At first glance he seemed ugly, but he was a giant, black as coal, rough despite the care manifestly bestowed upon him, long of body, ponderous of limb, huge in every way. A bystander remarked that he had a grand head. True, if only his head had been seen, he would have been a beautiful horse. Like men, horses show what they are in the shape, the size, the line, the character of the head. This one denoted fire, speed, blood, loyalty, and his eyes were as soft and dark as a woman's. His face was solid black except in the middle of his forehead where there was a round spot of white.

"Say, mister, mind tellin' me his name?" asked a ragged urchin with a born love of horses in his eyes.

"Bullet," replied the rider.

"Thet there's fer the white mark, ain't it?" whispered this youngster to another. "Say, ain't he a whopper? Biggest hoss I ever seen."

Bullet carried a huge black, silver-ornamented saddle of Mexican make, a lariat and canteen, and a small pack rolled into a tarpaulin. This rider apparently put all care of appearance upon his horse. His apparel was the ordinary jeans of the cowboy without vanity, torn and travel-stained. His boots showed evidence of an intimate acquaintance with cactus. Like his horse, this man was a giant in stature but rangier, not so heavy. Otherwise the only striking thing about him was his somber face with its piercing eyes and hair white over the temples. He packed two guns, both low down, but that was too common a thing to attract notice in the Big Bend. A close observer, however, would have noted a singular fact — this rider's right hand was more bronzed, more weather beaten than his left. He never wore a glove on that right hand.

He had dismounted before a ramshackle structure that bore upon its wide high-boarded front the sign: **Hotel**. There were horsemen coming and going down the wide street between its rows of old stores, saloons, and houses. Ord certainly did not look enterprising. Americans had manifestly assimilated much of the leisure of the Mexicans. The hotel had a wide platform in front, and this did duty as porch and sidewalk. Upon it, and leaning against a hitching rail, were men of varying ages, most of them slovenly in old jeans and slouched sombreros. Some were booted, belted, and spurred. No man there wore a coat,

230

but all wore vests. The guns in that group would have outnumbered the men.

It was a crowd seemingly too lazy to be curious. Good nature did not appear to be wanting, but it was not the frank and boisterous kind natural to the cowboy or rancher in town for a day. These men were idlers; what else, perhaps, was easy of conjecture. Certainly to this arriving stranger, who flashed a keen eye over them, they wore an atmosphere never associated with work.

Presently a tall man with a drooping sandy mustache leisurely detached himself from the crowd. "Howdy, stranger," he said.

The stranger had bent over to loosen the cinches. He straightened up and nodded. Then: "My Gawd, I'm thirsty!"

That brought a broad smile to faces. It was a characteristic greeting. One and all they trooped after the stranger into the hotel. It was a dark, ill-smelling barn of a place with a bar as high as a short man's head. A bartender with a scarred face was serving drinks.

"Line up, gents," said the stranger.

They piled over one another to get to the bar, with coarse jests and oaths and laughter. None of them noted that the stranger did not appear so thirsty as he had claimed to be. In fact, though he went through the motions, he did not drink at all.

"My name's Jim Fletcher," said the tall man with the drooping sandy mustache. He spoke laconically, yet there was a tone that showed he expected to be recognized. Something went with that name. The stranger did not appear to be impressed.

"My name might be Blazes, but it ain't," he replied. "What do you call this burg?"

"Stranger, this heah mee-tropolis bears the handle

231

Ord. Is thet new to you?"

He leaned back against the bar, and now his little yellow eyes, clear as crystal, flawless as a hawk's, fixed on the stranger. Other men crowded close, forming a circle, curious, ready to be friendly or otherwise, according to how the tall interrogator marked the newcomer.

"Sure, Ord's a little strange to me. Off the railroad some, ain't it? Damn' funny trails hereabouts!"

"How fur was you goin'?"

"I reckon I was goin' as far as I could," replied the stranger with a hard laugh.

His reply had a subtle reaction from that listening circle. Some of the men exchanged glances. Fletcher stroked his drooping mustache, seemed thoughtful but lost something of that piercing scrutiny.

"Wal, Ord's the jumpin' off place," he said presently. "Sure you've heard of the Big Bend country?"

"I sure have an' was makin' tracks fer it," replied the stranger.

Fletcher turned toward a man in the outer edge of the group. "Knell, come in heah."

This individual elbowed his way in and was seen to be scarcely more than a boy, almost pale beside those bronzed men, with a long expressionless face, thin and sharp.

"Knell, this heah's. . . ." Fletcher wheeled to the stranger. "What'd you call yourself?"

"I'd hate to mention what I've been callin' myself lately."

This sally fetched another laugh. The stranger appeared cool, careless, indifferent. Perhaps he knew, as the others present knew, that this show of Fletcher's — this pretense of introduction — was merely talk while he was looked over.

Knell stepped up, and it was easy to see, from the way

Fletcher relinquished his part in the situation, that a man greater than he had appeared upon the scene.

"Any business here?" he queried curtly. When he spoke, his expressionless face was in strange contrast with the ring, the quality, the cruelty of his voice. This voice betrayed an absence of humor, of friendliness, of heart.

"Nope," replied the stranger.

"Know anybody hereabouts?"

"Nary one."

"Jest ridin' through?"

"Yep."

"Slopin' fer back country, eh?"

There came a pause. The stranger appeared to grow a little resentful, drew himself up disdainfully.

"Wal, considerin' you-all seem so damn' friendly an' curious down here in this Big Bend country, I don't mind sayin', yes, I am on the dodge," he replied with deliberate sarcasm.

"From west of Ord . . . out El Paso way . . . mebbe?"

"Sure."

"Uh-huh! Thet so?" Knell's words cut the air, stilled the room. "You're from way down the river. Thet's what they say down there . . . 'on the dodge?' Stranger, you're a liar!"

With swift clink of spur and thump of boot, the crowd split, leaving Knell and the stranger in the center. Wild breed of that ilk never made a mistake in judging a man's nerve. Knell had cut out with the trenchant call and stood ready. The stranger suddenly lost his every semblance to the rough and easy character before manifest in him. He became bronze. That situation seemed familiar to him. His eyes held a singular piercing light that danced like a compass needle.

"Sure I lied," he said. "So I ain't takin' offense at the

233

way you called me. I'm lookin' to make friends, not enemies. You don't strike me as one of them four-flushers, achin' to kill somebody. But if you are . . . go ahead an' open the ball. You see, I never throw a gun on them fellers till they go fer theirs."

Knell coolly eyed his antagonist, his strange face not changing in the least. Yet, somehow, it was evident in his look that here was metal which rang differently from what he had expected. Invited to start a fight or withdraw, as he chose, Knell proved himself big in the manner characteristic of only the genuine gunman.

"Stranger, I pass," he said and, turning to the bar, he ordered liquor.

The tension relaxed; the silence broke; the men filled up the gap; the incident seemed closed. Jim Fletcher attached himself to the stranger, and now both respect and friendliness tempered his asperity.

"Wal, fer want of a better handle, I'll call you Dodge," he said.

"Dodge's as good as any. Gents, line up again . . . an', if you can't be friendly, be careful!"

Such was Buck Duane's debut in the little outlaw hamlet of Ord. He had been three months out of the Nueces country. At El Paso he'd bought the finest horse he could find and, armed and otherwise outfitted to suit him, he had taken to unknown trails. Leisurely he had ridden from town to town, village to village, ranch to ranch, fitting his talk and his occupation to the impression he wanted to make upon different people whom he met. He was in turn a cowboy, a rancher, a cattleman, a stock buyer, a boomer, a land hunter. Long before he had reached the wild and inhospitable Ord, he had acted the part of an outlaw, drifting into new territory. He passed on leisurely because

234

he wanted to learn the lay of the country, the location of villages and ranches, the work, habits, gossip, pleasures, and fears of the people with whom he came in contact. The one subject most impelling to him — outlaws — he never mentioned but, by talking all around it, sifting the old ranch and cattle story, he acquired a knowledge calculated to aid him much in his deeply laid plot. In this game time was of no moment; if necessary he would take years to accomplish his task. The stupendous and perilous nature of it showed in the slow, wary preparation. When he heard Fletcher's name and faced Knell, he knew he had reached the place he sought. Ord was a hamlet on the fringe of the grazing country, of doubtful honesty, from which no doubt winding trails led down into that free and never-disturbed paradise of outlaws — the Big Bend.

Duane made himself agreeable, yet not too much so, to Fletcher and several other men disposed to talk and drink and eat. Then, after having a care for his horse, he rode out of town a couple of miles to a grove he had marked and there, well hidden, he prepared to spend the night. This proceeding served a double purpose — he was safer, and the habit would look well in the eyes of outlaws who would be more inclined to see in him the lone-wolf fugitive.

Duane had fought out a battle within himself, won a hard-earned victory over longing and passion, and now he could think and dream of the woman he loved without agony. Jennie shared his sleeping and waking thoughts equally with this stern and desperate service he had set himself. His outer life, the action, was much the same as it had been, but the inner life had tremendously changed. He could never become a happy man; he could never shake utterly those haunting phantoms that had once been his despair and madness; but he had assumed a task impossible for any man save one like him. He had felt the meaning of it grow strangely and wonderfully, and through that there flourished up consciousness of how passionately he now clung to this thing which would blot out his former infamy. The iron fetters no more threatened his hands; the iron door no more haunted his dreams. He never forgot that he was free. Strangely, too, along with this feeling of new manhood, there gathered the force of imperious desire to run these chief outlaws to their dooms. He never called them outlaws — but rustlers, thieves, robbers, murderers, criminals. He sensed the growth of a relentless driving passion, and sometimes he feared that, more than the newly acquired zeal and pride in this ranger service, it was the old, terrible, inherited killing instinct lifting its hydra-head in a new guise. But of that he could not be sure. He dreaded the thought. He could only wait.

Another aspect of the change in Duane, neither passionate nor driving, yet not improbably even more potent of new significance to life, was the imperceptible return of an old love of nature, dead during his outlaw days. For years a horse had been only a machine of locomotion, to carry him from place to place, to beat and spur and goad mercilessly in flight; now, this giant black, with his splendid head, was a companion, a friend, a brother, a loved thing, guarded jealously, fed and trained and ridden with an intense appreciation of his great speed and endurance. For years, the daytime, with its birth of sunrise on through long hours to the ruddy close, had been used for sleep or rest in some rocky hole or willow brake or deserted hut, had been hated because it augmented danger of pursuit, because it drove the fugitive to lonely, wretched hiding. Now, the dawn was a greeting, a promise of another day to ride, to plan, to remember, and sun, wind, cloud, rain, sky — all were joys to him, somehow — speaking his freedom. For years the night had been a black space during which he had to ride unseen along the endless trails, to peer with cat-like eyes through gloom for the moving shape that ever pursued him. Now the twilight, and the dusk, and the shadows of the grove and cañon darkened into night with its train of stars, brought him calm reflection of the day's happenings, of the morrow's possibilities, perhaps a sad brief procession of the old phantoms, then sweet thought of Jennie, then sleep. For years cañons and valleys and mountains had been looked at as retreats that might be dark and wild enough to hide even an outlaw. Now, he saw these features of the great desert with something of the eyes of the boy who had once burned for adventure and life among them.

This night a wonderful afterglow lingered long in the west, and against the golden red of clear sky the bold black head of Mount Ord reared itself aloft, beautiful but aloof, sinister yet calling. Small wonder that Duane gazed in fascination upon the peak! Its name had come to him from the lips of Jennie Lee. Somewhere deep in its corrugated sides, or lost in a rugged cañon, was hidden the secret stronghold of the master outlaw, Cheseldine. All down the long ride from El Paso, Duane had heard of Cheseldine, of his band, his wealth, his fearful deeds, his cunning, his widely separated raids, of the many places he frequented, flitting here and there like a jack o' lantern but never a word of his den. How strange that Jennie should have borne him this secret, she to whom the strife that must come of it was most cruel! There in the shadow that blotted out the somber mountain, he saw her face, white, sweet, with the dark, staring, tragic eyes.

Next morning Duane did not return to Ord. He struck off to the north, riding down a rough, slow-descending road that appeared to have been used occasionally for driving cattle. As he had ridden in from the west, this northern direction led him into totally unfamiliar country. While he passed on, however, he exercised such keen observation that in the future he should know whatever might be of service to him if he chanced that way again.

The rough, wild, brush-covered slope down from the foot-hills gradually leveled out into plain, a magnificent grazing country upon which, till noon of that day, Duane did not see a herd of cattle or a ranch. About that time he made out smoke from the railroad and, after a couple of hours' riding, he entered a town which inquiry discovered to be Bradford. It was the largest town he had visited since Marfa and, he calculated, must have a thousand or fifteen hundred inhabitants not including Mexicans. He decided this would be a good place for him to hole up for a while, being the nearest town to Ord, only forty miles away. So he hitched his horse in front of a store and leisurely set about studying Bradford.

After he had made a number of small purchases in different stores, Duane came to the conclusion that total strangers were not rare in Bradford but were evidently waited upon without curiosity or interest. Duane found the habitants of the saloons different in this regard. He visited the depot, the stock yards, in fact looked Bradford over thoroughly, and his verdict was that the town was a trading point for a large grazing country northward and, as such, had its honest and prosperous citizens but was full of places and people about which he had his doubts. He found an innkeeper whom he believed trustworthy, an old fellow from eastern Texas who had drifted west and was now eking out a poor existence, and he was glad indeed to take charge of Duane and his horse. This innkeeper talked a great deal, a trait which Duane encouraged.

It was after dark, however, that Duane verified his suspicions concerning Bradford. The town was awake after dark, and there was one long row of saloons, dance halls, gambling resorts in full blast. Duane visited them all and was surprised to see wildness and license equal to that of the old river camp of Bland's in its palmiest days. Here it was forced upon him that the farther west one traveled along the river the sparser the respectable settlements, the more numerous the hard characters, and in consequence the greater the element of lawlessness. Duane returned to his lodging house with the conviction that MacNelly's task of cleaning up the Big Bend country was a stupendous one. Yet, he reflected, a company of intrepid and quick-shooting rangers could have soon cleaned up Bradford.

The innkeeper had one other guest that night, a long, black-coated, and wide-sombreroed Texan who reminded Duane of his grandfather. This man had penetrating eyes, a courtly manner, and an unmistakable leaning toward companionship and mint juleps. The gentleman introduced himself as Colonel Webb of Marfa and took it as a matter of course that Duane made no comment about himself.

"Sir, it's all one to me," he said blandly, waving his hand. "I have traveled. Texas is free, and this frontier is one where it's healthier and just as friendly for a man to have no curiosity about his companion. You might be Cheseldine of the Big Bend, or you might be Judge Little of El Paso, it's all one to me. I enjoy drinking with you anyway."

Duane thanked him, conscious of a reserve and dignity that he could not have felt or pretended three months before. And then, as always, he was a good listener. Colonel Webb told, among other things, that he had come out to the Big Bend to look over the affairs of a deceased brother who had been a rancher and a sheriff of one of the larger towns, Sheridan by name.

"Found no affairs, no ranch, not even his grave," said Colonel Webb. "And I tell you, sir, if hell's any tougher than this Big Bend country, I don't want to expiate my sins there."

"From what I see, I imagine sheriffs have a hard row to hoe out here," replied Duane.

The colonel swore lustily. "My brother was the only honest sheriff between Del Rio and El Paso. It was wonderful how long he lasted. But he had nerve . . . he could throw a gun . . . and he was on the square. Then he was wise enough to confine his work to offenders of his own town and neighborhood. He let the riding outlaws alone, else he wouldn't have lasted at all. What this frontier needs, sir, is about six companies of Texas Rangers."

Duane was aware of the colonel's close scrutiny. "Do you know anything about the service?" he asked.

"I used to. Ten years ago when I lived in San Antonio. A fine body of men, sir, and the salvation of Texas."

"Governor Stone doesn't entertain that opinion," said Duane.

Here Colonel Webb exploded. Manifestly the governor was not his choice for a chief executive of the great state. He talked politics for a while and of the vast territory west of the Pecos that seemed never to get a benefit from Austin. He talked enough for Duane to realize that here was just the kind of intelligent, well-informed, honest citizen that he had been trying to meet. He exerted himself, thereafter, to be agreeable and interesting, and he saw presently that

240

here was an opportunity to make a valuable acquaintance, if not a friend.

"I'm a stranger in these parts," said Duane finally. "What is this outlaw situation you speak of?"

"It's damnable, sir, and unbelievable. Not rustling any more but just wholesale herd stealing in which some big cattlemen, supposed to be honest, are equally guilty with the outlaws. On this border, you know, the rustler has always been able to steal cattle in any numbers, but to get rid of big bunches . . . that's the hard job. The gangs operating between here and Valentine evidently have not this trouble. Nobody knows where the stolen stock goes, but I'm not alone in my opinion that most of it goes to several big stockmen. They ship to San Antonio, Austin, New Orleans, also to El Paso. If you travel the stock road between here and Marfa and Valentine, you'll see dead cattle all along the line and stray cattle out in the scrub. The herds have been driven fast and far, and stragglers are not rounded up."

"Wholesale business, eh?" remarked Duane. "Who are these . . . er, big stock buyers?"

Colonel Webb seemed a little startled at the abrupt query. He bent his penetrating gaze upon Duane and thoughtfully stroked his pointed beard. "Names, of course, I'll not mention. Opinions are one thing. Direct accusation another. This is not a healthy country for the informer. There are a thousand men between here and Marfa who could tell things, but what's the use to risk so much? Whom could they tell? There's not even a pretense of law here. There never has been an honestly elected sheriff in this county. Every sheriff I know is richer than I am. No, stranger, I won't mention any names. But I gather that you're peculiarly interested, and I merely suggest that you go out in this town of Bradford and use your eyes. You look able to take care of yourself, which is important if you want to be curious yet still breathe this fine Texas air."

When it came to the outlaws themselves, Colonel Webb was disposed to talk freely. Duane could not judge whether the colonel had made a hobby of that subject, or the outlaws were so striking in personality and deed that any man would know all about them. The great name along the river was Cheseldine, but it seemed to be a name detached from an individual. No person of veracity known to Colonel Webb had ever seen Cheseldine, and those who claimed that doubtful honor varied so diversely in descriptions of the chief that they confused the reality and lent to the outlaw only further mystery. Strange to say of an outlaw leader, but as there was no one who could identify him, so there was no one who could prove he had actually killed a man. Blood flowed like water over the Big Bend country, and it was Cheseldine who spilled it. Yet the fact remained there were no eye-witnesses to connect any individual called Cheseldine with these deeds of violence. In striking contrast to this mystery was the person, character, and cold-blooded action of Poggin and Knell, the chief's lieutenants. They were familiar figures in all the towns within two hundred miles of Bradford. Knell had a record as a gunman with an incredible list of victims, but Poggin was supreme. If Poggin had a friend, no one ever heard of him. There were a hundred stories of his nerve, his wonderful speed with a gun, his passion for gambling, his love of a horse, his cold, implacable, inhuman wiping out of his path any man that crossed it.

"Cheseldine is a name, a terrible name," said Colonel Webb. "Sometimes I wonder if he's not only a name. In that case where does the brains of this gang come from?

No, there must be a master craftsman behind this border pillage. A master capable of handling those terrors, Poggin and Knell. Of all the thousands of outlaws developed by western Texas in the last twenty years, these three are the greatest. In southern Texas, down between the Pecos and the Nueces, there have been and still are many badmen. But I doubt if any outlaw there, possibly excepting Buck Duane, ever equaled Poggin. You've heard of this Duane?"

"Yes, a little," replied Duane quietly. "I'm from southern Texas. Buck Duane, then, is known of out here?"

"Why, man, where isn't his name known?" returned Colonel Webb. "I've kept track of his record, as I have all the others. Of course, Duane, being a lone outlaw, is somewhat of a mystery also but not like Cheseldine. Out here there have drifted many stories of Duane, horrible some of them, but despite them a sort of romance clings to that Nueces outlaw. He's killed three great outlaw leaders, I believe, Bland, Hardin, and the other I forget. Hardin was known in the Big Bend, had friends here. Bland had a hard name at Del Rio."

"Then this man Duane enjoys rather an unusual repute west of the Pecos?" inquired Duane with interest.

"He's considered more of an enemy to his kind than to honest men. I understand Duane has many friends . . . that whole counties swear by him . . . secretly, of course, for he's a hunted outlaw with rewards on his head. His fame in this country appears to hang on his matchless gun play and his enmity towards outlaw chiefs. I've heard many a rancher say: 'I wish to God that Buck Duane would drift out here! I'd give a hundred pesos to see him and Poggin meet.' It's a singular thing, stranger, how jealous these great outlaws are of each other."

"Yes, indeed, all about them is singular," replied Duane.

"Has Cheseldine's gang been busy lately?"

"No. This section has been free of rustling for months, though there's unexplained movements of stock. Probably all the stock that's being shipped now was rustled long ago. Cheseldine works over a wide section, too wide for news to travel inside for weeks. Then, sometimes, he's not heard of at all for a spell. These lulls are pretty surely indicative of a big storm, sooner or later. And Cheseldine's deals, as they grow fewer and farther between, certainly get bigger, more daring. There are some people who think Cheseldine had nothing to do with the bank robberies and train holdups during the last few years in this country, but that's poor reasoning. The jobs have been too well done, too surely covered to be the work of Mexicans or ordinary outlaws."

"What's your view of the outlook? How's all this going to wind up? Will the outlaw ever be driven out?" asked Duane.

"Never. There will always be outlaws along the Rio Grande. All the armies in the world couldn't comb the wild breaks of that fifteen hundred miles of river, but the sway of the outlaws, such as enjoyed by these great leaders, will sooner or later pass. The criminal element flocks to the Southwest but not so thick and fast as the pioneers. Besides, the outlaws kill themselves, and the ranchers are slowly rising in wrath, if not in action. That will come soon. If they only had a leader to start the fight, but that will come. There's talk of vigilantes, the same that were organized in California and are now in force in Idaho. So far it's only talk, but the time will come. The days of Cheseldine and Poggin are numbered."

Duane went to bed that night exceedingly thoughtful. The long trail was growing hot. This voluble colonel had given him new ideas. It came to Duane in surprise that he was famous along the upper Rio Grande. Assuredly he would not long be able to conceal his identity. He had no doubt that he would soon meet the chiefs of this clever and bold rustling gang. He could not decide whether he would be safer unknown or known. In the latter case his one chance lay in the fatality connected with his name, in his power to look it and act it. Duane had never dreamed of any sleuth-hound tendency in his nature, but now he felt something like one.

Above all others his mind fixed on Poggin — Poggin the brute, the executor of Cheseldine's will, but mostly upon Poggin the gunman. This in itself was a warning to Duane. He felt terrible forces at work within him. There was the stern and indomitable resolve to make MacNelly's boast good to the governor of the state — to break up Cheseldine's gang. Yet this was not in Duane's mind before a strange, grim, and deadly instinct arose — one which he had to drive away for fear he would find in it a passion to kill Poggin, not for the state, nor for his word to MacNelly, but for himself. His father's blood and the hard years had made Duane the kind of man who instinctively wanted to meet Poggin. He was sworn to MacNelly's service, and he fought himself to keep that and that only in his mind.

Chapter Eighteen

The following day Duane did indeed use his eyes, and that which interested him drew him by successive details to the stock yards. The corrals were full of dusty, bellowing cattle. There were trample and roar, the shouts of cowboys, the crack of ropes as the herds of steers were driven into the cattle train. Fenced runways led up to ten cars, and every narrow passage was jammed with wild cattle. Ten cars loaded at once! This was big business. Certainly there was no time lost in loading.

Duane sauntered closer to have a look at the brands. It was hard to make out anything clearly in the dust and jumble of the runways or box cars, so he directed his attention to the corrals. This big herd of steers had been driven in over night. Never in such close space had Duane seen such a diversity of brands, but the blotched and acid burned brands so common to the cheating stockman and sometimes to the rustler were here not in evidence.

Duane then sauntered over to the platform of the freight house. Both busy and idle men were there. It did not escape Duane that, as he lounged over toward them, there was a sharp glance directed toward him, and it came from one of the busy men.

"Big shipment," said Duane to one of the idlers.

"Shore is. Nigh on five hundred head in them corrals," replied the fellow.

"Who's the shipper?"

The idler made a wry face and cast a sly eye on Duane. "Reckon you air shore new hereabouts. Who else but Levitt? He's standin' over there."

Duane saw a tall man whose back was turned. He wore a black sombrero, a vest and scarf, and gun and boots like any cowboy, only they were of richer material than cowboys could afford. This man's spurs were made of gold.

"Wealthy feller?" went on Duane, as he watched Levitt.

"Shore aboot owns Bradford. Thet big saloon uptown is his. Then he has stores. An' everybody owes him. A free an' easy man with hosses, jobs, money, anythin' you want. He's only been heah about three years."

"Where'd he come from?" asked Duane.

"Some says Val Verde an' some says El Paso."

"Who buys all this stock for him?"

"Shore he goes all over hisself an' buys. Stands in with the rustlers, they say. It ain't no secret that Levitt buys some stock from rustlers. But anybody'd do thet in this country if a chanst was offered."

Duane sauntered away from his informant and carelessly approached Levitt. His keen eye caught a cowboy in the act of speaking to Levitt manifestly about him, for Levitt instantly wheeled. He had very light skin for so dark-eyed and dark-haired a person. He wore a long mustache and pointed beard. He was talking suavely as he turned, a cool, affable, handsome man with a look of concentrated power.

Duane's keen glance met Levitt's and held it. The old subtle instinctive thrill ran through Duane, only here it might have been that of a tiger. Duane had looked into the eyes of thousands of crooked men — outlaws and fugitives and criminals who had something to hide, whose nerve might have been magnificent, but whose souls were bare to him by reason of his strange instinct. To criminals

247

there was always in the encounter with a stranger that eternal question in the eyes — the searching, human curiosity — the inquisitive unconquerable habit of looking to quell an ever-present fear. Guilt! For Duane it was blazoned in the eyes of this stock buyer, Levitt. Then he returned his gaze to the dusty mêlée below. He was trying to account for this strange gift that had betrayed Levitt to him. The thing was baffling. Perhaps out of his years of agony and the endless flights, when his cunning and his sight and his hearing had been magnified, when all his life centered around that one hated fear of capture, out of all this there had grown a superhuman power to recognize the dread of his own soul in another guilty man's eyes. The guilt Duane divined. And this huge, hurried shipment of cattle gave him a stir of pulse and tingle of nerve rare indeed. When he shifted his gaze again, Levitt had taken a stride toward him and on the instant was in the act of waving back the cowboy who evidently wanted to join him.

"Hello, stranger," said Levitt, "looking for anything . . . to sell a bunch of steers, or get a job, or what?"

"Yes, I'm looking for. . . ."

"For what?" cut in Levitt sharply. His tone bore more than command. The power in it, the dominance of men that breathed there, drew from Duane an irresistible impulse. He leaned toward Levitt.

"I'm looking for Cheseldine!" he said, clearly and low.

Levitt stiffened ever so slightly. Otherwise the only change in him was a lightning-swift dilation and darkening of his eyes.

"*Hell!* Not so loud!" he hissed. "I'll kill somebody for this. What's Poggin mean . . . or Knell? What's up? Who sent you?"

"Came of my own accord," replied Duane.

A slow shade of white, barely perceptible, stole into Levitt's face. "Well, I don't know your man," he said, with narrowing eyelids. "I . . . I mistook you for a cowboy with . . . I've a cattle deal on."

"Save your breath," interrupted Duane in cool sarcasm. "You're Cheseldine!"

At that the soul of this man lay bare — a dark and terrible thing — the mind of a great criminal caught off guard — a vortex of passions chained by a will like steel. Duane read the man clearly. To any but close observers Levitt might have been holding a few casual words with a chance visitor. His right hand twitched on the paper he held, made it ring, and that little action meant the controlling of a dive for his gun. Duane actually admired him in that predicament, even though he stood ready to kill him.

Seldom had Duane seen in the eyes of any man more passion to kill; never had he seen it so controlled by intellect. The great outlaw manifestly saw two meanings in this encounter, and he could not so quickly choose between what might be sheer mindless effrontery or an unparalleled assurance.

"Who in the hell are you?" he asked hoarsely.

"I'm a stranger to the Big Bend," replied Duane. "I came in to join your gang. See you later."

Levitt stared, then recovered himself, and with a dark and sinister glance of eye, he turned away. Again he waved aside the eager cowboy. This fellow turned to look at Duane, and Duane saw in him an ally of the chief's. The others present appeared to be utterly deceived by the nature of that little by-play.

As Duane expected, Levitt hurriedly left the platform,

made his way to a saddled horse, unhitched him, but did not mount. He was followed by the earnest cowboy who likewise led a horse. Their heads were bent together, and Levitt was vehemently waving a hand when they passed out of sight around the corner of the freight house.

"I have located my man!" muttered Duane, and the words were like a deep thrumming in his ears.

Duane went to the station and, entering, seated himself in a quiet corner and composed himself for some hard thinking. It was difficult to decide upon a line of procedure until he new how Levitt would react to that meeting. Duane believed that nothing but an unheard of and amazing bluff would serve to carry his point with Levitt. The stockman could be easily killed or else, though not so easily, made prisoner. But that was not the game. Duane wondered if Levitt's craftiness was equal to his domineering egotism. Which would govern him in a case like this? The chances were that the man was so subtle and keen that he would sense some vague danger to himself in Duane's cool, blunt recognition. Also, he might have the failing common to so many of these violent, powerful leaders — a passionate refusal to brook even the slightest opposition to their wills. Duane concluded that, in a town so dominated as Bradford was, he would not have to wait very long if Levitt were at all like Bland or King Fisher.

Presently Duane sauntered up the main street, as keenly strung as on any walk he had ever made, but nothing happened. He passed Levitt's place, in front of which were dusty, booted men, all packing guns. None of them took any particular notice of Duane.

The day passed then without further incident. That night, however, as Duane was walking through a dark stretch of street someone took a shot at him from an obscure corner.

Duane caught the whistle of a bullet and then the swift shuffle of retreating footsteps. These did not sound as if they were made by boots but by moccasins or sandals. Probably a Mexican had taken a snap shot at him.

At the moment the only other person near was a man across the street, and from his cry and action it was evident the bullet had come nearer to hitting him than Duane. Certainly this other man believed he had been the one at whom the attack had been directed. Duane crossed to him and found him to be a young man, badly frightened. Duane reassured him and walked on toward the station with him.

"It's happened before," said the young man. "I'm the night operator. Was going on duty. If it happens again and I don't get plugged, I'll throw up the damn' job."

Duane made friendly advances toward the young operator, who said his name was Buell, and gave him some advice about how to avoid risks in the future.

"I'm scared to death of the town," declared Buell. "El Paso was tough enough. But this place's got El Paso skinned to death. Thanks for your advice, mister. I won't forget it in a hurry."

They parted at the station, and Duane went back uptown more pleased at the meeting than sore over being shot at, and he considered it would be a clever move on his part, every time he visited Bradford in the future, to look up the young operator. There might come a time when he would be useful. Returning to his lodgings, he found that the genial Colonel Webb had departed. He had supper, and then, as always a victim to suspense unable to remain inactive, he went out again. He walked up and down the street, and the more he pondered the matter, the more he became sure that delay would only make his task harder. A slow and cautious and observant approach to the scene

251

of his operations had been wise, but now that he was on the ground the quicker he worked the more chance he had of success. He believed he gauged the hazard, and to him it did not seem as great as MacNelly had intimated. Swift action, keen judgment, then a monstrous show of nerve, these it would take to make him a member of this outlaw band. But luck was a great factor, perhaps the greatest. If he would only have some flash of insight — if only some incalculable stroke of fortune would favor him!

Duane passed Levitt's place once, walking slowly. He passed again, still slower, and the third time he halted — then, with a stride like a leaf that marked his decision to force this game, he reached the door and entered.

His seeing, hearing, feeling faculties were at their old strong tension, but he had outlined no order or plan of action. This must develop from the sequence of events succeeding his bearding the lion in his den. The big gambling room was well lighted. There were a number of occupants, some at monte and faro tables, others at the bar. Among the latter Duane saw the cowboy who had been with Levitt at the stock yards. As Duane walked up, this man eyed him closely yet without hostility or impudence. Used to simple, elemental, direct natures such as characterized these outdoor men, Duane sensed only curiosity in Levitt's companion. Duane spoke amiably and brought up against the corner of the bar. The fellow answered the greeting shortly, however without rudeness.

"Drink with me?" asked Duane.

"Never turned down a drink in my life, 'ceptin' water," was the reply.

Both ordered and drank, with eyes steady and level over the rim of glasses. This apparent drinking good fellowship did not count for much with Duane. He had seen men meet, speak, laugh, raise their glasses to each other, then throw them down and go for guns. Nevertheless he gathered one favorable point from this cowboy's acquiescence.

"Did the boss mention me?" asked Duane easily, in a low tone.

The cowboy grinned. "Reckon he did."

"Hope I didn't give offense. I'm strange here, but I never was backward nowheres."

"My boss said you just paid him a doubtful compliment, but he wasn't the gent you took him for."

"That all?" queried Duane.

"About all, I reckon, 'cept he guessed you wasn't lackin' in nerve, if you really believed you was bracin' the gent mentioned."

Here Duane was confronted with the singular impression that this cowboy, evidently in Levitt's employ and a picked hand, treated the matter as a joke and had no inkling of the real character of his employer. Duane trusted these strange instinctive impressions. He had seldom found them false.

Duane made no further effort toward becoming acquainted and, as the cowboy maintained his disinterested manner, they naturally separated. Duane lounged around the room, watched the gamblers, even sat in a cheap monte game for an hour and stayed there till midnight, hoping Levitt might come in. When he did not, Duane left and went back to his lodgings.

Next morning he learned from his loquacious landlord that Levitt had left Bradford on the night train. He was in the habit of going away often, having big interests in other towns. If Duane had considered it a wise move, he would have tried to trace Levitt, but that probably would be futile. The stockman might return to Bradford the next day, and besides there was Duane's horse to be taken care of, and that horse might any time become indispensable to the success of this venture.

Duane waited a couple of days, visiting Buell several times, curbing his impatience, and then he thought of communicating with MacNelly. That matter appeared to be a vastly easier one than either MacNelly or he had anticipated. What would the ranger captain think when he learned that Duane had located the great outlaw in a good-size town, where there were honest people, post office, railroad, and telegraph? MacNelly had no intimation of what a deep and powerful rascal this Cheseldine was. After thinking over the several opportunities available, Duane decided to write a letter. This he did, using the cipher code MacNelly had given him, and he stated that he had located his man and might be ready any day for help. He had yet to plan the trap, but in case that plan could not be materialized in reasonable time, he wanted the rangers to join him at Bradford. For the present MacNelly was to assemble all his available rangers at San Antonio, and there await further advice, which would no doubt be a summons addressed to Nelson C. Mack. Duane set about the mailing of it. A little before the time the night mail going east was due, Duane went to the station. Buell, the young operator, was glad to see Duane.

"Say, son, I want you to do a favor for me," said Duane.

"Sure. Only too glad," replied Buell.

"Usually you have a lot of letters to go east on Number Six, don't you? I think I saw you with some the other night."

"Not usually. Sometimes I have a good many. Tonight, it happens, I've got a bunch."

"Do you know the mail clerk in Number Six?"

"Sure do. He's from my town, a fine chap. What's up? You're going to send money by letter. Better send it by Wells Fargo. Safer."

"Not money but an important letter. Now I want to know if this letter will go through any other hands besides the clerk's on Number Six?"

"Not till it reaches its destination. You can be sure of that, unless of course Number Six is held up by train robbers and the mail sacks taken. It's a safe bet that Number Six will be hit some day."

"I'll risk that. It's only the address that matters with my letter. The contents are unreadable."

Duane glanced casually around the little office and at the windows then laid the letter on Buell's desk. This move seemed another direct one in line with the forcing of this game. Buell read the address, and his sudden start showed he was familiar with the Texas Rangers, if not with Mac-Nelly's name. Likewise he showed an adroitness and presence of mind by slipping the letter into a packet as footsteps sounded without, and dark faces passed the windows. Presently he turned with bright eyes towards Duane.

"I savvy," he said. "By George! I wondered about you . . . say, tell me . . . ?"

"Son, I can't tell you anything now," replied Duane, "except you see I'm trusting you. Later perhaps you can help me. I want to know this. Suppose you wired San Antonio now . . . an important message to the address on that letter . . . would the message be read by anyone during transmission . . . particularly by any operator west of the Pecos?"

"The chances are the message might be heard but not read except by the operator called. The instrument grows monotonous. An operator hears only his call, you might say."

"Still, we can't be absolutely sure?"

"No. But it's a thousand to one chance."

"All right. Thanks. Keep this under your hat and look for me any time."

After that night Duane found waiting harder than ever. The temptation to ride to Ord was well-nigh overpowering, but he conquered it by the process of reasoning out his ever-growing desire to meet Knell and Poggin. These men haunted him as no dead man ever had. They represented so much brutal and vicious action. Their lives and deeds were the kind which were blamable for a burden of infamy such as had been shouldered upon him. He had been forced to suffer like a poisoned wolf because there were such outlaws alive.

As the days went by, Duane found it almost impossible to forget his old self in this new character of ranger, but he stayed at or near Bradford, never riding farther away than a day's journey, making a casual acquaintance with ranchers and learning the lay of different country. All this augured well for his eventual victory. Still his old implacable patience had begun to burn out under this mounting desire. Every night when he lay down, every morning when he rose, it was to earn a harder, dearer won battle over himself. Sometimes he grew angry. It was inconceivable that this pursuit should become personal, that he wanted Poggin and Knell more than Cheseldine, that when he thought of the two it was with no supposition of their capture but of their death. At length, driven into a corner with himself, he faced the truth — and with a shuddering renewed knowledge of himself realized that he wanted, more than anything he had ever wanted, to meet Knell, and then Poggin, to stand over them, to make them see him with their last fading sight. This was indeed not the service he had sworn to MacNelly, and Duane believed if he was anything it was honorable. The danger of failure now appeared to be in himself — in actually becoming what he had never yet been, despite his record — in the working out of that fatal heritage which yet, unless he fought with all his soul, might make him kill for the sake of killing. Not in lawful service, or self-defense, but because passion had claimed him! How horrible it would be now when he was free, no longer an outlaw, if that hellish instinct conquered him — that strange incomprehensible conjecture, doubt, anger concerning another man's speed with a gun. Duane dreaded while he longed for the climax and in spite of himself felt he would be true to his duty.

At the end of two weeks Bradford was amazed, and Duane startled, by inauthenticated news of Levitt's leaving and making deals to dispose of his Bradford property. Duane pondered over this rumor. If it were true, what did it mean? Levitt, if he were really Cheseldine, had shown himself a criminal of higher rank, of different caliber than any outlaw leaders Duane had ever studied. It was possible, of course, for Cheseldine to be as great as that colossal monster of evil, Plummer of Idaho, who became mayor and honored citizen while secretly he was the head of the most terrible and perfectly organized band of robbers and murderers ever known in the West. If Levitt were Cheseldine, then his possibilities must not be gauged and judged by those of lesser outlaws. The thing that blinded most leaders in crime was power. They rested upon violent deeds and felt safe by reason of the fear of them. They retrograded and became merely elemental, but one now and then, and perhaps Cheseldine, showed brains.

The night of the day that this news came to Bradford, Number 6, the mail and express train going east, was held up by train robbers, the Wells Fargo messenger killed over his safe, the mail clerk wounded, the bags carried away. The engine of Number 6 came into town minus even a tender, and engineer and fireman told conflicting stories. A posse of railroad men and citizens, led by the sheriff Duane knew was crooked, was made up before the engine steamed back to pick up the rest of the train. Duane had the sudden inspiration that he had been cudgeling his mind to find and, acting upon it, he got his horse and left Bradford unobserved. As he rode out into the night, over a dark trail in the direction of Ord, he uttered a short, grim, sardonic laugh at the hope that he might be taken for a train robber.

He rode at an easy trot most of the night and, when the black peak of Ord mountain loomed up against the stars, he halted, tied his horse, and slept until dawn. Then he took his time cooking breakfast. When the sun was well up, he saddled Bullet and, leaving the trail where his tracks showed plainly in the ground, he put his horse to the rocks and brush. He selected an exceedingly rough, round-about, and difficult course to Ord, hid his tracks with the skill of a long-hunted fugitive, and arrived there with his horse winded and covered with lather. It added considerable to his arrival that Fletcher and several others saw him come in the back way, through the lots, and jump a fence into the road. Duane led Bullet up to the porch where Fletcher stood wiping his beard. He was hatless, vestless, and evidently had just enjoyed a morning drink.

"Howdy, Dodge," said Fletcher laconically.

Duane replied, and the other men returned the greeting with interest.

"Jim, my hoss's done up. I want to hide him from any

chance tourists as might happen to ride up curious-like."

"Haw! Haw! Haw!"

Duane gathered encouragement from that chorus of coarse laughter.

"Wal, if them tourists ain't too durned snoopy, the hoss'll be safe in the 'dobe shack back of Bill's here. Feed thar, too, but you'll hev to rustle water."

Duane led Bullet to the place indicated, had care of his welfare, and left him there. Upon returning to the tavern porch, Duane saw the group of men had been added to by others, some of whom he had seen before. Without comment Duane walked along the edge of the road and, wherever one of the tracks of his horse showed, he carefully obliterated it. This procedure was attentively watched by Fletcher and his companions.

"Wal, Dodge," remarked Fletcher as Duane returned, "thet's safer'n prayin' fer rain."

Duane's reply was a remark, as loquacious as Fletcher's, to the effect that a long, slow, monotonous ride was conducive to thirst. They all joined him, unmistakably friendly, but Knell was not here and most assuredly not Poggin. Fletcher was no common outlaw, but whatever his ability it probably lay in execution of orders. Apparently at that time these men had nothing to do but drink and lounge around the tavern. Evidently they were poorly supplied with money, though Duane observed they could borrow a peso occasionally from the bartender. Duane set out to make himself agreeable and succeeded. There was card playing for small stakes, idle jest of coarse nature, much bantering among the younger fellows, and occasionally a mild quarrel. All morning men came and went until all told, Duane calculated, he had seen at least fifty. Towards the middle of the afternoon a young fellow burst into the saloon and yelled one word:

"Posse!"

From the scramble to get outdoors, Duane judged that word and the ensuing action was rare in Ord.

"What the hell!" muttered Fletcher as he gazed down the road at a dark compact bunch of horses and riders. "Fust time I ever seen thet in Ord! We're gettin' popular, like them camps out of Valentine. Wish Phil was here or Poggy. Now all you gents keep quiet. I'll do the talkin'."

The posse entered the town, trotted up on dusty horses, and halted in a bunch before the tavern. The party consisted of about twenty men, all heavily armed, and evidently in charge of a clean-cut, lean-limbed cowboy. Duane experienced considerable satisfaction at the absence of the sheriff who, he had understood, was to lead the posse. Perhaps he was out in another direction with a different force.

"Hello, Jim Fletcher," called the cowboy.

"Howdy," replied Fletcher.

At his short dry response and the way he strode leisurely out before the posse, Duane found himself modifying his contempt for Fletcher. The outlaw was different now.

"Fletcher, we've tracked a man to all but three miles of this place. Tracks plain as the nose on your face. Found his camp. Then he lit into the brush an' we lost the trail. Didn't have no tracker with us. Think he went into the mountains. But we took a chance an' rode over the rest of the way, seein' Ord was so close. Anybody come in here late last night or early this mornin'?"

"Nope," replied Fletcher.

His response was what Duane had expected from his manner, and evidently the cowboy took it as a matter of course. He turned to the others of the posse, entering into a low consultation. There was obviously a difference of

260

opinion, if not real discussion, in that posse.

"Didn't I tell you this was a wild goose chase, comin' way out here," protested an old hawk-faced rancher. "Them hoss tracks we follered ain't like any of them we seen at the water tank where the train was held up."

"I'm not so sure of that," replied the leader.

"Wal, Guthrie, I've follered tracks all my life. . . ."

"But you couldn't keep to the trail this feller made in the brush."

"Gimme time an' I could. Thet takes time. An' heah you go hell-bent fer election! But it's a wrong lead, out this way. If you're right, this road agent, after he killed his pals, would hev rid' back right through town. An' with them mail bags! Supposin' they was greasers? Some greasers has sense an', when it comes to thievin', they're shore cute."

"But we ain't got any reason to believe this robber who murdered the greasers is a Mexican himself. I tell you it was a slick job, done by no ordinary sneak. Didn't you hear the facts? One greaser hopped the engine an' covered the engineer an' brakeman. Another greaser kept flashin' his gun outside the train. The big man who shoved back the car door an' did the killin' . . . he was the real gent, an' don't you forget it."

Some of the posse sided with the cowboy leader and some with the old cattleman. Finally the young leader disgustedly gathered up his bridle.

"Aw, hell, thet sheriff shooed you off this trail. Mebbe he had reason! Savvy thet? If I had a bunch of cowboys with me . . . I tell you what . . . I'd take a chance an' clean up this hole!"

All the while Jim Fletcher stood quietly with his hands in his pockets.

"Guthrie, I'm shore treasurin' up your friendly talk," he said. The menace was in the tone not the content of his speech.

"You can . . . an' be damned to you, Fletcher!" called Guthrie, as the horses started.

Fletcher, standing out alone before the others of his clan, watched the posse out of sight.

"Lucky fer you-all that Poggy wasn't here," he said as they disappeared. Then with a thoughtful look he strode up on the porch and led Duane away from the others into the barroom. When he looked into Duane's face, it was somehow an entirely changed scrutiny.

"Dodge, where'd you hide the stuff? I reckon I git in on this deal, seein' I staved off Guthrie."

Duane played his part. Here was his opportunity and, like a tiger after prey, he seized it. First he coolly eyed the outlaw and disclaimed any knowledge whatever of the train robbery, other than what Fletcher had heard himself. Then at Fletcher's persistence and admiration and increasing show of friendliness he laughed occasionally and allowed himself to swell with pride, though still denying it. Next he feigned a lack of consistent will power and seemed to be wavering under Fletcher's persuasion and grew silent, then surly. Fletcher, evidently sure of ultimate victory desisted for the time being. However, in his solicitous regard and close companionship for the rest of that day he betrayed the bent of his mind.

Later when Duane started up, announcing his intention to get his horse and make for camp out in the brush, Fletcher seemed grievously offended.

"Why don't you stay with me? I've got a comfortable 'dobe over here. Didn't I stick by you when Guthrie an' his bunch came up? Supposin' I hadn't showed a cold hand to him?

You'd be swingin' somewheres now. I tell you, Dodge, it ain't square."

"I'll square it. I pay my debts," replied Duane. "But I can't put up here all night. If I belonged to the gang, it'd be different."

"What gang?" asked Fletcher bluntly.

"Why, Cheseldine's."

Fletcher's beard nodded as his jaw dropped.

Duane laughed. "I run into him the other day over at Bradford. Knowed him on sight. He was loadin' a big bunch of steers. Sure he's the king-pin rustler. Shippin' stolen cattle by train! I was some took back. But when he seen me an' asked me what reason I had for bein' on earth or some such like . . . why, I up an' told him."

Fletcher appeared staggered. "Who in all-fired hell are you talkin' about?"

"Didn't I tell you once. Cheseldine. He calls himself Levitt over there."

All of Fletcher's face not covered by hair turned a dirty white. "Cheseldine . . . Levitt!" he whispered hoarsely. "Gawd Almighty! You braced the. . . ." Then a remarkable transformation came over the outlaw. He gulped; he straightened his face; he controlled his agitation. But he could not send the healthy brown back to his face. Duane, watching this rude man, marveled at the change in him, the sudden checking motive, the proof of a wonderful fear and loyalty. It all meant Cheseldine — a master of men.

"Who air you?" queried Fletcher in a queer, strained voice.

"You gave me a handle, didn't you? Dodge. Thet's as good as any. Shore it hits me hard. Jim, I've been pretty lonely for years, an' I'm gettin' in need of pals. Think it over, will you? See you *mañana.*"

The outlaw watched Duane go off after his horse, watched

him as he returned to the tavern, watched him ride out into the darkness, all without another word.

Duane left the town, threaded a quiet passage through cactus and mesquite to a spot he had marked before, and made ready for the night. His mind was so full that he found sleep aloof. Luck at last was playing his game. He sensed the first slow heave of a mighty crisis. The end, always haunting, had to be sternly blotted from thought. It was the approach that needed all his mind.

He passed the night there, and late in the morning, after watching trail and road from a ridge, he returned to Ord. If Jim Fletcher tried to disguise his surprise, the effort was a failure. Certainly he had not expected to see Duane again. Duane allowed himself a little freedom with Fletcher, an attitude hitherto lacking.

That afternoon a horseman rode in from Bradford, an outlaw evidently well known and liked by his fellows. Duane heard him say, before he could possibly have been told the train robber was in Ord, that the loss of money in the hold-up was slight. Like a flash Duane saw the luck of this report. He pretended not to have heard.

In the early twilight, at an opportune moment, he called Fletcher to him and, linking his arm within the outlaw's, drew him off in a stroll to a log bridge spanning a little gully. Here, after gazing around, he took out a roll of bills, spread it out, split it equally, and without a word handed one half to Fletcher. With clumsy fingers Fletcher ran through the roll.

"Five hundred!" he exclaimed. "Dodge, that's damn' handsome of you, considerin' the job wasn't. . . ."

"Considerin' nothin'," interrupted Duane. "I'm makin' no reference to a job, here or there. You did me a good turn. I split my pile. If thet doesn't make us pards, good turns an' money ain't no use in this country."

Fletcher was won. The two men spent much time together after that day — ate, drank, smoked, gambled, hunted, rode, and all but slept together, for Duane held to his custom of going to the open at night. He made up a short fictitious history about himself that satisfied the outlaw, only it drew forth a laughing jest upon Duane's modesty. For Fletcher did not hide his belief that this new partner was a man of achievements. Knell and Poggin, and then Cheseldine himself, would be persuaded of this fact, so Fletcher boasted. He had influence. He would use it. He pulled a strike with Knell, but nobody on earth, not even the boss, had any influence on Poggin. Poggin was concentrated part of the time; all the rest he was bursting hell. But Poggin loved a horse. He had never loved anything else. He could be won with that black horse, Bullet. Cheseldine was already won by Duane's monumental nerve; otherwise, he would have tried to kill Duane.

Little by little, day by day, Duane learned the points he longed to know, and how indelibly they etched themselves in his memory. Cheseldine's hiding place was on the far slope of Mount Ord, in a deep, high-walled valley. He always went there just before a contemplated job where he met and planned with his lieutenants. Then, while they executed, he basked in the sunshine before one or another of the public places he owned. He was there in the Ord den now — getting ready to plan the biggest job yet. It was a bank robbery, but one about which Fletcher had not as yet been advised.

Then, when Duane had pumped the now amenable outlaw of all details pertaining to the present, he gathered data and facts and places covering the period of the ten years Fletcher had been with Cheseldine. And herewith was unfolded a history so dark in its bloody regime, so incredible in its brazen daring, so appalling in its proof of the outlaw's sweep and grasp of the country from Pecos to Rio Grande that Duane was stunned. Compared to this Cheseldine of the Big Bend, to this Levitt of Bradford, to this rancher, stock buyer, cattle speculator, property holder, all the outlaws Duane had ever known sank into insignificance. The power of the man stunned Duane; the strange fidelity given him, the intricate inside working of his great system, was equally stunning. But when Duane recovered from that, the old terrible passion to kill consumed him. It raged fiercely, and it could not be checked. If that red-handed Poggin, if that cold-eyed, dead-faced Knell had only been at Ord! But they were not, and Duane with help of time got what he hoped was the upper hand on himself.

Chapter Nineteen

Again inaction and suspense dragged at Duane's spirit. Like a leashed hound with a keen scent in his face, Duane wanted to leap forth, but he was bound. He almost fretted. Something called to him over the bold wild brow of Mount Ord but, while Fletcher stayed in Ord, waiting for Knell and Poggin or for orders, Duane knew his game was again a waiting one. Suddenly a thought flashed into his mind, bringing patience — the longer he was detained, the surer MacNelly was to have time to receive his message and act upon it.

Then one day there were signs of the long quiet of Ord being broken. A messenger, strange to Duane, rode in on a scout mission that had to do with Fletcher. When he went away, Fletcher became addicted to thoughtful moods and lonely walks. He seldom drank, and this in itself was a striking contrast to former behavior. The messenger came again. Whatever communication he brought, it had a remarkable effect upon the outlaw. Duane was present in the tavern when the fellow arrived, saw the few words whispered but did not hear them. Fletcher turned white with anger or fear, perhaps both, and he cursed like a madman. The messenger, a lean, dark-faced, hard-riding fellow, reminding Duane of the cowboy, Guthrie, left the tavern without even a drink and rode away, off to the west. This westerly direction mystified and fascinated Duane as much as did the southerly direction beyond

267

Mount Ord. Where were Knell and Poggin? Apparently they were not at present with the leader on the mountain. After the messenger left, Fletcher grew silent and surly. He had presented a variety of moods to Duane's observation, and this latest one was provocative of thought. Fletcher was dangerous. It became clear now that the other outlaws of the camp feared him, kept out of his way. Duane let Fletcher alone yet closely watched him.

Perhaps an hour after the messenger had left, not longer, Fletcher manifestly arrived at some decision, and he called for his horse. Then he went to his shack and returned. To Duane the outlaw looked in shape both to ride and fight. He gave orders for the men in camp to keep close until he returned. Then he mounted.

"Come here, Dodge," he called.

Duane went up and laid a hand on the pommel of the saddle. Fletcher walked his horse with Duane beside him till they reached the log bridge, where he halted.

"Dodge, I'm in bad with Knell," he said. "An' it 'pears I'm the cause of friction between Knell and Poggy. Knell never had any use fer me, an', Poggy's been square, if not friendly. The boss has a big deal on, an' here it's bein' held up because of this. He's waitin' over there on the mountain to give orders to Knell an' Poggy, an' neither one's showin' up. I've got to stand in the breach, an' I ain't enjoyin' the prospects."

"What's the trouble about, Jim?" asked Duane.

"Reckon it's a little about you, Dodge," said Fletcher dryly. "Knell hadn't any use fer you thet day. He ain't got no use fer a man unless he can rule him. Some of the boys here hev blabbed before I edged in with my say, an' there's hell to pay. Knell claims to know somethin' about you thet'll make both the boss an' Poggy sick when he springs

268

it, but he's keepin' quiet. Hard man to figger . . . thet Knell. Reckon you'd better go back to Bradford fer a day or so, then camp out till I come back."

"Why?"

"Wal, because there ain't any use fer you to git in bad, too. The gang will ride over here any day. If they're friendly, I'll light a fire on the hill there, say three nights from tonight. If you don't see it thet night, you hit the trail. I'll do what I can. Jim Fletcher sticks to his pals. So long, Dodge."

Then he rode away, leaving Duane in a quandary. This news was black. Things had been working out so well. Here was a setback. At the moment Duane did not know which way to turn, but certainly he had no idea of going back to Bradford. Friction between the two great lieutenants of Cheseldine! Open hostility — between one of them and another of the chief's right-hand men! Among outlaws that sort of thing was deadly serious. Generally such matters were settled with guns. Duane gathered encouragement even from disaster. Perhaps the disintegration of Cheseldine's great band had already begun.

What did Knell know? Duane did not circle around the idea with doubts and hopes — if Knell knew anything, it was that this stranger in Ord, this new partner of Fletcher's, was no less than Buck Duane. Well, it was about time, thought Duane, that he made use of his name, if it were to help him at all. That name had been MacNelly's hope. He had anchored his whole scheme to Duane's fame. Duane was tempted to ride off after Fletcher and stay with him. This, however, would hardly be fair to an outlaw who had been fair to him. Duane concluded to await developments and, when the gang rode in to Ord, probably from their various hiding places, he would be there ready to be denounced by Knell. Duane could not see any other culmination of this series of events than a meeting between Knell and himself. If that terminated fatally for Knell, there was every probability of Duane's being in no worse situation than he was now. If Poggin took up the quarrel . . . ! Here Duane accused himself again — tried in vain to revolt from a judgment that he was only reasoning out excuses to meet these outlaws.

Meanwhile, instead of waiting, why not hunt up Cheseldine in his mountain retreat? The thought no sooner struck Duane than he was hurrying for his horse. He left Ord, ostensibly toward Bradford, but once out of sight he turned off the road, circled through the brush, and several miles south of the town struck a narrow grass-grown trail that Fletcher had told him led to Cheseldine's camp. The horse tracks along this trail were not less than a week old and very likely much more. It wound between low brush-covered foothills, through arroyos and gullies lined with mesquite, cottonwood, and scrub oak.

In an hour Duane struck the slope of Mount Ord and, as he climbed, he got a view of the rolling black-spotted country, partly desert, partly fertile, with long bright lines of dry stream beds winding away to grow dim in the distance. He got among broken rocks and cliffs, and here the open, downward-rolling land disappeared, and he was hard put to find the trail. He lost it repeatedly and made slow progress. Finally he climbed into a region of all rock benches, rough here, smooth there, with only an occasional scratch of iron horseshoe to guide him. Many times he had to go ahead and then work to right or left till he found his way again. It was slow work; it took all day; and night found him half way up the mountain. He halted at a little side cañon with grass and water, and here he made camp.

270

The night was clear and cool at that height, with a dark blue sky and a streak of stars blinking across. With this day of action behind him he felt better satisfied than he had been for some time. Here, on this venture, he was answering to a call that had so often directed his movements, perhaps his life, and it was one in which logic or intelligence could take little stock. On this night, lonely like the ones he used to spend in the Nueces gorge and memorable of them because of a likeness to that old hiding place, he felt the pressing return of old haunting things — the past so long ago — wild flights — dead faces — and one quiveringly alive, white, tragic, with its dark, intently speaking eyes. To that last memory he yielded until he slept.

In the morning, satisfied that he had left still fewer tracks than he had followed up this trail, he guided his horse to the head of the cañon. There was a narrow crack in low cliffs and otherwise branches of cedar fenced him in. He went back and took up the trail on foot.

Without the horse he made better time and climbed through deep cliffs, wide cañons, over ridges, up shelving slopes, along precipices — a long, hard climb till he reached what he concluded was a divide. Going down was easier, though; the farther he followed this dim and winding trail, the wilder the broken battlements of rock. Above him he saw the black fringe of piñon and pine and above that the bold peak, bare, yellow like a desert butte. Once, through a wide gateway between great escarpments, he saw the lower country beyond the range, and beyond this, vast and clear as it lay in his sight, was the great river that made the Big Bend. He went down and down, wondering how a horse could follow that broken trail, believing there must be another and better one somewhere into Che-

271

seldine's hiding place.

He rounded a jutting corner, where view had been shut off, and presently came out upon the rim of a high wall. Beneath, like a green gulf seen through blue haze, lay an amphitheater walled in on the two sides he could see. It lay perhaps a thousand feet below him. Plain as all the other features of that wild environment there shone out a big redstone or adobe cabin, white water shining between green borders, and horses and cattle dotting the levels. It was a peaceful, beautiful scene. Duane could not help grinding his teeth at the thought of Cheseldine's living there in quiet and ease.

Duane worked half way down to the level and, well hidden in a niche, he settled himself to watch both trail and valley. He made note of the position of the sun and saw that, if anything developed, or if he decided to descend any farther, there was small likelihood of his getting back to his camp before dark. To try that after nightfall, he imagined, would be vain effort.

He bent keen and fascinated eyes in a downward gaze. The cabin appeared to be a crude structure, though large in size, and of course had been built by outlaws. There was no gardener, no cultivated field, no corral; excepting for the rude pile of stones and logs plastered together with mud, the valley was as wild probably as on the day of discovery. Duane seemed to have been watching for a long time before he saw any sign of a man, and this one apparently went to the stream for water and returned to the cabin.

The sun went down behind the wall, and shadows were born in the darker places of the valley. Duane began to want to get closer to that cabin. What had he taken this arduous climb for? He held back, however, trying to evolve further plans.

While he was pondering, the shadows quickly gathered and darkened. If he was to go back to camp, he must set out at once. Still he lingered. Suddenly his wide-roving eye caught sight of two horsemen riding up the valley. They must have entered at a point below, around the huge abutment of rock beyond Duane's range of sight. Their horses were tired and stopped at the stream for a long drink.

Duane left his perch, took to the steep trail, and descended as fast as he could without making noise. It did not take him long to reach the valley floor. It was almost level, with deep grass, and here and there clumps of bushes. Twilight was already thick down here. Duane marked the location of the trail and then began to slip, like a shadow, through the grass and from bush to bush. He saw a bright light before he made out the dark outline of the cabin. Then he heard voices, a merry whistle, a coarse song, and the clink of iron cooking utensils. He smelled fragrant wood smoke. He saw moving, dark figures cross the light. Evidently there was a wide door, or else the fire was out in the open.

Duane swerved to the left, out of direct line with the light, and thus was able to see better. Then he advanced noiselessly but swiftly toward the back of the house. There were trees close to the wall. He would make no noise, and he could scarcely be seen — if only there were no watch dog. All his outlaw days he had taken risks, with only his useless life at stake; now with that changed, he advanced stealthily and boldly as an Indian. He reached the cover of the trees and knew he was hidden in their shadows, for at few paces distance he had been able to see only their tops. From there he slipped up to the house and felt along the wall with his hands.

He came to a crack between logs and stones through which light shone. He peered in. He saw a room shrouded in shadows, a lamp turned low, a table, chairs. He saw an open door with bright flare beyond but could not see the fire. Voices came indistinctly. Without hesitation Duane stole farther along — all the way to the end of the cabin. Peering around, he saw only the flare of light on bare ground. Retracing his cautious steps, he paused at the crack again, saw that no man was in the room, and then he went in around that end of the cabin. Fortune favored him. There were bushes, an old shed, a woodpile, all the cover he needed at that corner. He did not even need to crawl.

Before he peeped between the rough corner of wall and the brush growing close to it, Duane paused a moment. This excitement was different from that he had always felt when pursued. It had no bitterness, no pain, no dread. There was as much danger here, perhaps more, yet it was not the same. Then he looked.

He saw a bright fire, a red-faced man bending over it whistling while he handled a steaming pot. Over him was a roofed shed built against the wall with two open sides and two supporting posts. Duane's second glance, not so blinded by the sudden bright light, made out other men, three in the shadow, two in the flare but with backs to him.

"It's a smoother trail by long odds but ain't so short as the one right over the mountain," one outlaw was saying.

"What's eatin' you, Pan Handle?" ejaculated another. "Blossom an' me rode from Faraway Springs where Poggin is with some of the gang."

"Excuse me, Phil. Shore I didn't see you come in, an' Boldt never said nothin'!"

"It took you a long time to get here, but I guess that's just as well," spoke up a smooth, suave voice with a ring in it.

Levitt's voice — Cheseldine's voice! Here they were — Cheseldine — Phil Knell — Blossom Kane — Pan Handle Smith — Boldt — how well Duane remembered the names! — all here, the big men of Cheseldine's gang, except the biggest, Poggin. Duane had holed them, and his sensations of the moment deadened sight and sound of what was before him. He sank down, controlled himself, silenced a mounting exultation, then from a less strained position he peered forth again.

The outlaws were waiting for supper. Their conversation might have been that of cowboys in camp, ranchers at a roundup. Duane listened with eager ears, waiting for the business talk that he felt would come. All the time he watched with the eyes of a wolf upon its quarry. Blossom Kane was the lean-limbed messenger who had so angered Fletcher. Boldt was a giant in stature, dark, bearded, silent. Pan Handle Smith was the red-faced cook, merry, profane, a short bowlegged man resembling many rustlers Duane had known, particularly Luke Stevens. Knell, who sat there tall, slim, was like a boy in build, like a boy in years, with his pale, smooth, expressionless face and his cold gray eyes. Cheseldine, who leaned against the wall, handsome, with his pointed face and beard like an aristocrat, resembled many a rich Louisiana planter Duane had met. The sixth man sat so much in the shadow that he could not be plainly discerned and, though addressed, his name was not mentioned.

Pan Handle Smith carried pots and pans into the cabin and cheerfully called out: "If you goddamn gents air hungry fer grub . . . don't look fer me to feed you with a spoon."

275

The outlaws piled inside, making a great bustle and clatter as they set to their meal. Like hungry men they talked little. Duane waited there a while then guardedly got up and crept around to the other side of the cabin. After he became used to the dark again, he ventured to steal along the wall to a crack and peeped in. The outlaws were in the first room and could not be seen.

Duane waited. The moments dragged endlessly. His heart pounded. Cheseldine entered, turned up the light and, taking a box of cigars from the table, he carried it out.

"Here you fellows, go outside and smoke," he said. "Knell, come on in now. Let's get it over."

He returned, sat down, and lighted a cigar for himself. He put his booted feet on the table.

Duane saw that the room was comfortably, even luxuriously furnished. There must have been a good trail, he thought, else how could all that stuff have been packed in there. Most assuredly it could not have come over the trail he had traveled. Presently he heard the men go outside and their voices became indistinct. Then Knell came to join Cheseldine and seated himself without any of his chief's ease. He seemed preoccupied and, as always, cold.

"What's wrong, Knell? Why didn't you get her sooner?" queried Cheseldine.

"Poggin, damn him! We're on the outs again."

"What for?"

"Aw, he needn't have got sore. He's breakin' a new hoss over there at Faraway, an' you know him where a hoss's concerned. That kept him, I reckon, more than anythin'!"

"What else? Get it out of your system so we can go on to the new job."

"Well, it begins back a ways. I don't know how long ago . . . weeks . . . a stranger rode into Ord, an' got down

276

easy-like, as if he owned the place. He seemed familiar to me, but I wasn't sure. We looked him over, an' I left, tryin' to place him in mind."

"What'd he look like?" asked Cheseldine.

"Rangy, powerful man, white hair over his temples, still, hard face, eyes like knives. The way he packed his guns, the way he walked an' stood, an' swung his right hand, showed me what he was. You can't fool me on the gun sharp. And he had a grand hoss, a big black."

"I've met your man," said Cheseldine. "Had a . . . a rather pleasant little chat with him."

"No!" exclaimed Knell. It was wonderful to hear surprise expressed by this man that did not in the least show any in his strange physiognomy.

"Yes. I saw him rather too interested in a cattle shipment of mine, so I asked him what he was looking for. I'll gamble you can't guess what he said."

"I'm not gamblin' on this man," replied Knell grimly.

"He said he was looking for . . . Cheseldine!"

Knell sat perfectly motionless, like a statue.

"You could have knocked me down with a feather," continued Cheseldine. "I made a blunder . . . was off my balance . . . mentioned you and Poggy before I got back my wits. Then he laughed in my face . . . called my bluff hard."

"He *knew* you!"

"I should smile," replied Cheseldine, and he showed his white teeth.

Knell's stiff body flashed into action as he banged his fist down upon the table. "Laugh! It's funny! Ho! Ho! Wait, Boss, *wait!* I'll spring in on him a minute. How'n hell did you miss gettin' it . . . that's what stumps me?"

"Getting what?" queried Cheseldine blankly.

277

Knell laughed a short, grim, hollow laugh, but he settled back in his seat without answering that.

"I interrupted your story," continued Cheseldine. "Make it short."

"Boss, this here big gent drifts into Ord again an' makes up to Jim Fletcher. Jim, you know, is easy led. He likes men. An' when a posse come along trailin' a blind lead, huntin' the wrong way for the man who held up Number Six, why, Jim . . . he up an' takes this stranger to be the fly road agent an' cottons to him. Got money out of him, sure. An' that's what stumps me more. What's this man's game? I happen to know, Boss, that he couldn't have held up Number Six."

"How do you know?" demanded Cheseldine.

"Because I did the job myself."

A dark and stormy passion clouded the chief's face. "Damn you, Knell! You're incorrigible. You're unreliable. Another break like that queers you with me. Did you tell Poggin?"

"Yes. That's one reason we fell out. He raved. I thought he was goin' to kill me."

"Why did you tackle such a risky job without help or plan?"

"It offered, that's all. An' it was easy. But it was a mistake. I got the country an' the railroad hollerin' for nothin'. I just couldn't help it. You know, Cheseldine, what idleness means to one of us. You know, also, that this very life breeds fatality. It's wrong . . . that's why. I was born of good parents an' I know . . . what's right. We're wrong, an' we can't beat the end, that's all. An' for my part I don't care a damn when that comes."

"Fine wise talk from you, Knell," said Cheseldine scornfully. "Go on with your story."

"As I said, Jim cottons to the pretender, an' they get

278

chummy. They're together all the time. You can gamble Jim told all he knew an' then some. A little liquor loosens his tongue. Several of the boys rode over from Ord, an' one of them went to Poggin an' says Jim Fletcher has a new man for the gang. Poggin, you know, is always ready for any new man. He says if one doesn't turn out good, he can be shut off easy. He rather liked the way this new pard of Jim's was boosted. Jim an' Poggin always hit it up together. So, until I got onto the deal, Jim's pard was almost in the gang, without Poggin or you ever seein' him. Then I got to figurin' hard. Just where had I ever seen that gent? As it turned out, I never had seen him, which accounts for my bein' doubtful. I'd never forget any man I'd seen. I dug up a lot of old papers from my kit an' went over them. Letters, pictures, clippin's, an' all that. I guess I had a pretty good notion what I was lookin' for an' who I wanted to make sure of. At last I found it. An' I knew my man. But I didn't spring it on Poggin. Oh, no! I want to have some fun with him, when the time comes. He'll be wilder than a trapped wolf. I sent Blossom over to Ord to get word from Jim an', when he verified all this talk, I sent Blossom again with a message calculated to make Jim hump. Poggin got sore, said he'd wait for Jim, an' I could come on over here to see you about the new job. He'd meet me in Ord."

Knell had spoken hurriedly and low, now and then with passion. His pale eyes glinted like fire in ice.

"Knell, unless you give good reasons, I'll back Poggin and Fletcher," said Cheseldine. "Rather liked the looks and nerve of that chap who called me."

The laugh Knell uttered had behind its scorn something absolute. Cheseldine dropped his cigar. Knell leaned over towards him.

279

"Did you say nerve? Who do you think called you that day?"

"No idea," snapped Cheseldine impatiently.

"Buck Duane!"

Down came Cheseldine's boots with a crash, then his body grew rigid. "That Nueces outlaw! That two-shot ace-of-spades gun-thrower who killed Bland, Alloway . . . ?"

"An' Hardin." Knell whispered, this last name with more feeling than the apparent circumstance demanded.

"Yes, and Hardin, the best one of the Rim Rock fellows. Buck Duane!"

Cheseldine was so ghastly white now that his black mustache seemed outlined against chalk. He eyed his grim lieutenant. They understood each other without more words — without asking why Duane was in the country. It was enough that he was there in the Big Bend. Cheseldine rose presently and reached for a flask from which he drank then offered it to Knell, who waved it aside.

"Knell," began the chief slowly, as he wiped his lips, "I gathered you have some grudge against this Buck Duane."

"Yes."

"Well, don't be a damn' fool now and do what Poggin or most any of you men would . . . don't meet this Buck Duane. Never mind if all the gang's backing you. They couldn't keep him from throwing his gun. And you want to live . . . and I need you. Here's a better way. Hit the trail early. Go to Ord and give Jim Fletcher a hunch. Then ride like hell to Bradford and tell Sheriff Bridger that I sent you . . . that I've located one of the men who held up Number Six, also suspected of safe-blowing. Bridger will do the rest. He'll come heeled enough to get even Buck Duane."

"All right. I'll do my best. But if I run into Duane. . . ."

"*Don't* run into him!" Cheseldine's voice fairly rang with the force of its passion and command. He wiped his face, drank again from the flask, sat down, resumed his smoking and, drawing a paper from his vest pocket, began to study it.

"Well, I'm damn' glad that's settled," he said, evidently referring to the Duane matter. "Now for the new job. This is October the eighteenth. On or before the twenty-fifth there will be a shipment of gold reaching the Rancher's Bank of Val Verde. After you return from Bradford with Bridger and get Duane out of the way, give Poggin these orders. Keep the gang quiet. You, Poggin, Kane, Fletcher, Pan Handle Smith, and Boldt are to be in on the secret and the job. Nobody else. You'll leave Ord on the twenty-third, ride across country by the trail till you get within sight of Mercer. It's a hundred miles from Bradford to Val Verde . . . about the same from Ord. Time your travel to get you near Val Verde on the morning of the twenty-sixth. You won't have to more than trot your horses. At two o'clock in the afternoon, sharp, ride into town and up to the Rancher's Bank. Val Verde's a pretty big town. Never been any hold-ups there. Town feels safe. Make it a clean, fast daylight job. That's all. Have you got the details?"

Knell did not even ask for the dates again. "Suppose Poggin or me might be . . . detained?" he asked.

Cheseldine bent a dark glance upon his lieutenant.

"You never can tell what'll come off," continued Knell. "I'll do my best."

"The minute you see Poggin, tell him. A job on hand steadies him. And I say again . . . look to it that nothing happens. Either you or Poggin carry the job through, but I want both of you in it. A big haul, Knell, a big haul! Don't miss it. Now a last word, then we'll play some monte.

281

I'll be in Bradford on the twenty-fifth, and next day I'll have business in Val Verde. I'll be across the street in the hotel when you pull off the job. Break for the hills and, when you get up in the rocks where you can hide your tracks, head for Mount Ord. When all's quiet again, I'll join you here. That's all. Call in the boys."

Like a swift shadow, and as noiselessly, Duane stole across the level toward the dark wall of rock. Every nerve was a strung wire. For a little while his mind was cluttered and clogged with whirling thoughts from which, like a flashing scroll, unrolled the long-baffling order of action. The game now was in his hands. He must cross Mount Ord at night. The feat was improbable, but it might be done — it *must* be done. He must ride to Bradford, forty miles from the foothills, before eight o'clock next morning, in time to catch Buell, the night operator, before he went off duty. He must telegraph MacNelly to be in Val Verde on the twenty-fifth. He must ride back to Ord to intercept Knell — face him — be denounced — kill him and, while the iron was hot, strike hard to gain Poggin's half-won interest as he had wholly won Fletcher's. Failing that last, he must let the outlaws alone to bide their time in Ord, to be free to ride on to their new job in Val Verde. Meanwhile, he must hide in the brush till the twenty-fifth then face Cheseldine in Bradford, arrest him or kill him, and go on to Val Verde to meet Poggin at the finish. It was a magnificent outline, incredible, alluring, unfathomable in its nameless certainty. He felt like fate. He seemed to be the iron consequences falling upon these doomed outlaws.

Under the wall the shadows were black, only the tips of trees and crags showing, yet he went straight to the trail.

282

It was merely a grayness between borders of black. He climbed and never stopped. It did not seem steep. His feet might have had eyes. He surmounted the wall and, looking down into the ebony gulf pierced by one point of light, he lifted a menacing arm and shook it. Then he strode on and did not falter till he reached the huge, shelving cliffs. Here he lost the trail; there was none; but he remembered the shapes, the points, the notches of rock above. Before he reached the ruins of splintered ramparts and jumbles of broken walls, the moon topped the eastern slope of the mountain and the mystifying blackness he had dreaded changed to magic silver illumination. It seemed as light as day, only soft, mellow, and the air held a transparent sheen. He ran up the bare ridges and down the smooth slopes and, like a goat, jumped from rock to rock. In this light he knew his way and lost no time looking for a trail. He crossed the divide and then had all downhill before him. Swiftly he descended, most always sure of his memory of the landmarks — having studied them in the ascent — and here they were, even in changed light, familiar to his sight. What he had once seen was pictured on his mind. He did not run but, true as a deer striking for home, he reached the cañon where he had left his horse.

Bullet was quickly and easily found. Duane threw on the saddle and pack, cinched them tight, and resumed his descent, leading his horse. The worst was now to come. Bare downward steps in rock, sliding weathered slopes, narrow black gullies, a thousand openings in a maze of broken stone, these Duane had to descend in fast time leading a giant of a horse. Bullet cracked the loose fragments, sent them rolling, slid on the scaly slopes, plunged down the steps, following like a faithful dog at Duane's heels.

Hours passed as moments. Duane was equal to his great opportunity, but he could not quell that self in him that reached back over the lapse of lonely, searing years and found the boy in him. He who had been worse than dead was now grasping at the skirts of life — which meant victory, honor, happiness. Yet, Duane knew he was not just right in part of his mind. *Small wonder that he was not insane,* he thought! He tramped downward, his marvelous faculty for covering rough ground and holding to the course never before even in flight so keen and accurate. Yet all the time a spirit was keeping step with him. A slender shape kept pace with him. He was descending once again as in the Nueces gorge, and Jennie walked with him. For months, except at long intervals, he had excluded her image from his mind. Thoughts of her, as he had left her, made him weak. But now, with the game near to its end, with the trap to spring, with success strangely haunting him, Duane let the memory of Jennie Lee come beating back to him. And that night became sweeter than any dream he had ever had in idle haunted hours. He saw her white face with its sweet, sad lips and the dark eyes, so tender and tragic. Time and distance and risk and toil were nothing.

The moon sloped to the west. Shadows of trees and crags now crossed to the other side of him. The stars dimmed. Then he was out of the rocks with the dim trail pale at his feet. Mounting Bullet, he made short work of the slope and the foothills and the rolling land leading down to Ord. The little outlaw camp, with its shacks and cabins and row of houses, lay silent and dark under the paling moon. Duane passed by on the lower trail, headed into the road, and put Bullet to a gallop. He watched the dying moon, the waning stars, and the east. He had time to spare, so he saved the horse. Knell would be leaving Cheseldine's camp about the time Duane turned back towards Ord. Between noon and sunset they would meet.

The night wore on. The moon sank behind low mountains in the west. The stars brightened for a while, then faded. Gray gloom enveloped the world, thickened, lay like smoke over the road. Then shade by shade it lightened, until through the transparent obscurity shone a dim light.

Duane reached Bradford before dawn. He dismounted some distance from the tracks, tied his horse, and then crossed over to the station. He heard the clicking of the telegraph instrument, and it thrilled him. Buell sat inside reading. When Duane tapped on the window, he looked up with startled glance then came swiftly to unlock the door.

"Hello, son. I'm here. Give me paper and pencil. Quick," whispered Duane.

With trembling hands, the operator complied.

Duane wrote out the message he had carefully composed. "Send this . . . repeat it to make sure . . . then keep mum. I'll see you again on the twenty-fifth. Good bye."

Buell stared but did not speak a word. Duane left as stealthily and swiftly as he had come. He walked his horse a couple of miles back on the road and then rested him till break of day. When the east began to redden, Duane turned grimly in the direction of Ord.

When Duane swung into the wide grassy square on the outskirts of Ord, he saw a bunch of saddled horses hitched in front of the tavern. He knew what that meant. Luck still favored him. If it would only hold! He could ask no more. The rest was a matter of how greatly he could make his power felt. An open conflict against odds lay in the balance. That would be fatal to him and, to avoid it, he had to trust to his name and a presence he must make terrible. He knew outlaws. He knew what qualities held them. He knew what to exaggerate.

There was not an outlaw in sight. The dusty horses had covered distance that morning. As Duane dismounted, he heard loud, angry voices inside the tavern. He removed coat and vest, hung them over the pommel. He packed two guns, one belted high on the left hip, the other swinging low on the right side. He neither looked nor listened but boldly pushed the door and stepped inside.

The big room was full of men, and every face pivoted toward him. Knell's pale face flashed into Duane's swift sight — then Boldt's — then Blossom Kane's — then Pan Handle Smith's — then Fletcher's — then others that were familiar, and last that of Poggin. Though Duane had never seen Poggin or heard him described, he knew him. For he saw a face that was a record of great and evil deeds.

There was absolute silence. The outlaws were lined back of a long table upon which were papers, sacks of silver coin, a bundle of bills, and a huge gold-mounted gun.

"Are you gents lookin' for me?" asked Duane. He gave his voice all the ringing force and power of which he was capable. And he stepped back, free of anything, with the outlaws all before him.

Knell stood quivering, but his face might have been a mask. The other outlaws looked from him to Duane. Jim Fletcher flung up his hands.

"My Gawd, Dodge, what'd you bust in here fer?" he said plaintively and slowly stepped forward. His action was that of a man true to himself. He meant he had been sponsor for Duane, and now he would stand by him.

"Back, Fletcher!" called Duane, and his voice made the outlaw jump.

"Hold on, Dodge, an' you-all, everybody," said Fletcher. "Let me talk, seein' I'm in wrong here."

His persuasion did not ease the strain.

"Go ahead. Talk," said Poggin.

Fletcher turned to Duane. "Pard, I'm takin' it on myself thet you meet enemies here where I swore you'd meet friends. It's my fault. I'll stand by you if you let me."

"No, Jim," replied Duane.

"But what'd you come fer without the signal?" burst out Fletcher in distress. He saw nothing but catastrophe in this meeting.

"Jim, I ain't pressin' my company none. But when I'm wanted bad. . . ."

Fletcher stopped him with a raised hand. Then he turned to Poggin with a rude dignity. "Poggy, he's my pard, an' he's riled. I never told him a word thet'd make him sore. I only said Knell hadn't no more use fer him than fer me. Now what you say goes in this gang. I never failed you in my life. Here's my pard. I vouch fer him. Will you stand fer me? There's goin' to be hell if you don't. An' us with a big job on hand!"

While Fletcher toiled over his slow, earnest persuasion, Duane had his gaze riveted upon Poggin. There was something leonine about Poggin. He was tawny. He blazed. He seemed beautiful as fire is beautiful. But looked at more closely, with glance seeing the physical man instead of that thing which shone from him, he was of perfect build, with muscles that swelled and rippled, bulging his clothes, with the magnificent head and face of the cruel, fierce, tawny-eyed jaguar.

Looking at this strange Poggin, instinctively divining his

287

abnormal and hideous power, like his person, Duane had for the first time in his life the inward quaking fear of a man. It was like a cold-tongued bell ringing within him and numbing his heart. The old instinctive firing of blood followed but did not drive away that fear. He knew. He felt something here deeper than thought could go. And he hated Poggin.

That individual had been considering Fletcher's appeal. "Jim, I ante up," he said, "an' if Phil doesn't raise us out with a big hand . . . , why he'll get called, an' your pard can set in the game."

Every eye shifted to Knell. He was dead white. He laughed, and anyone hearing that laugh would have realized his intense anger equally with an assurance that made him master of the situation.

"Poggin, you're a gambler, you are, the ace-high straight-flush hand of the Big Bend," he said with stinging scorn. "I'll bet you my roll to a greaser peso that I can deal you a hand you'll be afraid to play."

"Phil, you're talkin' wild," groused Poggin, with both advice and menace in his tone.

"If there's anything you hate it's a man who pretends to be somebody else when he's not . . . ! That so?"

Poggin nodded in slow-gathering wrath.

"Well, Jim's new pard . . . this man Dodge . . . he's not who he seems. Oh, no! He's a hell of a lot different. But *I* know him. An' when I spring his name, you, Poggin . . . you'll freeze to your gizzard. Do you get me? You'll freeze, an' your hand'll be stiff when it ought to be lightnin' . . . all because you'll realize you've been standing there five minutes . . . five minutes *alive* before him."

If not hate then assuredly great passion toward Poggin manifested itself in Knell's scornful fiery address, in the shaking hand he thrust before Poggin's face. In the ensuing silent pause Knell's panting could be plainly heard. The other men were pale, watchful, cautiously edging either way to the wall, leaving the principals and Duane in the center of the room.

"Spring his name, then, you bastard," said Poggin violently, with a curse.

Strangely, Knell did not even look at the man he was about to denounce. He leaned towards Poggin, his hands, his body, his long head all somehow expressive of what his face disguised.

"Buck Duane!" he yelled suddenly.

The name did not make any apparent difference in Poggin, but Knell's passionate, swift utterance carried the suggestion that the name ought to bring Poggin to quick action. It was possible, too, that Knell's manner, the import of his denunciation, the meaning back of all his passion held Poggin bound more than the surprise. For the outlaw certainly was surprised, perhaps staggered at the idea that he — Poggin — had been about to stand sponsor with Fletcher for a famous outlaw hated and feared by all outlaws.

Knell waited a long moment, and then his face broke its cold immobility in an extraordinary expression of devilish glee. He had hounded the great Poggin into something that gave him vicious, monstrous joy. *"Buck Duane!* Yes," he broke out hotly, "the Nueces gunman! . . . that two-shot, ace-of-spades lone wolf! You an' I . . . we've heard a thousand times of him . . . talked about him often. An' here he is *in front* of you! Poggin, you were backin' Fletcher's new pard, Buck Duane. An' he'd've fooled you both but for me. *I* know him . . . an' I know why he drifted in here. To flash a gun on Cheseldine . . . on you . . . on me! Bah!

Don't tell me he wanted to join the gang. You know a gunman, for you're one yourself. Don't you always want to kill another man? An' don't you always want to meet a real man, not a four-flusher? It's the madness of the gunman, an' I know it. Well, Duane faced you . . . called you! An' when I sprung his name, what ought you have done? What would the boss . . . anybody have expected of Poggin? Did you throw your gun, swift, like you have so often? Naw, you froze. An' why? Because here's a man with the kind of nerve you'd love to have. Because he's great . . . meetin' us here alone. Because you know he's a wonder with a gun, an' you love life. Because you an' I an' every damned man here had to take his front, each to himself. If we all drew, we'd kill him. Sure! But who was goin' to lead? Who was goin' to be first? Who was goin' to make him draw? Not you, Poggin! You leave that for a lesser man . . . me . . . who've lived to see you a coward. It comes once to every gunman. You've met your match in Buck Duane. An', by God, I'm glad! Here's once I show you up!"

The hoarse, taunting voiced failed. Knell stepped back from the comrade he hated. He was wet, shaking, haggard, but magnificent.

"Buck Duane, do you remember Hardin?" he asked in a scarcely audible voice.

"Yes," replied Duane, and a flash of insight made clear Knell's attitude.

"You met him . . . forced him to draw . . . killed him?"

"Yes."

"Hardin was the best pard I ever had."

His teeth clicked together tightly, and his lips set in a thin line. The room grew still. Even breathing ceased. The time for words had passed. In that long moment of suspense

Knell's body gradually stiffened, and at last the quivering ceased. He crouched. His eyes had a soul-piercing fire.

Duane watched them. He waited. He caught the thought — the breaking of Knell's muscle-bound rigidity. Then he drew. Through the smoke of his gun he saw two red spurts of flame. Knell's bullets thudded into the ceiling. He fell with a scream like a wild thing in agony.

Duane did not see Knell die. He watched Poggin. And Poggin, like a stricken and astounded man, looked down upon his prostrate comrade.

Fletcher ran at Duane with hands aloft.

"Hit the trail, you liar, or you'll hev to kill me!" he yelled.

With hands still up he shouldered and bodied Duane out of the room. Duane leaped on his horse, spurred, and plunged away.

Chapter Twenty

For Duane the twenty-fifth of October seemed a whole lifetime in coming. When that day dawned, he left a lonely camp in the brush and rode into Bradford. He went to the old innkeeper with whom he had made acquaintance and, leaving his horse in the stable, set off in search of Buell. Inquiry discovered the night operator asleep at his boarding house. Duane had him awakened. Buell came in heavy-eyed but curious, half expectant.

"Buell, I'm sorry to disturb you," said Duane, "but my business is urgent. You can aid me. I'm going to arrest a man here today, a prominent citizen. Now it's likely some of his friends . . . somebody, at any rate . . . will shove a gun in your face, or the day operator's, and make you send telegrams east along the line. This will probably happen after I take the train with my man. What I want you to do is to post the other operator. In case this does happen to either of you, be cool and pretend to send the message given you but send the wrong message . . . anything at random. Bluff the thing so these allies of my man will think they can stall operations east."

Buell promised with a heightened color and considerable show of pleasure to go at once and relieve the day operator who, he said, wanted some time off duty and to stay by his instrument as long as needed.

"Who're you after?" he asked excitedly.

"You'll know presently. Another thing. My horse is over

at the inn. I'll have to leave him, and I'd like you to take care of him till you hear from me. If you don't hear . . . , he's yours."

Then Duane kept out of sight. He learned from the innkeeper that Levitt was not in Bradford but was expected sometime that day. The property had changed hands, and final settlement was not to be made until after his arrival.

Duane had waited hours and weeks and months, so a little additional time, more or less, ought to have been borne in patience. Outwardly he was calm; inwardly he was in a tumult. He wanted to get to Val Verde; he wanted the twenty-sixth to come; he wanted the last scene at the bank. That tawny Poggin had never left his mind. Was MacNelly ready? Would his rangers hide and wait as Duane had planned? Duane seemed to put no value on the arrest or death of Cheseldine. He had scarcely given that a thought. When he met the outlaw leader, he meant to give him one chance — a chance for his life and no more. Duane went to the station, sat in a secluded corner, and waited. The hours wore so slowly. Westbound train — eastbound train — and no Levitt! There was only one more train from the west and that was Number 6. It was due at nine o'clock at night. Would Levitt come on that and transact his business so late? The afternoon was endless. Twilight — dusk — darkness — a pin point of light far out in the black west — at last the whistle of an engine. Number 6 came thundering in, a long gray-dusted train.

The first passenger to alight was Levitt who gaily called to waiting friends. From the obscure background Duane watched, felt all his fears vanish at the sight of this man's dark powerful face, and let him go with his friends. Duane thought that he might have spared himself such suspense. This man had acted according to his plan. He had said he would be in Bradford on that day, and here he was. Likewise he might be expected to keep to all his decisions. He would come down to take the eastbound train in the morning for Val Verde.

Duane went to the room he had engaged, lay down dressed as he was, slept a few hours, then awoke and lay there, wide eyed, waiting, thinking, as he had so many lonely nights of his life. Day dawned — the twenty-sixth of October! With it came a serenity that quivered to one mortal stab — a thought of Jennie Lee — and then he was cold, unhurried, ready. Today he would pay — bring back his honor and good name.

He did not think of eating. He waited. At eight he went to the station. Buell was pale from loss of sleep.

"On time!" he said to Duane's questioning look. "She's due eight-fifty."

Duane repaired to his old seat. He meant to remain there until the last quarter of an hour then go up street to get his man.

The time passed. When he went out, he saw several Mexicans, a cowboy, and two men; and they all watched him curiously. Next he ran into Sheriff Bridger. He laid a heavy hand on Bridger.

"I want Cheseldine. Is he coming?"

The sheriff gasped, and his swarthy face turned green. He looked sick. He could not speak. Over his shoulder Duane saw Cheseldine coming with a group of men, all intent upon themselves.

"I'm Buck Duane, Texas Ranger," he said, close to Bridger's ear. He drew his gun and pressed it against the sheriff. "Look down!" he added.

Bridger saw the gun and almost collapsed.

"Give me your handcuffs," went on Duane.

Bridger produced them and held them out with shaking fingers. Duane snatched them and, with a look at Bridger that meant death, he shoved him back. Then Duane with gun high leaped in front of the approaching men.

"Cheseldine!" he yelled piercingly.

All of them halted, as if the word had petrified them. One of them turned a ghastly stricken white.

"Hands out! Not up! In front of you! *Quick!*"

As Duane's look had meant death, so here did his voice. The manacles clicked. Cheseldine was a prisoner. Duane turned to the paralyzed men.

"Gentlemen, you look honest," he said, "but I can take no chances. You must be judged by your company. I'm Duane, Texas Ranger. I arrest this man, Cheseldine. I advise you all to be careful with your hands."

He grasped Cheseldine and, backing away, led him up to the station, pushed him against the wall. Duane's eyes covered every point before him. Bridger had disappeared. Cheseldine's friends, recovering from their stupefaction, broke into a frenzy of excitement, but they did not approach any closer. One by one the little crowd of astounded men was enlarged by others. Sight of Duane and his gun were enough both to make them gape and hold them back.

Cheseldine remained white but calm. He had nerve. He seemed to want to hide his manacled hands. "Duane, why did you make an exception of me?" he asked.

Duane did not reply. At the moment he heard the train whistle. Probably Cheseldine was wondering why he had not met the same fate as Bland, Alloway, Hardin. Duane wondered grimly the same thing.

The eastbound rolled into the station. Duane, waving the crowd back with his gun, made Cheseldine walk ahead of him, climb the steps of a car.

"Hurry this train!" called Duane to the amazed conductor. Then he got on, entered the car, put Cheseldine in a seat, and sat facing him and all the passengers.

The train started up almost immediately and left behind on the platform a yelling, gesticulating crowd. Duane had a glimpse of Buell waving his hand from the station window.

Chapter Twenty-One

It was a fast train, yet the ride seemed slow. Duane, disliking to face Cheseldine and the watching, conjecturing passengers in the car, changed his seat to one behind his prisoner. They had not spoken. Cheseldine sat with bowed head, deeply in thought. Occasionally the train halted briefly at a station. The latter half of that ride Duane had observed a road running parallel with the railroad, sometimes right alongside, at others near or far away. When the train was about twenty miles from Val Verde, Duane saw a dark group of horsemen trotting eastward. His blood beat like a hammer at his temples. The gang! He thought he recognized the tawny Poggin and felt a strange inward contraction and a significant jerk of his right arm. He thought he recognized the clean-cut Blossom Kane, the black-bearded giant, Boldt, the red-faced Pan Handle Smith, and Fletcher. There was another man strange to him. Was that Knell? — no! it could not have been Knell.

Duane leaned over the seat and touched Cheseldine on the shoulder. "Look!" he whispered.

Cheseldine was stiff. He had already seen. The train flashed by; the outlaw gang receded out of range of sight.

"Cheseldine, did you notice Knell wasn't with them?" whispered Duane.

The outlaw bent a malignant glance upon the ranger. "By God it took one of our kind . . . and a traitor . . . to turn the trick!" he said with terrible fierceness.

Duane did not speak to Cheseldine again till the train stopped at Val Verde. Then he felt for a weapon upon the outlaw, took charge of a pearl-handled gun, removed the handcuffs and said: "Cheseldine, I want things to look natural. Use you head now. No signals to anybody!"

They got off the car. The station was a good deal larger than that at Bradford, and there was considerable action and bustle incident to the arrival of the train. Duane's sweeping gaze searched faces, rested upon a man who seemed familiar. This fellow's look, too, was that of one who knew Duane but was waiting for a sign, a cue. Then Duane recognized him — MacNelly, clean-shaven. Without mustache he appeared different, younger.

When MacNelly saw that Duane intended to greet him, he hurried forward. A keen light flashed from his eyes. He was glad, eager, yet suppressing himself, and the glances he sent back and forth from Duane to Cheseldine were questioning, doubtful. Certainly Cheseldine did not look the part of an outlaw.

"Duane! Lord, I'm glad to see you," was the captain's greeting. Then at closer look into Duane's face his warmth fled — something he saw there checked his enthusiasm or at least its utterance.

"MacNelly, shake hands with Cheseldine," said Duane, low voiced.

The ranger captain stood dumb, motionless, but he saw Cheseldine's instant action, and he reached for the outstretched hand.

"Any of your men down here?" queried Duane sharply.

"No. They're uptown."

"Come. Cheseldine, walk between us and look straight ahead. Don't see anybody."

They set off uptown. Cheseldine walked as if he were

298

with friends on the way to dinner, except that his lips were mute. MacNelly walked like a man in a trance. There was not a word spoken in the four blocks.

Presently Duane saw a stone building on a corner of the broad street. There was a big sign — **Rancher's Bank**. Duane touched Cheseldine's elbow, pointed to the bank. The outlaw looked but made no sign. He was imperturbable. Somehow Duane resented Cheseldine's silence, his nerve. It seemed that the outlaw had not given up.

"Cheseldine, do you want to go in the bank and see if the shipment of gold has come . . . *the big haul?*" asked Duane sarcastically. He hated to taunt the man but could not resist that much.

Cheseldine gave a violent start. Perhaps in that moment he understood. He made no reply.

"There's the hotel," said MacNelly. "Some of my men are there. We're scattered around."

They crossed the street, went in through lobby, office, saloon, to a large room like a hall, and here were men reading and smoking. Duane knew them — rangers! When he snapped the handcuffs back upon Cheseldine, it was with a strange air of finality. It was as if he renounced his prisoner. MacNelly, the rangers, and certainly Cheseldine, all noted Duane's strange action and look.

"There, Cheseldine!" And with something almost of passion and violence, he pushed the outlaw toward MacNelly. He was done with him. Did that action mean that, as ranger, he was turning Cheseldine over to the law, when as Buck Duane he wanted to meet him, to face him, to make him draw, to kill him?

MacNelly beckoned to his men. "Boys, here he is. Cheseldine! Russell, you and Mills take him in the small room and guard him. Don't take your eyes off him till we decide what to do."

The rangers led Cheseldine away.

"Duane, what had we better do with him for the present?" queried MacNelly. "There's a jail here. We can put him away till we're through, but would that be best? We've been laying low."

"No. How many men have you?"

"Fifteen."

"Keep two men here guarding Cheseldine."

MacNelly left to go into the other room and returned closing the door. Then he almost embraced Duane, would probably have done so but for the dark grimness that seemed to be coming over the man. Instead he glowed; he sputtered; he tried to talk, to wave his hands. He was beside himself. And his rangers crowded closer, eager, like hounds ready to run. They all talked at once, and the word most significant and frequent in their speech was Cheseldine.

MacNelly clapped his fist in his hand. "This'll make the adjutant sick with joy. Maybe this'll show the governor? We'll show all of them about the ranger service. Cheseldine! . . . how'd you ever do it? Oh, I knew you were a wonder, but I was sure you'd kill him."

"He didn't give me a chance," replied Duane. "Now, Captain, not the half nor the quarter of this job's done. The gang's coming down the road. I saw them from the train. They'll ride into town on the dot . . . two-thirty."

"How many?" asked MacNelly.

"Poggin, Blossom Kane, Pan Handle Smith, Boldt, Jim Fletcher, and another man I don't know. These are the picked men of Cheseldine's gang. I'll bet they'll be the fastest, hardest bunch you rangers ever faced."

"Poggin! That's the hard nut to crack! I've heard their records since I've been in Val Verde. Where's Knell? They say he's a boy but hell and blazes."

"Knell's dead."

"Ah!" exclaimed MacNelly softly. Then he grew business-like, cool, and of harder aspect. "Duane, it's your game today. I'm only a ranger under orders. We're all under your orders. We've absolute faith in you. Make your plan quick, so I can go around and post the boys who're not here."

"You understand there's no sense in trying to arrest Poggin, Kane, and that lot?" queried Duane.

"No, I don't understand that," replied MacNelly bluntly. "It can't be done. The drop can't be got on such men. If you meet them, they shoot and mighty quick and straight. Poggin! That outlaw has no equal with a gun unless . . . ? He's got to be killed quick. They'll all have to be killed. They're all bad . . . desperate . . . know no fear . . . are lightning in action."

"Very well, Duane, then it's a fight. That'll be easier, perhaps. The boys are spoiling for a fight. Out with your plan now."

"Put one man at each end of this street just at the edge of town. Let him hide there with a rifle to block the escape of any outlaw that we might fail to get. I had a good look at the bank building. It's well situated for our purpose. Put four men up in that room over the bank . . . four men, two at each open window. Let them hide till the game begins. They want to be there in case these foxy outlaws get wise before they're down on the ground or inside the bank. The rest of your men put inside behind the counters where they'll hide. Now go over to the bank, spring the thing on the bank officials, and don't let them shut up the bank. You want their aid. Let them make sure of their gold, but the clerks and cashier ought to be at their desks

301

or windows when Poggin rides up. He'll glance in before he gets down. They make no mistakes, these fellows. We must be slicker than they are, or lose. When you get the bank people wise, send your men over one by one. No hurry . . . no excitement . . . no unusual thing to attract notice in the bank."

"All right. That's great. Tell me, where do you intend to wait?"

Duane heard MacNelly's question, and it struck him peculiarly. He had seemed to be planning and speaking mechanically. As he was confronted by the fact, it nonplused him somewhat, and he became thoughtful, with lowered head.

"Where'll you wait, Duane?" insisted MacNelly, with keen eyes speculating.

"I'll wait in front . . . just inside the door," replied Duane with an effort.

"Why?" demanded the captain.

"Well," began Duane slowly, "Poggin will get down first and start in. But the others won't be far behind. They'll not get swift till inside. The thing is . . . they *mustn't* get clear inside, because the instant they do, they'll pull guns. That means death to somebody. If we can, we want to stop them just at the door."

"But will you hide?" asked MacNelly.

"Hide?" The idea had not occurred to Duane.

"There's a wide-open doorway. A sort of round hall, a vestibule, with steps leading up to the bank. There's a door in the vestibule, too. It leads somewhere. We can put men in there. You can be there."

Duane was silent.

"See here, Duane," began MacNelly nervously. "You shan't take any undue risk here. You'll hide with the rest of us?"

"No!" The word was wrenched from Duane.

MacNelly stared, and then a strange comprehending light seemed to flit over his face.

"Duane, I can give you no orders today," he said distinctly. "I'm only offering advice. Need you take any more risks? You've done a grand job for the service . . . already. You've paid me a thousand times for that pardon. You've redeemed yourself. The governor, the adjutant general . . . the whole state will rise up and honor you. The game's almost up. We'll kill these outlaws or enough of them to break forever their power. I say, as a ranger, need you take more risk than your captain?"

Still Duane remained silent. He was locked between two forces. And one, a tide that was bursting at its bounds, seemed about to overwhelm him. Finally that side of him, the retreating self, the weaker, found a voice.

"Captain, you want this job to be sure?" he asked.

"Certainly."

"I've told you the way. I alone know the kind of men to be met. Just *what* I'll do, or *where* I'll be, I can't say yet. In meetings like this the moment decides, but I'll be there!"

MacNelly spread wide his hands, looked helplessly at his curious and sympathetic rangers, and shook his head. "Now you've done your work . . . laid the trap . . . is this strange move of yours going to be fair to Jennie Lee?" he asked in a deliberate, low voice.

Like a great tree chopped at the roots, Duane vibrated to that. He looked up as if he had seen a ghost.

Mercilessly the ranger captain went on. "Jennie Lee came to me in Austin. She was heartbroken. She reproached me. She begged me. She told me of your mother. She did all she could to get me to fetch you back and, if I hadn't been powerless, I would have done so. You can go back to

303

her, Duane! It never seemed possible, but now it's true. Fight with us from cover . . . then go back to her. You will have served the Texas Rangers as no other man has. I'll accept your resignation. You'll be free, honored, happy . . . and rich. Jennie's rich, Duane. And she loves you! My God! how that girl loves you! She's. . . ."

But Duane cut him short with a fierce gesture. He lunged up to his feet, and the rangers fell back. Dark, silent, grim as he had been, still there was a transformation singularly more sinister, stranger.

"Enough. I'm done," he said somberly. "I've planned. Do we agree . . . or shall I meet Poggin and his gang alone?"

MacNelly cursed and again threw up his hands, this time in baffled chagrin. There was deep regret in his dark eyes as they rested upon Duane. "I accept, Duane," he rejoined quietly. "I'll go about arrangements at once."

Duane was left alone. Never had his mind been so quick, so clear, so wonderful in its understanding of what heretofore had been intricate and elusive impulses of his strange nature. His determination was to meet Poggin. Meet him before anyone else had a chance — Poggin first — and then the others! He was unalterable in that decision as if, on the instant of its acceptance, he had become stone.

Why? Then came realization. He was not a ranger now. He cared nothing for the state. He had no thought of freeing the community of a dangerous outlaw — of ridding the country of an obstacle to its progress and prosperity. He wanted to kill Poggin. It was significant now that he forgot the other outlaws. He was the gunman, the gun-thrower, the gunfighter — passionate and terrible. His father's blood, that dark and fierce strain, his mother's spirit, that strong and unquenchable spirit of the surviving pioneer — these had been in him and the killings, one

304

after another, the wild and haunted years, had made him absolutely in spite of his will the gunman. He realized it now, bitterly, hopelessly. The thing he had intelligence enough to hate he had become. At last he shuddered under the driving, ruthless inhuman blood lust of the gunman. Long ago he had seemed to seal in a tomb that horror of his kind — the need, in order to forget the haunting sleepless presence of his last victim, to go out and kill another. But it was still there in his mind, and now it stalked out, worse, more powerful, magnified by its rest, augmented by the violent passions peculiar and inevitable to that strange wild product of the Texas frontier — the gunfighter. And those passions were so violent, so raw, so base, so much lower than what ought to have existed in a thinking man. Actual pride of his record! Actual vanity in his speed with a gun! Actual jealousy of any rival!

Duane did not want to believe it, but there he was without a choice. What he had feared for years had become a monstrous reality. Respect for himself, blindness, a certain honor that he had clung to while in outlawry, all, like scales, seemed to fall away from him. He stood stripped bare, his soul naked — the soul of Cain. Always, since the first brand had been forced and burned upon him, he had been ruined. Now with conscience flayed to the quick yet utterly powerless over this tiger instinct, he was lost. He said it. He admitted it. And at that utter abasement, the soul he despised suddenly leaped and quivered with the memory of Jennie Lee.

Then came agony. He would never go back to her — she had said it. She had divined. As he could not govern all the chances of this fatal meeting — as all his swift and deadly genius must be occupied with Poggin, perhaps in

305

vain — as hard-shooting men whom he could not watch would be close behind, this almost certainly must be the end of Buck Duane. That did not matter. He loved the girl. He wanted her. She needed him. All her sweetness, her fire and pleading, her abandonment returned to torture him. If she had been there to put her arms around him, to press him close, to lay her wet cheeks on his, her fragrant hair in his eyes, to kiss him with those tremulous drowning lips — to love him as she had that last hour, then he might be . . . he could be saved. But she was not there, and all her remembered charm and appeal availed nothing but to add to his agony.

To forget her, to get back his nerve, he forced into mind the image of Poggin — Poggin, the tawny haired, the yellow eyed, like a jaguar with his rippling muscles. He brought back his sense of the outlaw's wonderful presence — his own unaccountable fear and hate. Yes, Poggin had sent the cold sickness of fear to his marrow. Why, since he hated life so? Poggin was his supreme test. And this abnormal and stupendous instinct, now deep as the very foundation of his life, demanded its wild and fatal issue. There was a horrible thrill in his sudden remembrance that Poggin, likewise, had been taunted into fear of him. So the dark tide overwhelmed Duane and, when he left the room, he was fierce, implacable, steeled to any outcome, quick like a panther, somber as death in the thrall of his strange passion.

There was no excitement in the street. He crossed to the bank corner. A clock inside pointed to the hour of two. He went through the door, into the vestibule, looked around, passed up the steps into the bank. The clerks were at their desks, apparently busy, but they showed nervousness. The cashier paled at sight of Duane. There were men — the rangers — crouching down behind the low partition. All the windows had been removed from the iron grating before the desks. The safe was closed. There was no money in sight. A customer came in, spoke to the cashier, and was told to come tomorrow.

Duane returned to the door. He could see far down the street, out into the country. There he waited, and minutes were eternities. He saw no person near him; he heard no sound. He was insulated in his unnatural strain.

At a few minutes before half past two a dark, compact body of horsemen appeared far down, turning into the road. They came at a sharp trot — a group that would have attracted attention anywhere at any time. They came a little faster as they entered town — then faster still. Now they were four blocks away — now three — now two. Duane backed down the middle of the vestibule, up the steps, and halted in the center of the wide doorway. There seemed to be a rushing in his ears through which pierced the sharp, ringing clip-clop of iron hoofs. He could see only the corner of the street, but suddenly into that shot lean-limbed dusty bay horses. There was a clattering of nervous hoofs pulled to a halt.

Duane saw the tawny Poggin speak to his companions. He dismounted quickly. They followed suit. They had the manner of ranchers about to conduct some business. No guns showed. Poggin started leisurely for the bank door, quickening his step a little as he came. The others, close together, came behind him. Blossom Kane had a bag in his left hand. Jim Fletcher was left behind, and he had already gathered up the bridles.

Poggin entered the vestibule first, with Kane on one side, Boldt on the other a little behind him. As he strode in he saw Duane.

"Hell's fire!" he cried.

Something inside Duane burst, piercing all of him with cold. Was it that fear?

"Buck Duane!" echoed Kane.

One instant Poggin looked up, and Duane looked down. Like a striking jaguar, Poggin moved. Almost as quickly Duane threw his arm. The guns boomed almost together. Duane felt a blow just before he pulled trigger. His thoughts came swiftly, like the strange dots before his eyes. His rising gun had loosened in his hand. Poggin had drawn quicker! A tearing agony encompassed his breast. He pulled — pulled at random. Thunder of booming shots all about him! Red flashes — jets of smoke — shrill yells! He was sinking. The end — yes — the end! With fading sight, he saw Kane go down, then Boldt. But supreme torture — more bitter than death — Poggin stood, mane like a lion's, back to the wall, bloody-faced, grand, with his guns sporting red!

All faded — darkened. The thunder deadened. Duane fell, seemed floating. There it drifted — Jennie Lee's sweet face, white, sad, with dark tragic eyes . . . fading . . . fading . . . fading.

Chapter Twenty-Two

Light shone before Duane's eyes — thick, strange light that came and went. It seemed a long time with dull and booming sounds rustling by, filling all. It was a dream in which there was nothing. Drifting under a burden — darkness — light — sound — movement. Obscure struggling thought — vague sense of time — a long time.

There was blackness and fire, creeping, consuming fire. He was rolled and wrapped in it — and a dark cloud carried him away, enveloped him. He saw then, dimly, a room that was strange, strange people moving about, over him, with faint voices, far-away things in a dream.

He saw again, clearly, and consciousness returned, still strange, still unreal, full of these vague and far-away things. He was not dead, then. He lay stiff, like a stone, with a weight ponderous as a mountain upon him. And slow, dull, beating, burning agony racked all his bound body.

A man bent over him, looked deeply into his eyes, and seemed to whisper from a distance: "Duane . . . Duane? My God! He knew me!"

After that another long time of darkness and, when the light came again, more clearly, this same dark-eyed, earnest man bent over him. It was MacNelly — and with recognition the past flooded back.

Duane tried to speak. His lips were weak and limp. Their movement was barely perceptible. "Poggin!" he whispered

in the ear close to his face. The first real conscious thought
— Poggin! — ruling passion — eternal instinct!

"Dead. Poggin's dead, Duane . . . shot to pieces," replied
MacNelly. "God! What a fight he made! I lost three men
. . . others badly wounded."

"Who . . . got away?"

"Fletcher, the man with the horses. We got the others.
Duane, it's done . . . done! And you . . . you . . . ?"

"Have you sent . . . for her?"

"No, oh, no. It's not that bad. You've a chance. Why, man,
you'll get well. You'll pack a sight of lead all your life, but
what's that? Fight now. Fight to live, Duane. The whole
Southwest knows your story. You need never be ashamed
again of the name Buck Duane. It'll live in Texas with
that of Davy Crockett. Think of Jennie . . . home . . .
mother!"

The rangers took Duane home to Wellston. A railroad
had been built since Duane had entered upon his exile.
Wellston had grown, it appeared. A great crowd surrounded
the station — a noisy, cheering mob that suddenly stilled
as Duane was carried from the train to a gaily decorated
vehicle. Kind, strong arms lifted him — made him comfortable. A sea of faces pressed close — some were faces
he remembered. Schoolmates — friends — old neighbors.
There was an outstretching of many hands. Duane was
being welcomed home to the town from which he had fled.
That deadness in him broke. This welcome hurt him somehow, yet through his cold being, his weary mind, passed
a change. His sight dimmed and did not clear during the
ride.

Then there was a white house — home — and his heart
beat thickly. How familiar it all was — how strange, too!
And all seemed magnified.

They carried him in, these ranger comrades, and laid him down, and lifted his head upon pillows. The house was still, though full of people. Duane's eyes sought the open door. Someone was coming — someone in white, leading an old lady, gray haired with a strong, bitter face — his mother. She was feeble, but she walked erectly. She was pale, shaking, yet wore an austere dignity.

The someone in white cried low and knelt by his bed. His mother flung wide her arms with strange gesture.

"That man . . . that's his father! Where is my boy? My son, oh, my son!"

It was sheer pleasure to lie by the west window and watch Uncle Jim whittle his stick and listen to him talk. He was old now and broken. He told so many interesting things about people Duane had known, people who had grown up and married, failed, succeeded, gone away, died. But it was hard to keep Uncle Jim off the subject of guns, fights, outlaws. He could not seem to divine how mention of these things made Duane shrink. Uncle Jim was old, childish now, and he had a pride in Duane. He wanted to hear it all — all of Duane's exile. If there was one thing more than another that pleased him, it was to speak of the bullets Duane carried in his body.

"Nine bullets, wasn't it? Nine in that last scrap. By gum! A man's a man to carry them. And you had three before?"

"Yes, Uncle," replied Duane.

"Nine and three . . . that makes twelve. An even dozen. You could pack more than that, my boy, and get away with them. There's Cole Younger. I've seen him. He's got twenty-three. But he's a bigger man than you . . . more flesh. Funny, wasn't it, about the doctors only cuttin' one bullet out of you . . . that one in your breast bone? It was a Forty-One caliber, an unusual cartridge. I had it, but Jennie took it from me. There was one bullet left in Poggin's gun, and it was the same kind as the one cut out. By gum! Boy, that bullet would have killed you, if it'd stayed there."

"It would have indeed, Uncle," said Duane, and the old haunting, somber mood returned.

Jennie was with him most of the time and, when she was nearby, there was a deep quiet joy such as had never been his. She knelt by him at the window, her sweet face still white but with warm life beneath the marble, her dark eyes still intent, haunted by shadows but no longer tragic.

"The pain, Duane . . . is it any worse today, dear?" she asked.

"No, it's the same. It will always be the same, Jennie. I'm full of lead, you know. But I don't mind that."

"It's the old mood . . . the fear?"

"Yes. It haunts me. I'll be able to go out soon. Then it'll come back."

"No . . . no, Duane," she said.

"Some drunken cowboy . . . some fool with a gun will hunt me out," he said miserably. "Buck Duane! To kill Buck Duane!"

"Hush! Listen to me," she whispered, with tender arms around him. "I understand, but you will never have to draw again, Duane. You'll never kill another man, thank God! For you will have me with you always. Soon you'll be well. Then, Duane, we'll . . . we'll be married. We'll take Uncle Jim and Mother and go far from Texas, north somewhere, to Indiana, Michigan, anywhere that we want. I have money, Duane. Isn't it wonderful? The little ragged girl you met in Bl . . . out on the Rio Grande! Do you remember my Mexican sandals? . . . no stockings! And I

312

was lame then. Oh, it all comes back! But that's past. We'll buy a farm, and you will be busy with horses and cattle and sheep. You'll forget. I'll love you so. Maybe . . . I . . . I hope . . . oh, I pray . . . there'll be children. We'll be happy, Duane."

They watched the sun set golden over the line of low hills in the west, down over the Nueces, far beyond the wild country of the Rio Grande which they were never to see again. It was then that Duane faced life, accepted happiness, trusted in this brave and tender woman to be stronger than the dark and fateful passion that had ruined him. It would come back — that instinct of fire — that madness to forget — and those drifting haunting faces with the fading eyes, but Jennie need never know.

THE END

About the Author

Zane Grey was born Pearl Zane Gray at Zanesville, Ohio in 1872. He was graduated from the University of Pennsylvania in 1896 with a degree in dentistry. He practiced in New York City while striving to make a living by writing. He married Lina Elise Roth in 1905 and with her financial assistance he published his first novel himself, BETTY ZANE (1903). Closing his dental office, the Greys moved into a cottage on the Delaware River, near Lackawaxen, Pennsylvania. Grey took his first trip to Arizona in 1907 and, following his return, wrote THE HERITAGE OF THE DESERT (1910). The profound effect that the desert had had on him was so vibrantly captured that it still comes alive for a reader. Grey couldn't have been more fortunate in his choice of a mate. Trained in English at Hunter College, Lina Grey proofread every manuscript Grey wrote, polished his prose, and she effectively managed their financial affairs. Grey's early novels were serialized in pulp magazines, but by 1918 he had graduated to the slick magazine market. Motion picture rights brought in a fortune and, with 108 films based on his work, Grey set a record yet to be equaled by any other author. Zane Grey was an author who charted the interiors of the soul through encounters with the wilderness. He often provided characters no more realistic than one finds in Balzac, Dickens, or Thomas Mann, but nonetheless they have a vital story to tell. "There was so much unexpressed feeling that could not be entirely portrayed," Loren Grey, Grey's younger son and a noted psychologist, once recalled, "that, in later years, he would weep when re-reading one of his own books." More than stories, Grey fashioned psycho-dramas about the odyssey of the human soul. They may not be the stuff of the real world, but without them the real world has no meaning — which may go a long way to explain the hold he has had on an enraptured reading public ever since his first Western romance in 1910. LAST OF THE DUANES is his first Five Star Western.

FIC
Grey, Zane.   16.95
Last of the Duanes.

DATE			